Bold, str...
willing to p...
the lin...

Dark &
Dangerous

**Don't miss these tall, handsome
strangers…they'll make you want
to beg to take them home—two
classic, full-length stories of wild
desire and deception by bestselling
authors Suzanne Brockmann and
Linda Turner.**

We're proud to present

SILHOUETTE SPOTLIGHT

a second chance to enjoy two bestselling novels by favourite authors every month— they're back by popular demand!

November 2003
Dark & Dangerous
featuring

A Man To Die For by Suzanne Brockmann
The Lady in Red by Linda Turner

December 2003
His Christmas Bride
featuring

The Surprise Christmas Bride by Maureen Child
A Very Convenient Marriage by Dallas Schulze

January 2004
Holding Out For Her Hero
featuring

Wild Mustang Woman by Lindsay McKenna
Defending His Own by Beverly Barton

Dark & Dangerous

Suzanne Brockmann
Linda Turner

SILHOUETTE®

DID YOU PURCHASE THIS BOOK WITHOUT A COVER?

If you did, you should be aware it is **stolen property** as it was reported *unsold and destroyed* by a retailer. Neither the author nor the publisher has received any payment for this book.

All the characters in this book have no existence outside the imagination of the author, and have no relation whatsoever to anyone bearing the same name or names. They are not even distantly inspired by any individual known or unknown to the author, and all the incidents are pure invention.

All Rights Reserved including the right of reproduction in whole or in part in any form. This edition is published by arrangement with Harlequin Enterprises II B.V. The text of this publication or any part thereof may not be reproduced or transmitted in any form or by any means, electronic or mechanical, including photocopying, recording, storage in an information retrieval system, or otherwise, without the written permission of the publisher.

This book is sold subject to the condition that it shall not, by way of trade or otherwise, be lent, resold, hired out or otherwise circulated without the prior consent of the publisher in any form of binding or cover other than that in which it is published and without a similar condition including this condition being imposed on the subsequent purchaser.

Silhouette and Colophon are registered trademarks of Harlequin Books S.A., used under licence.

First published in Great Britain in 2003 as a 2-in-1 volume Silhouette Books, Eton House, 18-24 Paradise Road, Richmond, Surrey TW9 1SR

DARK & DANGEROUS © Harlequin Books S.A. 2003

The publisher acknowledges the copyright holders of the individual works as follows:

A Man To Die For © Suzanne Brockmann 1995
The Lady in Red © Linda Turner 1997

ISBN 0 373 04955 2

64-1103

*Printed and bound in Spain
by Litografia Rosés S.A., Barcelona*

A Man To Die For

SUZANNE BROCKMANN

SUZANNE BROCKMANN

wanted to be a cowboy, an astronaut, a spelunker and a rock-and-roll singer when she grew up. Allergic to horses, too short-sighted for NASA and slightly claustrophobic, she took up writing instead and has successfully gone with her characters on trail rides, into outer space and deep beneath the earth. She actually was a rock singer, forming and fronting an original band while attending college in Boston. Suzanne still lives in the Boston area, surrounded by the best family and the coolest group of friends in the world.

. . . of the . . . couple nights . . . loaded and placed in
. . . . . the . . . door behind her and hurried down a
. . . woods . . . into the hot, humid summer night. That
. . . . . . Simon . . . no doubt left the gun loaded and returned
. . . the Sea Cliffe . . . where even rather He safely set . . .

Chapter 1

July

It was quarter past midnight before Carrie Brooks turned off the computer in the Sea Circus office, twenty past before she turned off the lights.

With the laser printout of her environmental coastal report safely tucked in her backpack, Carrie stopped only to pick up the tranquilizer rifle she was borrowing for tomorrow's expedition to the edge of the Everglades. She was leading one of her well-known wildlife preserve tours for a group of college professors from Ohio. The rifle wasn't really necessary. She wasn't planning on using it, but it made for good show, and it *would* be pleasant to have on hand should any of the 'gators get nasty, or should one of the professors get careless.

One of the rifle's double barrels was loaded, she realized as she locked the office door behind her and headed down the rickety wooden steps into the hot, humid summer night. That wastecase, Simon, had no doubt left the gun loaded, and returned it to the Sea Circus office without even putting the safety on.

Didn't he realize it was a weapon? Just because it shot tranquilizer darts meant for sharks or 'gators didn't mean it couldn't hurt or even kill a human.

Carrie put the safety on, locking it into place as she started across the Sea Circus grounds.

She had to be up and alert and at the marina by six in the morning. By the time she got to her car, drove to the gate, punched in her security code, opened the gate, drove her car out, closed the car, restarted the alarm system and drove all the way home to her little apartment on the other side of town, she'd stand a chance at getting four solid hours of sleep.

Four wasn't too bad, she thought as she cut across the lawn next to the main aquarium tank. She'd be able to nap tomorrow afternoon, maybe take the boat back out and just let it drift. She'd close her eyes in the soft sunshine and work on her tan....

Carrie froze. Was that the sound of laughter that had floated across the sandy grounds, or had it been some lonely seabird, or the sound of the surf?

Listening hard, Carrie heard it again. Laughter. Laughter, followed by a stream of rapid-fire Spanish, then a plaintive voice, complaining clearly in English, "Yo, man, talk American, wouldja?"

Teenagers on the beach, she decided. No one could have gotten onto the Sea Circus grounds without triggering the alarm system. And even if they had somehow managed to get in without setting off all the bells and whistles and bright flashing lights, the fail-safe silent alarm would ring down at police headquarters, and a patrol car would be out in a matter of minutes.

Carrie rounded the corner of the main aquarium tank, heading to her parked car.

And came face-to-face with a group of men.

Good Lord! How the hell had they gotten in?

The scientist that she was, quickly assessed the facts.

There were four of them—that she could see anyway—and they were *not* teenagers. They were grown men in their midtwenties. Several of them may have been even older.

The take-no-bull Montana rancher's daughter that she'd been for the first eighteen years of her life planted her feet firmly on the ground and cradled the rifle in her arms, making sure they could see it clearly.

"I believe you gentlemen are trespassing," she said coolly. "I suggest you allow me to escort you off Sea Circus property before the police arrive."

One of the men wore a red bandanna tied around his head. On closer examination, he looked to be in his late thirties, with deep-set eyes and gaunt, hollow cheekbones. He merely smiled at her words.

"But we're not ready to leave," he said with a thick Cuban accent.

Another of the men had a nose ring the size of a quarter. He was tall, taller than the rest of them by a good six inches, and he towered over Carrie. He had greasy blond hair pulled back into a messy ponytail at his nape. He kept his eyes carefully hidden behind a pair of mirrored sunglasses despite the fact that it was the middle of the night.

A third man was standing slightly to the left of Bandanna. He had short red hair in a crew cut and a face that still bore the scars of teenage acne. He was wearing a faded Nirvana T-shirt and a pair of cutoff jeans that revealed a pair of skinny legs. "Yeah, baby," he said, leering at her. "Iceman wants to look at the fishies."

"Then he should come back tomorrow," Carrie said tartly, "when Sea Circus is open to the general public."

"We ain't the general public," Nose Ring sneered.

The men seemed undaunted by the rifle she was holding. They moved slowly, spreading out around her, and Carrie realized in another few seconds she'd be completely surrounded. She slipped the safety off the rifle and took several steps backward until her shoulder blades hit the rough concrete of the main aquarium building. Better to have a wall behind her than God-knows-who and his even uglier brother.

In one quick movement, she hoisted the solid barrel of the rifle to her shoulder and cocked the trigger, closing one eye and squinting to aim directly at Bandanna—the man who was clearly the leader. At this proximity, shooting the tranquilizer dart at his head would probably kill him. The dart would shatter the bones in his skull, then penetrate his brain. He'd be tranquilized—permanently.

Bandanna seemed to realize this, too, and he gave a brief command in Spanish.

"Back off," another man translated, a man who had been standing slightly out of Carrie's sight, in the shadows behind Bandanna.

Carrie glanced in his direction.

He was the only one of the four who looked as if he might actually be nice to stand downwind of. He was more than average height—which meant that he stood a good nine inches taller than Carrie—and his clothes were pure American Urban. Despite the heat, he was wearing a black leather biker's jacket over a white T-shirt, and a pair of faded blue jeans that fitted him like a second skin. Snakeskin cowboy boots with pointy toes and silver-chained boot bracelets added the final touch.

His hair was long and thick, curling down around and past his shoulders. He had wide, angular cheekbones that spoke as clearly of his Latin heritage as did his gentle Hispanic accent.

He was a handsome man. No, forget handsome. He wasn't handsome. He was drop-dead gorgeous, Carrie realized as he stepped out into the light—but not because of his cheekbones or his shiny hair or his trim, muscular body.

It was his eyes.

Soft and black, his eyes were incredible—the color of the midnight sky—surrounded by a fringe of thick, dark, almost femininely long lashes. They held a gentle serenity, a quiet confidence, like that of a priest or a minister, that contradicted his macho leather-and-chains getup. But then that look shifted, and there was something else in his eyes, too—a glint of excitement, a flare of fire and power, a sense of very real danger. Part priest maybe, but also part devil.

This was not a man to mess with.

Holding Carrie's gaze, he stepped in front of Bandanna, shielding the older man from her rifle. But he didn't stop there. He kept going, slowly moving closer and closer to her.

"We were only cutting through. We *will* leave, but first you must give me the gun," he said. He smiled at her, showing a set of white, perfect teeth, and added, "Please?"

"Pwetty pwease?" Crew-cut said, then laughed loudly. "Yo, Carlos, man, you forgot to say 'Mother, may I.'"

Carlos. The man with the midnight eyes was named Carlos.

"Freeze, Carlos," Carrie ordered him, training the gun on the center of his forehead.

But he just kept coming. "Give me the gun, miss," he said again, "so that no one gets hurt."

"You don't want anyone to get hurt?" she asked, her anger making her sound breathless and afraid. "Then turn around right now and leave."

Bandanna spoke again in Spanish.

"Iceman says we will," Carlos said, translating. "But only when we are ready." Was that genuine remorse that flashed in his eyes? Or was it amusement?

He was almost within an arm's reach of her rifle. Carrie moved the barrel down slightly, so it was aimed steadily at his stomach. He smiled, and she knew *he* knew she didn't have the nerve to kill him. But if he came any closer, she *would* pull the trigger. And God only knows how the human body would react to the fast-acting tranquilizer intended for a four-hundred-pound marine mammal.

"Take another step and I'll shoot," she warned him.

He stopped. And laughed. "You would, too, wouldn't you?"

"Damn straight," she said grimly.

"And then what?" Carlos asked his eyes glittering, reflecting the dim glow of the floodlights that lit the park grounds. "I fall." He shrugged. "But there are three others. And I doubt that my friends will wait patiently while you reload your gun. No, if you shoot me, you will be in serious trouble. I cannot recommend it."

"Let's skip the trouble, shall we?" Carrie said. "Now, you boys just hop back over that fence and clear on out of here, and we'll call it a night."

"You sound like one of them thar Western movies," Crew-cut said, mimicking and exaggerating Carrie's drawl. "Like a cute little cowgirl." He smiled, revealing a variety of cracked and broken teeth. "Come on, baby, why don't you show us your spurs and whips?"

Carrie glanced at Crew-cut for only a fraction of a second, but that was all it took to give Carlos an edge.

He moved, faster than she thought it was possible for a man of his size to move, quickly closing the gap between his hands and her gun.

She squeezed the trigger, but it was too late. He knocked the barrel of the gun up, and the dart shot harmlessly into the night sky.

The recoil caught her off-balance, and Carrie went down, hard, into the sandy dirt. She scrambled quickly to her feet, straining her ears for the sound of police sirens. But there was only silence.

Bandanna, Crew-cut and Nose Ring stood in a semicircle around her, just watching. Carlos was looking at her gun, releasing the spent cartridge and making sure there wasn't another round in the second barrel.

"She was gonna shoot ya, man," Crew-cut said to Carlos.

Carlos just smiled serenely.

Now what? Carrie was still breathing hard, trying to control the crazy hammering of her heart. The situation wasn't looking very good. She was unarmed, in a deserted spot, in the middle of the night, with four scary-looking men. Could things get much worse?

Bandanna said something to Carlos in Spanish.

Carlos answered evenly.

Bandanna spoke again, gesturing toward Carrie.

Carlos smiled at Bandanna, smiled at Carrie and nodded his head. "*Sí,*" he said. *That* she understood. "*Sí*" meant yes. But yes *what?*

A police siren wailed faintly in the distance, and Carrie held her breath. But it was moving away from her, getting softer and softer until she couldn't hear it anymore. Dammit, where *were* those police?

And still the conversation in Spanish went on.

Crew-cut finally exploded, voicing all of Carrie's frustration, letting out a stream of foul language. "I'm feeling left out here," he added. "If you guys aren't discussing the balmy weather, then translate, for chrissake."

"Iceman said he wants to see the dolphins now," Carlos said, clearly tongue in cheek.

Nose Ring scowled. "Cut the crap, Carlos."

"Time to go," Carlos said evenly.

"What about her?" Crew-cut asked, pointing to Carrie with his chin. "We can't just leave her here."

"Sure you can," Carrie lied. "You clear out of here, I'll forget I ever saw you. No harm done, right?"

Carlos laughed, humor lighting his face.

"What?" Carrie said defensively. But she could tell from his eyes that he knew if they simply left her here, she'd run up to the office and call the police faster than they could sneeze.

"I'll take care of her," he said to Crew-cut. "You go with Iceman. I'll catch up."

Bandanna and Nose Ring were already walking away, heading for the other side of the park.

"No way, man," Crew-cut said, his voice cracking. "Why do I want to go on ahead when *you're* having all the fun?"

Carlos shrugged. "Suit yourself." He turned to Carrie. "Do you have a car?" he asked.

Her blood felt icy cold despite the evening's heat. Take care of her? How was Carlos going to "take care of" her? Still, she stuck out her chin. "Maybe."

"Please give me the car keys."

"I don't have 'em," she lied.

He leaned the rifle against the side of the aquarium and stepped toward her. "Give me the keys, please," he said, "or I'll have to take them from you."

"And I'll help," Crew-cut said with an ugly smile.

Carrie crossed her arms. "You boys planning to steal my car now, too? Aren't breaking-and-entering charges good enough for the lot of you?"

One arm. That's all it took for Carlos to hold her while he quickly searched her pockets for her car keys. Both her arms were pinned and her face was pressed against the sweet-smelling leather of his jacket. If he hadn't been wearing that jacket, she would've bitten him, but she didn't even try, since all she would've gotten was a mouthful of cowhide. She pulled back her leg to kick him, but he found the keys in the front pocket of her shorts and let her go before her boot connected with his shin.

Carrie was gasping indignantly, but Carlos was unruffled.

"Thank you," he said politely, as if she'd handed him the keys. He slipped them into his own pocket.

A strand of her long blond hair had come free from her pony-tail, and she pushed it back off her face, looping it behind her ear. "I have three more payments on that car," she said hotly. "If you think I'm just going to let you steal it—"

"No one's going to steal your car," Carlos told her.

"Wait a minute, man." Crew-cut looked at Carrie. "What kind is it?"

Even Carlos looked exasperated. "Get lost, man," he said to Crew-cut. "You're cramping my style, you know?"

But Crew-cut didn't budge. "If *you* get to have fun," he said with a petulant set to his square jaw, "*I* get to watch."

Watch? Watch what? The fear was back, fear for her personal safety, fear for her very life. But the fear brought a new wave of anger—anger that her father and brothers were going to be proven right. She *couldn't* take care of herself. She had had no right to leave the safety of their isolated Montana ranch and move to a crime-riddled Florida city. Dammit, she could just imagine them saying "We told her so," as they morosely gathered around to identify her body at the St. Simone morgue.

Carlos took her gently by the arm, but she pulled free, glaring at him.

"Where are you taking me?" she asked.

He countered with a question. "Where's your car parked?"

She didn't answer, so he answered for her.

"Not in the parking lot outside the gate," he said, "or I would have seen it there. It's probably somewhere inside the fence, no?"

She stared at him silently. If he so much as touched her, she'd throw up on him. That's what she'd always been told to do in the event of a sexual assault, right? It sure wouldn't take much effort on her part. She was already feeling queasy.

"Are you going to walk?" Carlos said patiently, "or perhaps I should carry you?"

"Yo, Carlos, *I'll* carry her," Crew-cut volunteered.

"I'll walk," Carrie said quickly.

"Oh, man," Crew-cut said, exaggerating his whine. "I don't think she likes me." He pretended to pout. "But, baby, you know, I like *you*...."

He reached out to touch her, and Carrie jerked back out of his grasp. "Don't you come near me," she said sharply, including Carlos in her glare.

What were her options here? She could stand passively by and wait to see what they were going to do with her. Or she could run. She could dart away into the shadows and hide. She could slip into the seal tank and swim to the covered hutch that could only be accessed underwater.

She glanced toward the seal tank. It was more than a hundred yards away. If she was smart, she'd run in the other direction first, lose these jerks in the shadows underneath the main aquarium bleachers, and then head back to the seal tank. Once she was under the water, they'd never find her. Not in a million years.

"Don't even think about it," Carlos murmured, as if he could read her mind.

"Think about what?" she asked innocently. And bolted toward the bleachers.

Seven steps. That's all it took before Carlos tackled her, pulling her down onto the hard sand with him. He pinned her to the ground, her hands above her head, the full weight of his body pressing against her.

Carrie struggled to get away, struggled to bring her knee up to kick him, but she couldn't move. Her heart was pounding and she was nearly blind with panic.

"*Madre de Dios,*" Carlos said. "You are a handful and a half, aren't you?" He brought his mouth closer to her ear, lowering his voice. "Look, I'm not going to hurt you. I'm a—"

Carrie bit him between his shoulder and his neck, right through the white cotton of his T-shirt collar.

He swore sharply, and pulled away from her. She scrambled into a sitting position and tried to back away, but he grabbed her ankle with one hand. With the other he rubbed his neck.

"A biter, huh?" Crew-cut said, crouching down next to them. "Oh, baby, you can bite *me* anytime."

Carrie was shaking uncontrollably, and she couldn't stop the tears that had flooded her eyes. One spilled down her cheek and she wiped it fiercely away. She'd be damned if she was going to let these bastards see her cry.

Carlos muttered something in Spanish, pushing his hair out of his face. One dark, curly lock caught on his eyelashes, but he didn't seem to notice. The priest look was back in his eyes, making his entire face seem warm and compassionate and full of remorse. Would he look at her that way after the devil took over again, after he'd forced himself on her?

Carrie spit at him, and he closed his eyes as the spittle hit him full in the face.

"Oh, gross," Crew-cut exclaimed. "Slap her, man. Don't let the bitch get away with that. Hell, I'll slap her for you."

"No, thank you."

"Aw, come on—"

"I said, *no*." Carlos kept his eyes closed until he'd wiped his face clean with his hand. When he opened his eyes again, Carrie could see no anger there—only patience. He smiled apologetically at Carrie. "I'm sorry," he said. "I didn't mean to frighten you."

"You're telling her you're *sorry?*" Crew-cut said. "*She's* the one who should be apologizing."

Carlos exchanged his hold on Carrie's leg for a steady grip on her arm and got to his feet, pulling her up with him.

She tried to pull free, but he wouldn't let go. "If I let you go, you'll just run again," he said, "so I'm not going to do it."

"You're hurting me," Carrie said.

"Don't pull, and I won't have to hold you so tightly," Carlos said.

He led her around the corner of the main aquarium, and there was her little sports car, bright red and very shiny, even in the dimly powered floodlights.

Crew-cut gave a low whistle. "Nice wheels."

The trunk was open, the way she'd left it when she'd come to the office that evening. She'd been airing out the fishy smell that seemed to follow her around.

"I guess I didn't need those keys after all," Carlos said, pulling her around to the back of the car. He was still holding her arm with his right hand, so he gestured grandly toward the trunk with his left. "Get in."

Carrie stared at him, not understanding. What did he want her to do?

"That's it?" Crew-cut sputtered, disappointed. "You're just going to lock her in the trunk? Man, if it was me, I'd've taken her right here, in the front seat of her car."

Carlos was going to lock her in the trunk of her car. He wasn't going to force himself on her; he was just going to make sure she couldn't call the police. He *wasn't* going to hurt her; she was going to be all right. Except, Lord, that trunk was awfully tiny, and with the hood down, it would be incredibly dark and hot and…

Crew-cut reached out and ran one grubby finger down the side of Carrie's face. She pulled away, slapping at his hand, disgusted by his touch. On further thought, maybe being locked in the trunk wasn't such a bad idea.

Crew-cut drew back his hand to slap her, but Carlos caught his wrist.

"Rumor has it," he said dryly, "that sex is more pleasurable when the woman is willing."

"Yeah, well, this would be better than nothing," Crew-cut said with a shrug, jerking his hand free.

"No," Carlos said firmly. "In a case like this, *nothing* is best."

"Aw, come on, man," Crew-cut said. "I think she's kind of cute, so little and pretty. Look at all this blond hair."

Her hair had come free from its ponytail, and it hung around her face in a smooth blond sheet. Crew-cut ran his fingers through it, and Carrie yanked her head back, nearly toppling over. Carlos steadied her, and she realized she was grateful for his presence, grateful for the warmth of his body behind her. Crew-cut was the one she was afraid of. Carlos didn't want to hurt her. At least she *hoped* he didn't.

"Come on," Crew-cut said again. "Take me five minutes, ten minutes tops. I bet she's a real screamer." He leered at Carrie. "I bet you'd like to sink those sharp little teeth in me, huh, baby?"

"If you so much as touch me," Carrie snapped, "I'll kick your family jewels through the roof of your mouth."

"And that's after *I* get finished kicking your family jewels through the roof of your mouth," Carlos said mildly. "Back off, T.J."

"Why? You don't want her—"

"I didn't say that," Carlos corrected him. "On the contrary. You're right. She *is* very pretty. And I like her spirit. Very much so. No, I didn't say I didn't want her."

Carrie's eyes flew to Carlos's face. Her heart was pounding so loudly she could barely hear. She searched his eyes, looking to see if he was serious, or if he was joking—or if he'd been joking all along and he really meant to force himself on her, and then let his horrible friend take a turn.

"Shh," he said softly, as if he could see the sudden flare of panic in her eyes. "No one's going to hurt you."

His eyes were unreadable, an odd mix of heat, excitement and...*kindness?* Carrie was confused, and terribly frightened again. If this was some kind of head game Carlos was playing with her, he was winning, hands down.

"Just do her, man," Crew-cut urged. "You know you want to."

"But the real question is, does *she* want to?"

"Try it, and I'll kill you," Carrie whispered.

"Unlike you," Carlos said to Crew-cut, "I am quick to recognize a no when I hear one, and that sounded like a very definite no to me." He turned to Carrie. "Get in the trunk, please."

But Carrie couldn't do it. She couldn't move. As much as she wanted to be away from Crew-cut and Carlos, she couldn't bring herself to climb into that tiny, dark, airless trunk. Never mind her childhood claustrophobic fears of being locked in a closet or trapped in her parents' camper's tiny bathroom. Lord, in a few hours, the hot Florida sun would rise, and that trunk would turn into an oven. She'd bake. She'd dehydrate. Her body temperature would soar, and she'd be dead in a matter of hours.

Carlos scooped her up, holding her, one arm behind her shoulders, the other supporting her knees, and lifted her easily into the trunk.

"No!" She clung to his neck, afraid to let go, afraid that his would be the last face she'd ever see, afraid of the hood closing down on her, trapping her, entombing her.

"You'll be safest here, *cara*," Carlos murmured, prying her fingers loose. "Trust me," Carlos said to Carrie, his dark brown eyes so gentle, so kind. "You have to trust me."

The hood of the trunk closed with a frightening finality. She was alone, alone in the dark.

"C'mon, man, we're going to be late," T.J. said, running his hand anxiously across his crew cut as he looked across the dark marine park. "Iceman's gonna start the meeting without us."

"I'm not ready to go," the man known as Carlos said calmly, stopping at a row of pay phones near the closed and shuttered concession stand.

"This ain't the time to call your girlfriend," T.J. said, watching him dial. "911? What the hell...?"

"Someone's got to get the girl out of the trunk before the sun comes up," Carlos said in his gentle Hispanic accent.

"Yo, we can let her out on the way back." T.J. smiled. "*I'll* come back this way and—"

"Yeah," Carlos said into the phone. "I'd like to report a woman locked in the trunk of a red Miata inside the grounds of Sea Circus. Yeah, that's Sea Circus—down on Ocean and Florida Streets? The car's *inside* the park, not out in the lot."

T.J. shook his head. "You're a stupid sonuva—"

"No, I wish to remain anonymous," Carlos said.

"We gotta go," T.J. growled.

Carlos put his finger in his ear, blocking the sound of T.J.'s voice. "How do I know there's a woman in the trunk of a red

Miata?'' He laughed. ''Because I put her there. Just send a patrol car down to let her out, okay?'' There was a pause. ''Good,'' he said.

He hung up the phone and smiled at T.J. ''Now I'm ready to go.''

Chapter 2

January—six months later

Felipe Salazar adjusted his bow tie in the mirror of his furnished suite at the ritzy Harbor's Gate Apartments, then wiped imaginary dust from the shoulder of his tuxedo.

It was a very nice tuxedo, carefully tailored so that his shoulder holster and gun didn't disrupt the lines of his jacket.

This penthouse suite was very nice, too. It was four times bigger than his tiny one-bedroom apartment on the other side of town. Of course, the monthly rent was much higher than four times that of his little, airless apartment. But luckily for him, he wasn't paying it.

In fact, he wasn't paying for anything these days. The hotel, his expensive clothes, his meals, the two thousand dollars in spending money he carried around in fifties and one hundreds were all courtesy of the St. Simone Police Department.

It was one of the perks of working a round-the-clock dangerous job. In fact, it was the only perk most people would understand. Very few people would call the danger, the risk, the *thrill* of being an undercover police detective a perk.

But Felipe Salazar wasn't most people.

And tonight, he wasn't even Felipe Salazar.

Tonight, as he'd been for the past five months, he was Raoul Tomás Garcia Vasquez. Raoul Tomás Garcia Vasquez had quite good taste in clothes. He wore expensive suits and Italian shoes and underwear that cost more than a police detective's daily salary.

Felipe looked at himself again in the mirror. Yes, the tux fitted him very nicely. It was a far cry from the leather jacket and worn-out blue jeans he'd worn on his last assignment. He'd been called Carlos for that one, and he'd infiltrated an uneasy alliance of street-gang leaders out to make a fortune in the world of illegal drugs. As Carlos, he'd come face-to-face with Caroline Brooks, that intriguing blonde at Sea Circus and…

He shook his head. This was no time to think about blondes, particularly about *this* blonde. Unfortunately, there was never any time. He'd gone straight from being Carlos to being Raoul Vasquez. He couldn't remember the last time someone had actually called him Felipe. But such was the nature of his job. Felipe glanced into the mirror again, and Raoul Vasquez looked back at him.

Raoul was fresh out of prison, and ready to start over. He'd come to St. Simone—or so his story went—after cashing in some favors, some *big* favors. His old boss, Joseph Halstad, the head of a minor crime syndicate in Washington, D.C., had offered him his old job back, but Raoul wanted a fresh start, someplace new, someplace where the police didn't recognize his face.

So Halstad had phoned Lawrence Richter, the man who ran Western Florida's organized-crime outfit, and called in a few favors of his own.

Of course, Richter didn't know that Halstad had made that phone call as part of a deal struck with the Washington D.A. over certain racketeering charges.

And Richter *wouldn't* know—at least not until Felipe had gathered all the proof he needed to cement this case shut and send Richter and all the men and women in his syndicate to jail for a long, long time.

After five months, Felipe was immersed in Richter's organization deeply enough to put Richter and many of his underlings away. Strangely enough, even with all the drug and weapons sales, the prostitution, gambling and racketeering that went on, it was the importation of illegal aliens that was going to bring Richter down.

On the surface, it seemed innocent enough, benevolent even. Lawrence Richter, humanitarian, was helping the poor and impoverished into America. He was helping them get a start, helping them find that American Dream.

Felipe knew all about the American Dream. His own parents had made the move from Puerto Rico to Miami, searching for a better life for themselves and their five children. But Miami had been hot and angry, and they'd moved on, across to the west coast of Florida, to the city of St. Simone.

Some American Dream.

Felipe's father had worked himself into an early grave, trying to keep his floundering auto shop afloat. Raphael, Felipe's older brother, had run with the wrong crowd, nearly overdosed on drugs and ended up doing time in a state maximum security prison. His oldest sister, Catalina, had married a man who'd been killed in a car accident by a drunk driver, leaving her alone to raise their two small children. His other sister, Marisela, had given up her own dream of going to college and had taken over their father's garage with the help of Roberto, their youngest brother, who was still in high school.

And Felipe? Felipe had become a cop.

He smiled wryly at himself in the mirror. His father, the dreamer, had been disappointed in Felipe's choice of profession. Yet it was Felipe who was most like the old man. Out of all his brothers and sisters, it was Felipe who was the idealist. It was Felipe who still believed in good versus evil, in right over wrong. It was Felipe who still believed in the criminal justice system and the rule of law. It was Felipe who was keeping alive the American Dream.

And that meant putting away Lawrence Richter, who was bringing entire families of illegal immigrants into the country and turning them into little more than slaves. In exchange for safe passage into America, the land of opportunity, Richter would squeeze years of indentured servitude from these people. He'd contract them out to work in factories and sweatshops at much lower than the legal minimum wage. Then he'd keep most of their paycheck, giving them only barely enough to get by. If they complained, they'd get delivered into the hands of the immigration department, speaking hardly any English and knowing only the assumed names of the men who had brought them into the country.

Felipe had seen many of these people, trapped into working sixty-hour weeks for money that they would never see, money that would line Lawrence Richter's pockets. Felipe had looked into their eyes and seen the despair and desperation—and utter hopelessness.

For them, the American Dream had become a nightmare.

Shutting Richter's operation down would mean deportation for many of them. But some would slip through the cracks, free at last to pursue that elusive American Dream.

Still, as close as Felipe was to nailing Richter, he had to wait. Because last week, something he'd suspected for quite some time had become more than a mere suspicion.

Richter had a partner.

And Richter's partner was someone relatively high up in St. Simone's government. He was someone with power, someone with clout, someone who, it seemed, could make the entire police force turn their heads and look the other way if need be.

And before he took Richter down, Felipe Salazar, faithful believer in right over wrong and staunch defender of his father's American Dream, was going to make sure that this other man, this man Richter had nicknamed "Captain Rat," whoever he was, fell, too.

Bobby Penfield III was *the* most boring man Carrie Brooks had ever met in her twenty-five years of life.

Yet she sat across from him at their table in Schroedinger's, St. Simone's most elegant restaurant, located on the ground floor of the glamorous Reef Hotel, and tried to smile. *This* was why she didn't go out on dates, she reminded herself sternly. The next time some relatively nice-looking man that she didn't know asked her to dinner, she would definitely find some excuse to stay home.

Sure, some women might have found Bobby Penfield III and his endless stories about the ad agency wars exciting. But frankly, Carrie couldn't see how choosing a man over a woman to plug some paper towel on TV could really make that much difference in the future sales of those paper towels. And it certainly didn't warrant nearly an hour of dinner conversation. Besides, as an avid environmentalist, she'd prefer it if the entire world stopped using paper and turned to reusable cloth towels instead.

Carrie wished that he'd change the subject. She wished that he'd talk about *any*thing else. Hell, she'd rather discuss last week's sensational mob-related killings—the "Sandlot Murders," the press had so cleverly dubbed them. Everyone across the state was talking about it. It had even made the national news. Two mobsters, Tony Mareidas and Steve Dupree, had been executed in a vacant lot downtown—a vacant lot that happened to be next to an elementary school. Children had discovered the bodies, and the city was in an uproar, searching for the man or men responsible for the bloody crime.

But Bobby Penfield III rambled on about his paper products, and Carrie was forced to smile cheerfully back at him. She was here because Bobby's ad agency was going to produce a series of commercials and print ads about Sea Circus, at quite a discount off their regular rates. Or so Hal Tompkins, the aquarium's business manager had told her. And when Hal had brought Bobby over to see the dolphins run through their afternoon training session with Carrie, and when Bobby had asked Carrie to dinner and Hal had widened his eyes at Carrie in a silent plea to be nice to Bobby, Carrie had stupidly accepted the date.

So here she was in her own personal level of hell, in a much too posh restaurant, underdressed in the fanciest dress she owned—a simple blue-flowered sleeveless dress with a short, swingy skirt—sitting across the table from a man she had nothing, absolutely *nothing* in common with. Except maybe for the fact that they both liked the new two-piece bathing suit Carrie had been wearing during that afternoon's dolphin training session.

Across the restaurant, a long banquet table caught Carrie's eye. It was filled with men in tuxedos and their beautiful wives. Or dates. Dates, Carrie decided cynically. Their wives were probably all home with the children.

A silver-haired man sat at one end of the table, smiling benevolently at his guests. Yes, this was his party, Carrie decided. Silver-hair was definitely the man who'd be picking up tonight's check.

Bobby Penfield droned on about marketing disposable diapers, unaware that Carrie's attention had long since wandered. As she watched, across the room, Silver-hair stood up and made a toast. Another man, a man who had his back to her, stood also and bowed graciously to polite applause.

Carrie leaned forward, trying to get a closer look. Something about this man, something about the set of his shoulders—or maybe the way his tuxedo fit those broad shoulders—was oddly familiar. She studied the back of his head, silently willing him to turn around.

But he didn't. He sat back down without giving her a chance to see his face. Whoever he was, he wore his long, dark hair pulled tightly into a ponytail at his nape.

Carrie knew plenty of men with long, dark hair that they wore in a ponytail. But none of the men *she* knew had ever worn a tuxedo—let alone a tuxedo that had so obviously been altered to give its wearer such an incredibly precise fit.

Carrie looked up, startled, suddenly aware that Bobby had stopped talking. He was looking at her as if he was waiting for her to answer a question.

She did the only thing she could. She smiled at him. And asked him where he went to college.

Bobby was only too happy to keep talking about himself. He didn't even notice she'd never answered his question. Carrie wasn't sure he'd heard a single thing she'd said all night—except the questions she'd asked about him.

Lord, somewhere, someplace in the world, there had to exist a man who actually listened to the words another person spoke.

But whoever he was, he sure as all hell wasn't named Bobby Penfield III.

Of course, she wasn't exactly listening to *him,* either. She sighed. She'd known from the moment she'd gotten into his car that this entire evening was going to be a disaster. She'd picked up on their incompatibility that early and wished now that she'd had the nerve to bow out gracefully.

Except Bobby still seemed to harbor hopes that Carrie would go home with him after dinner. She could see it in his eyes, in the way his gaze lingered on her breasts and on her mouth.

Carrie sighed again. This was truly the pits.

But it sure wasn't as bad as being trapped in the trunk of her car for two endless, nightmarish hours, the way she'd been back in July.

It still haunted her, even after all these months.

Those two hours had seemed more like two years.

Carrie had gone ballistic at first, flashing temporarily back to the time she was locked in the tiny bathroom of her parents' camper when she was nine years old. Just as she'd done when she was nine, she'd cried as if the world were coming to an end. She'd cried, and kept crying, until she'd groped around and found the old flashlight she kept in the trunk of her car for emergencies. The main bulb was out, but it was one of those big box flashlights with a bullet-shaped red light attached to the handle, and *that* light was working.

The trunk had been absurdly tiny and terrifyingly confining in the red glow from the flashlight. But at least the darkness hadn't pressed in on her anymore, suffocating her. And there had been fresh air—or at least there had been after she'd pulled the foam sealing strip from between the trunk hood and the frame. Her trunk would probably never be watertight again, but fresh air had been her immediate concern.

Then, lying on her back with her legs scrunched up and her face only a few inches from the inside of the hood, Carrie sang. She sang to keep herself from losing her mind. She sang every song she'd ever learned, and some she hadn't. She sang all of the top forty hits from the year she'd entered eighth grade. She sang all of those annoying Broadway musical show tunes that her mother had loved so much. She sang every song from Patty Loveless's two most recent compact discs. She sang until her throat was raw.

It truly had been hell, lying there, sweating, trying to keep the panic from engulfing her, feeling the walls closing in even tighter....

Carlos.

Her thoughts continued to return to him every now and then, even after all this time. In the first few weeks after he'd locked her in the trunk, she'd thought about him often.

Oddly enough, he still sometimes showed up in her dreams, too. Even odder, those dreams were steamy and erotic, filled with entangled legs, and cool, smooth, muscular skin, and long, dark hair hanging down around her face as he slowly bent to kiss her, as he sensuously, languorously, exquisitely moved inside of her—

She'd wake up with a start, surprised and sometimes a little disappointed to find that she'd only been dreaming.

Six months ago, she'd gone to the police station and sworn out a complaint, but the man named Carlos and his three friends still hadn't been caught.

Lucky for them, she told herself fiercely. If she so much as set eyes on any of those sons of bitches again...

Across the room, Silver-hair's guests stood up, stretching their legs. The women moved off, almost in one body, toward the ladies' room. The men shook hands and—

No.

It couldn't be.

Could it?

Carrie had gotten only the briefest glimpse of the man's face, but those exotic cheekbones were unmistakable.

She wouldn't be absolutely positive until she saw his eyes, but either she was going crazy or the man with the long dark ponytail, the man in the well-tailored tuxedo, was *Carlos*.

Of course, it was entirely possible that she *was* going crazy.

It had been six months, and Carrie *still* thought she spotted Carlos everywhere—in the mall, in the grocery store, at the movies, and even in the crowd at Sea Circus. She'd see a tall man with long, dark hair and she'd stare and take a closer look. But then the man would turn his head and she'd realize it wasn't Carlos after all. It was just someone who looked a little bit like him.

But *this* man didn't turn around and give her a second chance to see his face. He stared toward the lobby door with his back to her.

"Excuse me," Carrie said to Bobby Penfield as he paused to take a much-needed breath. She folded her napkin and set it down next to her salad plate. "Excuse me for just one minute. I'll be right back."

She pushed back her chair and hurried toward the lobby after the tuxedo-clad men.

Schroedinger's lobby was splendorous, with lots of plants and high ceilings and chandeliers and big wall mirrors that seemed to make the room twice the size it really was. The man who might be Carlos was standing near the checkroom, talking to Silver-hair. Several of the other men stood nearby.

Carrie stopped short at the sight of the long-haired man's face in one of the mirrors.

It *was* Carlos. Lord in heaven, it really was him.

He was smiling, with that gentle, priestly smile, at something Silver-hair had said to him. Silver-hair said something else, and the smile exploded into a devilish laugh, complete with a full view of perfect white teeth.

Despite all her dreams and various pseudo-Carlos sightings, Carrie had forgotten exactly how handsome this man was.

At that exact instant, his gaze flickered in her direction, then landed squarely on her face. For the briefest second, Carlos froze, recognition darkening his eyes as he looked at Carrie.

She'd known him six months ago for all of half an hour, but during that time, even when she aimed her rifle directly at his head, she'd not seen anything besides confidence and calm control in his eyes. But now, suddenly, she could see panic. Sheer, total panic. It flared for an instant, and then it was gone, and his face and eyes were oddly expressionless.

He was afraid of something. Afraid of *her,* probably.

Damn straight he had a reason to be. He'd locked her in the

trunk of her car, for Pete's sake. All she had to do was point her finger and scream loud enough, and the entire St. Simone police force would be down upon his head.

Slowly, deliberately, Carrie started toward him.

Chapter 3

He was looking at the cause of his death.

Felipe Salazar was standing in the lobby of Schroedinger's, and looking directly at the cause of his certain death.

It was the dolphin-riding cowgirl from Sea Circus, and she was heading toward him, a small, tight smile on her perfect lips, and the fires of hell gleaming in her pretty blue-green eyes.

She'd traded her clunky boots for a pair of brown leather sandals, and her grungy shorts and T-shirt for a sleeveless, short, blue-flowered dress that would have sent his heart into his throat—if it hadn't already been there for an entirely different reason.

Her blond hair was longer than it had been six months ago, and she wore it down around her shoulders, parted on the side, a straight sheet of gold that shimmered in the light from the chandeliers.

She wasn't wearing much makeup, just a hint of eye shadow and lipstick, maybe a touch of rouge. She hadn't tried to hide the charming splash of freckles that dotted her delicate nose and softly rounded cheekbones.

Madre de Dios, but she was even lovelier than he remembered. And dear God, he'd spent an awful lot of time remembering, those first few weeks after the showdown with Iceman and the rest of his gang. Felipe had even gone back to Sea Circus, just to see for himself that the girl was really all right.

Her name was Caroline Brooks, nickname Carrie.

He'd caught most of her dolphin show, and seeing her dive into the huge tank with the enormous sea creatures, seeing her actually ride on their backs, seeing the gentle way she treated them, seeing her smile and laugh without that tinge of panic on her pretty face, and yes, seeing her in that amazing red, form-fitting Speedo bathing suit, he'd almost approached her. He'd almost gone up to her and finished that sentence he'd started, that sentence she'd interrupted with a bite from her sharp teeth.

I'm a cop.

So why hadn't he told her?

Because he liked her way, *way* too much. Because in his heart, he knew that even if he were able to seduce her, one or two nights simply wouldn't be enough. Because he knew in a matter of days, he'd be gone, deep under cover, infiltrating Lawrence Richter's crime syndicate as Raoul Tomás Garcia Vasquez. And, most of all, because he knew that any romantic involvement with him would place her in potential danger.

So he'd made himself forget about her.

Or at least he'd tried.

At the very least, he'd stayed far, far away from Sea Circus and pretty Caroline Brooks.

How very ironic to realize now that *not* approaching her, *not* telling her he was a cop, *not* revealing his true identity to her, was going to result in his own death. And, dear God, probably her death, too.

Because, coming over here the way she was, with that bright light of justice and retribution in her eyes, Felipe had no doubt that she was going to blow his cover to kingdom come.

And if Lawrence Richter had the slightest reason to believe that Felipe was a cop, then Felipe was soon going to be a very dead cop. There was no way—not knowing what Felipe knew— that Richter would let him live.

Felipe hadn't spoken to his best friend, Jim Keegan, in more than four weeks. That thought flashed crazily into his head and he wondered briefly how Jim—or Diego, the Spanish version of James, as Felipe was fond of calling him—would take the news of his friend's death.

The best defense is a strong offense. That's what Jim always used to say back when they were partners on the vice squad, before Jim took a coveted spot on the force as a homicide detective. *There's always a way out. You've just got to find it,* and *Keegan's Rule Number One: Nothing is impossible.*

If there was a way out of this mess, it would involve somehow keeping Caroline's smart mouth tightly shut.

And that wasn't going to be easy.

"Excuse me, please," Felipe murmured to Lawrence Richter. "I have to head off an…old girlfriend."

If the older man saw the bead of sweat drip down the side of Felipe's face, he didn't mention it. He merely looked from Felipe to Caroline and back, and smiled.

"Of course," Richter said.

Felipe moved quickly then, intercepting Caroline Brooks a good ten feet away from Richter. Maybe, just maybe, they were far enough away to keep him from overhearing their conversation.…

"Well, what do you know?" the tiny blond woman said, gazing coolly up at Felipe as if she were the one who was almost ten inches taller. "We meet again, C—"

Carlos. She was going to call him Carlos, in a voice loud enough to carry around the entire lobby. But he wasn't Carlos now. He was supposed to be Raoul Vasquez.

Felipe shut her up the only way he could.

He covered her mouth with his and kissed her.

She tasted like the house salad dressing, fresh and spicy and delicious. She drew her breath in sharply, pulling back to look him in the eye, and Felipe knew in that one fraction of a second he hadn't imagined the electricity that had sparked between them that night at Sea Circus. It was still there, still fierce and hot. And he also knew without the slightest doubt that if he'd gone to her the way he'd longed to, if he'd told her the truth, told her he was a cop and apologized for treating her so roughly, he would've been able to seduce her. Or, *Madre de Dios,* maybe she would've seduced him.

Regret coursed through him, regret that he'd missed his chance, regret that he'd probably never have another opportunity to kiss Caroline Brooks, let alone make love to her. Because unless Felipe took her arm and dragged her away from Lawrence Richter and his right-hand triggerman, Tommy Walsh, his life was about to end.

"Darling," he said smoothly, while she was temporarily silenced, "how nice to see you again. Come, let's step outside where we can talk privately."

He took her by the arm and drew her toward the main entrance.

But she wasn't having any of it. She pulled her arm free and laughed. "You're crazier than I thought if you think I'd go *any*-where with you," she said coldly in her Western twang.

Felipe could feel Richter's eyes on him, watching. Richter was always watching, always aware of every little thing that went on around him. It was one of the reasons he was so successful, and one of the reasons he'd never been apprehended.

"I know you've missed me," Felipe said, loudly enough for Richter to overhear. "And I'm sorry I haven't called you, but I've been busy. Please don't be angry—"

"*Missed* you?" She laughed in disbelief. "You locked me in the tr—"

Near desperation, Felipe kissed her again. Anything, *any*thing, to make her stop talking. He kissed her harder this time, drawing her body completely against his and holding her tightly in his arms.

Again she was temporarily silenced, and he took advantage of those few precious seconds.

"Please," he said, again loudly enough for Richter to hear. "I know you'll find this difficult to believe, but I've stayed away because I care for you so very much and—"

She hit him. She pulled her right arm free and hauled off and punched him, hard, in the stomach. Felipe saw it coming and tightened his stomach muscles. She probably hurt her fist more than she hurt him. But it was enough to catch the attention of the restaurant staff.

"Mister, you are *so* full of crap," Carrie said, her coolness gone. She was livid with anger.

"Is there a problem here?" the maître d' said, smoothly sidling up.

"No, no," Felipe said almost desperately. "Everything is fine—"

"Yes, there most certainly *is* a problem," Carrie said. "This…this…*con* man is trying to make it seem as if he and I have known each other for longer than the thirty minutes we spent together over at—"

"Caroline," he said quickly, interrupting her. Con man. Better than cop, but not by much. One glance at Richter told Felipe that the older man was still watching him. Watching and listening. "I think the gentleman would like us to continue this discussion outside and—"

Carrie's eyes narrowed. "How do you know my name?"

"She gets like this sometimes," Felipe said in a low voice to the maître d'. "Too much to drink. Will you help me take her outside?"

"Touch me again and I swear I'll scream," Carrie warned him, glaring at both men.

The maître d' backed off, eager to keep the young woman from having a fit in the lobby of his four-star restaurant.

Richter nodded once and Tommy Walsh stepped forward, his pale blue eyes bored and flat. "Raoul," he said in his thick Brooklyn accent, "you need some kind of help here?"

Carrie turned her wide blue-green gaze back on Felipe. "*Raoul?*" she said in disbelief. She turned indignantly to Tommy. "Funny, six months ago I knew him as Carlos."

Six months ago, Raoul Vasquez was supposedly in prison.

"Oh, really?" Tommy said to Carrie. "Is that right?"

"It was August," Felipe said, talking fast and low. "I was just out on parole. It had been eighteen months, man. I didn't want to get married. I just wanted a little relief, you know? I told her my name was Carlos and—"

"It was *not* August. It was July," Carrie said sharply. "And you didn't touch me. You locked me in the trunk of my car, remember?''

She sounded loco. The way she said it, it sounded as if Felipe—or Raoul or Carlos or whoever he was—had turned down an opportunity to spend the night with her. And standing there in that enticingly simple blue-flowered dress that accented her near-perfect figure, with her slender, tanned arms and shapely legs, her shining golden hair, her eyes the color of the ocean and her sweetly pretty face, it didn't seem possible that any man in his right mind would have turned her down.

So Felipe laughed, praying hard that Tommy would get the joke.

He did. Tommy's beefy boxer's face crinkled slightly in a tight smile that didn't reach his eyes. But then again, Felipe had never seen Tommy truly smile.

''She's crazy, man,'' he said to Tommy, grateful at least for that half smile. He turned back to Carrie. ''Sweetheart, I know you must've been upset when I was gone in the morning but—''

Carrie crossed her arms and turned her imperious gaze on the maître d'. ''Call the police. I want this man arrested.''

''You must be confusing me with someone else,'' Felipe said, in a last-ditch effort to keep her from revealing his true identity. But he knew it was too late. Yes, Tommy was smiling, but he was smiling as if the joke was on Felipe.

''Oh, no,'' Carrie said with certainty. ''You're Carlos, all right. And it wasn't August. It was July. July 22. You were with that son of a bitch you called T.J. And that other guy you called Iceman and—''

Carrie kept talking, but Felipe didn't hear her. He didn't hear her because she'd just told Richter clear as day that he was a cop.

Iceman. Her mention of Iceman had given him away.

Iceman had been one of St. Simone's hardest-working drug pushers.

And Iceman had owed Richter a cool quarter million at the time of his death. The money had been borrowed in order to make an investment in what was quite possibly the biggest small-time drug shipment to hit the west coast of Florida. The money had been borrowed and never paid back, because when Iceman and T. J. Cerrone and big, nose-ring-bedecked Randall Page, a.k.a. Mule, went to pick up the shipment of cocaine, the police went, too.

Although surrounded and clearly outgunned, Iceman had pulled his weapon and started a gun battle that had injured four police officers and left himself and his two business associates dead.

It had happened last summer, on the night of July 22, to be precise. And if Felipe had been with Iceman on July 22 before his death, it could only mean one thing.

Richter was a smart man. Tommy Walsh, despite the fact that he looked like an aging boxer, was a smart man, too. They could add one plus one, and in this case, one plus one equaled cop.

Richter looked at Tommy and Tommy looked at Richter, and Felipe knew that they'd come to the obvious conclusion.

"You were good," Tommy said quietly to Felipe, speaking to him in the past tense as if he were already dead. "You just weren't lucky enough."

Tommy's pale blue eyes flickered once toward Caroline, and Felipe knew with dreadful certainty that Richter's right-hand man was going to use the petite blonde to make sure Felipe cooperated. Tommy was going to threaten to blow Caroline's brains across Schroedinger's lobby if Felipe didn't go quietly with him out to the parking lot and Richter's waiting limo.

But if Felipe went along for the ride, it would be his last ride. He had no doubts that Tommy would take him into the Everglades and kill him. And then he'd kill Caroline, too, because by then, *she'd* have seen and heard too much. Dear God, she'd probably already witnessed enough to warrant her death in Tommy's mind.

From the corner of his eye, Felipe could see the big glass doors that led out of the restaurant. Outside, a valet pulled an expensive-looking car under the brightly lit awning.

As if in slow motion, Tommy reached under his jacket for his gun.

The valet got out of the car, leaving the door open. He crossed to the other side and opened the front passenger door as the owners of the car, a middle-aged couple, started out into the Florida night.

It was now or never.

Felipe turned, scooped Caroline into his arms and ran for the door.

She screamed in outrage, just as he knew she would. He prayed that drawing attention to themselves this way would keep Tommy from pulling out his gun right there in the lobby and shooting Felipe in the back.

Felipe heard the muffled thud of a gunshot, then a bullet whizzed by his left ear, and he knew with a sinking heart that Tommy wanted him dead badly enough to risk going to prison himself. He shielded Caroline Brooks with his body and moved even faster, hoping desperately that Tommy would miss again. But Tommy didn't often miss, and Felipe knew without a doubt that the gunman's next shot was going to hit him.

The car's owner was still holding the glass door open for his wife, and Felipe knocked them both aside, praying they wouldn't get caught in the cross fire.

Tommy was using some kind of silencing device—most of the people around them were unaware of the gun, unaware of the danger.

"Get down," Felipe shouted, shifting Caroline easily into one arm, drawing and brandishing his own gun. "Everyone down!"

The valets scattered.

As Felipe threw Caroline into the front seat of the waiting car, slamming the door behind her, he felt a slap hit the back of his leg. He scrambled up and over the hood of the car and into the driver's seat. The keys were in the ignition and the motor was idling, and he threw it into gear.

The tires squealed on the pavement as the powerful engine responded. Felipe knew he'd been shot. He knew his leg was bleeding, but the pain hadn't registered yet. It was masked by the adrenaline surging through his veins. Besides, a bullet in the leg was nothing compared to what might have been.

He was alive. He was still alive.

Tommy's aim was usually unerringly accurate, and Felipe knew that it had only been good fortune that had kept the bullets from slamming first into the back of his head, and then into the small of his back. Or maybe somebody was listening to his prayers.

But that somebody wasn't listening to all of them.

In the rearview mirror, Felipe could see Richter's limousine leave the parking lot, bouncing as it took the slope of the driveway too quickly. Tommy was following them. This wasn't over yet.

Next to him in the car, Caroline Brooks had stopped screaming. One glance in her direction told Felipe that she was watching him. Her face was pale and her eyes were big. That and her rapid breathing revealed the fear she was trying so hard to hide.

"Fasten your seat belt," he told her curtly over the roar of the engine.

"Just let me out of the car," she said, talking low and fast, working hard to keep fear from raising the pitch of her voice. "I don't know what your game is, mister, but you don't need me to play it."

"I don't need you," Felipe agreed, taking a hard right turn that took an inch of rubber off the tires. Caroline lost her balance and was thrown across the seat nearly onto his lap. "But you need me."

"Like hell I do." She scrambled back, away from him, and quickly fastened her seat belt.

Sixty miles an hour. He was going sixty miles an hour on shadowy back streets. His mind was going even faster.

Tommy was right behind them. It would take quick thinking and a great deal of luck to lose him—Tommy Walsh was one of the best when it came to pursuit. And even if Felipe *did* lose him, he couldn't be sure he'd actually succeeded. He couldn't be certain that Tommy hadn't simply faded into the background, unseen but ready to blow Felipe away the moment he stepped out of the car.

Even if Felipe drove directly to police headquarters, Tommy would gun him and Caroline down in the parking lot.

There wasn't too much Felipe could do short of driving this expensive car up the front steps and through the double doors of the St. Simone Police Department's Fourth Precinct.

No. He had only one option here. And that was to lead Tommy to a place where Felipe would at least have a fighting chance at defending himself.

Felipe went through a red light, swerving to avoid hitting a pickup truck, and Caroline yelped in fear.

"Look," she said sharply. "Just pull over and let me out."

"I can't do that," Felipe said.

"Whatever you're wanted for," Caroline said sharply, "kidnapping me will only make it worse."

Felipe took a sharp left at Ocean Street, leaving more of the car's tires behind on the street. There was heavier traffic in this part of town, and he kept his eyes on the road, praying that no cars would pull out in front of him.

"I'm not wanted for anything," he told her matter-of-factly. "I'm a cop."

Carrie stared at the man sitting so calmly next to her.

He was a cop?

He'd stolen a car and kidnapped her and now was driving like a lunatic, violating every traffic law in the book. And she was supposed to believe that he was a cop?

She laughed, but it had nothing to do with humor. "Try another one, Carlos. Or Raoul—or whoever you are."

"Felipe," he said in his gentle Hispanic accent, raising his voice only very slightly to be heard over the sound of the racing engine. "Salazar. I'm an undercover detective with the Fourth Precinct. You blew my cover back there, Miss Brooks. Those men I was with, they're very dangerous. We're lucky we're still alive."

Carrie stared at him as she braced herself against the dashboard. "Just pull over to the side and let me out," she said tightly. "And then you can get back to whatever little fantasy you've got going here, okay?"

He glanced at her with those deep chocolate brown eyes, those dark, penetrating eyes she'd seen so many times in her dreams, then looked back at the road ahead of them. His face was glazed with perspiration, and his hair curled damply around his face where it had come free from his ponytail. A bead of sweat traveled down past his ear and plopped onto the lapel of his tuxedo jacket.

"I'm sorry," he said apologetically. His eyes flickered up to the rearview mirror. "I can't do that. I can't stop. There's a man—Tommy Walsh—chasing us. He's not a very nice man. He wants me dead, and I think he's going to try to kill you, too."

Carrie loosened her hold on the dashboard and turned around. She looked over the back of the plush leather seat, through the rear window.

There *was* a car following behind them. It, too, was driving at breakneck speed. Tommy Walsh. He must be the balding man with pale eyes and a boxer's scarred face and muscular build who had approached them in the lobby.

"Well, I think *he's* the cop and *you're* the bad guy," she said. "That's usually how these chases work, isn't it?"

"Not this time," Felipe told her. "I've been under cover for five months and I've witnessed some things that would put Walsh—and his boss—into prison for years. They aren't going to let me get away without a fight."

Carrie looked at the car that was following them, at Mr. Muscles, and then at Felipe. How could she possibly believe *any*-thing this man told her?

"All right," she said abruptly. "Show me your ID. If you're a cop, prove it."

But he shook his head, still watching the road. "Do you know what it means to be deep under cover?"

They were rapidly approaching a red light. Carrie could see the traffic crossing the intersection in front of them, but Felipe didn't hit the brakes.

"Lord in heaven," she gasped. "Slow down!"

"Hold on," Felipe said, and gunned the car even faster.

They were going to die. Forget about Mr. Muscles in the car behind them. Forget Mr. Muscles, who Carlos—or Felipe or whoever he was—said wanted to kill them. They were going to die all by themselves, without anyone's help.

Carrie shrieked and held on as they roared through the red light, but her voice was drowned out by the sound of squealing tires and blaring horns as first one, then another and another car swerved. Then one vehicle went into a skid and slid sideways into them. Metal scraped against metal, creating a chilling, awful, screeching sound.

And then it was over. They were through the intersection, once more going sixty down Ocean Street.

Carrie glanced back through the rear window. Unbelievably, the big, dark limousine was still behind them.

"When a detective goes deep under cover," the dark-eyed man said calmly, as if nothing were wrong, as if they hadn't just nearly been killed in a car accident, as if he hadn't just removed all the paint from one side of this expensive car—this *stolen* car, "when he intends to infiltrate an organized-crime outfit, he does not bring any police identification with him. Hold on again, please."

Felipe yanked the steering wheel hard to the left, cutting across the oncoming traffic to pull into a narrow side street. The car skidded on loose gravel and dirt, hitting a metal garbage can with a bang and a crunch. The windshield was instantly covered with a layer of rotten vegetables.

"Oh, Lord," Carrie breathed, and for the first time since she'd seen the panic in Felipe's eyes at the restaurant, the man seemed unsettled.

He muttered in Spanish, alternately searching the dashboard for the controls to the windshield wipers and peering at the narrow road through a tiny hole in the muck.

Carrie saw it first. Loosening her grip on the dashboard, she reached over next to the steering wheel and switched on the wipers.

"Gracias," Felipe said. "Thanks."

"Don't bother," Carrie said tersely. "It was pure self-preservation."

"I'm sorry you had to become involved in this," Felipe said, glancing at her, then back in the rearview mirror at the car still following them. "It was an unfortunate coincidence that we were both at that same restaurant."

The neighborhood they were roaring through was run-down and unkempt, with crumbling stuccoed apartment buildings, their wooden porches sagging and rotten. The road, too, had seen far better days. Carrie's teeth rattled as they hit another pothole.

"I *had to* become involved?" Carrie said skeptically. "You really expect me to believe that Mr. Muscles would *kill* me simply for talking to you at Schroedinger's?"

"You were a witness," Felipe said.

"A witness to *what?* A conversation?"

"When I turn up dead or missing," Felipe said, taking another sharp right turn, "there'll be a great deal of publicity. You're the only one who can place me in that restaurant lobby with Tommy Walsh—Mr. Muscles, if you will—and Lawrence Richter. It's not enough to base a murder case on, but Walsh is known for his caution."

Carrie glared at him. "There were twenty other people in that lobby," she said. "Is Muscles going to kill them, too? That is, assuming he really does want to murder you."

"Hold on," Felipe said.

"Lord, I hate when you say that," Carrie muttered, bracing herself by bending her knees and putting her feet up against the dashboard.

They were coming to the end of the side street. Felipe could turn either left or right onto Clark Road. For once, the light was green.

Felipe took a left, and then an immediate right, going the wrong way down a one-way street.

Carrie bit back a shout. There was no need to point out his mistake. Because it was no mistake. He knew exactly what he was doing.

"With the exception of the maître d'," Felipe said calmly as if their conversation hadn't been interrupted, "who's probably on Richter's payroll, you were the only one in that lobby who knew me well enough to make a positive ID."

"Know you?" Carrie said. "I don't know you at all. And there's no reason for anyone to think that I do."

"But you're wrong," he said.

He glanced at her again, and in a flash, Carrie remembered those kisses. He had kissed her—twice—there in Schroedinger's lobby, and she knew just from looking at him, that he was remembering it, too. His gaze dropped to her legs, to where her ungainly position had caused her skirt to fall away from the tops of her thighs.

They were barreling, sixty miles an hour, the wrong way down a one-way street, and he was sneaking looks at her legs?

No, not sneaking. He wasn't sneaking anything. There was nothing even remotely clandestine about the way he looked at her legs. His gaze was almost leisurely, appreciative and very, *very* male. And he glanced up and met her eyes afterward, as if he wanted to make sure she knew that he'd been looking at her legs.

That's when she saw it. The car phone. It was in a special case between their seats. Carrie pointed at it. "If you're a cop," she said, "why don't you call for backup?"

"Because I don't have the telephone's access code," Felipe said. "I've already checked. It's got a valet lock. You know, so the parking-lot attendant doesn't make a hundred dollars' worth of long-distance phone calls while the owner's having dinner?"

"You have an answer for everything, don't you?" Carrie observed tartly.

"Unfortunately, no," Felipe said. "I haven't figured out a way to get rid of Tommy Walsh without putting you in real danger."

Real danger? *Real* danger? Their current situation wasn't *really* dangerous? If this wasn't real danger, then what was?

The rear window shattered with a crash.

"Get down!" Felipe shouted, grabbing Carrie and pushing her onto the seat.

The right passenger mirror was blown completely off the car door.

He was shooting at them.

Mr. Muscles, the guy in the car behind them—Tommy Walsh or whoever he was—was *shooting* at them.

With a gun.

With bullets.

Real bullets.

The kind that could kill you.

"Hold on!" Felipe shouted again, and for the first time, Carrie was glad to hear him say those words. For the first time, she actually *wanted* him to drive even faster.

But the way she was down on the seat, there was no place to hold on to, nowhere to get a good grip.

The tires squealed as Felipe turned another corner and Carrie started to slide.

Felipe reached out with one hand and held her tightly, pulling her against him, anchoring her in place.

"He must've stopped and picked up a shooter," he said. "I saw him slow down, but I didn't see him stop."

Another bullet made a hole in the windshield and Felipe ducked.

And then the car phone rang.

Chapter 4

Caroline Brooks turned to look up at Felipe from her rather indelicate position, sprawled out on the seat across his legs, her head down. Normally, the sight of long, fine hair like spun gold fanned out across his lap would trigger rather powerful sexual fantasies. But at the moment, Felipe could allow himself only the very briefest possible flash of pleasure. And even if he had allowed himself to dwell on the possibilities, the fear and alarm in Caroline's blue-green eyes would have quickly brought him back to the task at hand.

Somewhere underneath beautiful Caroline Brooks, the car phone was ringing and Felipe knew exactly who was on the other end.

Caroline scrambled off him, her head carefully kept down behind the protective barrier of the seat back. Gunning the car to over seventy, Felipe picked up the phone.

"*Hola,* Tomás," he said.

There was a brief moment of silence. Then Tommy Walsh spoke.

"Give it up, Vasquez," he said. "Or should I call you *Detective Salazar?*"

Felipe's hand tightened on the phone. He wanted desperately to swear. He wanted to let loose a long stream of the blackest curses, but instead he kept his mouth tightly shut. By knowing his real identity, Tommy Walsh was already one giant step ahead of him. If Felipe vented his frustration by swearing, that would only reveal to Walsh just how badly he was rattled.

Before the silence stretched on too much longer, Felipe made himself laugh.

"Very good, Tomás," he said, taking the entrance ramp to the interstate and pushing the car even faster. Seventy-five. Eighty. "Please extend my admiration to Mr. Richter. His efficiency is—as usual—quite remarkable. Of course, it helps to have an inside man in the police force, does it not?"

It was Tommy Walsh's turn to let the silence turn stale.

"Here's how it's gonna work," Walsh finally said. "You give up and pull over, and I'll make it quick and painless. One bullet in the back of the girl's head, nice and neat."

Felipe glanced at Carrie. She was watching him, her eyes wide in the light from the dashboard, listening only to his side of the conversation.

"I recommend you stop and pick up a dictionary, Tomás," Felipe told Walsh, "and look up the definitions for both 'nice' and 'neat.' A bullet in the head is neither. It's ugly, in fact."

"No," Tommy Walsh said. "Ugly is what happens when I have to chase you all over kingdom come. Ugly is when I make you spend the last few hours of your life listening to your little girlfriend scream."

Eighty-five. Felipe shot past a row of semis that were themselves going well above the sixty-five miles-per-hour speed limit.

"So that's it," he said. "Option A or option B?"

"That's what it boils down to," Walsh replied.

Ninety.

"You know, man, there's always option C," Felipe said. "You give yourself up to me and plea bargain for your freedom in return for testifying against Richter—"

"Three more miles," Walsh interrupted him. "You pass the next exit, and we do it the ugly way."

The phone line was cut as Walsh hung up.

Carrie was still watching him. Felipe smiled ruefully. "I don't think he liked option C," he said, reaching over to put down the telephone.

"I want to get out," she said. "Just pull over and let me out. I'd rather take my chances with him." She gestured with her head back toward the car that was still following them.

One hundred. How much faster could this car go? Or a better question—how much faster could the limo Walsh was in go?

"I'd reconsider," Felipe said. "He just offered to put a bullet into your brain."

"That's what *you* say," Carrie said. "And we both know I have absolutely no reason to trust *you.*"

Felipe nodded. "That's right," he said. "You don't. But if I were you, I'd test this situation with something smaller and less important than my life."

One hundred and five. One hundred and ten.

The exit was approaching, the green sign reflecting their headlights in the darkness. It was the point of no return. *Madre de Dios,* don't let him regret this. The thought of having to watch and listen as Walsh tortured Caroline Brooks was excruciating. But to simply pull over and quit... No. If they were going to die, they'd die fighting.

They shot past the exit, and sure enough, the shooter in the limo opened fire, trying for one of their tires.

At nearly one hundred and twenty, if they lost a tire, they'd be smeared across the road. But at nearly one hundred and twenty, the limo was hard-pressed to keep up. If only this car could go a little faster, they'd lose Walsh. Unfortunately, Felipe, too, had maxed out, with the gas pedal to the floor. Now all he could do was pray.

Pray, and turn off the headlights and rear running lights. Why give them a lighted target?

They were barreling into the darkness, with only the lights from the other cars and trucks to guide them.

But then, suddenly, the shooting stopped.

Felipe glanced into what was left of his rearview mirror.

He could see inside the limousine. The interior lights were on and Tommy Walsh was on the phone again. Walsh hung up and the limo began to slow.

As Felipe watched, Walsh moved into the right lane. As he raced up to the crest of a hill, he looked back and saw the limo's headlights turn away as the car exited the highway.

What the hell…? Was Tommy Walsh giving up? Man, what just happened here?

Felipe had a sudden bad feeling in the pit of his stomach as he lifted his foot from the accelerator and the car began to slow. Something was wrong. Something was *seriously* wrong. The only time he'd ever seen Walsh back away was when his prey was dead. The implication was that in Walsh's eyes, Felipe and Caroline were already dead.

Still, Felipe hit the brakes and turned his lights back on. He could feel Caroline's eyes on his face as he searched the rear-view mirror, watching for some sign of a trap. But there was nothing. There was no sign of the limousine, no sign they were being followed by anyone else.

He exited at a rest stop, pulling onto the ramp at the last instant, keeping his signal light off.

Caroline peeked over the back of the seat. "Did we lose them?"

"No," Felipe said tersely. "They lost us. Something's wrong."

"Something's *wrong?*" she echoed. "They're not shooting at us anymore. I'd consider that to be something *right.*"

"Tommy Walsh shouldn't have given up so easily," Felipe said, glancing at her. He had to make a phone call, find out what the hell was going on.

He saw a row of pay and credit-card telephones that could be accessed without leaving the car. That was good, because now that the immediate danger had passed, Felipe's leg was starting to hurt like hell. He parked next to one of the phones, leaving the car engine idling.

But even before the car had stopped moving, Carrie was out the door like a shot.

Felipe swore. He'd pulled up to these phones because he hadn't wanted to get out of the car. His pants were wet with blood and his leg was throbbing with an unholy pain. Despite the agony, he slid across the bench seat, leaving a smear of blood on the fancy leather upholstery. Carrie hadn't closed the door, and as he left the car after her, he hit the pavement running. *Man!* His leg hurt like a *bitch,* but he ran after her anyway. If he didn't catch her, she was as good as dead. Worse, he thought, remembering Walsh's threats.

The parking lot was mostly empty. There were a few cars but no people around. She headed toward a brightly lit fast-food restaurant.

"Caroline, wait!" Felipe called, but she only ran faster, harder.

She was fast, but she was small, and her stride was only three-quarters the size of his, even with a bullet in his leg.

He caught her before she reached the wheelchair ramp up to the front door of the restaurant, and pulled her down with him onto the soft grass that lined the sidewalk.

"No!" she cried. "Let me *go!*"

She took in a deep breath to scream and he covered her mouth with his hand, trying desperately to ignore the fire of pain shooting up and down his thigh.

"Stop it!" he hissed into her ear. "I'm not going to hurt you, but Tommy Walsh will. By now, he and Richter know who you are and where you live. You go home, you're *dead.*"

There was fear in her eyes as she looked up at him. But was it his words, or was it he, himself, that frightened her?

He realized with a sudden stab of awareness that he was on top of her, covering her with the full weight of his body. Mother of God, she was so very female, so very soft, and he was crushing her.

Keeping a tight hold on her arm, he rolled off her.

"I'm sorry," he said. "I didn't mean to…"

But now she was looking at him with new horror in her eyes. "Are you bleeding?" she breathed. "My Lord, you *are.*"

Her dress and part of her leg were streaked bright red with his blood.

Still holding her with one hand, Felipe pulled himself to his feet before helping her up. "I need to make a phone call," he said, "and then we need to get out of here. We're not out of danger yet, Caroline."

He winced as he put his weight on his wounded leg. But he tried not to limp as he led her back across the parking lot toward the car. On the off chance someone was watching, he didn't want them to know he was injured.

"Lord above," Carrie said, "you were *shot*."

He glanced at her. The expression in her eyes begged him to tell her otherwise, but Felipe nodded his head. "Yes," he said. He had her full attention, and he pressed his advantage. "This is not a game we're playing here. The bullets are very real, and Tommy Walsh is saving one or two of them especially for you, do you understand?"

He watched her steadily, seeing the doubt and mistrust on her face. What he would have given simply for her to trust him. But she didn't believe him. She didn't buy into what he was telling her. Even so, behind all that mistrust, he could see her concern.

In her mind, he was the enemy, yet she was concerned for his health. Felipe found himself smiling as he gazed at her. Despite her tough-guy exterior, she was softhearted. She was as sweet as she looked. Dear heaven, even with her dress rumpled and stained, and her hair windblown and messy, she still managed to look incredibly sweet.

"You better do something to stop the bleeding," she said, glancing up at him. She quickly looked away, but not before Felipe caught the answering heat of attraction in her eyes. Maybe sweet wasn't quite the right word....

"You know," he said softly, "instinctively, you want to trust me, Caroline. Instinctively, there is this powerful attraction between us—"

Carrie laughed. "I'd be willing to bet that instinctively, there's a powerful attraction between you and every woman on earth," she said, carefully not meeting his eyes.

He smiled again. "Not like this," he said. "Never like this." He closed the car door and led her around to the other side. He opened that door and, still holding her wrist, shrugged out of his tuxedo jacket. He handed it to Carrie. "Use this to wipe off the seat, please, and then get in."

To his surprise, she took it and tore it cleanly down the middle. She handed him back one of the halves. "Use this to tie around your leg to try to stop the bleeding," she said. "It *is* your leg that's hurt, isn't it?"

Felipe nodded, once again touched by her concern. Still, she wouldn't meet his eyes. "Yes," he said. "Thanks."

But he wouldn't let go of her wrist to tie the jacket around his leg.

"I won't run away," Carrie said.

Felipe just laughed.

In frustration, she took the torn fabric from him and tied it herself, folding a piece of the sleeve against the gash on his upper thigh, forming a bandage that applied pressure to the wound. Damn, it hurt. He had to grit his teeth to keep from crying out. He must have made some sort of sound, though, because she glanced up at him.

"Sorry," she whispered.

And she was. She was tending to him with as much compassion as she'd give a wounded manatee—or shark. Yes, Felipe could imagine her coming to the aid of an injured shark and disregarding its sharp, deadly teeth in the name of compassion.

Her hands were unquestionably gentle, but there was a hole in his leg where the bullet had entered. A hole, with a bullet still inside, that hurt like *hell*.

If she noticed the new layer of sweat that was glazing his face, she didn't mention it. "I've never been shot," she said, tying the bandage into place, "but my brother has—in a hunting accident. It was barely a scratch, but my other brothers had to carry him down from the mountains on a stretcher."

Brothers. Felipe realized in a flash just where they could go to hide. To his brother's. Of course. He'd cut himself off so thoroughly from Raphael, no one in the police force, including Jim Keegan, knew he had an older brother. Not even Richter would be able to track him there.

The pain had subsided to a dull, throbbing ache. Felipe forced his face to relax, then even managed to smile at Caroline. "Well, my brothers are not here right now," he said, "so I'll have to carry myself."

"You should go to the hospital," she said. "I didn't get a really good look at your leg in this light. I can't tell if the bullet's still in there. If it is, you're risking serious infection. If it's not, you still need stitches."

"The hospital can't treat a bullet wound without reporting it to the police," Felipe said. "I can't go in yet. Not until I know that it's safe for both of us."

"Please," she said, still looking up at him. "Just turn yourself in. You're clearly a man of integrity—"

"I'm so glad you've recognized that," Felipe said with a wry laugh.

"I'll go with you," she said. "I'll make sure no one hurts you. I'll help you get an attorney—"

"Caroline, I'm a cop," he said. "I don't need a lawyer."

"If you let me go right now," Carrie said as if she hadn't heard him, "I'll ask them to dismiss any kidnapping charges."

"I'm cop, a police detective," Felipe said again, looking down at her. "There will be no kidnapping charges. I wish you would believe me."

She still gazed up at him. "If you're a police detective, then let's go to the police station," she said beseechingly. "Right now. Let's just get in the car and drive over—"

"I can't."

She stood up. "Because you're not a cop."

Felipe shook his head. "No, because we're dealing with organized crime," he explained, "and they've bought someone in the department. Neither of us would last a day in local protective custody. Richter would be tipped off as to our every move, and he'd bring in a hit man to finish the job. And God knows how many good men and women would die trying to protect us."

Caroline didn't buy it—he could tell from the set of her mouth. "That's a convenient excuse," she said.

They were standing so close, she was forced to tilt her head to look up at him.

"I'm telling you the truth," he said.

She only laughed. "Are you sure you even remember the truth?" she asked. "Or maybe you simply change it with your name, Carlos. Or should I call you Raoul? No, wait, it's Felipe, isn't it? Yeah, Felipe Salazar, undercover cop.''

"If you would get in the car, please, and sit down," Felipe said, feeling his patience start to slip, "then I could sit down, too. And I really, *really* would like to sit down.''

She climbed into the car, and still holding tightly to her wrist, he followed her, closing the door behind him.

It was cool inside. With the engine running, the air conditioner kept the temperature down to a comfortable level. Caroline was silent as Felipe pushed the button that lowered the window, then reached outside the car for the telephone. He dialed Jim's direct number, glancing over at her.

It was so easy to imagine this woman sitting next to him in his own subcompact car, smiling instead of looking at him with this mixed expression of wariness and mistrust. He could imagine the sound of her laughter; he could picture amusement dancing in her beautiful eyes. And he could imagine bending to kiss her smiling mouth, her face upturned in anticipation of his lips.

"Jim Keegan, Homicide," said a familiar, husky voice on the other end of the line.

Felipe pulled his gaze away from Caroline's face. "Diego, it's me.''

"Phil! Jesus! Thank God you're alive.''

"Look, man, I need—''

"I'm sure you realize that this line's tapped," Jim said, cutting Felipe off and talking fast, "and that I've got to try to keep you on as long as possible so we can track you.''

"Of course," Felipe said. My God, he'd had no idea. His heart sank. Obviously, Jim wasn't in any position to help him.

"An APB came in just a few minutes ago," Jim said. "All available men are looking for you and a stolen car, New York plate HTD-761.''

In other words, ditch the car.

Jim Keegan was one of the few people who knew that Felipe had been trying to infiltrate Richter's organization. Why would he make hints for Felipe to stay away, to keep running, to stay hidden?

"You're wanted for the Sandlot Murders, pal," Jim said. "It's not my case, but the word is we've got evidence that ties you to the crime scene.''

The Sandlot Murders? They'd happened less than a week ago. Two men with mob connections had been killed in a vigilante-style execution after they'd been released from prosecution on a technicality. Word on the street was that they'd been prepared to deal with the D.A. Now they were D.O.A. and a very obvious warning to the other underlings who worked for the crime bosses.

The media had sunk their teeth into the case because the murders were committed in a vacant lot next to an inner-city elementary school. The children were traumatized, the parents were in an uproar and the newspapers and TV stations were searching for someone to blame.

The triggerman could've been any one of a number of hired assassins. It was a high-profile case with virtually no chance of being solved.

It was the perfect case to use to create a frame.

It was so obvious. Richter's man in the police department, this partner of his, this "Captain Rat," had worked hard and fast to set Felipe up. It was such an obvious frame, it was almost laughable.

Almost.

But maybe, if he could stay alive long enough, the last laugh could be Felipe's. He may not know exactly who Captain Rat was, but he *did* know that there was a planned meeting between this man and Richter in less than three days, at three-thirty in the afternoon. But he couldn't tell Jim about it—not with the line being tapped and God only knows who listening in.

"I'm supposed to try to talk you into turning yourself in," Keegan said. "Just stay where you are, stay on the line and we'll come to you, you hear me?"

In other words, get out of there fast.

"I hear you, man," Felipe said. "Loud and clear." He hung up the phone.

Caroline Brooks watched him in silence.

"Diego can't help us," he told her, even though she had no idea who Diego was.

Diego couldn't help him, but maybe Raphael could.

It was time for a Salazar family reunion.

Chapter 5

Carrie heard the sirens in the distance at the same time Felipe did.

But instead of starting the car the way she expected, he opened the door.

"You're wearing sandals, not heels, am I right?" he asked, looking down the length of her legs to her feet. "Good," he added, not even waiting for her to answer. "Come on."

He was still holding on to her wrist, and he tugged her gently out of the car.

"Where are we going?" she asked.

"The police are looking for this car," he answered, leading her across the parking lot toward a grove of trees, beyond which shone the lights of a suburban street. "We're better off on foot."

"The police," she said. "I thought you *were* the police."

"I am," he said.

"Then how come they're looking for this car?" she asked. "And you, too, I assume?"

"Because they don't know that I'm one of the good guys, and that one of the bad guys is in the department," Felipe said.

His hair had come free from his ponytail, and it curled around the shoulders of his snowy white tuxedo shirt. He'd untied his bow tie and unbuttoned the top few buttons of the shirt, its perfection now marred by darkening stains of blood. He was still shockingly handsome, despite the lines of pain Carrie could see on his face.

His eyes were as soft and as dark as the night sky above her, and equally mysterious. If she could suspend all disbelief, it would be easy to see him as one of the good guys. In a more perfect world, no criminal could possibly have eyes so kind, so warm. If she looked at him for too long, she felt as if she were being pulled into some kind of vortex—spinning, imprisoning, consuming.

She looked away, and from the corner of her eye, she saw him smile at her confusion.

"You really don't want to like anything about me, do you?" he asked as he led her into the cover of the trees. "Careful where you step," he added.

"Let me go," Carrie countered, "and I'll be your best friend."

It was dark in among the trees, away from the lights of the parking lot. The ground was spongy and wet. Mud squished up over the soles of Carrie's sandals and between her toes.

He'd slid his hand down so that he was no longer holding her wrist. Instead, he was holding her hand, their fingers interlocked as if they were lovers rather than captor and hostage.

She could no longer see his face in the darkness, but she could hear his ragged breathing. His leg must hurt him. He stumbled slightly, and his grip on her hand tightened and she heard his quick inhale. He was clearly in serious pain.

But when he spoke, his voice was even. "I can't let you go, Caroline. I'm sorry."

"Then I can't be your best friend," she said.

"That's too bad," he murmured.

Yes, oddly enough, it was.

The sirens were louder now, and despite his injury, Felipe picked up the pace. Together they half ran, half skidded down an embankment to the street below.

One dim street lamp illuminated a row of shabby houses, blue television light flickering from most of the windows. In one of them the volume was up too high. Canned laughter echoed among the cars parked along the side of the road. Farther down the street, a dog barked, but other than that, nothing moved.

Here in the darkness, Felipe didn't try to hide his limp. Still, he moved quickly along the line of cars.

"What are you looking for?" Carrie asked.

He turned toward her, putting one finger to his lips. "Shh." Bringing his mouth up close to her ear, he said very softly, "We need transportation. I'm afraid I'm not up to walking back to St. Simone."

She pulled back to stare at him. "You're going to *steal* a car…?"

"Shh," he said again. "Not steal. Borrow."

Carrie nodded. "Right. Tell that to the guy who owns the car."

Felipe ran his hand across his face. "If there was another way, I wouldn't do this," he said. "But I believe a life—*your* life— is worth more than a 1979 Subaru, don't you?"

He tugged at her arm, and she knelt next to him as he opened the driver's-side door and quickly turned off the interior light. He pulled her in front of him, pinning her between the car and his body so he could use both of his hands.

"I'm worth a vintage Ford Mustang convertible," Carrie said. "Preferably from 1966 and cherry red."

He glanced at her and smiled, his teeth a flash of white in the darkness.

"I'm glad your sense of humor is back," he said, disconnecting a panel from the steering column.

"It's hard for me to keep my sense of humor when I'm being held hostage," Carrie said.

It was also hard to keep her sense of humor with his body pressed against hers the way it was. As he worked to hot-wire the car, his arms were on either side of her, his weight against her. Carrie tried to shift away, but only succeeded in wedging herself more firmly against him.

He pulled back slightly to look down at her. "You're not a hostage," he said.

"Are you sure?"

He didn't hesitate. "Yes. You're in protective custody."

"Assuming you are who you say you are, Carlos-Raoul-Felipe," she said.

Felipe shifted his position, then winced as his weight came down more fully on his injured leg. He wiped the sweat from his upper lip. "I'm tempted to take you to my apartment in St. Simone, just to show you my police identification," he said.

"But no doubt you've got some dramatic excuse to keep us from going there, too," Carrie said, trying to ignore the fact that his face was mere inches from her own. If he leaned forward another four inches, he'd be kissing her.

"They're looking for me. My apartment is one of the first places they'll stake out," he said. "It's no dramatic excuse. It's a fact."

"They who?" Carrie asked. "The police?"

"The police and Richter's men," Felipe said. "They'll both send someone around to watch my apartment, assuming I'd be stupid enough to show up there." The car started with a roar. "Quick, get in."

Carrie scrambled across the stick shift and into the passenger seat. She reached for the opposite door and was about to throw it open, when Felipe firmly put his hand on her left knee.

"Give me a break," he said.

"Let me go," she countered.

"Haven't you been listening to *any*thing I've told you?" Felipe said. "Put the car in first gear, please."

With her left hand, Carrie pushed the stick shift up into first position.

With a jerk, Felipe pulled away from the curb.

"If I let you go," he said, trying hard to be patient, "you're dead. Second, please."

Carrie shifted into second gear as Felipe rounded a corner onto a secondary road heading south toward St. Simone.

"I do not want you to be dead," Felipe said, "therefore, I will not let you go. As long as you're with me, I'll keep you safe. Third gear, please."

Carrie snorted, shifting gears. "Oh, you've kept me really safe so far."

Felipe turned to look at her. His eyes were dead serious. "A lot of it's been luck, and circumstance," he said, "but yes, so far, I have."

His hand was still resting on her knee. She looked down at it pointedly. "You can have your hand back," she said. "I'm not going to jump out of a car going forty."

He glanced at her and grinned. "Thirty-five, you'd try it, but not forty, huh?" He squeezed her knee slightly, then put his hand on the stick, shifting into fourth gear. "Short of driving to the precinct or going to my apartment to get my ID, what can I do to make you believe me, Caroline?"

Nothing. Carrie shook her head. "If Silver-hair—this Richter guy—if he's such a threat, how come I haven't heard about him before?"

"He's very low-key," Felipe said. "Some mob bosses, they get off on people knowing who they are and how powerful they are, you know? But not Lawrence Richter. Instead of taking a seat on the city finance committee, or some position where the media would check into his background, Richter joined the public library's volunteer board of directors. The papers and TV reporters don't pay him any mind—he's not paid after all—and, through the contacts he's made, he has the ears of some of St. Simone's most powerful politicians."

"Lawrence Richter," Carrie mused. "Doesn't exactly sound like he's Old-World Mafia."

"The Mafia controls only a portion of organized crime," Felipe said. "These days, organized crime is an equal-opportunity employer."

He used the back of his arm to wipe the sweat from his face. This car's air conditioner wasn't anything to write home about. He glanced at her and tried to smile, but she could tell it was getting harder for him to hide his pain. His face was pale—it looked almost gray in the headlights from the oncoming traffic. She wondered how much blood he'd lost.

"Do you want me to drive?" she asked.

He looked at her in surprise. "No," he said. "I'm okay. Thanks."

She studied his face in the dim light from the dashboard. With his exotic cheekbones and liquid brown eyes, with his elegantly shaped mouth and sensuous lips, with that trim, athletic body, he could have made a fortune modeling for perfume ads or loose-fitting-jeans ads or, hell, even underwear ads. Maybe especially for underwear ads. Or, if he could dance even just a little bit, he could surely have made a bundle every night over at the Chippendale's club at the corner of Gulf and Garden Streets. But he didn't even seem aware of his striking looks— well, except for the fact that somewhere down the line, he'd learned that women responded to his smile. Or maybe that wasn't learned. Maybe it was instinctive.

He could have slid along in life, getting by with that smile and those warm, expressive eyes. Instead—so he claimed—he'd chosen to become a cop.

"What made you decide to join the police force?" Carrie asked.

He glanced at her again. "Is this a test?" he asked. "If I don't have an answer ready, that proves that I'm lying?"

"You're stalling," she returned. "Do you need more time to make up your story?"

"I became a cop," Felipe said without further hesitation, "because of my brother, Rafe. Raphael. He was a robber. I figured someone had to go in the other direction and balance the family out."

"That's it?" Carrie asked. "You just woke up one morning and decided that you had to be Wyatt Earp because your brother was Jesse James?"

He looked over at her. "You really want to hear the whole story?"

She pushed her hair back behind her ear. "Yeah," she said. Oddly enough, she did. "Is Rafe older or younger?"

"Older, by about five years," Felipe said. "He first started using when he was fourteen—I was nine."

"Using?"

"Drugs."

He stared at the road. Carrie could see the sudden tension in his jaw.

"We shared a bedroom," Felipe continued, "and he used to come in wasted and tell me not to tell our parents. He was my hero—how could I tell? Besides, it was a laugh at first. He was funny when he drank or when he got stoned. But then it stopped being funny when he started using the hard stuff.

"It happened real fast—he was an addict at fifteen. By the time I realized what was happening, I couldn't stop him. I don't know how many times I tried to talk sense into him, but you can't reason with an addict.

"I could only pick him up off the street when he was too high to walk, and carry him home. I could only hide his stash from my father. I could only give him the money from my paper route when he was broke and hurting and needing drugs to ease his pain. And I could keep my mouth shut when he started stealing."

Felipe glanced at Carrie, but she didn't speak. She simply waited for him to continue.

"Rafe didn't know it," he said, "but I gave back most of the stuff he stole. He thought he was getting ripped off by some of the other guys in the 'hood, but it was just me, covering his ass." He laughed, but the sound was devoid of humor. "Man, I was the perfect little enabler but I didn't even know the definition of the word. I was Rafe's worst enemy, second only to himself." He turned to glance at her again. "You sure you want to hear more?"

Carrie nodded. His words rang with a certain bitter truth. She actually wanted to believe him.

"Rafe and I did the addict-enabler dance for eight years," Felipe said, his gentle accent like music accompanying the soft hiss of the car's tires against the road. "Then, the summer I turned seventeen, one of the detectives in the local precinct started an outreach program designed to help kids like me—and indirectly, help kids like Rafe.

"By that time, Rafe had a few priors, nothing too big, and no punishment bigger than a reprimand. Still, this detective, Jorge Gamos, added up Rafe's record with what he saw going on in the neighborhood. Gamos actually came out on the street and hung with the kids. He got to know us. He saw that Rafe had a habit, and he also saw my stress levels, which were pretty high by that time. I was seventeen—going on forty-five. I hadn't been a kid since Rafe lit his first crack pipe. Anyway, Jorge Gamos saw what was going on, and he figured out—correctly— that my brother couldn't have lasted so long on the street if it hadn't been for me.

"It took Gamos nearly a year, but he finally talked me into going to a meeting that he helped run—a counseling session for kids who'd lost a brother or sister to drugs. It was…eye-opening, particularly when he told me that I was going to end up right there, with those kids, talking about my brother Rafe. My *dead* brother Rafe."

Carrie wanted to believe him, but his story was probably fictional. Still, it was one hell of a good tale. "Did Rafe die?" Carrie found herself asking, as if Rafe were a real person, as if Felipe really had been a kid who'd lost his childhood to drugs.

He glanced at her, a fleeting smile touching his lips. "Not yet," he said. "I virtually turned him in. He came to me for an alibi, but I wouldn't lie anymore. He was convicted and served an eight month sentence. During that time, he detoxed. When I went to see him in the jail, he thanked me for helping him, and he swore he'd never touch crack again. He was clean and he was going to stay clean. I was attending the police academy by that time. I was going to be a cop. With Jorge Gamos's help, I got Rafe an early release."

Felipe shook his head. "Raphael hit the streets and in a matter of weeks, he was using again. It nearly broke my heart. He'd conned me into getting him out of prison. His apology, everything he'd told me had been nothing but crap. None of it had been sincere. *None* of it." He laughed bitterly. "He ended up back in prison, but after he scammed me, I washed my hands of him. I haven't seen him in years. Apparently, Rafe's been out of jail for a while now. Jorge tells me he's really clean these days, that he runs a halfway house and works as a counselor for addicts and ex-cons. I've heard that counselors who've been addicts and ex-cons themselves are the most compassionate.

Man, I guess he's got that covered because he's been there and back." He leaned over and tried to turn the air conditioner's fan higher. "That's where we're heading, by the way."

Carrie blinked. "You mean…right now?"

"Yes. To Raphael's halfway house." Felipe glanced at her, his dark eyes even more mysterious. "It's time for my brother to pay some old debts."

By the time Felipe pulled up in front of the A Street Halfway House, his left leg was on fire. He should have ripped off a car with an automatic transmission. Borrowed, he corrected himself. The car was only borrowed. And he'd memorized the plates so that when this was over, he could track down the owner and give him or her money for the mileage, gas and inconvenience.

If he was still alive when this was over.…

He looked over at Caroline Brooks who sat quietly in the passenger seat, gazing back at him, unmindful of the fact that they were parked in the most run-down, dangerous part of the city.

"Are you all right?" she asked quietly.

Her blue eyes were colorless in the shadowy darkness. Her hair looked silvery, reflecting what little light there was. He could smell her perfume—no, that wasn't perfume. It was sun block that he smelled. Carrie wasn't the type to wear perfume. The fresh tang of the lotion suited her better than any flowery fragrance could have. She smelled like blue skies and white sand and warm gulf water. She smelled like paradise.

He'd had a bigger whiff when he'd kissed her back at the restaurant. He thought back to the way her lithe body had fitted against his.… Paradise indeed. Oh, what he would give to kiss her again.

"I must be all right," he said, finally answering her question. "The thoughts I am thinking are those of a healthy man."

She turned away. It was too dark for him to see the blush tingeing her cheeks, but he knew it was there.

She was such a contradiction, this Caroline Brooks. Part of

her was a tough-talking, rifle-wielding, no-nonsense fighter. But another part of her blushed at his sweet talk.

Felipe reached over and took her hand, and she nearly jumped out of her seat.

"I know it's an inconvenience to hop over the stick shift," he said, "but I need you to come out of the car this way. I can't risk your running again."

Still holding tightly to her hand, he opened the car door and stiffly pulled himself to his feet. Pain hit him in one solid wave and that, with his light-headedness, nearly made him black out. But Caroline was right behind him, and she held him up, looping his arm around her neck and supporting most of his body weight.

"Can you make it inside?" she asked, "or should I get help?"

Felipe tried to straighten up. "No way in *hell* am I going to face my brother on anything but my own two feet," he declared, then realized he had spoken in Spanish. God, he was losing it fast. The concern in Caroline's eyes was growing. "I can make it," he said, this time in English. He forced a smile. "Thanks for not running away."

Regret passed briefly across her eyes. "Yeah, well, I should have," she said, helping him around the car and onto the cracked sidewalk. "I'm leaving as soon as I get you inside."

"No, you're not," he countered. "I can't let you."

"Watch it," she said sharply, "or I'll drop you right here and run."

"If you do," he said, "somehow, someway, I will find the strength to follow you."

She turned to look up into his eyes, and he knew that she believed him. She may not have believed his story about his brother, she may not have believed that he was a cop investigating Lawrence Richter, she may not have believed that Tommy Walsh would kill her as easily as blinking, but she *did* believe that he would follow her.

It was a start.

Chapter 6

Raphael Salazar was bigger than his brother. He was older, harder, leaner to the point of being wiry, and several inches taller. His hair wasn't quite as long, though he, too, wore it pulled severely back from his face in a ponytail at his nape. But the biggest difference was in his eyes. Unlike Felipe's, Rafe's eyes were flat, cold and expressionless.

He didn't bother to greet his brother but simply came into the linoleum-tiled waiting room. Two other men, the two who had answered the door, stood slightly behind him. One was almost as broad as he was tall, his Bugs Bunny T-shirt stretched tight across his belly; the other was just a kid, looking barely even eighteen years old.

Rafe didn't move, didn't even blink. He just stared at Felipe, who was sitting on a hard bench against the far wall, Carrie at his side.

"Yes," Felipe said. "That's right, man. It's me."

Rafe took in the bloodstains and the makeshift bandage on Felipe's leg. Then his cold eyes flickered toward Carrie. He spoke softly, but in rapid-fire Spanish.

"In English, please," Felipe said. "Or she won't understand."

"Figures you'd get a gringa girlfriend," Rafe said. His voice was raspier, harsher than Felipe's. "Our kind's not good enough for you, eh, little brother?"

"My kind is human," Felipe said evenly. "Besides, she's not a girlfriend. She's in my protective custody."

"Does she have a name?" Rafe asked, looking back at Carrie. His face was similar to Felipe's in shape, but because he was older, or maybe because he was thinner, his cheekbones looked angular, his nose sharp. He was dangerous-looking, like a wolf or an attack dog.

"She has one," Felipe said pleasantly. "But you don't need to know it. The fewer people who know her name, the fewer who can spread the word on the street that she was here, no?"

Carrie looked from Rafe to Felipe. "*She* doesn't like people talking about her as if she wasn't in the room, *if* you boys don't mind."

Rafe said something to Felipe in Spanish.

Felipe shook his head. "Stop," he said quietly.

Rafe turned again to Carrie. "Even though you are not one of our kind, I was pointing out your obvious physical attributes to my little brother," he said. "Sometimes he gets so caught up in being superhuman, he forgets that the people he's dealing with are mere flesh and blood."

Carrie looked at Felipe, but he was staring down at the floor. Even though this building was air-conditioned, he was still perspiring. His face was expressionless but his jaw was tightly clenched. Whether it was from his brother's harsh words or the pain from his bullet wound, Carrie couldn't tell.

As if he felt her eyes on him, Felipe glanced up. There was sadness in his eyes. He tried to force a smile, but failed miserably.

"I don't think I've ever seen him with his hair this long," Rafe continued. "He usually wears it well above his ears, you know? And I'm certain I've never seen him with his jacket off and trousers torn. What's the deal with my little brother? He under cover?"

"I don't know." Carrie stood up. "I'd like to leave," she said, lifting her chin and staring straight into Rafe's peculiar, lifeless eyes.

Felipe reached out and took her arm. Rafe, of course, didn't miss the move.

"But you're in 'protective custody,' no?" he said. "Maybe you don't think you need to be? Ah, but Felipe, he always knows what's best for everyone else. Felipe, he's always right. Except…" Rafe's gaze flickered back to the bandage on Felipe's leg, and all the blood that covered what was left of his tuxedo. "Maybe this time Felipe was a little *too* right, huh? And maybe someone with a gun doesn't like being wrong. Was it anyone I know, *niño?* One of our other brothers and sisters perhaps? Maybe you've betrayed one of them lately, the way you've betrayed me, huh?"

That one hurt. Even though Felipe's expression didn't change, his fingers tightened around her wrist, and Carrie knew that the barbs from Rafe's sarcastic comment had struck hard.

Still, when Felipe spoke, his voice was even. "You don't know the man who shot me," he said. "But you probably know *of* him."

Rafe laughed, but it was humorless. "I know of half a dozen men who'd probably like very much to shoot you or any one of the men in blue you work with," he said, "and that's without thinking very hard."

"This one's real trouble, man," Felipe said.

He spoke quietly, but there was something in his tone that made Rafe pause. He turned to the two men who were standing behind him and spoke to them in Spanish. They went out of the room, closing the door behind him.

"Tommy Walsh," Felipe said. He glanced at Carrie. "He wants us both dead."

"Walsh," Rafe said. His thin face became even more wary and aloof.

Carrie felt fear flicker in the pit of her stomach. Rafe's quiet response to Walsh's name told her more than any louder reaction could've done.

"I need help," Felipe said quietly. "I'm in deep, man. I've

been shot, Walsh is after us and Richter's got a man in my department, ready to get rid of me the minute I resurface at the precinct.''

"So you come to me," Rafe said softly, sarcastically. "I'm touched."

"All I want is to get cleaned up," Felipe said. "A shower, and maybe some clean clothes for both me and…" He looked at Carrie. "Her."

Rafe smiled, a bitter twist of his lips that attempted to hide his anger. "You don't even trust *me* with her name, huh?"

"I'm sorry," Felipe said. "I don't."

Rafe's temper exploded. "You're not sorry, you self-righteous, holier-than-thou son of a—"

"You're wrong," Felipe interrupted him, his cool vanishing, too. His voice shook with passion and he pulled himself clumsily to his feet. "I spent more years sorry than you even have memories of. Sorry for *your* mistakes, sorry for *your* pain. Sorry for you, and sorry for myself, too, because your mistakes and your pain were mine to share. They were *my* burden, too. I *am* sorry I don't trust you, but I don't. That's one thing you taught me well, Raphael—that you were not to be fully trusted, *never* to be fully trusted.''

"If you don't trust me," Rafe snarled, "why the hell did you bother to come here? How do you know I'm not going to run out and tip Walsh off that you and little Miss No-name are here?"

"I don't know that you're not going to," Felipe said. "I can only hope that you won't. I can only pray you'll remember everything I've done for you—"

"You kept me from hitting bottom on my own," Rafe countered hotly. "Because of you, it took me another three years to come clean."

"When some people hit bottom, they hit with enough force to kill themselves," Felipe said. "I knew you were going to hate me for doing it, but I loved you and I didn't want you to *die*." He shook his head in resignation and turned to Carrie. "Come on, we're getting out of here. He's not going to help."

"I don't hate you," Rafe said, suddenly quiet.

To Carrie's surprise, his eyes were filled with tears, tears and a depth of emotion that made his eyes look so much more like Felipe's. But then he blinked, and both the tears and the emotion were gone, leaving his eyes oddly flat again.

"My apartment's on the second floor," Rafe continued, his voice still quiet. "You can take a shower there. There're clothes in the closet. Help yourself. I'll have Highboy show you up."

And with that, Rafe turned and walked out of the room.

Raphael Salazar's apartment consisted of one small room with a tiny attached bathroom. He had a sofa bed with a small coffee table in front of it and a cheap television set and a VCR on a stand in front of that. There was nothing on the walls—no pictures, no photos, nothing to personalize the room.

A dresser stood in the corner, with shaving supplies and a brush and comb neatly arranged on top, a small mirror attached to the wall above it. Several days' worth of newspapers were on the coffee table, but they, too, were neatly stacked.

In the other corner was a makeshift kitchen area, with a tiny sink built into an equally tiny counter area. A small table and a pair of cheap kitchen chairs sat nearby. On top of the table was a hot plate and a plastic sugar bowl. Underneath the table was a small, square refrigerator.

There was one window, with bars both on the inside and the outside.

Felipe locked the door behind the man in the Bugs Bunny shirt—Rafe had called him Highboy. He limped to the window and pulled down the shade.

"So, you see? My brother Rafe's real," he said to Carrie. "Any chance you're starting to believe what I've told you about Walsh and Richter?"

Carrie could see herself in the mirror over the dresser. Her hair was tangled and limp. She had a smudge of blood—Felipe's blood—across her cheek. *Was* she starting to believe him? She didn't know what to think anymore.

Felipe sat down on one of the kitchen chairs. He didn't wait for her to answer. "Why don't you take a shower?" he suggested gently. "You'll feel better. It'll clear your head."

"We need to—*you* need to get your leg cleaned up," Carrie said. "You should go first."

His eyes were warm as he looked up at her. "Thanks," he said. Then he peered at his roughly bandaged leg and grimaced. "But it's going to take me a while to get undressed. So go ahead. Just don't use up all the hot water, okay?"

He started unfastening the mother-of-pearl buttons of his tuxedo shirt, and Carrie turned away. A shower seemed like an especially good idea—particularly since the alternative was to stand and watch Felipe strip down to his underwear. Or beyond.

Carrie quickly went into the bathroom.

It was as Spartan as the rest of the apartment. The white tile floor was spotless. The sink, tub and toilet were gleaming white porcelain. The shower curtain looked fairly new. It was clear plastic, and it hadn't yet been fogged up by mildew and age. The room was devoid of any personal items—with the exception of a copy of *Off Road Cycle* magazine on the top of the toilet tank. A small cabinet held clean white towels in a neatly folded stack.

There was no window for her to climb out of and escape.

Carrie wasn't quite sure whether to feel disappointed or relieved. Because the truth was, Rafe's reaction to the name Tommy Walsh *had* made her start to wonder if Felipe's story wasn't true.

Lord above, maybe Felipe *was* a cop.

Carrie locked the door securely behind her and quickly stripped off her clothes.

The shower felt good, and she washed her hair with Rafe's inexpensive shampoo, wondering if maybe everything Felipe Salazar had told her was the truth.

If that was the case, he'd saved her life more than once tonight. And with no thanks from her.

She came out of the shower and toweled herself dry. She didn't want to put her bloodstained dress back on, but she had no choice.

She also had no comb, so she ran her fingers through her wet hair, trying to untangle it. When she'd done the best she could, she put her hand on the doorknob.

Taking a deep breath, Carrie opened the door. She opened it slowly, then peeked around to see if Felipe had moved from his seat in the far corner of the room.

He had. He was standing in front of the tiny kitchen sink, his back to her. He'd undressed down to an expensive-looking pair of dark green and navy blue paisley silk boxer shorts and a white tank undershirt that contrasted with the rich darkness of his tanned skin. He was wearing more than he would have had she run into him on the beach. Still, he was in his underwear, and Carrie felt uncomfortable—possibly because she had dreamed about him wearing even less.

His body was as trim and athletic as she'd imagined. The sleek muscles in his shoulders and arms rippled as he supported his weight on the kitchen counter. The water was running, and he didn't hear her as she approached.

Without his pants on, she could clearly see the wound that the bullet had made on the side of his thigh, just under the edge of his shorts. He was lucky that the bullet hadn't hit an artery. The wound was still bleeding slightly, or maybe it was bleeding again from his attempts to clean threads of tuxedo fabric from the gash. Bright red blood trickled slowly down his leg.

As she watched, he reached into the sink to wring water and blood from a washcloth he was rinsing out. He swayed slightly and caught himself on the edge of the sink, closing his eyes and trying to breathe deeply.

"Why don't you sit down?" Carrie said. "I'll do that."

He opened his eyes and turned to look at her. "Ah," he said, "you're out of the shower."

"Sit down," she said again. She took the washcloth from his hands and finished rinsing it in the sink.

Felipe didn't move. He stood there, inches away from her, so close she could feel the heat from his body.

"So," she said, turning off the water and wringing the cloth out, "what on earth made you decide to be a detective in the vice squad? I figure you're vice, right? That's where organized crime fits in, doesn't it?"

She looked steadily up into the warmth of his brown eyes. He looked back searchingly, and then he smiled, a real genuine smile despite his pain. It softened his face and made him seem so much younger.

But he *was* young, Carrie realized. He probably wasn't much older than she was—twenty-five. He was twenty-six or twenty-seven at the most.

"You believe me." It was a statement, but his eyes were full of questions.

"God help me," Carrie said. "I think I'm starting to. But…" She shook her head, pulling away from the hypnotizing heat of his eyes, turning back to the sink.

"What?"

He touched her. It was just a light hand on her shoulder, just the gentlest of caresses.

"You have a question?" he asked. "I'll answer anything you want to know, if I can."

Carrie moved out of reach, crossing her arms in front of her, afraid of the way that touch made her feel. "I still can't believe anyone would want to kill *me*," she said. "I didn't even get a good look at that muscle man—you know, Tommy Walsh." She shook her head. "I probably wouldn't even be able to pick him out in a lineup."

"Probably," Felipe said. "Probably's not good enough for Tommy. He'd kill a blind man at a crime scene simply on the off chance that the man caught a whiff of his cologne. Promise me something, Caroline."

She looked up at him, and once again was sucked into the intensity of his gaze.

"Promise me you'll ask Rafe—or anyone else here—about Tommy Walsh," Felipe said. "Please don't leave until you hear what the word on the street is about him. Promise me you won't leave."

Carrie swallowed. He was so serious, so intense. His hair was slick with perspiration and several stray curls clung to the side of his handsome face. With his midnight eyes, he was willing her to agree.

"Promise me," he whispered again.

She nodded, not sure whether or not she was lying. "All right."

But he believed her and relief made him sag. She moved quickly beside him, holding him up.

"Come on," she said. "You better sit down."

"Part of my problem," Felipe said ruefully, "is that I've got a bullet where I sit down."

He did, too. Still have a bullet in his leg, that is. There was an entry wound, but no exit wound. That was bad. That was *really* bad, especially since he refused to go to the hospital. Carrie helped him into one of the kitchen chairs.

He swore softly in Spanish. The change in his position must've hurt like hell. Carrie knelt next to him.

"You're going to need to get that bullet out," she said, examining the back of his leg. "This already looks infected."

He nodded slowly. "Unfortunately, I can't do it myself."

"You need a doctor," Carrie said.

"That's going to have to wait," Felipe said.

"Until when?" Carrie asked. "Until after you get so sick you can't even stand, or until after you die?"

Felipe pushed himself up off the chair. "I need a shower," he said. "Then I'll figure out what to do."

"You'll need antibiotics, too," Carrie said. "Where are you going to get them?"

"I don't know." Painfully, he reached down to where he'd thrown his pants onto the floor, and dug through his pockets. He pulled out a key.

"Since you trust me," he said, handing her the key, "it's only fair that I trust you." He gestured to the key. "It's for the dead bolt on the apartment door."

Carrie glanced at the door, then back at the shiny key in her hand.

"You promised me you wouldn't leave," Felipe reminded her.

He turned, carrying his bloody clothes and his shoulder holster and gun with him to the bathroom. He pushed the door shut behind him, but didn't latch it.

Carrie heard the water turn on. Slowly, she sat down on the sofa.

Felipe needed a doctor. They both needed some kind of protection from this Tommy Walsh. And—if Felipe's story really was true—Felipe needed to figure out exactly who in the police department was on Lawrence Richter's payroll.

Carrie shook her head. It was too much. A few hours ago, her biggest problem had been how to ditch her date without hurting his feelings. Now she was neck-deep in intrigue and murder attempts…and undercover police detectives with charming smiles that could make her melt.

It was getting more and more difficult *not* to believe Felipe. Was his story really becoming more convincing, or was she simply falling victim to his persuasive eyes?

Still, if she truly were his hostage, he wouldn't have given her a key to the door. He wouldn't have risked the possibility of her running away.

A sharp knock on the door broke into her thoughts and made her jump up.

"Who's there?" she asked, aware once again that she was holding the key. She could actually unlock the door if she wanted to.

"Rafe," Felipe's brother's voice replied. "I've brought something for you to eat. Open up."

Carrie slipped the key into the dead bolt's lock, but it didn't fit. She tried again. No, it was definitely the wrong key. "They key doesn't work," she said.

"There are two keys," Rafe said impatiently. "One has a round head, the other is square. The round one opens the dead bolt. The square is for the bathroom door."

Carrie looked down at the key in her hand. The head was square. Felipe hadn't given her the key to unlock the apartment door after all.

"The food's outside the door," Rafe said, his voice already fading as he walked away.

So much for Felipe trusting her…

Carrie turned and looked at the bathroom door. It was ajar, and she could clearly hear the shower still running.

Lord, maybe she *was* his hostage. Maybe everything he'd told her was one great big lie.

Angrily, she marched to the bathroom door and pushed it open.

Felipe was in the shower, eyes closed, hands braced against the tile wall as he let the water stream down onto his head. She could see him clearly through the plastic shower curtain. He was naked, of course. He was very, *very* naked.

Which made sense, again of course, because he was in the shower.

The bathroom door slowly swung all the way open and hit the wall with a thud.

Felipe looked up and directly into Carrie's eyes.

For one heart-stopping moment, the rest of the world ceased to exist. Tommy Walsh and Lawrence Richter and all the car chases and gunfire and anger and mistrust vanished, swirling down the drain with the blood-tinged water. Carrie was all that was left behind—Carrie, and this incredible-looking man, with his seemingly perfect, gentle smile and kind brown eyes.

But he wasn't smiling now, and his eyes couldn't possibly be described as kind. Hot, yes. Intense, definitely. Passionate, absolutely.

He made no effort to cover himself. Clearly, he was comfortable with his body—and why shouldn't he be, with a body like that? He had muscular legs, narrow hips, a flat stomach with a full array of washboardlike muscles. His chest was wide, his shoulders were broad and his arms were powerful-looking.

His skin was smooth and slick with water, accentuating the planes and angles and curves of his muscles. He didn't have a tan line—either he sunbathed nude, or his skin was naturally a beautiful golden brown.

Felipe slicked his hair back out of his face and turned off the water. With one movement of his hand, he pushed the shower curtains open. Steam billowed into the tiny bathroom, following him as he stepped out of the tub, making him seem mystical and savage.

He reached for a towel and wrapped it around his waist, careful of his injured leg. "Is there a problem?" he asked in his gentle, musical accent.

For heaven's sake, she was standing there like a ninny, with her mouth hanging open, just staring at him as if she'd never seen a naked man before in her life.

She'd never seen one like Felipe, that was for sure.

"You gave me the wrong key," she said. Her voice came out sounding squeaky, not accusing or outraged the way she'd intended.

Water ran in tiny rivulets from his shoulders, down his neatly sculpted chest, up and down the ripples of his abdominal muscles and into the towel, knotted casually beneath his belly button. He had an exceptionally nice-looking belly button.

"You promised you wouldn't leave," Felipe said.

Carrie jerked her eyes up from where she'd been staring at his smooth, perfect stomach. "I didn't promise I wouldn't let your brother in," she said. "He brought up some food, and I couldn't unlock the door."

"You couldn't?" He sounded surprised.

"You knew perfectly well I couldn't," she said. He took another towel and began drying his dripping hair. "There were two keys—you purposely gave me the wrong one."

He was watching her. His eyes didn't give away either his guilt or his innocence. "My mistake," he said quietly.

A mistake? Carrie wasn't so sure. She couldn't believe this man ever made *any* mistakes.

Felipe had hung his torn and dirty tuxedo pants on the back of the bathroom door, along with his holster and gun. He reached into the pants pocket and took out another key.

"I'm sorry," he said, handing it to Carrie. "Please don't mistrust me because of this."

The key in her hand had a round head. It would unlock the dead bolt and let her out of Rafe's apartment.

"You're going to let me walk out of here?" she asked.

"You promised not to leave," he said. "You're a smart lady, Caroline. I don't think you will leave—not after you hear what my brother and his friends have to say about Tommy Walsh. And if you do decide you have to leave, I hope you'll be smart enough to go home to Montana."

"How did you know I'm from Montana?" she asked suspiciously.

He looped the second towel around his neck and sat gingerly on top of the closed toilet. He was hurting, but he still managed to smile at her. "After our first meeting at Sea Circus," he said, "I was...intrigued, shall we say? I went back—and not just to make sure you were all right, although I went back for that reason, too."

"If you're really a cop," Carrie said, searching his eyes for something, *any*thing that would convince her he was telling the truth, "why didn't you say something? Why didn't you introduce yourself to me?"

"I should have," he said simply. There were pages of meaning compressed into those three little words. His eyes caressed her face and Carrie had to look away. "I loved watching you with the dolphins," he added. "I've always wanted to swim with dolphins, but I think I'd draw the line at getting into the tank with the killer whales—what were their names? Biffy and Louise?"

She looked back up at him. "You really *were* there," she said. "Weren't you?"

Felipe nodded. "I came more than once," he said, "although I tried not to. I thought knowing me would be dangerous for you." He smiled ruefully. "Looks like I was right."

"Nothing at Sea Circus mentions that I'm from Montana," Carrie said. "Was that just a good guess?"

"No," he said. "Don't be angry, but I looked you up in the police computer. I also found out that you have the habit of driving too fast on I-75. Two speeding tickets in the course of one week. Eighty-one one day, seventy-nine the next." He shook his head, making tsking sounds. "Shame on you, Miss Brooks."

He was hiding a smile, but that smile finally slipped out. Carrie found herself smiling back at him.

"I have no excuse," she said, "and obviously I didn't learn my lesson, did I? I slowed down, but not by much."

"I took care of the tickets for you," Felipe said. "It was the least I could do after locking you in your trunk."

Carrie's smile faded. "Was that really necessary?" she asked. "I mean, assuming you really are a police detective, and assuming you really were under cover that night at Sea Circus. What do you really think would have happened if you hadn't locked me in the trunk of my car?''

Felipe sighed. ''I *am* a police detective,'' he said, clearly disappointed that she still doubted him. ''I *was* under cover that night. And if I hadn't put you in the trunk where you were safe, well, those men I was with? They were not very nice men. I would have had to hurt them. Or worse. Because I would not have let them hurt you.''

It was very hard not to believe him, not when he sat there, gazing up at her with that protective light in his eyes.

I would not have let them hurt you.

Carrie could almost believe it. She *wanted* to believe it.

''Talk to Rafe,'' Felipe said. ''Talk to some of the other men who live here. Ask them about Tommy Walsh. Then come back and talk to me. Okay?''

Carrie nodded. Okay.

She turned and walked out of the bathroom. She could feel his eyes watching her as she crossed to the apartment door. She could feel him watching as she turned the key, unlocking the bolt. She glanced back once, then slipped out the door.

Felipe scrambled for the living room, searching for a clock. There was one on the VCR—it read 9:36 p.m.

Thank God.

The halfway house was locked up tight from 9:30 every night until 6:00 in the morning.

Carrie wouldn't be able to leave the building even if she wanted to—not without a great deal of trouble anyway. She certainly wouldn't be able to simply walk away.

And that was good, because Felipe couldn't let her leave. He would not let her get killed, even if that meant locking her up, holding her prisoner. Even if it meant that she would hate him.

Better that she hated him and stayed alive, than loved him and died.

Chapter 7

Carrie hadn't really noticed when she'd first come in, but now she realized the entire halfway house was as spotlessly clean and orderly as Rafe's apartment. The halls and stairway were swept and brightly lit, and the walls wore a fresh coat of paint.

She wandered down past a large common room and into the kitchen. Highboy was cleaning the stove, an apron tied carefully around his wide expanse.

Rafe was sitting at the kitchen table, drinking a diet cola straight from the can. He looked up as Carrie lingered in the doorway.

"Is he okay?" Rafe asked without greeting. They both knew who he was talking about. Felipe.

Carrie shook her head. "He's still got a bullet in his leg," she said. "Not only does it hurt him, but it's going to make him sick."

Rafe blinked. "I know what a bullet does, what it can do," he said. He turned to the man cleaning the stove, and spoke to him in Spanish.

The man nodded and left the room, squeezing past Carrie, who still stood in the doorway.

"Gracias," Rafe called after him. He looked at Carrie. "We have a former medical doctor in residence. He spent about four years in service in 'Nam. He'll know how to take care of a bullet wound. He owes me, big time. This will make us even."

"May I sit down?" Carrie asked.

Rafe shrugged. "It's a free country. Sit where you want."

Carrie came into the kitchen and sat down at the table across from him. The kitchen was as immaculate as the rest of the house—maybe even more so. From somewhere, maybe the common room down the hall, came the sound of canned TV laughter.

"This is a nice place," Carrie said.

Rafe laughed derisively. "That surprises you," he said. "No, don't deny it, I know it does. You think, ex-cons, recovering addicts and alcoholics, and you automatically think dump, right? Yeah." He laughed again. "The problem is, some of the time you're right. But not here." He sat forward, leaning toward her across the table, his flat brown eyes oddly alight. "One of the things you need to learn when you're an addict is self-respect. You think anyone who truly respects themselves would shoot themselves full of crap? No way. So how do you learn to respect yourself? One of the things you do is take pride in where you live. You *don't* live in a dump. You keep your place clean. And then you look around and you say, 'Hey, I live in this nice place, so maybe I'm worth something after all. What do you know?'"

Carrie didn't speak. She wasn't sure what to say. She could feel Rafe Salazar's eyes studying her.

"Forty-eight hours," he said suddenly.

She looked up at him. "Excuse me?"

"That's my prediction," he said with a wolfish grin. "My little brother's gonna get you into bed with him in the next forty-eight hours."

Carrie felt herself blush, but she held her chin up and looked him straight in the eye. "You're wrong," she said. "But wrong or right, I really don't think that it's any of your business."

"You look like one of those little blond angels we used to hang on our Christmas tree," Rafe mused. "Even when he was a kid, Felipe liked the little blond angels. He's not going to be able to resist you, angel. If you don't want him in your bed, you're gonna have to work hard at keeping your distance.''

"Thanks for the tip," Carrie said dryly. "You have any additional words of wisdom to share with me about this Tommy Walsh guy?"

"Why's he after you?" Rafe asked.

Good question. "I was there when Felipe's cover was blown," Carrie said. "I think your brother had infiltrated some crime boss's organization—"

"Lawrence Richter," Rafe broke in, supplying the name.

"That's right," Carrie said. "Felipe says he has enough information to put both Walsh and Richter away."

"And you were there when Felipe's cover was blown?" Rafe repeated. "How much 'there'?"

Carrie made herself steadily meet his eyes as she confessed, "I, um, blew his cover."

Rafe didn't say anything for several long moments. He took a sip from his can of soda and put it carefully down on the table, turning it so that the label was directly in front of him.

"Well, angel," he finally said, "if I were you, I'd think about getting my personal effects and last will and testament in order."

Carrie had been holding her breath, but now she let it out in a ragged swoosh of air. "That bad, huh?"

"You have two options," Rafe said. "Either you change your identity and disappear, or…Walsh finds you and you die."

"Even though I'm not positive I could ID him?" Carrie asked.

"Walsh wasted a six-year-old for witnessing a hit," Rafe said. "He's got to do Felipe—he's got no choice, not if Felipe can put Richter in jail. But my little brother's a cop. Killing him's a capital offense. We're talking mandatory death sentence. You'd be able to tie Walsh to Felipe's death. Walsh probably doesn't like the idea of the electric chair, so he's got to do you, too."

"But Felipe's not dead," Carrie said.

"Yet," Rafe finished grimly. "I knew the *estúpido* sonuvabitch would get himself into something like this someday. I swear to God—" He looked up at Carrie, stopping abruptly.

"There's something that you should know about my little brother."

Carrie waited for him to explain.

"He expects everybody to be the same kind of saint that he is," Rafe said. "It's impossible to live up to his expectations." He smiled, but it was humorless. "No doubt you'll disappoint him too, angel, when he finds out you're just human, a mere mortal like the rest of us."

"Can you really blame him for being disappointed and mistrustful of you?" Carrie asked Rafe quietly.

Her words struck home. She could see it in the tension in his face and shoulders, but Rafe shook his head. "He scorns me because I am an addict. A recovering addict, but an addict just the same. But you know what?" Rafe added. "Felipe, he's an addict, too. He's addicted to living on the edge. He's addicted to danger. Either that, or he's got some kind of sick death wish, no? What kind of man would try to bring Richter and Walsh down? What kind of man would put himself eyeball-deep in that kind of danger?"

"A brave man," Carrie answered. "A man who wants to help and protect innocent people."

As she spoke those words defending Felipe, Carrie realized that she believed him. She believed he was a cop. She believed what he'd said about Richter and Walsh. She believed everything Felipe had told her.

Rafe laughed and laughed. "Ah, angel, you've already bought into the saint story, huh?"

It was something of a relief, believing Felipe. She could rely on him to protect her from Tommy Walsh. She could quit fighting him, quit searching for a way to escape. She could let herself trust him. And she could stop worrying so much about the powerful attraction that sparked between them every time their eyes met....

"You're not so different from your brother," Carrie observed. "You help people, too."

"Felipe doesn't see it that way," Rafe said. "To him, I'm just a time bomb, ready to explode and start smoking crack again. He can't see past what I was."

"That's because you hurt and disappointed him when he was a child," Carrie said. "You can't expect him just to forget that."

"He'll never forget," Rafe said bitterly. "He'll never forgive me."

Exasperated, Carrie stood up, shoving her chair away from the table with a screech. "If you really want him to forgive you, you might try being a little nicer to him," she said sharply. "Good Lord, Felipe walks in here with a bullet in his leg, needing help, and you insult him and argue with him and are downright *mean* to him. Maybe *you're* the one who won't forgive and forget."

She pushed her chair back under the table and strode out of the room.

Rafe's harsh laughter followed her down the hall. "An angel for the saint," he said. "It's perfect. Did I say forty-eight hours? I'm gonna change that prediction to twenty-four."

Carrie ignored him, hurrying up the stairs.

Felipe's leg was throbbing, and he was so nauseated he was sure he must look green. But the bullet was out of his leg, thanks to a tall, heavyset man who called himself Doc Bird.

He'd given Felipe something to bite down on as he dug for the bullet. It had been a grueling two minutes, but only two minutes. One hundred and twenty seconds of hell. It could've been far worse.

Once more, Felipe was drenched with sweat. But he doubted he could stand up and take another shower. Besides, the stitches Doc Bird had put into his leg had come with instructions not to get them wet for at least a day if not two.

He pushed the hair out of his eyes and tried to focus on the clock on the VCR. It was nearly ten o'clock. Where was Caroline?

Another ten minutes, and pain or no pain, nausea or no nausea, he was going to go looking for her. Until then, he had to find something to distract himself.

He checked out the pile of newspapers on the coffee table. The top paper had a headline about St. Simone's newly appointed chief of police, a man named Earley.

Felipe knew him. He'd met him at least half a dozen times, maybe more. He was a little too conservative, a little too old-fashioned and probably exactly what the city needed in a police chief.

He picked up the paper, but the tiny print made his eyes swim and he threw it back on the table. Instead, he picked up the remote control and switched on the television.

The Fox affiliate carried a ten o'clock news program. Curious to see if the news had been released about his so-called connection to the Sandlot Murders, he switched to that station.

The program was just starting. The lead story concerned an outbreak of salmonella poisoning at a local nursing home. Three elderly people had already died, dozens more were ill.

Next came the story about newly appointed Chief Earley. Felipe was surprised. He'd been almost positive that the fact that he was suspected of committing the Sandlot Murders would've been leaked to the media. But there was no mention of it. Nothing at all.

There was a brief interview with Earley, then a background profile. The police chief had served in Vietnam as a demolitions expert. Felipe hadn't known that. Apparently, Earley had worked clearing booby traps from the labyrinth of underground tunnels that Vietcong guerrillas hid in during the daytime. His was one of the most dangerous and terrifying jobs in the marines. It was not a job for the faint of heart or the claustrophobic, that was for sure.

Felipe heard a sound in the hallway, and pushed the mute button on the TV remote control. The apartment door swung open, and…thank you, Lord.

Caroline was standing there.

She came into the apartment, closing the door behind her.

She seemed embarrassed, almost shy, and Felipe realized that he was wearing only his boxer shorts. He hadn't had the energy to make it over to Rafe's closet to find a pair of jeans or a T-shirt to put on.

Still, she crossed over to the sofa, looking down at him. "You look awful," she said.

He tried to smile. "*Gracias,*" he said. "I *feel* awful. But the bullet's out. My brother sent someone up, someone who I think was a doctor at one time.''

Carrie nodded. "I know," she said. She knelt on the floor next to the sofa. "It must really hurt. I'm sorry."

"I'm not," Felipe said. He took a deep breath in and released it slowly. He found that now he *could* smile at her. "I don't mind the pain. In fact, I like it. It reminds me that I'm alive. And I really like being alive—particularly after an evening like this one."

Carrie smiled tentatively back at him. How beautiful she was. Felipe had to hold on tightly to the remote control to keep himself from reaching out and drawing her into his arms. What he would have given for one small, comforting embrace. Except there was no way on earth an embrace between them would have remained either small or comforting for long.

"I don't think you realize how close we both came to being killed tonight," Felipe said quietly, searching the depths of her sea green eyes.

But she didn't look away. She didn't turn her head. She didn't shut him out. Instead, she nodded. Yes.

"Yes, I do," she said. "I talked to your brother about Walsh."

"And...?"

"I believe you," she said.

"About Walsh?"

"About everything."

Heat coursed through him at her words. She believed him. Even though he knew that he shouldn't, Felipe let go of the remote and reached for Carrie. He touched the side of her face and her skin was so smooth, so soft. And she didn't pull away.

He could see her pulse beating at the delicate base of her neck, he could see her chest rising and falling with each breath she took, he could see her lips, parted slightly and moistened with the tip of her tongue, and still she didn't pull away.

She looked the very way he felt—hypnotized.

Knowing quite well that he shouldn't, but unable to stop himself, he leaned forward to kiss her. How he wanted to kiss her! He truly didn't have a choice.

He brushed his lips against hers in the smallest, gentlest, most delicate of kisses.

Her eyelids fluttered, and she looked up at him. She looked scared to death, terrified, but she still didn't pull away.

So he kissed her again, knowing that he shouldn't, knowing absolutely that kissing this woman was a gigantic mistake. He liked her too much—*way* too much. He couldn't afford to have any kind of relationship with her. He couldn't bear the fact that just *knowing* him would put her in danger. And, maybe for the first time in his entire life, he knew that he wouldn't be able to keep the physical, sexual side of a relationship with Caroline from becoming entangled with the emotional. And that truly frightened him.

No, Caroline was not the only one who was scared to death. But he couldn't stop himself. And this time, she met him halfway. She reached up and threaded her arms around his neck and kissed him as if there were no tomorrow.

And maybe, just maybe, she was right.

But the danger they were in, the risk of impending death, wasn't the real reason Felipe pulled her even closer and deepened the kiss. He did it for one reason only—because he so desperately wanted to. He could no sooner resist Caroline Brooks than he could stop breathing.

Her mouth was so sweet, her lips so inviting. Her hair was like silk as he ran his fingers through it. And her soft, fragile body was neither entirely fragile nor entirely soft. She was slight and slender, yes, but still quite strong. He slid one hand down her back to the curve of her firm derriere and pulled her toward him.

Man, five minutes ago, he'd been lying here on the sofa, feeling like death warmed over, uncertain whether or not he'd even be able to stand. It was funny what desire could do to a man. Because now he knew without a doubt that he could stand. He could stand. He could walk. Man, he could run laps if he needed to.

His fingers found the edge of Caroline's dress, and the soft, smooth warmth of her thigh. Felipe heard himself groan, and she pulled back, alarmed.

"Did I hurt you?" she whispered, her voice husky. Her hair was tousled and her cheeks were flushed. It didn't take much imagination to picture her amid the rumpled sheets of a bed....

"Oh, yes," he said, barely hiding his smile. "You can't imagine my pain. Although it has nothing to do with my leg."

She blushed and laughed, then leaned forward to kiss him again.

And then the door burst open.

Felipe reacted. He found his gun almost instinctively, remembering he had thrown the holster over the back of the sofa. As he drew it out, he pulled himself off the sofa so that his body was shielding Carrie's.

"Jesus, it's only me," Rafe said. "Put that thing away, Superman. Lois Lane's still safe."

Felipe sagged with relief. It was only his brother. Relief turned sharply to annoyance. "Didn't our mother teach you to knock?" he asked, dragging himself back onto the sofa.

Rafe smiled humorlessly at his brother. He looked pointedly at Carrie, who was running her fingers through her disheveled hair. "Yeah," he said. "She also taught us not to play with fire—a rule you've obviously forgotten, little brother."

Felipe reached down to help Carrie onto the sofa next to him. He kept his arm behind her, his fingers lightly touching her shoulder. She glanced at him, and he nearly felt burned. Rafe was right. He *was* playing with fire. But what a way to go.

He looked up at Rafe. "Was there something you needed?"

Rafe looked at the television, which was still on, but muted. A commercial for a dishwashing liquid was showing.

"Were you watching the news—no, obviously not," Rafe said, answering his own question.

Felipe sat up a little straighter. "Why?" he asked.

Rafe glanced at him. "I think you know why," he said. He bent down and picked the remote control off the floor. As the commercial ended, he pressed the mute button.

"To recount a story just in," the news anchor said, looking seriously out from the television screen, "police sources have revealed that they are searching for a suspect in the controversial Sandlot Murders case."

A rather grainy picture of Felipe appeared at the top right of the screen, with the words Rogue Cop in jagged letters underneath.

"Police Detective Felipe Salazar," the anchor reported, her voice still solemn, "being labeled a rogue cop by the supervisors in his department…"

"Good Lord!" Carrie cried, leaning forward to look more closely at the screen. Felipe's hand fell away from her shoulder.

"…is wanted in connection with last week's double slaying in a downtown sandlot, next to the East 43rd Street Elementary School. Salazar, described in the official police statement as being a twenty-five-year-old Latino male, is six feet tall, one hundred seventy pounds, with dark hair and eyes. He is believed to be armed and extremely dangerous."

Caroline was staring at the television, clearly aghast. She looked up at Felipe, and he knew with a sinking heart that all her doubts about him had come flooding back.

"It's a frame," Felipe told her, but the news broadcast had once again caught her attention.

"We're going to the Fourth Precinct where we have a reporter standing by," the anchor said, reaching up to adjust a tiny speaker in her ear. "Hello, Walt, are you there?"

The picture switched to that of a man standing in the brightly lit lobby of the police station.

"This is Walter Myers reporting from downtown at the Fourth Precinct, where Felipe Salazar is a member of the police force," the man said, staring into the camera. "Newly appointed Police Chief Jack Earley will be arriving shortly to hold a press conference. We'll be breaking into regular programming to bring you that live report."

The camera followed Walter Myers down the corridor.

A man stepped into camera range. "Gentlemen, I'm going to have to ask you to leave," he said.

"That's Diego," Felipe said. His friend and former partner had gotten a haircut since he'd seen him last. But other than that, Jim Keegan looked the same. He was wearing his standard uniform—jeans and rumpled button-down shirt, with a loosened tie around his neck to make it look a little more businesslike.

Carrie glanced at him. "That's the man you called?"

"Yeah."

"And you are...?" the reporter asked.

"Detective James Keegan," Jim replied patiently. "I'm afraid you're going to have to continue your news report outside, sir."

"His name's not Diego, it's James," Carrie said, her eyes still glued to the screen.

"Diego's Spanish for James," Rafe told her.

"Can you comment on the latest suspect in the Sandlot Murders?" the reporter asked Jim.

"No, I cannot," he replied firmly, herding them back to the door.

"Do you know Salazar?" the reporter asked.

"Yes, I do," Jim said.

"Do you believe he committed this crime?"

Jim was about to respond, then he glanced toward the camera. It was almost as if he'd decided to change his answer. "You never know," he told the reporter. "That's one thing I've learned in all my years on the force. You just never know."

The reporter looked into the camera. "Back to you, Mary."

The news anchor reappeared with another story, and Rafe reached over and turned off the television.

Carrie didn't move. "You don't seem surprised by this," she said tightly to Felipe.

"It's a setup," he said again. "A frame. And yes, you're right. I'm not surprised. I knew they were going to try to pin these murders on me."

She turned and looked at him. He could see anger in her eyes. Anger and hurt. "You knew," she said. "And you didn't tell me. This is really why you can't go to the police, isn't it? Because you're wanted for *murder*."

"I didn't do it," Felipe said. How could she think that he would kill someone in cold blood? "I wouldn't kill anyone."

"Not anyone who didn't deserve it," Rafe cut in. "But a vigilante-style execution...? Maybe."

"Stop it," Felipe said sharply. "You know damn well—"

"I only know you're a big fan of justice," Rafe retorted. "You'd send your own brother back to prison, two years hard labor. You're probably capable of delivering this kind of justice, no?''

Carrie was looking at Felipe as if he'd just been accused of slaying infants. "Even your friend, what's his name—Keegan—wouldn't stand up for you," she said.

Felipe reached for her hand. She didn't pull away fast enough, so he held it, wishing that she could somehow get inside his head and see for herself that he was telling the truth.

"Caroline, don't you see?" he said quietly, intensely. "This is why Walsh let us get away. Richter's man in the police department set up this frame, somehow making me look like a suspect in this murder case. They may not even have any evidence against me, I don't know. If they *do* have anything, it's trumped up or fake. But the case is never going to go to court, because as soon as they find me and bring me in, Walsh will be tipped off. He'll wait until I'm being transported and then he'll put a bullet in my head. Everyone will assume my death was some kind of mob counterhit, and the case will be closed."

Carrie didn't look convinced. She was staring down at her hand, entrapped by Felipe's larger hand.

"I need you to leave," Rafe said. "Your being here is jeopardizing everything I've worked hard for—including my own freedom. I won't serve time for aiding and abetting. Not even for you, little brother."

Caroline pulled her hand free.

Felipe looked up at Rafe. "Don't you mean *especially* not for me?" he asked bitterly, then ran his hand across his face. "I'm sorry. I didn't mean that."

"Yes, you did," Rafe said. He sighed. "Look, I had one of my staff get rid of the car you drove over here. I can't risk giving you one of my vans, but I'm going to tell you where I keep the keys, do you follow?"

Felipe nodded.

"They're in the kitchen, top cabinet, left of the microwave. I'll give you seventy-two hours, then I'm going to report the van stolen," Rafe continued.

"Do you have a tape recorder I can borrow, too?" Felipe asked.

"There's a tape deck in the van," Rafe told him, "though this is hardly the time to be thinking about tunes, little brother."

Felipe ran a hand back through his hair. "No," he said, "I need to make a recording, to make a tape telling what I know about Richter and Walsh. You know. In case…"

Rafe nodded curtly. "I'll find you something," he said. "The bastard's gonna blow you away, least you can do is leave behind incriminating evidence, right?"

"Wrong," Felipe said. "It wouldn't be evidence. A taped statement wouldn't hold up in court. No, it would just be information to help the next guys nail Richter."

"You mean…" Rafe stared at him. "If you're dead, that's it? No case against Richter?"

"That's why he's so hot to waste me," Felipe said.

"Jesus," Rafe said. "You don't stand a chance."

Carrie was silent. She stared down sightlessly at the floor.

Rafe crossed to the closet and pulled out a pair of jeans and some worn-out black leather boots. "Here," he said, handing them to Felipe. He took a T-shirt and a clean pair of socks from his dresser and tossed them onto the sofa. He gestured toward Carrie. "I don't have anything in her size," he said. "But she can put a shirt on over that dress. And you, you probably need something to cover up that holster and gun," he added, crossing back to the closet.

He took out a black leather biker's jacket.

Felipe shook his head. "I can't take that," he said. "That's your jacket, man."

Rafe looked down at the jacket in his hands. When he looked up again, the lines in his face seemed deeper, the seat of his mouth even tighter than normal. "I don't have anything else to give you, Felipe," he said, for once all the sarcasm gone from his voice. "I *am* sorry that I can't let you stay. Do you have somewhere to go?"

Felipe nodded. "Yeah. I've got someplace in mind, someplace to lie low for a day or two until I feel like running again."

"Then what?"

"Then I find out who Richter's mysterious partner is," Felipe said. "Richter called him Captain Rat. I thought there was some connection to the wharf, the harbor authority, maybe the Coast Guard, but now I think this 'Rat' is a captain in the police department. Who else could have engineered this kind of a frame-up so quickly?''

Stiffly, gingerly, Felipe pulled on the jeans. They were a little loose—his brother was taller than he was—but they fitted just fine over his bandaged leg. He pulled the T-shirt over his head and slipped on his shoulder holster.

That little bit of movement exhausted him, and he had to stop and gather his strength. Only God could help them if Walsh came after them now.

He opened his eyes and found Caroline watching him, wariness still on her face. She looked away, unable to hold his gaze.

She didn't trust him, didn't believe him again.

They were back to square one.

Chapter 8

Carrie stood in the hallway with Rafe, waiting while Felipe limped into the kitchen. He was taking the keys to one of the halfway house's vans, with Rafe supposedly unaware.

She still couldn't believe the news report they'd just seen on the television.

The man she was with was indeed Felipe Salazar—that much had been established without a doubt. He *was* a detective with St. Simone's Fourth Precinct—that was true, too. And he could kiss exactly as she'd imagined in her dreams—better, in fact.

Good grief, one kiss, and she'd been ready... Well, she wasn't sure exactly *what* she'd been ready for, but she certainly hadn't been ready to find out that this handsome, charismatic man who could kiss like a dream was wanted for murder.

Felipe was wanted for *murder*.

He said he didn't do it. He said it was a setup, a frame. Carrie wanted to believe him, but she couldn't ignore the fact that if the man was a cold-blooded killer, he certainly wouldn't balk at lying.

Rafe was watching her, his flat, expressionless eyes studying her face.

"Do you believe Felipe?" she asked him.

He shrugged, holding his arms out wide. "I don't know," he said. "Used to be my brother couldn't even fib. He was the straightest kid you ever met, you know? He was the kind of kid who'd break something and then stick around to face the music. No running or hiding." He glanced toward the kitchen door, but there was no sign of Felipe. "But working under cover, he's had to learn to lie. I mean, when you think about it, an undercover cop does nothing *but* lie, huh?"

Carrie nodded.

"Do *you* believe him?" Rafe asked.

But Carrie didn't have a chance to answer. Felipe came out of the kitchen.

Part of her *did* believe him. When he told her he'd been set up, his words had been very persuasive. And the look in his eyes had begged her to trust him. She ought to trust him, considering the way they'd connected. And they had really connected—the proof was in that kiss they'd shared.

Hoo boy, what a kiss....

But just because Felipe Salazar had the power to knock her socks off with a kiss didn't mean that she should simply trust him. And the truth was, her belief in him was based on instinct, on gut reaction alone. It had nothing to do with logic or provable facts.

And that scared her. How could she believe him when there was no proof to back his words? How could she trust him when all of the data implied that he was not to be trusted?

She couldn't. Despite her gut reaction, despite their obvious attraction, she couldn't let herself trust him. It was that simple.

"You get what you need?" Rafe asked Felipe, leading them to the front door.

Felipe nodded. His expression was almost as guarded as Rafe's. Carrie thought he was trying to hide the pain in his leg until he glanced at her. But with one look at his eyes, she could see that his pain wasn't from the bullet wound. It was from his disappointment. In her.

Rafe had stopped in the entry hall. He held a key, but he didn't attempt to unlock the front door.

Felipe looked incredible in those blue jeans and that black leather jacket, with his hair loose and flowing around his shoulders. It was different from the way he'd looked in his tuxedo, but no less commanding.

"Highboy's got the other key," Rafe explained. "Until he gets down here, we're locked in."

Locked in?

Felipe was studying the tips of his borrowed boots, his hands jammed deep into the pockets of his jeans as he leaned against the wall.

"Locked in?" Carrie asked.

Felipe still didn't look up, so she turned questioningly to his brother.

"Yeah," Rafe said. "That's the way the halfway house operates. Door doesn't open unless both guys who hold the keys can be talked into opening it. See, night can be the worst time for some of the addicts. I know it always was for me—still is sometimes. If the door is locked, and you can't get out of the house, you can't give in to the devil. We keep the door locked tight from 9:30 at night until 6:00 in the morning. It helps everyone stay clean. No one comes in or goes out unless it's an emergency. And it has to be one mother of an emergency."

The doors were locked after 9:30. Carrie looked at Felipe, who was still studying his boots as Highboy came down the stairs carrying the key.

Felipe had given her the key to get out of Rafe's apartment—but only after 9:30. She'd thought that he'd set her free, but she had still been a prisoner. She simply hadn't realized it at the time.

Highboy unlocked the top bolt; Rafe undid the bottom. The door swung open and Felipe and Carrie stepped outside.

Carrie's head was spinning. She took a deep breath, trying to clear it, but the night was warm and the air was tainted with the smell of trash.

"Raphael," Felipe said, turning back to his brother. *"Gracias."* He held out his hand, but Rafe turned away.

"Dejame," Rafe said flatly, closing the door in Felipe's face. The hurt that flashed in Felipe's eyes was heartbreaking. But

Carrie didn't have time to feel bad. If ever there was an opportunity to get away, it was right at this very moment.

She started down the sidewalk at a brisk pace, hoping Felipe wouldn't even notice that she was walking away. But he caught up with her before she'd gone ten yards. He took hold of her arm. "The van's parked in the alley," he said. "It's the other direction."

"That's real nice," Carrie said, "but I'm not going in the van with you."

"Yes," he said, "you are." His patience was wearing thin— she could hear it in his voice. He led her around the side of the house to the alley where the van was waiting.

"So I *am* your hostage," she said, steadily meeting his eyes and refusing to be seduced by the heat she could see there. "I have been all along, haven't I?"

"Caroline, you're not a hostage."

She looked pointedly down at his hand holding her arm. "Coulda fooled me," she said.

Something snapped. She could see it in his eyes, in the tenseness of his jaw.

"You believed me a half hour ago," he said tightly.

"You should have told me you were wanted for murder," she countered.

"I didn't really think they could pull off a frame-up this big— not until I saw it myself," he said. He laughed harshly. "Ah, the power of television. You'd rather believe what you see on the screen than believe me, no?"

"How can I believe you?" Carrie asked, "when I don't even know you?"

"You know me," Felipe said, his voice suddenly soft. His dark eyes glittered in the moonlight. "I think you know me quite well, in fact. Trust your heart, Caroline."

She closed her eyes, afraid of the hypnotizing power of his gaze, afraid of the magnetic pull of this man, afraid of the way his hold on her arm suddenly felt like a caress.

But then he let her go. "Okay," he said, still quietly. "You're free to go."

Carrie opened her eyes in surprise, and he dropped the keys to the van into her hand.

"There's one condition," he said. "You have to get on the interstate heading north. You have to go directly to your father's home in Montana, tell your father and your brothers everything that's happened here tonight, and then ask them to protect you. If you won't let me do it, you've got to let them."

"I'm just supposed to leave you here?" Carrie asked incredulously. "With a bullet wound in your leg?"

He shook his head. "I don't have time to argue with you," he said. "Especially not out here in the open like this, where anyone can see me. I've got an awful lot to do tonight. My first priority is to make sure you're safe. My second is to stay alive so that tomorrow I can get to my third priority—clearing my name. So kiss me goodbye and get the hell out of here."

Carrie looked from the keys in her hand, to the van, then back to Felipe. His number-one priority was her safety. In fact, he'd given up his one means of escape for her. Without the van, he'd be forced to take public transportation and risk being spotted by some vigilant citizen who'd seen the evening news. Of course, he could always travel by foot—although how far he'd get on his injured leg was uncertain.

He looked pale in the moonlight, and she could see that he was perspiring again. The pain from his bullet wound had to have been excruciating. He was just barely standing on his feet. How could she just drive away from him?

His eyes held no reproach, no recriminations. She could see only gentleness and warmth.

"Go," he whispered. "Godspeed, Caroline Brooks."

But Carrie didn't want to go. She wanted to stay. She didn't want to have to rely on her family for protection—not when she had the best possible protection right here in St. Simone.

Her feelings weren't scientific. They weren't based on fact or data or any kind of proof. For the first time in years, Carrie was rejecting the obvious and trusting her heart.

She took several steps forward, closing the gap between them, stood on her toes and kissed him.

She could taste his surprise. Nevertheless, he pulled her to him and kissed her, too. It was a long, slow, deep kiss, a sweet kiss, perhaps the sweetest she'd ever known.

He was kissing her goodbye, Carrie realized suddenly. He was giving her a kiss to last a lifetime, a kiss to remember him by.

He held her close, as if gathering his strength to push her away. "Don't stop for anything until you're out of state," he said, his voice husky.

She looked up at him and could actually see tears in his eyes.

"After you're out of Florida," he continued, "get rid of the van—leave it in some neighborhood just parked on the street. Then take a bus. Pay in cash and don't use your real name." He released her, digging into the back pocket of his jeans for his wallet. "I'm going to give you some money—"

"No," Carrie said. There were tears in her own eyes now. He was giving her the van *and* some money, too? She wiped at her eyes fiercely with the back of her hand.

Felipe shook his head. "Caroline, you're going to need—"

"Get in the van," she said, unlocking the passenger-side door. "I'm driving."

He stepped forward and touched the side of her face. "As much as I'd like to, I can't go to Montana with you."

"I'm not going to Montana," she said, then smiled at the hope that sprang into his eyes. He was trying to control it, trying not to allow himself to assume anything. "I'm safer with you," she added. "My brothers are lousy shots."

He nodded slowly, as if he was taking her words very seriously. "You've decided to believe me?" he said.

"Is there anything else that you've neglected to tell me?" she asked. "Any other sensational murders or maybe a kidnapped child or two in your basement? Or maybe you've been keeping secrets from me about your health. Any brain tumors or terminal illnesses you've been hiding?"

He smiled and shook his head. "Nothing of that great a magnitude."

"Then get in the van," she said, hoping to hell that she wasn't going to regret this.

Felipe sat low in the passenger seat of the cargo van so that no one could see him. He didn't like that he wasn't driving. In fact, he couldn't remember the last time he'd been in a car but not behind the wheel—excluding rides in Richter's limousine, of course.

He watched Carrie as she drove. She'd had to shift the driver's seat way up close to the steering wheel, but she drove the over-size vehicle with all the confidence and skill of an experienced truck driver.

This was a far cry from the little red sports car she'd had all those months ago at Sea Circus, when they'd first met. Still, someone who owned a precision automobile like Carrie's had to care about her car. And, in Felipe's experience, people who cared about their cars tended to know how to drive, and drive well. And usually fast. Her two speeding tickets verified that fact—although at the moment she was keeping their speed slightly below the limit. The time they'd save by going faster wasn't worth the risk of getting pulled over.

Carrie glanced over at him. He tried to smile, but the muscles in his face weren't working quite the way they should have been.

"You okay?" she asked, concern thickening her already husky voice, accentuating her slight Western drawl. She sounded a little bit—just a *little* bit—like Lauren Bacall trying to imitate John Wayne. On a woman of her less-than-imposing size, with all that silky blond hair and those enormous blue eyes, the effect was utterly charming.

"My leg hurts," Felipe admitted. *Hurts* was an enormous understatement. The damn thing throbbed steadily with a knife-like pain. And, as a bonus, he felt nauseated from the antibiotic Doc Bird had given him. He was supposed to take one of the capsules four times a day to keep his wound from becoming infected. Doc Bird had given him a ten-day supply of the medicine.

Ten days. He could only hope he lived that long.

Man, he was exhausted.

"Is there anything I can do?" Carrie asked quietly. She glanced at him again, and this time he managed to smile.

"You're doing it," he said.

"Where are we going?" she asked. "Besides south?"

"Sanibel Island," he told her. "Diego's in-laws own a beach house out there. It's empty at this time of year. We can hide there, at least overnight."

She nodded, her eyes carefully on the highway.

He took out the tape recorder that Rafe had given him. It was small and cheap and at least twenty-five years old. But it would get the job done.

"If you don't mind," Felipe said, "I'd like to record that information about Richter's operation."

"In case you're not around to do it in person," Carrie said, glancing over at him.

He nodded. "Yeah."

"But you will be," she said.

"Yes," he said with more certainty in his voice than he felt. "But I would hate not to make this tape, and then be wrong."

"Rafe thinks we don't stand a chance, doesn't he?"

We. Felipe liked the sound of that. She was on his side. "My brother is a pessimist," he said.

"But you're not," she answered back.

"We're still alive, aren't we?" he declared. "Against all odds, our hearts are still beating. Either we're lucky, or God's got a reason for keeping us around."

"God?" she said, turning to look at him in the darkness.

"Don't you believe in God?" he asked. "Some god, any god? Some force bigger than we are?"

She turned her head away from him as if she was embarrassed. "Gee, I don't know."

"Too bad," Felipe said, studying her profile as she drove. He adored the way her nose turned up very slightly at the end. "I've found believing is helpful in times like this."

She glanced back at him again. "I'm…surprised," she said.

Felipe smiled. "That's good," he said. "I'd hate to be boring."

Caroline laughed, a low, husky sound that hit him low in the gut and spread all the way out to his fingers and toes. Man, bullet wound or not, he would have sold his soul right at that moment for a chance to finish what they'd started with a kiss back in Rafe's apartment. His borrowed blue jeans were getting tighter and more uncomfortable by the second. But at least it took his mind off the pain in his leg.

"Believe me," she said. "You're not boring." She looked over at him, but quickly focused on the road again, as if she could see his desire simmering in his eyes. She probably could. He wasn't very good at hiding that sort of thing. "Go on and make your tape," she added. "I'd like to know why someone's trying to kill you—and me."

Felipe looked down at the tape recorder, and ejected the tape that his brother had put inside. It needed to be rewound to the beginning, so he put it back in and pushed the rewind button. Then he pressed Record and Play and silently counted to five to let the leader run out.

"My name is Felipe Ricardo Salazar, and I am a police detective with the Fourth Precinct in St. Simone," he said, speaking clearly into the machine's built-in microphone, still watching Caroline as he talked. "Today is January 17, 11:45 p.m.

"Early August of last year, I went under cover to infiltrate Lawrence Richter's crime syndicate. Posing as Raoul Tomás Garcia Vasquez, I have spent the past five months winning both Tommy Walsh's and Lawrence Richter's confidence."

Felipe took a deep breath. "Two months ago, I learned of a scam that I believe Richter has been operating for nearly a decade here in Florida. He imports illegal aliens from Cuba and Haiti and other Caribbean islands, and even from as far away as Mexico, charging them exorbitant prices for a so-called safe passage and entry into the United States. After they arrive, having spent every penny of their life savings, they are told of other, equally exorbitant fees for forged green cards that will enable them to stay. Richter's men sign a contract with these people, trading their future wages for these coveted—and counterfeit, therefore worthless—green cards."

Carrie drew in a sharp breath, again glancing over at Felipe.

"In short," he said, nodding grimly at her, "it's a form of indentured servitude, or should I say slavery? Richter currently has a work force of over twenty-two hundred illegal aliens—including children. Child labour laws don't apply to children who technically don't exist."

"That's awful," Carrie murmured.

"I've seen the below-poverty conditions that these people live in," Felipe continued, watching the impact his words had on her through the expressions on her face. "Most of them are housed in run-down buildings that Richter has bought in the worst neighborhoods in the city. These buildings have no running water, no electricity and no hope of ever being renovated. They are scheduled to be torn down, but Richter has orchestrated a series of delays in the legal proceedings surrounding their condemnation. It could literally be years before the buildings are destroyed, and by that time, Richter will have purchased—dirt cheap— other equally squalid buildings.

"Most of these apartment buildings are between Howard and Stern Streets, on First and Second Avenues." He sighed. "Although by the time you hear this tape, all the illegal tenants will probably have been moved.

"Garrett Hedford and Stuart Tiffler are two of Richter's men who use intimidation to keep the work force in line," he continued. "They also schedule the arrival of additional boatloads of people. In the past two months, I've seen ships arriving in both Miami and Fort Myers." Quickly, he rattled off the information on the ships' names and ports of call.

"I've seen copies of Richter's books," he said, shifting in his seat, trying to ease the endless throbbing in his leg. "He grosses over two hundred thousand dollars each *month* from these people, his *slaves*. I've witnessed him giving orders to both Hedford and Tiffler, as well as Tommy Walsh. I've witnessed the production of the counterfeit green cards, and their distribution to the illegal aliens. I've witnessed the signing of contracts, indenturing these people to Richter— although his name is not used. A corporate front, called L&R Co. is used, and it virtually cannot be traced to Lawrence Richter. At least not without me around. I've witnessed Richter transferring funds from the L&R account to his Swiss bank account."

"Felipe."

He turned off the tape recorder, looking up at Caroline. "Yes?"

"If you know all this," she asked, "what were you waiting for? You'd seen enough to put Richter away."

"His partner," he reminded her. "I found out that Richter wasn't working alone. The more I found out, the more I wanted to catch this other man, too." He smiled ruefully. "The more I found out, the more I realized I *had* to nail this guy. I'd guessed he was someone in St. Simone's government, someone who'd have access to my whereabouts after I went into protective custody while awaiting Richter's trial. I was the chief witness against Richter—the *only* witness. If I didn't bring a case against this other guy, too, this inside guy, I'd end up dead. I'm lucky I found out about this Captain Rat. If I hadn't, I probably never would have heard the bullet coming."

Caroline swallowed. "You say that so casually."

"It's my job," he replied.

"It's an awful job," she said.

"No, it's not," he returned gently.

"In my opinion it is," she said. She looked at him. "And I'm entitled to my own opinion."

Felipe leaned back against the headrest, just watching her. She believed him. Oh, she didn't believe him one hundred percent, but she believed him enough to stick around. And that was what counted.

Is there anything else that you've neglected to tell me? Her words echoed in his mind as he watched her drive.

Nothing of that great a magnitude.

But his answer had been a lie. And not just because there was something that he hadn't told her. It was true, there *was* something, but he couldn't possibly have told her about it, because he wasn't sure yet himself exactly what it was. It was difficult to pinpoint, harder even to define, these feelings, this *emotion* that seemed to swirl around him, enveloping him in a chaos both perfect and terrible whenever she looked in his direction, whenever he caught her eye.

What was it? He didn't know. Man, he didn't *want* to know.

But whatever it was, something told him it was of a far greater magnitude than he could ever imagine.

* * *

"I want to tell you...why I didn't come back and explain who I was and what I was doing that night at Sea Circus," Felipe said softly.

Carrie glanced at him, startled. He'd been quiet for so long, she was certain he'd been asleep.

"You know I went under cover as part of the Richter investigation back in August," he said. "One week I was pretending to be Carlos and running with some of the leaders of the most powerful gangs in St. Simone, and the next I was Raoul, driving a Jaguar and living in a penthouse at the Harbor's Gate. I had maybe three days between the two assignments. It...wasn't long enough."

"Long enough for what?" Carrie asked, looking over at him again. "It was certainly long enough for you to come and apologize."

He shifted in his seat. "It wasn't long enough for what I wanted," he said bluntly. "And I didn't think you deserved to be a one-night stand."

Carrie laughed, afraid to look at him, afraid of what she knew she'd see in his eyes. Desire. He'd stopped trying to hide it from her ever since they'd shared that kiss. "How gallant of you," she said. "You were saving me from my own lack of control, huh?"

"At the risk of sounding conceited," he said, "you would not have been able to resist me."

Coming from any other man's lips, his words would have been outrageous and disgustingly egomaniacal. But when Felipe said them, those words, combined with the rueful look in his eyes, were merely a statement of fact.

It was, however, no less disconcerting.

"Your brother thinks I'm going to sleep with you within the next twenty-four hours," Carrie said tightly. "But that's not why I'm here, and I intend to prove him wrong. In fact, I think we should ignore this...this...physical attraction until after you clear your name and Lawrence Richter and Tommy Walsh are in jail."

Felipe was silent. One mile, then two, sped by under their

wheels before he spoke. "That's probably best," he agreed quietly.

It was. It was best. Still, Carrie couldn't help but remember the power of his kisses. If Rafe hadn't interrupted them, she very likely would have made love to Felipe right there on the sofa, injured leg and all. No, forget twenty-four hours. It would have been more like four hours. Four hours after they'd met—not counting the half hour or so at Sea Circus six months ago, and the dozens of dreams she'd had about him since then—and she would have had sex with this man. Did he have some special power over her specifically, she wondered, or did he experience this phenomenon with every woman he met?

"I'm sorry if Rafe offended you," Felipe said. He shook his head. "He had no business saying that to you." His dark eyes were lit with anger and embarrassment. "I *am* sorry, Caroline."

"It's okay," she said. "He was just trying to rattle me." She laughed. "It worked, too."

"I don't understand him," Felipe said, shaking his head again. He ran one hand across his forehead, applying pressure, as if he had a headache. "Sometimes I think I never will." He looked up at her. "It's not as if he didn't know that crack was addictive. It's not as if he didn't know it could kill him. So what the hell made him do it? What pushed him over the edge? And what kind of man cares more about getting a rush than he does about his life?"

"Rafe seems to think you get a similar rush from being an undercover cop," Carrie said.

His gaze sharpened. "You talked to him about me?"

"Only a little," Carrie said. "He wants you to forgive him."

"He sure as hell has a funny way of showing that," Felipe muttered. "And I *do* forgive him," he added. "I just don't trust him. How do I know he's going to stay clean? How can I be sure he won't start using again?"

All his frustration and anger and hurt—deep, deep hurt—showed on his face. He was speaking to her from his heart, sharing his darkest fears and innermost secrets with her.

She liked him, Carrie realized suddenly. There were so many

sides to him, so much more than a handsome face, more than those exotic cheekbones and the long, curly hair.

Who would've guessed that such a powerful, independent, self-sufficient man would believe so firmly in the idea of a god? And in this day and age, when religion was a low priority in most people's busy lives?

Who would've guessed that talk of his brother could reduce him in part to the little boy that he'd once been, badly hurt, and afraid of being hurt again?

And who would've guessed that he'd let her see that pain, rather than try to conceal it from her?

Yeah, she liked him, despite the fact that he'd locked her in the trunk of her car, despite the fact that he'd put her life in jeopardy.

He was waiting for her to say something, watching her with those liquid eyes.

"Sometimes," Carrie said softly, her eyes on the highway, talking about more than Rafe—*much* more than Rafe, "you've just got to have faith."

Chapter 9

Carrie drove past the darkened beach house three times before Felipe nodded his head.

"Okay, no one's there," he said, his gentle Hispanic accent like velvet in the darkness. "Let's park over on the next block. I don't want to leave the van out front, or even in the driveway."

"Maybe I should drop you off," Carrie said, "so you don't have to walk that far."

He didn't say anything. He just looked at her, one eyebrow slightly raised.

"Bad idea?" she asked.

"Bad idea. I can't protect you if I'm here and you're a block away."

You can't protect either of us if you're too tired and in too much pain to walk, she wanted to say. But then she thought better of it, remembering the way he'd run after her when he'd stopped to make that phone call. He'd had a bullet in his leg, yet he'd still managed to chase her across the parking lot. And he'd caught her—with a flying tackle and total disregard for his injury.

Yes, dropping him off *was* a bad idea. If mobsters with guns wanted her dead, then maybe it was a good idea if Felipe Salazar stayed near her at all times, healthy or injured, awake or asleep.

Awake or…

The image of Felipe asleep next to her in the clean white sheets of a cozy double bed was a powerful one. His wavy black hair spread out across the snow-white pillow, his eyes closed, his long, dark eyelashes like fans against his tanned cheeks, his body relaxed but his muscles still hard as steel under silky smooth skin.…

Thinking this way wasn't going to help her one bit. And sleeping with him would be rash and reckless—and possibly a knee-jerk reaction to the danger they were in. Yes, he was sexy as hell. Yes, he was sensitive and compassionate and he seemed to know exactly what she was thinking when he looked deeply into her eyes. Yes, he was quite possibly the most complicated, interesting and exciting man she'd ever met.

But imagine what would happen if—heaven forbid—she let herself fall in love with this man. Could she imagine them together, having breakfast every morning for the rest of their lives?

Actually, the image was not as difficult to conjure up as she'd thought. In fact, it was a nice picture, a comfortable picture. He'd be sitting at the kitchen table, drinking a glass of orange juice and eating a bowl of cereal. She'd be sitting across from him, spreading jam on her toast. He'd look up, meet her eyes and smile and…

Carrie shook her head, trying to dispel the warm feeling that had somehow invaded her body. So, okay, the thought of Felipe Salazar eating breakfast with her every morning wasn't such an alien one.

But imagine her taking him home to meet her father. Imagine Felipe Salazar in the mountains of Montana. Well, actually, that wasn't such an incongruous picture, either. She could imagine teaching him to ride a horse, imagine him loving it, imagine them riding up into that meadow above the house and sharing a picnic lunch spread out on a blanket. A picnic lunch and a whole lot more.…

As for her dad, well, he'd be put off at first by Felipe's accent, by his long hair and the diamond stud he wore in his left ear.

But her father was a fair man, and he'd quickly see that Felipe was everything he could want for his only daughter—

Good grief. What was she doing? One kiss, and she was daydreaming about happily-ever-after.

Happily-ever-after could end permanently and quite abruptly in a matter of days, considering the danger they were in. And even if it didn't, even if Walsh didn't find them and kill them…well, Felipe Salazar wasn't exactly the happily-ever-after kind.

Sure, he had a certain steadiness, a certain serenity about him that counteracted the risks he took. But he *did* take risks, and it was clear that he loved the danger and excitement. What had Rafe said? He'd said that Felipe was addicted to danger.

No, if she wanted to dream up some image to help keep her resolve to stay away from this man, all she had to do was picture his being led away from her in handcuffs. *That* was a much more likely scenario than any she'd imagined. Yes, she had no doubt that he would make love to her exquisitely. It would be desperately exciting, incredibly thrilling, considering both their adrenaline levels were already quite high. But the reality was, this man was wanted by the police. For murder.

He said he didn't commit the crime.

She wanted to believe him. She *did* believe him.

But what if she was wrong? What if he *was* a cold-blooded killer? What if he wanted her around only as a hostage, not for her protection? What if…?

Carrie parked the car and turned off the engine. He was watching her as if he could read her mind, as if he knew her every thought. She handed him the keys, which he pocketed.

Carrie cleared her throat. "Do we have a way to get into the house?" she asked.

"I know where a key is hidden," Felipe said, opening his door and swinging his legs out.

He winced as his feet hit the ground, and Carrie quickly got out of the van and went around the front to help him.

"I'm okay," he insisted. But he swayed slightly, and she slipped his arm around her shoulders.

He surely outweighed her by more than sixty pounds, and the

leather jacket he was wearing added even more to that. But Carrie was strong. Besides, she didn't try to carry him; she merely offered support.

Slowly, they moved down the street and around the corner toward the beach house.

Carrie's head was tucked up almost underneath Felipe's arm, and her own arm went around his waist under his jacket. As they walked, his thigh brushed against hers.

She tried to ignore the heat that coursed through her. After all, it had been her idea to suppress the physical attraction they both obviously felt toward each other. And *he* seemed to have no trouble doing just that.

But then she stumbled slightly, and he reached for her to keep her from falling. The movement made his T-shirt go up, and all of a sudden her fingers were against the smoothness of his bare back. He inhaled sharply, and she quickly pulled her hand away.

"Sorry," she said, not certain which she was apologizing for—nearly tripping and taking him down with her, or touching him that way.

He didn't say a word, he just looked at her, the moonlight failing to fully light his face. His eyes were in shadows, not that she could have deciphered the mysteries in his hooded gaze even if they hadn't been. But one thing was very clear. He wasn't finding it easy to keep his distance from her. He was simply better at hiding it.

But he wasn't hiding it now. She could hear him breathing, smell his warm, masculine scent, feel his heart beating—racing, really—in his chest.

Her own pulse was pounding just as hard and fast. Soon they were going to be inside the beach house. Soon they'd be behind the closed door. Alone. Together. With the world and all of its threats and dangers and realities carefully shut outside.

She could do anything, *any*thing, and no one would ever know. Except…*she* would know. She could make love to this man whom she wanted to trust and believe in, and then hope beyond hope that he *wasn't* the man the police were looking for.

But if he was…

Carrie walked down the driveway around to the rear of the house with her arm still tightly encircling Felipe's waist. He stopped at the bottom of the stairs leading up to the back porch, pulling her more fully into his arms, turning what might have been called support into an undeniable embrace.

"Caroline," he said, his mouth a whisper away from hers. He touched her hair, moving it back from her face in the gentlest of caresses.

Carrie stood staring up into the darkness of his eyes, unable to move, unable to speak. He was going to kiss her. He was going to…

Instead, he released her, stepping away and using the stair railing for support.

"The key's under the flowerpot next to the back door," Felipe said, his voice husky. He cleared his throat. "We must remember not to turn on any lights inside. We don't want to catch the neighbors' attention."

As Carrie watched, he pulled himself up the stairs. He found the key exactly where he'd said it was and unlocked the door. Motioning for her to be quiet, he went inside first.

She followed him into the dark house and stood silently in the coolness. He stood several feet in front of her, his black jacket and jeans making him little more than a dark shape. He was listening intently, and Carrie found herself listening, too.

There was a clock somewhere in the room, and the sound of it ticking seemed thunderously loud. Outside the closed windows, the surf murmured, but other than that and the clock, the house was silent.

The air-conditioning unit came on with a hum, and Carrie nearly jumped out of her skin.

Felipe vanished, his dark shape moving out of the room they were in—the kitchen, Carrie saw as her eyes became more accustomed to the dark. But he reappeared a moment later.

"It's all right," he said, still whispering even though he had no need to. "There's no one here."

He opened one of the drawers and rummaged around, coming up with a box of matches. He lit one, and the tiny light seemed unnaturally bright.

The beach house was gorgeous—at least the kitchen was. The shiny finish of blond pine cabinets gleamed in the match's glow. White and blue Mexican tile made up the countertops and floor.

A candle stood on the windowsill, and as Carrie watched, Felipe lighted it. "Come," he said, leading the way into the living room, shielding the candle's flame with his hand.

The living room was as splendid as the kitchen. More so. A huge fan hung from a beamed cathedral ceiling. Big glass windows and sliding doors covered nearly one entire wall. A huge stone fireplace was in the corner. White wicker furniture had been grouped around the room, creating an airy, spacious feeling.

Perfect. The beach house, the candlelight—it was all incredibly romantic. In fact, she couldn't remember anything quite so utterly romantic. And she was here, alone, with the most charismatic, attractive, *irresistible* man she'd ever met.

Absolutely perfect.

But Felipe didn't stop in the living room. He led her down a hallway, toward a trio of bedrooms. He stopped outside of one of them. "Check to make sure the shades are pulled down," he said, still speaking softly in the hush of the quiet house.

Carrie went into the room and crossed toward the windows. She pulled first one and then the other shade down.

"Those windows face the neighbor's," Felipe said.

Carrie nodded, not daring to meet his gaze. Instead, she looked around.

This was the master bedroom. It was big, with the same high ceiling as the living room. A king-size bed with a heavy oak frame was set against one wall. There were two doors in the far wall. One led to an open walk-in closet that was nearly as big as her entire apartment. The other opened into an adjoining bathroom. Carrie could see the gleam of tile and mirrors, shiny and clean and new.

The other wall, the same wall that in the living room held all those windows, was covered by curtains. She was willing to bet there were sliding glass doors behind them, doors leading out onto a private deck, with maybe a hot tub overlooking the backyard, which was in fact the moonlight-kissed beach.

It was too much. It was all way too much.

She wasn't going to be able to resist him. She was going to turn around, and he would be watching her with those black velvet eyes. And then she would fall headlong, with no hope of landing on her feet, off the dizzying cliff of desire and need.

She turned to look at Felipe. He stood in the doorway holding out the candle, offering it to her.

Carrie crossed toward him and took it. Their fingers brushed, and she jerked her hand away as if she'd been burned.

Holding her gaze, he backed away from her into the hallway. "Good night," he said, and closed the door.

He was gone.

Carrie stood there for a moment, staring at the rich wood of the door.

He was gone.

Obviously, he'd taken seriously her request to keep their relationship platonic.

Carrie looked around the room—at that enormous bed, at the luxurious plush carpeting, at the rich fabric of the draperies.

It wouldn't have taken much effort on Felipe's part to change her mind. In fact, another one of his high-powered kisses would've surely done the trick.

But he hadn't tried. He'd respected her decision.

Carrie wasn't sure whether to feel happy or sad.

Happy, she told herself fiercely as she went into the bathroom. She was happy.

Happily, she washed her face. Happily, she brushed her teeth with her finger and some borrowed toothpaste. And happily, she climbed into that great big bed all by herself and blew out the candle.

And lay there.

Felipe stared at the ceiling, listening to the sounds of the house, wishing he could fall asleep.

From his bed, he heard the sound of water running as Caroline Brooks drew herself a bath. It was one in the morning. She'd been quiet for a while, but now she was up and moving around. He guessed she couldn't sleep, either.

It wasn't hard to imagine her lying back and soaking in that bathtub. He'd stayed here at this beach house before, slept in the master bedroom. He'd soaked in that tub himself.

He'd been alone at the time. Come to think of it, he'd never brought any of his lady friends here to Sanibel Island. He'd never wanted to share either the peaceful solitude when he was alone, or the friendly atmosphere that prevailed when Diego and Emily Keegan were also here.

True, he'd once or twice brought Jewel Hays and her little boy, Billy. But Jewel was like a sister to him. They were old friends, nothing more.

But Caroline...

He closed his eyes, remembering the taste of her, the feel of her in his arms, the touch of her fingers on his neck and in his hair. Truthfully, his wounded leg wasn't the only thing that was throbbing.

He could go to her. Right now. He could stand up and walk the few feet down the hall and into the master bedroom. He could push open the bathroom door and she would look up at him in the candlelight, her huge blue-green eyes wide with surprise.

He would move closer and look down at the graceful lines of her body through the clear, warm water of the tub. She would sit up, water falling off her in a sheet, her small, firm breasts like some delicious, exotic, mouth-watering fruit.

Please, he'd say. It would be all he'd have to say, and she'd hold out her arms to him. He'd slip off his boxer shorts and join her in the water...

Felipe's eyes opened. No, he wouldn't. He wasn't supposed to get his stitches wet—at least not with more than a quick shower. Certainly he wasn't supposed to soak them in a tub.

He smiled ruefully at his overactive imagination. Like hell she would hold out her arms to him and welcome him. Like hell she would urge him to make love to her. She'd told him in no uncertain terms that she didn't want their relationship to become sexual.

Sure, he could seduce her. He knew that was a fact from looking into her eyes earlier tonight. He could kiss her and ignite the rocket fuel of their mutual attraction, and the earsplitting roar would drown out her protests. He'd kiss her again, and those protests would fade away. It wouldn't take long before she'd help him undress her, before she'd undress him, all her reservations forgotten.

At least temporarily.

And therein lay the reason he didn't stand up and go into the master bedroom, he thought with another smile. Caroline had asked him specifically to back off. She'd said no, quite distinctly and directly to his unspoken question, to the look she'd surely seen in his eyes. No. And no didn't mean maybe. No didn't mean catch me later when I'm more vulnerable. No meant no.

In the other room, on the other side of the wall, came the sound of water swirling around and then the pipes thumped as the water was turned back on. Caroline was adding hot water to the tub. Too bad. Felipe could think of a dozen or so ways to warm her up. He shifted his position in the bed, trying desperately to get comfortable.

He couldn't blame her for wanting to keep her distance. Until just a few hours ago, she'd thought he was some kind of criminal, some gang leader named Carlos who ran with an ugly bunch of friends. And just when she finally believed that he was who he said he was, she found out that he was wanted for murder. No, he couldn't blame her.

Quite honestly, Felipe was amazed she'd come here with him. He was grateful and relieved that she had. Because as he'd watched that news broadcast, as he'd watched her face as *she'd* watched it, he had been certain that she would never trust him again. And if he hadn't talked her into going to Montana, he *would* have had to make her his prisoner, his hostage, just the way she feared. And God, what a mess *that* would have been. But no way was he going to let her walk around without protection. No way was he going to let Tommy Walsh kill her. No way. No *way*.

The savage rush, the intensity of his feelings, made him grip the bedsheet like a rope that kept him from falling into some terrible abyss. Dear God, what was wrong with him?

He tried to tell himself he'd feel the same about any woman, about any *person* who was in danger of being killed, who was a target for Tommy Walsh's bullets.

But that wasn't true.

Caroline Brooks was special. If she died, he'd more than mourn the loss of a human life. He'd grieve deeply for himself, for his own loss. And he would miss her desperately, even though he'd only known her for a short time.

She fit. In his arms, she fit perfectly. And she fit in his heart. *His* heart? Heaven help him, he realized with a sudden flash of icy fear, it wasn't his heart anymore. Sure, it still beat in his chest, but it was hers. She had stolen it. She'd stolen it all those months ago during that night at Sea Circus. Why else had he gone back all those times to watch her from a distance? Why had he told Diego and Emily about her? Why had she haunted his dreams for months?

No, he tried to tell himself. That had been attraction. Nothing more. Attraction, simple lust. Well, maybe not simple. But it was entirely sexual. Wasn't it? Just a case of raw sexual attraction. Just as this…this…odd feeling in his chest was nothing more than a case of being overtired. Or it was heartburn, from the antibiotic. Sure. That was probably it.

He closed his eyes, willing himself to sleep. In the morning, in the light of day, he'd feel better. He'd be back on track.

From the other room he heard the sound of water going down the drain. With sudden clarity, he could picture Caroline Brooks, stepping from the bathtub, reaching for a towel, her lithe body wet and shivering with cold and…

Felipe stared at the ceiling, listening to the sounds of the house, wishing he could fall asleep.

Chapter 10

A car pulled into the driveway, and Felipe was instantly awake and reaching for his gun.

He sat up and threw the sheet from his legs before the engine was turned off.

It was morning. Daylight seeped in around the shades. He hit the well-polished floorboards running, his mind racing even faster. Hide. They had to hide. But where? He remembered a crawl space underneath the house with an access door on the floor of the closet in the master bedroom. *Yes.*

Felipe ignored the sudden pain in his injured leg as he scooped his jeans, his shirt and his holster off the chair he'd thrown them over the night before, and snatched his boots from the floor.

He could hear the sound of a car door—one car door—as he moved swiftly and silently down the hall toward the master bedroom and Caroline.

He could hear the sound of footsteps—one set of footsteps—on the back porch as he pushed the bedroom door open.

Caroline was fast asleep, sprawled diagonally across the king-size bed. She'd kicked one tanned leg free from the sheets and her face was partially hidden under a cloud of golden hair. Her arms were spread wide as if she were embracing the world. She was wearing blue cotton high-cut panties and an old white tank top she must've found in one of Emily's father's dresser drawers.

His body began to tighten, an instant reaction to her state of dishabille, or maybe just a reaction to her presence. But he had no time to consider this, no time to do more than get them out of there, to keep them safely hidden from whoever was coming inside.

Felipe jammed his gun into the holster that was over his shoulder. With one hand, he swept Caroline's hair back from her face. The other he clamped firmly down over her mouth.

She woke up immediately. Her eyes were wide as she stared at him for a moment, a scream at the back of her throat securely stopped by his hand.

"It's okay," he whispered. "It's me. Someone's outside— they're coming in."

Instant understanding filled her eyes and he helped her sit up. She untangled herself from the sheets as he searched in vain for her clothes. Damn, he couldn't find them. Where had she put her dress and sandals?

But then there was no time. As a key turned in the back door, there was no time for anything but hiding.

Still carrying his own clothes, Felipe took Carrie's hand and tugged her toward the big walk-in closet. Motioning for her to be silent, he pulled back the carpet, revealing the access to the crawl space. He pulled up the inset brass ring, and the small trapdoor opened with a squeak.

"Go on," he whispered to Caroline. "It's a crawl space. It's not deep—it's less than three feet down. Just climb in."

But she didn't move. She stared down into the darkness, her eyes wider than ever, her hair a golden tangle around her face. She heard the back door open, and she turned, glancing over her shoulder toward the sound, then looked at Felipe.

He threw his clothes and holster into the crawl space, keeping his gun in his hand.

"Quickly," he urged. "I'll be right behind you."

Wordlessly, she shook her head.

The back door closed behind whoever had come inside.

Felipe grabbed Caroline around the waist and pulled her down with him into the crawl space.

It was dark and damp and tight and hot and filled with cobwebs and other things he didn't want to think about. He closed the access door over their heads, taking care to flip the carpet back over it.

And then it was *really* dark.

There was barely enough room for him to lie on his side without his shoulder brushing the support beams for the floor above. Gingerly, Felipe shifted around, one arm still encircling Caroline's waist, the gun in his other hand pointed up through the blackness at where he knew the access door to be. Carrie's back was against his chest, her head tightly nestled below his chin. He could feel her heart pounding and hear her ragged breathing in the pitch darkness.

And then he could hear footsteps.

In his arms, Caroline held her breath as if she was afraid whoever was up there might be able to hear her.

She was terrified. Her entire body was trembling. But she tried to stop herself from shaking, entwining her smooth legs with his as if to anchor herself. It didn't help.

It certainly didn't help him.

Her round little bottom was pressed intimately up against him, and now his thigh was wedged firmly between her legs. His left hand was up underneath her shirt, and his thumb rested against the swell of her breast.

Felipe felt many trickles of sweat begin their journeys. One traveled down his back, others slid past his ear, another rolled down his collarbone.

The footsteps moved across the floor again. Whoever was up there was not overhead. The sound was coming from the other side of the house—where the kitchen and living room were located.

Caroline seemed to realize that, too, and she let herself breathe again. She took short, fast breaths as if she were running a marathon—or as if she were nearing sexual release.

That particular image was nearly too much for Felipe to bear. He tried to concentrate on the concentric waves of pain that were radiating from his wounded leg rather than his growing arousal.

But it was no use. Despite the imminent danger, despite his pain, he couldn't stop himself from being turned on. Afraid of offending Caroline, knowing his silk boxers did little to hide his state, he tried to loosen his hold on her and back away from her just an inch or two.

But she wouldn't let him go. "No,' she breathed almost inaudibly in the silence, turning her head toward him. "Felipe, please, stay with me!"

There was such desperation in her voice, such fear—and such total trust that his presence could make it all okay. He stopped trying to pull away.

"I'm here, sweetheart," he whispered. He was experiencing a jumble of emotions he could barely recognize. Protectiveness—he felt fierce, almost savage protectiveness. And he felt possessiveness, yes, there was plenty of that, too. Only God could help Tommy Walsh, or whoever else tried to take this woman away from him. And gluing everything together was sort of an odd tenderness, making all these powerful emotions stick like a painful lump high up in his chest, making his eyes burn and his heart hurt.

And the really loco part of it was, despite the fact that he wanted her so badly, these things he was feeling had absolutely nothing to do with sex, with the desire that was making his blood boil.

Above their heads the telephone rang.

The footsteps moved rapidly toward the kitchen.

In the total darkness of the crawl space, Felipe strained to listen.

"Hello?" a faint voice said. "No, who's callin'?"

Female. Southern belle accent. Anywhere from thirty to sixty years old. Not Tommy Walsh. Not a threat.

"No, I'm sorry," the voice said. "The Marshalls aren't here right now. They'll be down in February. I can take a message and call the daughter if you wish. She and her husband are in and out all the time." There was a pause, and then the gentle tinkling of a delicate laugh. "No, no. I live next door. I'm just over to water the plants. Uh-huh. That's right." Another laugh. "Bye now."

Felipe lowered his gun to the floor, suddenly aware how much his arm ached from holding it up for so long. He let himself relax slightly, twisting his head to get the kinks out of his neck.

But in his arms, Caroline still shook.

"Hey," he said softly, putting the safety on his gun. He set it down, away from them on the hard dirt floor and wrapped his other arm around her. Maybe in her fear she hadn't heard the phone conversation; maybe it hadn't sunk in. "It's all right— we're all right. We're not in any danger. Even if she sees the unmade beds, even if she calls the police, we'll still have time to get away."

Carrie took in a deep breath and tried to let it slowly out of her mouth. But that still didn't stop her trembling. "It's so dark," she whispered, her husky voice cutting through the pitch black. "I can't see anything."

"But that's good," Felipe said soothingly. "If we can't see anything, than no one can see us, right?"

"No," she said. Her voice sounded choked, unnatural, her breath still coming in sobs. God in heaven, was she crying? Felipe reached up and felt the tears on her face. She *was*. She was crying. His heart lurched.

"Caroline," he whispered, his voice nearly cracking with his concern. "*Cara*, my God, are you hurt? What's wrong?"

"I'm okay," she whispered. But it sounded as if she was trying to convince herself as well as him. "It's okay. See, I'm claustrophobic, but I'm okay."

Claustrophobic?

Man, to a claustrophobic, the past ten minutes had to have been a total nightmare, a living hell. And she was still living it. Squeezed tightly together in a narrow crawl space, without any light...

"My God," he said, hardly aware he was speaking aloud. "My *God*—"

"Shh," she said, turning toward him, trying to comfort *him*.

"It's all right. I'm all right. It's okay, because you're with me. I'm not alone. Really, it's not so bad."

Not so bad? She was still trembling. He could feel her heart drumming in her chest. And she couldn't stop the tears that were flowing down her face, wetting his neck.

And, oh, God, give him strength! At Sea Circus, he'd locked Caroline in the trunk of her car. He'd locked her in the tiny, dark airless trunk of her little sports car, all by herself.

Felipe felt sick. His stomach churned and tears burned his eyes. Two hours. She'd been in there for two hours, she'd told him. He knew 911 calls were often dangerously backed up, but *two hours!* What he'd done to her was tantamount to torture.

"Oh, Caroline," he whispered raggedly, holding her tightly. "I'm so sorry."

The footsteps upstairs had been silent for a while. From outside the house, Felipe heard the sound of a car engine. The voice, the neighbor, had left.

He found his gun in the darkness, then moved toward the access door. He was careful to bring Caroline with him, careful to keep as much of his body in contact with hers as he possibly could, aware that such obvious proof of his presence helped her.

With a heave, he pushed the trapdoor open, and light—brilliant, glorious, golden light flooded down on top of them.

Caroline scrambled toward the light, and Felipe helped her up and out. Gathering his clothes and holster from where he'd thrown them, he climbed stiffly after her.

She lay on the floor of the master bedroom. Her eyes were closed and her hair had tumbled forward to hide her face.

Felipe holstered his gun and tossed aside the pile of clothes he'd been holding. He knelt next to her and brushed her hair back from her face.

"I'm sorry," he said again. "At Sea Circus, when I put you in your trunk... God help me, I had no idea."

She opened her startlingly sea green eyes and looked directly up at him. "I know that," she said, still breathing hard. "How could you have known? Besides, you did what you had to do to save me."

He was miserable, and he realized that every bit of his misery showed clearly on his face. No wonder she had been so angry with him at Schroedinger's restaurant. No wonder she was adamant about keeping her distance. "How you must hate me," he said.

She pushed herself up off the floor. Reaching out with one hand, she touched the side of his face. "No," she said quietly. She took a deep breath in, then let it slowly out. "No, I don't."

The tears that were in Felipe's eyes threatened to overflow. He reached up, pressing her hand tightly to his cheek. "I'd never do anything to hurt you," he said. "Please believe that."

She nodded, her own eyes luminous. Her face was smudged with dirt, and her tears had made clean tracks through it. Still, she looked beautiful. Lord, the torment he'd put her through...

She tried to smile and actually succeeded. "That was a heck of a way to wake up," she said. "A hand over my mouth to scare me to death, and then a trip to my own personal hell. Tomorrow you might try something a little lower key—maybe like this."

And then she kissed him.

She kissed *him.*

It started out feather light, the gentlest of butterfly kisses.

Felipe pulled back, surprised and even embarrassed. Had she really kissed him? Or maybe he'd kissed her, and maybe—certainly—he shouldn't have.

But she leaned forward again, and this time there was no mistaking. She *did* kiss him.

Her mouth was warm and soft, her lips opening under his, pliant and willing and...oh, *yes.*

He pulled her against him, turning his head to kiss her deeper, harder, longer. She molded her body against his and wrapped her arms around him.

Dizzy with desire, Felipe sank down onto the floor, pulling her with him. Their legs intertwined, and this time, he let himself truly enjoy the sensation of her smooth, silky skin against his. He kissed her again and again, exploring her mouth with his tongue, taking his time, content just to kiss her for hours and hours.

But then she moved against him, the softness of her belly

against him. Her legs tightened around his thigh and he heard himself groan.

Her heart was beating as fast and hard as it had been down in the crawl space—faster, even. She tugged at him, and he rolled over so that he was on top of her.

This was not a case of him seducing her. This was not a case of him taking advantage...or was it?

Felipe pulled back. "Caroline," he said, shaking his head, unable to speak.

She looked up at him, fire in her sea green eyes. He reached for her hand, pulling her so that she was sitting up. Confusion and then trepidation replaced the fire in her eyes.

"You don't want to...?" she whispered.

"*You* don't want to," he replied, hardly believing he was saying those words, hardly believing he was denying himself what would surely be a first-class trip to heaven. "You told me that yesterday, *cara,* remember?"

She looked at the obvious sign of his arousal. He couldn't hide it, so he didn't bother to try. He could feel her eyes studying him, searching his face. He looked back at her, steadily meeting her gaze.

"Is it okay if I changed my mind?" she asked softly, and his heart leaped.

"Oh, yes," he said huskily. "It's very okay."

"I changed my mind," she said.

He wanted to touch her. But right at this moment, it was enough to look, knowing that soon, very soon, he would be touching her.

For the first time, he let himself really see her in that ridiculous excuse for a shirt. The thin material was nearly transparent as it hung loosely on her slight frame. The armholes dipped down almost to her waist, revealing the soft, round sides of her breasts. Her nipples were dark, tight points that the shirt did little to conceal. It was sexy as hell and her smile told him that she knew it. She liked knowing that she turned him on. That was good, because he couldn't have hidden his attraction to her even if he had wanted to.

She was beautiful, and she was to be his. That knowledge made his body nearly hum with desire.

"Do you have any protection?" she asked. "A condom?"

"I keep one in my wallet." He smiled. "I kept it there in hopes that I'd meet up with you."

She laughed. "I know that's supposed to be romantic," she said, her eyes dancing with amusement. "But, really, Felipe, that's *such* a total crock of—"

"Do you know for sure it's not true?" he countered, his eyes sliding down her body, across those perfect breasts, down her shapely legs then up again to meet her eyes. "I've met you in my dreams quite often these past six months, Caroline Brooks."

Her smile faded, leaving only heat in her eyes. She moistened her lips with a nervous flick of her tongue. "Why don't you call me Carrie?" she asked.

"Because Caroline is more beautiful," he said. "It suits you."

She rolled her eyes. "Ease up on the B.S., Salazar," she said, "or I might change my mind again."

He watched her steadily. "It's not bull," he said serenely. "And, you know, if you change your mind again, that's okay, too."

She smiled at his words, but then stopped as she realized he wasn't kidding. It *was* okay. *Every*thing was okay.

"There is more to the way I feel about you than sex," Felipe said quietly. His words were true but purposely vague. He couldn't get more specific. He was afraid to delve more deeply into his own feelings. But even though it scared him—both the words he spoke and the feelings that prompted those words—she had the right to know.

She looked down, away from him, and he was struck by how sweet, how young and innocent she looked. She was only twenty-five—that was his age, too, he realized. But she was still young and he was not. He'd grown up a lot faster, a lot harder. They came from different neighborhoods, he and Caroline. The mountains of her father's ranch couldn't be compared to the rough, unforgiving city streets where he'd spent his childhood— what little of it he'd had. He'd been twenty-five for the past fifteen years. She'd been twenty-five only since last October 16—at least that was what had been listed on her driver's license.

But then she glanced up at him from underneath her long eyelashes and smiled. It was a smile that promised paradise, a dazzling contrast to her seeming shyness moments before. She was full of surprises, full of contradictions, a living kaleidoscope of mercurial energy and emotion. He liked that. He liked *her*.

He leaned forward to kiss her and she met him halfway.

The explosion of passion was nearly instantaneous. He heard her moan as he pulled her, hard, against him. As he kissed her again, he felt her hands in his hair, on his back, touching, caressing, drawing him yet closer.

They were back exactly where they'd been several minutes earlier. Only this time, when Caroline pulled him down on top of her, she opened her legs, pressing the heat of her most intimate self against him.

Oh, *yes.*

The pain in his leg no longer existed. St. Simone and Lawrence Richter and Tommy Walsh and this whole damned mess they were in no longer existed. The world—the entire *universe*—no longer existed.

There was only Caroline.

Felipe rolled over onto his back, pulling her along so that she was straddling him. She kissed him, her tongue dancing with his, mimicking the movement of their bodies as she slowly, sensuously moved on top of him. Her hair fell around his face, a curtain of gold, as his hands cupped her buttocks, fixing her more tightly against him. Only the silk of his shorts and the cotton of her panties kept him from entering her.

"Oh, Caroline," he breathed. "This is…" He couldn't find the words. But he didn't have to.

She stopped kissing him long enough to gaze down into his eyes and he knew that whatever it was he was feeling—this euphoria, this sense of perfection, of completeness—she was feeling it, too.

He found the edge of her shirt and pushed it up and over her head. Her breasts were small and round and perfectly proportioned to the rest of her body. He covered them with his hands, groaning at the pleasure of touching her soft flesh. She moaned, too, pressing herself forward.

With one swift move, he flipped her onto her back, moving to touch one taut, pink nipple with his lips. Gently, so gently, he kissed her, then touched her lightly with his tongue.

Her skin smelled fresh and clean and ever so slightly of sun block. Yes, now more than ever, he would associate that scent with paradise.

Felipe could feel his pulse racing. He tried to bring it under control, to slow down his breathing and ease this feeling of an imminent explosion that tightened his throat and his gut and made him ache even lower. He wanted to rip off her panties and his boxer shorts and plunge himself deep inside her.

Instead, he forced himself to move deliberately, unhurriedly. He drew languid circles around her nipple with his tongue while his hands swept slowly up and down her tanned, flat stomach to the edge of her panties and then up and across her other breast. She touched him the same way, too, almost reverently, as if she couldn't believe she was finally getting her heart's desire.

Her fingers felt cool and delicate against the burning heat of his skin. Could she feel his heartbeat? he wondered. Did she know that the gentleness of her touch had the power to make him tremble? As he drew her more fully into his mouth, pulling, sucking, laving her with his tongue, she gripped his shoulders with a strength that surprised him. She arched her back, wanting more. Her response nearly did him in, nearly pushed him over the edge.

By sheer willpower, he managed to hang on to his sanity and his control. He closed his eyes, counting slowly to ten. When he opened them, she was watching him. She smiled and his heart nearly burst. If it wasn't one part of him ready to explode, it was another.

She pushed his hair back from his face in a gentle, loving caress. It warmed him and he smiled back at her, whispering words of endearment in Spanish—words he wouldn't have dared say to her in a language she could understand.

He broke away from the spell her ocean-colored eyes had cast over him, gazing down at her beautiful body, clad only in those blue panties.

She was tanned all over, he realized. At least on the top. She did have a tan line where she'd worn bathing-suit bottoms, and another line of shading where she'd worn shorts, but her breasts had the same perfect, golden tan as her shoulders and arms and stomach.

More contradictions. Somehow he couldn't imagine Caroline driving south down the coast from St. Simone to hang out at Tamiami Beach, the area's only topless sunbathing spot. Still, she'd obviously spent some time—quite a bit of time—in the sun without her top on.

"Nice tan," he murmured, and she blushed. More contradictions. But then he lowered his mouth to her other breast, and she forgot her embarrassment. He felt her hands in his hair as she ran her fingers through his dark curls. He ran his hand down her stomach again, and when he would've stopped short of her panties, she lifted her hips, pressing herself up and into his hand. She couldn't have been any clearer about what she wanted if she'd announced it through a megaphone.

So he slipped his hand beneath the elastic waistband of her panties, lifting his head to gaze into her eyes as he touched first the nest of her curls and then her soft heat. The light of pleasure on her face was sinfully delicious as he explored her most intimately.

This would be enough, he realized. Even though he was straining against his shorts, even though he wanted to be inside this woman more than he'd ever wanted anything in his life, simply giving her pleasure would truly be enough.

She closed her eyes, moving against him as he stroked her harder, deeper.

He murmured to her in Spanish, telling her of the strange sensations in his heart, urging her on, right there, right now, as he held her in his arms.

But Caroline had an entirely different idea.

She reached for him, encircling his shaft with her hand right through the silk of his shorts. "This is what I want," she whispered. She moved her hand along his length and he bit back a cry of pleasure.

She reached for the waistband of his boxers, pulling them down, freeing him from their restraint. And then she was touching him, her fingers against his hardness, and once again he fought for self-control.

But she wasn't going to let him get it back.

She sat up, pulling away from him, getting up on her knees to drag his shorts down his legs, careful to lift them over the bandage that covered his stitches, touching him all the while. Feverishly, he reached for his jeans, for the wallet that was still in the back pocket, and for the condom that was stored there.

His hands shook as he tore open the foil package. She pushed off her panties—how beautiful she was!—then quickly helped him cover himself. Helped? Not really. She stroked him, squeezed him, caressed him as he blindly tried to put on the damned condom.

All of his English had left him, every single blasted word of it. He tried to tell her that he wanted to make love to her this first time in the traditional way. The first time, the man should be on top, giving the pleasure.

But she didn't understand. She murmured something to him about his leg, something about not wanting him to hurt himself, something he didn't understand because he wasn't hurting—he was feeling absolutely no pain. She kissed him, still straddling him, moving her hips so that she touched him with her moistness and heat. Oh, man, at this rate, he'd be finished in seven seconds. Felipe lifted her up, about to turn her and lay her down on her back, wincing when all at once the pain from his leg cut through. And, then, "No."

The single word penetrated and he froze.

No?

He looked into her eyes through the fog of desire, and she shook her head.

Yes, that was definitely a no.

Stopping like this was going to kill him, but if she'd changed her mind, then he'd stop. He was holding his breath, he realized, and he let it out with a long, ragged sigh, trying desperately to regain his equilibrium. What had happened? Had he done something wrong?

Slowly he lowered her back down, but instead of moving away from him, she moved toward him. With one smooth thrust, she unsheathed him.

Oh, *yes.*

It was a lot like being thrown a surprise birthday party. He was caught totally off guard, but instantly able to adjust to the shock. And just as quickly, he understood what she had been saying no to. She wanted to be on top.

It went against the grain of everything he believed about making love to a woman. The man gave and took the pleasure. The man was in control.

And he was not in control here.

But as she moved on top of him, as she rode him, her eyes half-closed with pleasure, her long, blond hair loose around her shoulders, covering all but the tantalizing tips of her breasts, Felipe realized an awful truth.

When it came to making love to Caroline Brooks, he would never truly be in control.

The only consolation was that she was not in control, either.

He moved his hips, thrusting up to meet her downward movement, driving himself deep into her. Her eyes widened, then shut tightly, and she threw her head back, crying out her pleasure at the sensation.

He was lost, swept away by passion and pleasure and an ache in his heart he was beginning to fear would never let up.

Time blurred, and he pulled her down to kiss him as they moved together. *Together.* He wasn't making love to Caroline, he was making love *with* her. The thought exploded in his head as clearly as the flash of light from fireworks. Suddenly, all of his previous beliefs about making love seemed old-fashioned and obsolete. Because as sure as he was born, he'd never in his life felt anything even remotely like what he was feeling right now. It was delicious ecstasy, wild abandon, pure pleasure. And he was sharing it with Caroline. It was dizzying, consuming, terrifying. Could he actually feel this way for more than the briefest moment and not disintegrate?

And still they moved together.

She pulled away from his kiss to sit up, still atop him, and the movement sent him plunging harder and deeper into her again and again. Her head went back and she clutched at his arms, and feeling something close to disbelief, Felipe fell over the side of a cliff.

He felt the last shred of his ragged control dissolve as his body took full command. He exploded with a violent rush as, for the only time since he'd first made love at age sixteen, he finished before his lover.

He heard the hoarse sound of his voice crying out her name, heard her answering cry, felt her shudder of pleasure as she, too, found her release.

His ears were ringing as she slumped on top of him, her hair covering his face. He closed his eyes, breathing in the sweet scent of her shampoo, feeling their two hearts racing, pounding a syncopated tattoo.

His breathing slowed, and his pulse finally returned to near normal. But the dizzying, consuming emotions that had been let loose in his mind and in his heart at their coupling wouldn't fade away.

Perhaps they never would.

That thought scared him to death.

What could it mean? Why was he feeling this way?

They swirled around him like a tornado, those almost palpable emotions, forming a pattern of words that repeated over and over in his mind.

Te amo. Te adoro.

I love you.

His eyes opened and he stared at the ceiling through a haze of golden hair.

He was in love with Caroline Brooks.

No. He couldn't be. He wouldn't let himself be. It was not possible. Not now. Especially not now. But not later, either. There was no room in his life for such a thing.

And there was no room in *her* life for both him and the danger he would bring with him. How many gang members, mobsters and crime lords had he angered over the past few years? How many contracts were there on his life right now? And how many people wouldn't think twice about ripping the life from an innocent young woman, simply to get back at the undercover police detective who had given them their due?

No.

If he cared about her at all, after this was over and he knew that she was safe, he would walk away. And if he loved her, he'd run.

Te amo. Te adoro.

No. It wasn't true. And even if it was, he couldn't tell her. He'd never tell her.

Never.

Chapter 11

"I'm sorry," Felipe said quietly, his mouth up against her ear.

Carrie turned her head to look at him, pushing her hair back off her face.

He gazed up at her, his dark eyes mysterious and unreadable. "Sorry?" she asked.

She could have sworn she saw a flash of embarrassment in those eyes. He looked away from her, but then forced his gaze back up, steadily meeting her inquisitive stare.

He moistened his lips. "I, uh…" he said, then he cleared his throat. "Usually…I'm not so…inconsiderate. Usually…I allow my partner to…reach, uh, satisfaction first."

Carrie felt herself start to smile as the meaning of his words penetrated. She couldn't hide a laugh. "Are you *apologizing* for the way you just made love to me?" she asked, her voice dripping with disbelief.

He *was* embarrassed. He closed his eyes briefly, then nodded his head.

Carrie couldn't keep from laughing. "Mister, are you telling me that this is just an off day—that you've done that even *better?*"

"I came before you," he said. He wasn't laughing.

"Was it a race?" she asked. "And were you trying to let me win?"

Unblinkingly serious, he gazed up at her. "It's important to me," he said. And then he blushed slightly, looking away, unable to meet her eyes. "This hasn't happened since… It hasn't happened ever."

Carrie's heart flip-flopped in her chest. The tinge of red across his high cheekbones was utterly charming, despite the slightly archaic and macho tinge to his words.

He was still inside her and she didn't move off him. She didn't want to. The glow from the perfection of their joining still surrounded her. She nestled her head on his shoulder, careful that her hair didn't fall across his face, marveling at how well they fit together, even now, even after.

He stroked her back almost absentmindedly, his fingers trailing lightly from her neck to her derriere and up again.

"Do you know," she murmured, lifting her chin so that her breath touched his ear, "what it felt like to me just now?"

His hand stopped moving. He swallowed, then shook his head once slightly. He'd closed his eyes, but he was listening to her very carefully, absorbing each of her words.

"Do you know," she asked, stopping for a moment to brush her lips lightly along the line of his jaw, "what a turn-on it is when the man you're making love to loses control like that?"

Again, he shook his head.

"It's unlike anything you can imagine," she said, her voice husky with the memory and the emotion. "At the risk of feeding your ego, I've never been made love to like that before. *And* as far as I'm concerned, we were together. You started first. Big deal. I was a millisecond behind you. Who's counting?"

He opened his eyes and turned his head to look at her. "You're very sweet," he said, pressing a kiss to her forehead.

"You don't believe me?" Carrie shook her head, feeling impatience rising in her. Impatience, and something else. Hurt? How could he not think that the love they'd just shared was anything but sensational? "I can't believe we're arguing about this. Can you honestly tell me that that entire experience gets stamped *rejected* because of one minute detail that didn't happen exactly the way you'd planned? Or are you telling me that the whole thing was lousy—and if that's the case, I better take a good long look at my sex life, because if *that* was lousy, I've been missing something all these years!''

"Caroline—"

"And if that's the case, we're on very different wavelengths, Detective, with you thinking that was lousy sex, and me thinking…" She took a deep breath and let it slowly out. "And me thinking it's never been so perfect, so complete," she finished miserably.

She rolled off him, wishing she could crawl away and hide. How had this happened? Two minutes ago, she'd been laughing, euphoric. Then this man whom she thought she was finally beginning to know and understand, this man who had been so amazingly in tune with her every want and need as he'd made love to her, this man had mutated into some kind of rigid caveman who needed to follow an extremely macho set of rules when making love. She began to search almost frantically for her clothes.

Felipe caught her arm. "Please," he said. "I was being stupid." He pulled her close to him and cradled her in his arms. "I was being *really* stupid. You were right. I was…stupid."

"Damn straight you were," Carrie muttered.

He gently moved her chin so that she was facing him. "I was frightened," he murmured. "The power of the feelings… It still frightens me. Forgive me, Caroline."

And then he kissed her.

He may have voiced some very old-fashioned ideas about male and female roles in bed, but his apology sounded sincere, and he could kiss like no one else in the world.

Most men that Carrie had known had kissed her for a reason. To placate or apologize. To get on her good side. To get her into bed.

But even though Felipe had just apologized to her, his kiss was very separate from his words. He kissed her purely for the sake of kissing her, for the pleasure of her mouth against his.

He kissed her slowly, lazily, his tongue sweeping possessively into her mouth, claiming her, staking out his territory.

Carrie heard herself sigh, felt herself melt, felt the world tilt and disappear. Maybe having a lover who could be an absolute caveman at times *wasn't* such a terrible thing. She laced her fingers up through his long, gorgeous hair, slanting her head to grant him easier access to her mouth.

He drew in a breath and murmured to her in Spanish. She couldn't understand the words, but his voice sounded like poetry in the hush of the quiet room. And still he kissed her.

She felt dizzying heat pooling in her stomach. Was it really possible that she wanted him again? Already?

He lifted his head, supporting his upper body with one elbow as he looked down at her. "I love kissing you," he said.

Carrie's heart pounded in her chest. For a moment, when he'd started that sentence, she had been so sure he was about to tell her something else. *I love you.* But how could she expect him to say that? He barely knew her.

They were undeniably compatible—especially physically. They'd certainly proved that. And despite Felipe's momentary slip revealing his old-fashioned beliefs, she honestly liked him more and more with each passing moment. Heck, she liked him more *because* of his slip. Before she'd seen that side of him, he'd been too damn perfect. She liked him better because now she knew that he was human and that he had his weaknesses and doubts.

He was stroking her, his strong, warm hand sliding up her hip and over the curve of her waist. His eyes were hooded as he looked at her. Carrie felt the tips of her breasts harden into tight little beads under the weight of his gaze. He glanced into her eyes and smiled.

"Do you really go out to Tamiami Beach?" he asked.

Tamiami…? Where…? The nude beach, Carrie remembered. No, not nude, topless. He was referring to her nearly allover tan. She felt her face heat with a blush.

"No," she said, shaking her head. "No. I…do a lot of re-search work out on my boat, all by myself." Did he really want to hear the entire story? He was listening, waiting for her to continue, so she did.

"I always used to just wear my bathing suit, but one day I was out doing some work along the coast near one of the swamps, and I forgot to bring my suit or even a change of clothes. I was bringing in a sampling of the marine life that had died as a result of an oil spill, and I ended up with tar all over my T-shirt." An angry alligator had surprised her near an illegal garbage dump and she'd tripped in her haste to get back into her boat. "It was hotter than hell that day, and the sun was heating the tar on my shirt. Obviously, it wouldn't rinse out, and I was actually afraid it was going to burn me. My options were to take off the shirt, or turn and head for home. I figured if I were a man, I'd have had my shirt off hours earlier, so…I took off the shirt and put in five more hours of work. And got a great tan."

She smiled up into his eyes. "I also got a…certain sense of liberation. Ever since then, when I'm alone on my boat, I go topless. No one knows but me. And now you."

He leaned forward to touch the peak of her breast with the tip of his tongue. "The thought of you working like this is…stimulating," he murmured. "Someday, will you let me come and help?" But then he shook his head, as if he thought better of his words. "Or maybe that's not such a good idea," he added. "It would be too distracting, at least for me."

He pulled back from her, no longer meeting her eyes. He ran his fingers through his hair, then rubbed his forehead as if he had a headache. She could see the sudden tension in his neck and shoulders. Even the well-defined muscles in his arms seemed tighter. He hadn't moved an inch, but mentally he was stepping back, away from her. Was he doing that because he thought she wanted him to? Did he think she still wanted him to keep his distance?

"I'd love for you to come out on my boat someday," Carrie said quietly, trying to read his reaction.

But Felipe shook his head, still looking away from her. "We don't have someday, *cara,*" he said just as quietly. "We only have right here and right now." He looked up at her then. The deep sadness was back in his eyes.

"Walsh and Richter aren't going to be looking for us forever," Carrie said. "And you're going to prove that you didn't kill those men in the sandlot—"

"Even then," he said, interrupting her. "Even if this ends and we're both still alive…" He took a deep breath. "I can't make you any promises, Caroline. I probably should have told you this before we made love, but…I can't fall in love with you."

His words filled her with a disappointment that was a great deal stronger than she'd expected. And his words proved how deceptive good sex could be. She'd interpreted his caresses, his sighs, those long looks he gave her, and especially the way he'd clung to her and called out her name, as a measure of his feelings. In truth, those things were merely a measure of *what* he was feeling. Physical sensations, not love in any way, shape or form.

But what the heck, she told herself, she hadn't *really* thought Felipe Salazar would fall in love with her, had she?

Yes. The word rose in her throat like a bubble that had to break free.

No, she told herself harshly. No, she hadn't. And it was good he'd told her this, because now that she knew, she'd make damn sure she wouldn't fall in love with him.

She forced her mouth into a smile. "Well, that's fine," she said to Felipe. "Because I have no intention of falling in love with you, either. You know, I don't even really trust you entirely."

Now, why the hell had she said that? She saw the flash of hurt leap into his eyes, and knew that her words had stung. She *knew* that his innocence was a sticky subject for Felipe, that he wanted her to trust him.

But what she'd said was true, she told herself. For all she knew, he really had killed those men. Or maybe he hadn't actually pulled the trigger himself. Maybe he was just involved in some other awful way. She had seen no proof that he wasn't involved. She only had his word.

*You said it because you wanted to hurt him. You said it be-
cause you want him to fall in love with you, because you've
already fallen in love with him.*

"You must trust me on some level," Felipe said, "or you
wouldn't have made love to me."

Carrie lifted her arms over her head and stretched, pretending
desperately to be casual and noncommittal while her brain and
her heart were going in twenty different directions. He followed
her movement with heat in his eyes, like a cat watching a bird
and ready to pounce. Was it desire or anger glowing there?

"I trusted that sex with you would be great," she said, keeping her voice light. Inside, she felt heavier than lead. She *wasn't*
in love with him. She *wasn't*... "I wasn't wrong, was I?" She
pushed herself off the floor and stood. "I'm going to take a
shower, maybe take another soak in that tub." She stopped at
the bathroom door, looking back at him. "Too bad you can't
get your stitches wet for another day or so."

Then it was all desire that flared in his eyes. "Maybe I can—"

"You told me nothing but a quick shower until tomorrow,"
Carrie said, pretending that she actually *wanted* him to shower
with her, pretending that his admission that he didn't love her,
would *never* love her, was something that she took casually in
stride, pretending that her heart wasn't breaking. "And if you
get in the shower with me, it won't be quick. You better wait
out here."

He smiled at her, a smile that held a promise of paradise. But
no, he'd said he couldn't promise her anything. Nothing but
sexual pleasure anyway, and certainly not paradise. Paradise was
more than pure, raw sex. Paradise was murmured words of love,
promises of forever. He wasn't even going to pretend to give
her that.

Carrie supposed she should be grateful that he wasn't trying
to deceive her. At least he'd been up-front and honest about his
feelings—or lack of feelings in this case.

He was so utterly handsome, lying there on the floor buck
naked, his long, muscular legs stretched out in front of him. His
hips were narrow, leading up to his equally narrow waist and
the washboard muscles of his stomach. He didn't have much

hair on his chest. He didn't need it; it would have hidden the near perfection of his pecs and other steel-hard muscles. His skin was smooth and golden brown, his nipples a darker shade of that same delicious color. A line of dark hair started at his belly button and spread downward toward the thick thatch of black curls between his legs and…

He was fully aroused.

She did that to him, Carrie knew. With her talk of showering together, her stories of working on her boat without a top, and with the way she'd just looked at him—as if she were starving and he was a five-course gourmet meal.…

He was more than willing to let himself make love to her. *Make* love, yet not love her. He wouldn't let himself love her.

It didn't seem fair.

It *wasn't* fair.

Carrie went into the bathroom and turned on the shower. Stepping under the rush of water, she closed her eyes.

He *could* be a killer, she reminded herself. Maybe if she repeated that over and over, she'd stop loving him. Maybe she should take precautions against further hurt and take care not to make love to Felipe again.

Yeah, right. And maybe alligators could fly.

Rafe's prediction had come true, she realized ruefully. Less than twenty-four hours had passed since she'd sat with Felipe's brother in the kitchen of the halfway house, and sure enough, she'd gone and slept with Felipe. Slept with. It was a funny expression, considering neither of them had ever had the slightest intention of sleeping. Gone to bed with? That wasn't true, either, since they'd made love on the plush carpeting on the bedroom floor. Made love to. Only half-true—her half, not his. Still, a half truth was better than none, wasn't it?

Any predictions for the next twenty-four hours? she wondered as she turned her face up to the stream of water. Where was Rafe when she needed him? Too bad he hadn't warned her she was going to fall in love with his little brother. Of course, if he'd as much as suggested the possibility, she would've laughed that off, too.

The water falling on her face hid her tears. As long as she

stood there in the shower, Carrie could pretend that she wasn't crying.

Predictions for the next twenty-four hours? She had one that she knew so damn well to be true, it would make Nostradamus look like a cheap carnival palm reader.

Sometime in the next twenty-four hours or less—and probably many, many hours less—she was going to make love again to that man, that beautiful, exciting, charismatic, dangerous man that she'd so foolishly, and against all her better judgment, fallen in love with.

Chapter 12

Untangling her wet hair with a brush she'd found in the bathroom, and dressed in a too-big pair of cutoffs and a man's dress shirt that nearly covered the legs of the shorts, Carrie walked down the hall toward the living room. Felipe was nowhere in sight.

She stood looking out through the big glass doors at the turquoise blue ocean. The private beach was deserted and picture postcard perfect. She could see why someone would want to build a beach house on this spot. The sun reflecting off the white sand filtered in through the tinted glass of the windows, illuminating the living room with an unearthly golden light.

A sound from behind her made her turn around.

Felipe stood in the doorway that led to the kitchen. His hair, too, was wet from his own quick shower, and he ran his fingers through the tight curls, loosening them and letting the air dry them. His eyes were gentle, so soft and serene as he looked at her. There was no sign of the fire that had threatened to consume her only an hour or so earlier. But then his gaze traveled down her body, grazing her breasts, taking in the fact that she wasn't wearing a bra underneath her shirt, reminding her that both her bra and panties were hanging in the bathroom, drying. His eyes caressed the length of her legs, lingering, heating her with just a look.

The fire was still there, Carrie realized as he glanced back into her eyes. He was just very, very good at keeping it hidden.

"Are you hungry?" he asked, his soft accent like velvet in the quiet room.

Carrie's stomach clenched with a sudden rush of desire, and inwardly she kicked herself for her body's blatant reaction to this man. Hungry? Yes, sir, but not for food.

He was wearing only a pair of dark blue, knee-length shorts. A size or more too large, they hung low around his waist. He looked as if he were on vacation at the beach, as if he'd just come in from a morning of swimming in the surf. His muscles rippled as he gave his hair one last shake dry. Carrie remembered the feel of those arms around her, the incredible smoothness of his skin. She wanted to touch him again, but he stayed in the doorway all the way across the room.

"There wasn't much in the kitchen," Felipe said, "but I found some frozen vegetables and a bag of rice. The rice should be done in about five minutes. The vegetables are already hot."

He was going to play it normal, pretend that nothing between them had changed. He was going to be polite and friendly and keep his distance until the heat between them got too intense, until they ended up making love again. He wasn't going to hold her in his arms just for the sake of holding her, for the sake of closeness and comfort and warmth. And, oh, how she needed that right now.

To Carrie's horror, she felt her eyes fill with tears. Why? Why was she crying now? She never cried—well, hardly ever. And she was *damned* if she was going to cry in front of Felipe again. Fiercely blinking, she quickly turned away from him, pretending to study the view of the ocean. The blues of the water and the sky blurred together and she blinked even harder, forcing back her tears.

"Are you all right?" There was concern in his warm voice, and she heard him start to limp toward her. Heaven help her if he got too close. She'd end up crying in his arms, and that was the *last* thing she wanted. She wanted him to hold her, but not out of pity.

She took a deep breath and turned to face him, forcing her mouth into a smile. He wasn't fooled—she could see that from his eyes, but he stopped on the other side of the couch that bisected the room.

"The thought of rice and vegetables always gets me choked up," she said breezily.

He smiled at her words, but the concern didn't leave his eyes. No doubt he'd figured out that she'd fallen in love with him. No doubt it was a common occurrence. Every woman he'd ever slept with probably fell in love with him. And no doubt the concern in his eyes came from his imagining all the grief she was going to give him—the jealous phone calls, the tears, the desperate visits to him at work....

Except that he was a suspected murderer on the run. And *she* wasn't like all the other women he'd ever known. She had backbone. She had grit. She had pride.

"What happens now?" she asked, holding her chin high, letting him see that her eyes were dry as she walked past him into the kitchen. It was a big room, with cabinets and tiled counters lining the walls, a center island with a sink in the middle of the room, and a huge, round, butcher-block-style table off to the side in a breakfast nook. Windows and skylights were everywhere, letting in the sunshine, but the trees and shrubs outside provided a screen for privacy. No one could see inside.

"We'll have lunch." He followed her.

"That's not what I meant." There were two pots on the pristine white stove and the fragrant smell of basmati rice filled the air.

"We'll stay here another night," he said, crossing to the stove and turning off the burners.

Another night here at the beach house, alone in the candlelight. Heat rushed through Carrie at the thought of Felipe with her in that king-size bed...but tonight was too far away. She didn't want to wait until tonight. Man, she was shameless.

But here and now was all she had. He'd told her that himself.

"And then what?" she asked. Her voice sounded husky, so she cleared her throat again.

"Then I try to contact Diego," Felipe said. He leaned forward, bracing his arms against the back of one of the chairs that surrounded the big wooden table, taking the weight off his injured leg. The muscles in his arms and shoulders tightened and stood out. "Hopefully, he'll be able to tell me something new, something that will tip me off as to who in the police department set this frame up."

"And if he can't?"

"If he can't, we find someplace else to hide while I figure out a way to get past the security system in Richter's mansion and—"

Shocked, Carrie's mouth dropped open. "That's incredibly dangerous." As she stared across the room at him, she remembered Rafe's words. *Felipe, he's an addict, too. He's addicted to danger.* "It's *crazy*."

"This whole thing is crazy," he countered.

"You're planning to go—no, *break into*—the house of a man who wants you dead?" She started to pace. If Felipe went into Richter's house, did he really stand a chance of coming out alive?

"I'll go there if necessary," he said, his eyes following her as she moved back and forth across the cool tile floor. "But I'll have to do it soon. If I wait too long, Richter and Walsh will be expecting me to show up. Right now, they know I've been shot because of all the blood in that car. They'll expect me to lie low, to recuperate." He smiled tightly. "They're probably hoping I'll die from infection."

Carrie stopped pacing. "How *is* your leg?"

"Better."

"Honestly?"

"Well, it's not getting any worse."

"Are you really going to be ready to leave here tomorrow?" Carrie asked.

"I have to be," Felipe said. "We can't stay here much longer. It's only a matter of time before someone finds the van and the police connect it to us."

"I could go out and drive it farther away from this house," Carrie suggested.

"Without me? Bad idea, remember?" he said, softening his words with a gentle smile.

Bad idea. It wasn't as bad an idea as falling in love with him. Falling in love with Felipe Salazar was about the worst idea she'd had in all of her twenty-five years.

Carrie crossed her arms and looked down at the floor. "It seems all my ideas are bad ones these days," she said.

He was silent for a very, *very* long time. In fact, he didn't speak until she glanced up at him. His expressive eyes held real sadness and disappointment.

"Caroline," he said, "are you having regrets? About making love to me?"

She couldn't hold his gaze. "I don't know what I'm feeling," she admitted.

"I never meant to take advantage of you—or of our situation," he said quietly. "Although I guess I must have—"

"Oh, cut the macho attitude," Carrie said, exasperated. "How do you know I didn't take advantage of *you?* How do you know I didn't intend to seduce you?"

"Are you saying you worked out a plan to seduce me while we were down in that crawl space?" he said. "Nice try, but…" He shook his head. "I don't buy it."

He was smiling, and despite the heaviness in her heart, that smile was contagious. Carrie found herself smiling back.

"With your wounded leg, you couldn't exactly run away from me," she observed, putting her hairbrush down on a wicker telephone stand.

"I *did* run," he said with a broader smile that exposed his straight white teeth. "Last night. And it was *after* you, if I remember correctly."

His smile faded as he gazed at her. Carrie looked down at the floor, suddenly embarrassed by his scrutiny. She could feel his eyes studying her, watching, trying to read her mind. "I didn't want you to have any regrets," he said softly. "I'm sorry."

Her lips were dry. She moistened them with her tongue, feeling his eyes follow the slight movement. "I don't regret making love to you," she whispered. "How can I regret something that I'm dying to do again?"

She turned to look at him and found he'd silently closed the gap between them. He was standing only inches away, yet not touching her.

"Maybe you were right," he mused, gazing into her eyes. "Maybe you did seduce me this morning. Because I think you are about to seduce me again, no?"

"What about lunch?" she breathed, lost in the whirl of heat in his eyes as he moved even closer but still didn't touch her.

"Lunch can wait," he said, watching her mouth.

He was waiting for her, Carrie realized. He was waiting for her to make the first move, to touch him, to kiss him. To seduce him.

But he didn't love her. He liked her, and he lusted after her, but he didn't love her. He said he wasn't going to let himself fall in love with her, either. Not now, not ever. That hurt. To think that he could control his emotions as easily as he controlled his body and—

But he'd lost control. When they made love this morning, Felipe had *lost control*. Who was to say the same wouldn't happen to the tight rein he held on his emotions?

Carrie wanted him to love her. It was crazy. For all she knew, he was going to spend the rest of his life in a maximum security penitentiary or—God help her—on death row for the crime of first-degree murder. For all she knew, he *had* pulled the trigger two times, sending bullets into the heads of those mobsters. Oh, she didn't *think* he was guilty. Naturally, she didn't want to believe him capable of such a thing. But she didn't truly *know*. There were no hard facts or any proof to placate the scientist that she was. And her faith in Felipe wouldn't help him in a court of law.

Yeah, she was probably certifiable for wanting this man to fall in love with her. But she wanted it. And she was *damned* if she was going to sit back and just give up, just settle for his here and now.

At the very least, she was going to give him something to remember her by—and quite vividly—for the rest of his life.

The rays of light streaming in through the windows gave Felipe a golden glow. He looked otherworldly with his long, dark hair curling around his broad shoulders, his muscular chest gleaming and smooth. Carrie wondered if that same light accentuated her pale hair and lightly tanned skin. She wondered if she looked even half as exotic, half as sexy as he did. She sure *felt* sexy as he watched her, desire churning in his eyes.

But if she *was* going to seduce him, if she *was* going to try to loosen the hold he had on his emotions, she had to move fast before she chickened out.

With one swift movement, she pulled her shirt over her head.

His quick smile and quiet laugh told her he hadn't been expecting her to do that. That was good. She wanted to keep him off-balance.

He gazed at her silently but his eyes spoke volumes as they caressed her breasts and the curve of her smooth, tanned shoulders. She truly felt beautiful when he looked at her that way. Beautiful and sexy and powerful and capable of damn near anything. There wasn't a chance in hell she'd chicken out now. She'd set the wheels in motion, and now she'd see it through.

But he didn't reach for her. Instead, he jammed his hands hard into the front pockets of his shorts as if not touching her was a difficult task. She knew, suddenly, what he was doing. She knew why he wasn't touching her.

No regrets.

This time, he was making damn sure that it was clear *she* initiated their lovemaking. Of course, she could still regret it afterward, but this way, his own sense of guilt would be much lighter.

She could smell his clean, fresh, masculine scent. His nostrils flared, and she knew he could smell her, too. He could surely smell the faint, herbal scent of the shampoo she'd used to wash her hair, the tangy sweetness of the sun lotion she'd found in the bathroom and used in place of a moisturizer, and the fresh mint toothpaste she'd used to clean her teeth.

Felipe's eyes followed her fingers to the button of her shorts. She undid it slowly. *Very* slowly. Then she pulled the zipper down slowly. *Very* slowly. The look on his face was incredible.

Every muscle in his body was tight with tension as he waited. Carrie knew he was keeping himself from reaching out and speeding the process along.

Watching him, she pushed the shorts off her hips and they fell to the floor with a soft rustle. He inhaled sharply, a reaction to her lack of underwear. She stepped out of the shorts totally naked. Except, of course, for the slight blush that heated her cheeks. Damn her fair skin anyway.

Still, she held her chin high, steadily meeting his gaze. The heat in his eyes was fast approaching a nuclear meltdown. Still, he kept his hands in his pockets. Still, he didn't move.

"We could have lunch first," she whispered, unable to hide her smile. "Are you sure you're not hungry?"

He wet his lips. "Not for rice," he countered. His gaze dropped to the golden brown curls between her legs, then back to her face.

His message couldn't have been more clear.

The sudden rush of heat that shot through her caught her off guard. She swayed toward him, and at that same moment, she saw his control snap.

He reached for her, *lunged* for her, taking her into his arms and carrying her over to that huge, wooden table.

His hands and his mouth were everywhere, touching, kissing, suckling, licking. The sensation of his tongue in her belly button made her cry out, her voice echoing through the quiet of the house. She tried to sit up, but he held her firmly in place, using his tongue to try to drive her as deliriously insane as she'd driven him.

She writhed in pleasure, and her arm knocked a sugar bowl onto the kitchen floor with a crash. But she didn't care. She didn't care about anything except that she was making love to this man whom she adored.

She tried to reach for the button that fastened his shorts. He obliged by moving closer. Her hand fumbled with the button, and he reached down, wrapping her fingers tightly around him.

He undid the button himself, and the zipper, and then his shorts were sliding off. From somewhere, maybe out of thin air—and she wouldn't have been surprised if he were capable of such magic—maybe from the depths of his wallet, he procured a condom.

And then he was on top of her, inside her, filling her completely with each urgent thrust. He groaned as he kissed her, and she moved with him, in a rhythm of love as old as time.

You're going to love me, Carrie told him with her eyes, her hands, her body. I'm going to make you love me.

But she couldn't talk, couldn't form words let alone sentences. She could only grip his shoulders more tightly and moan her pleasure.

Felipe pulled back to look at her. His eyes were wild and tinged with shock. He spoke to her. His words were in Spanish, but his meaning was clear. Now. *Now.*

Now, like this morning, he was unable to hold back. Now, like this morning, *she* had driven him to a place of wild abandonment, a place where he had absolutely no control.

That knowledge sent her soaring, rockets of pleasure bursting through her as her body tightened and clenched in a culmination too intense to be real. But it *was* real. Waves of hot and cold rushed through her, colors exploded in her head as she wrapped her legs around Felipe and tried to draw him closer, even closer to her.

She heard him cry out her name, and then something else in Spanish as he exploded, thrusting harder and deeper inside her.

And then it was over. Carrie closed her eyes as Felipe let his head fall forward next to hers. He rolled off her so as not to squash her, but then quickly gathered her into his arms in a tender embrace. Oh, how she loved him.

Together they lay there on the kitchen table.

Carrie started to laugh.

They were *lying* on the kitchen table. They'd just made *love* on the kitchen *table.* Heaven help them if they were ever invited back to this beach house for dinner. Carrie would never make it through the meal without breaking into hysterical laughter.

"You must be thinking what I'm thinking," Felipe said, kissing the top of her head.

"Dinner here," Carrie said. "With the Marshalls."

"That's what I'm thinking," he said with a laugh.

"I wonder if they'll know," Carrie mused. "Just from…I don't know, the aura, the cosmic waves of sex that will ripple forth from this table from now on."

"Hmm," Felipe said, cupping her breast with his hand.

"Or maybe," Carrie said, "the Marshalls do exactly what we just did on this table all the time."

Felipe laughed, tipping her face up so he could kiss her on the mouth. "Maybe not," he said.

Carrie gazed up into his eyes. "That was *great* sex," she said. "Are we in agreement?"

He didn't answer—not right away. Finally, he nodded. "Yes," he said. "We're in agreement."

Chapter 13

Great sex.

Caroline's words echoed in Felipe's head.

Great sex. Was that all it really was to her?

She was curled up on the other end of the long couch, her head resting on a throw pillow, her eyes tightly closed. She looked like an angel as she slept, with her lips slightly parted, her long eyelashes fanned out against her smooth cheeks, her hair a tangle of unearthly gold around her face. She was enveloped in what was probably Jim Keegan's old white terry-cloth robe. If she stood up with it on, it would trail behind her like the train of a wedding gown.

A wedding gown. Now that would be a vision to behold: Caroline, resplendent in a white gown, her long, blond hair elegantly arranged up off her shoulders, a whisper-thin veil covering but not hiding her beautiful smile.

The groom would be a lucky man, his destiny a life of laughter and love, sweet kisses and sleepy blue-green eyes smiling up at him after wonderful, endless, sinfully delicious nights of loving.

Felipe's destiny, on the other hand, promised a procession of cold and lonely nights, stakeouts and time spent under cover with another identity, another name and no real future. Of course, he'd still have Caroline's blue-green eyes smiling at him—they'd haunt his dreams for the rest of his days.

Suddenly chilled and feeling desperately alone, Felipe stretched his leg down the couch toward Carrie, wanting their connection to remain unbroken for as long as it possibly could.

He slipped his foot under her robe, touching the warmth of her leg with his toes. She smiled and opened her turquoise eyes, and a hand appeared from beneath the mound of white terry cloth. She rested it gently on his leg, stroking him slightly as she closed her eyes again.

Great sex.

It had been incredibly great sex. In fact, that was the way Felipe had always preferred to think of it in the privacy of his own mind. He spoke to his lovers of "making love," but love never really entered into it—at least not more than the rather general love he had for all beautiful women. Sure, he'd imagined himself in love a time or two back when he was a teenager. But either it hadn't lasted or he'd been spurned and his broken heart had quickly healed. So quickly, in fact, that he'd soon come to doubt the truth of what he'd felt.

But this thing he'd been feeling lately, this lump of emotion that was lodged in his chest was unlike anything he'd ever felt before.

Maybe it wasn't love, he told himself. Maybe he was mistaken.

Caroline sighed and opened her eyes again. "What time is it?" she murmured.

He didn't need to glance at the clock on the wall. He could tell by the angle of the sun on the horizon. "Nearly six."

She yawned and stretched, her legs entwining with his on the couch, her arms reaching for the high, beamed ceiling.

Caroline folded her hands behind her head, elbows in the air, and looked down the couch at him. With one foot, she played with the edge of his shorts. "What does 'tay-yamo' mean?"

Her question made him freeze. Even his heart seemed to stop beating for a few solid seconds.

"What did you say?" he said.

"Tay-yamo," she said again.

Te amo.

I love you.

He kept his shock carefully hidden from her curious gaze.

"You said it more than once," Caroline said. She lowered her arms and began fiddling with the belt of the robe, aware of his sudden complete silence and clearly uncertain how to interpret it. "You remember, back when we *weren't* having lunch. Remember, the kitchen table…?"

Her smile was half shy, half wicked and utterly charming.

"I remember the kitchen table." He would always remember the kitchen table. In fact, he would probably be thinking of it, ninety-five years old and on his deathbed. That is, if he lived that long.

"I was just wondering if…" She looked at him from underneath her long lashes. She wasn't being coy or trying to act cute. Her nervous shyness was as real as the sweet blush that often tinged her cheeks. It totally contradicted the woman who had brazenly and openly tempted him in the kitchen this noon, but that wasn't a shock. She was a nest of contradictions and surprises. He expected it by now.

She took a deep breath. "I was wondering if Tay-yamo was someone's name. Like an old girlfriend. Or maybe a not-so-old girlfriend…?"

Felipe shook his head. "It's not a name," he said.

"Then what does it mean?" she asked. She said it again, practicing the unfamiliar Spanish words. "Tay-yamo. Am I saying it right?"

Te amo.

I love you.

Felipe could only nod. Had he really told her that he loved her?

"What does it mean?" she asked again.

He cleared his throat. "It's…rather difficult to translate."

He'd told her he loved her as they made love. He closed his eyes, and he could hear the echo of his voice calling out those words. *Te amo.* Yes, he'd really said it.

Worse than the shock of realizing he'd slipped, of realizing it was only chance that he'd said those words in a language Caroline didn't understand, worse than that was the sudden glaring knowledge that those words he'd cried were true.

He loved her.

She tucked her legs back underneath her robe, moving away from his foot. The sudden loss of her warmth, of the sensation of the closeness was too much for Felipe. He reached forward and pulled her so that she was sitting toboggan-style between his legs, her back against his chest. He wrapped his arms around her, holding her tightly.

He couldn't deny it anymore. He loved her.

He was doomed.

"Tay-yamo," she said again, and his heart clenched. She didn't know what she was saying, and she probably wouldn't say it if she *did* know what it meant. "You really can't translate it, huh?"

He shook his head. No.

How ironic that the tables had turned on him so absolutely. Here he'd gone and fallen in love, and *she'd* had "great sex."

"Tay-yamo. You were…exuberant when you first shouted it," she mused, that same wicked light in her eyes. "Is it kind of like, I don't know…yabba dabba do?"

Felipe laughed, holding her closer, loving her, wishing with all his heart that she loved him, too. But if she did, man, what a mess that would be. A double heartbreak instead of a single one. Because he was going to leave her when this was over. He *had* to leave her. He wouldn't risk putting her in danger. It would be easier for her, much easier, if she simply didn't fall in love with him, if she simply continued to consider their relationship a source of friendship and "great sex."

"Yes," he told her, pulling up her chin and kissing her soft lips. "It's *exactly* like yabba dabba do."

Felipe woke up at nine-thirty with Caroline in his arms.

Morning sunlight was streaming in around the edges of the shades and curtains in the master bedroom, and had been for quite some time.

He'd never slept so late before.

But it didn't surprise him. These past few days had been full of firsts.

Take, for example, the fact that he was lying here with the woman that he loved in his arms. Loved. That was a very big first.

Caroline was still fast asleep. He smiled despite the tension in his stomach and shoulders that his thoughts had created. She slept fiercely, her eyes tightly closed and her fists clenched, as if she was fighting to stay asleep.

He'd kept her up late last night. But then she'd woken him up at dawn.... She was as insatiable as he.

They'd stumbled around in the gray half-light, searching the master bedroom for condoms. They'd used up the one he'd carried in his wallet, *and* the others his brother had slipped him before they'd left the halfway house.

Felipe had been prepared to improvise, or heaven help him, even risk it—now *there* was another first—when Carrie had dug up a nearly full box. They were Jim's, and they'd been buried—hidden—way, way back underneath the sink.

Felipe was going to take every single one with him when they left. Jim wouldn't need them for a while—his wife, Emily, was five months pregnant.

He looked down at Caroline again, studying the pattern of freckles that splashed across her nose and cheeks, imagining her pregnant with his child. The want that rose in him was so intense he had to close his eyes and breathe deeply until it faded.

The baby would look like him, dark hair, dark eyes. He would be big—all of the Salazar babies were big—maybe even too big for Caroline to deliver safely. She was so tiny that the thought of her heavy with child and in possible physical danger because of it, because of *him,* was nearly overwhelming. If he got her pregnant, he'd spend nine months terrified that she would somehow be hurt...or worse.

Another reason not to tell her that he loved her. Another reason to walk away and never let her know the way she made his heart sing.

But—and it was time for yet another first—Felipe was starting to wonder if, when the time came, he'd actually have the strength to leave her.

Jim Keegan was married. Of course, he spent most of the time worried to hell about Emily. And Jim took precautions, too. He had a state-of-the-art security system and a dog the size of a small horse trained never to leave their yard. When he worked late at night, patrol cars would drive past his house, occasionally checking in with his wife. Felipe had stopped by himself, many times, as a favor to his old friend.

All that worry, all those precautions, and Jim only worked straightforward homicide. He rarely went under cover. His job was known to be far less dangerous than Felipe's.

Infiltrating street gangs and organized crime, which was what Felipe was so very, very good at, included a certain risk of retaliation or revenge. If he stayed with Caroline, if he let himself live the kind of life he longed for with her, he'd never be free from worry. His concentration would be off, and he'd probably get himself killed. Or *her* killed. And God help him, if anything happened to her, he'd never forgive himself.

No. When the time came, Felipe would find the strength to leave Caroline. Somehow, he'd manage to do it.

His leg started to ache, and he closed his eyes. Caroline snuggled against him, and he held her tighter, breathing in the sweet, familiar scent of paradise.

It wasn't going to be easy. God, even if *she* was the one who turned and walked away, it wouldn't be easy. Easier, but not easy.

Nothing would ever be easy again.

The bloodstains hadn't quite washed out of Carrie's dress, but the blue-flowered pattern managed to hide them, at least at a distant inspection. Now that the dress was clean and dry, she'd put it back on. Despite the stains, it fit far better than anything else she'd found in this house of tall people.

She stripped the sheets from the beds they'd used and put them and their dirty towels in a laundry basket. She left a note on top, apologizing for not taking the time to wash the linens.

Felipe was in the kitchen, washing up the pots and dishes.

He'd been oddly quiet all morning, a strange shadow darkening his eyes. Whether it was the thought of leaving the sanctuary of the beach house or something else, Carrie didn't know. But he was tense—more so than usual—and seemed lost in his thoughts.

Making love in a bed had seemed almost anticlimactic after the kitchen table. Still, it had been…lovely. He'd made love to her slowly, so exquisitely slowly. She could have sworn she'd seen love in his eyes, but she was probably mistaken. It was more likely only a reflection of the candlelight.

She sighed. Felipe glanced up at her and she forced her mouth into a smile.

"Ready to go?" he asked, wiping his hands on a dish towel, then hanging it on a hook near the sink. He walked toward her.

"No," she said.

He pushed her hair back from her face so very gently. "Neither am I," he said. "But we have to."

He was wearing the jeans, T-shirt and jacket he'd borrowed from his brother Rafe. He'd pulled his hair into a ponytail and his face looked sterner and harder without the softening effect of his long, dark curls. But his eyes were soft and his lips were even softer as he leaned forward to kiss her.

"Where are we going?" Carrie asked.

The shadow came back, flitting quickly across his gaze, and he looked away, toward the door that would lead them out of the house. "To a friend's," he said vaguely. "I have to get my hair cut. I need to look as different as I possibly can."

Carrie reached up and touched his ponytail. "Cut short?" she asked, unable to hide her disappointment.

He smiled, amusement in his dark eyes. "What? You like it long like this?"

"Yes," she said, freeing his hair from the ponytail and running her fingers through it. "It's…sexy."

"Hmmm," he said, closing his eyes, letting her know he enjoyed her touch. "I'm sorry. I won't get it cut too short." He looked at her and smiled. "The police have two kinds of pictures of me—some are with my hair long, like this. The others are with it cut short. You know, I always wore my hair really short until about two years ago.'' He looked down at his clothes and made a face. ''And this is not my normal wardrobe. I always wore designer suits and ties.''

Carrie laughed. She just couldn't picture it. Although he had worn that tuxedo with a certain ease and familiarity.... ''I'll believe that when you show me the pictures.''

He stepped slightly away from her, putting the rubber band back in his hair. ''Time to go.''

Carrie watched him open the kitchen door. She didn't want to walk through it, afraid of whatever might be waiting for them in the harsh world outside. She stalled. ''What if the van's not there? What if it's been towed?''

''We're not taking the van.''

''We're not?''

Clasping her hand, he led her out the door onto the back porch. He locked the door and slipped the key back under the flowerpot. ''We're taking Diego's bike.''

His...*bike?*

Carrie followed Felipe down the stairs and around the house to a detached garage. He pulled up the garage door, and there it was. A big, shiny, chrome-and-black Harley-Davidson motorcycle. Diego's bike. Of course.

''Do you really know how to ride that thing?'' Carrie asked.

Felipe wheeled it out into the sunlight, then closed the garage door.

He glanced at her and smiled. ''Yes.''

''I've never ridden one before,'' she said.

''Think of it as riding a horse with a powerful engine and a narrower saddle,'' he said. ''You did ride horses in Montana, right?''

''Of course.''

He smiled at the faintly insulted tone in her voice. ''You know how when you let your horse run, really run, you feel it inside? You move together, you even think together—''

She interrupted him. ''You ride?''

''My uncle Manny works at the racetrack,'' he said. ''I still sometimes go over there and pick up a few extra dollars exercising the horses that are boarded in their stables.''

"I don't really know that much about you, do I?" she said.

The shadow came flitting back into his eyes. He shook his head. "No, you don't."

"I mean, I had no idea... Are you a good rider?"

"*I* think so. But I'm better at riding one of these," he said, turning away from her and slapping the seat of the motorcycle.

He swung one long leg over the bike, straddled the monster and slipped a key into the ignition.

"Climb on behind me," he said, handing her own of the helmets that had been hanging on the bike's handlebars. "Put your arms around my waist and hold on tight. Lean when I lean, move with me, okay? And careful where you put your legs and feet. The engine gets pretty hot."

She nodded, about to put the helmet on, when he suddenly pulled her tightly to him and kissed her on the mouth. It was a passionate kiss, filled with deep yearning and need, yet it was still sweetly, achingly tender.

Carrie's knees felt weak and her bones turned to jelly. When he released her, she nearly fell over. He put the helmet on her head, strapping it securely under her chin.

He started the motorcycle with a roar, wincing as he jarred his injured leg. The motor turned and caught. "Climb on," he shouted, strapping on his own helmet.

She wasn't too happy about getting on the motorcycle, but after a kiss like that, she'd probably follow him damn near anywhere.

Carrie took a deep breath, then swung her leg over the seat. The dress she was wearing wasn't exactly made for riding astride. She tried to secure it underneath her, then locked her arms around Felipe's waist.

As he drove slowly down the driveway, she looked back over her shoulder at the beach house, wishing they could have stayed there forever.

Chapter 14

St. Simone hadn't changed one bit during the two days they'd been away. The sun still shone endlessly down from a perfect blue sky, warming the cracked sidewalks and the tiny one- and two-bedroom houses that lined the street. This was the part of town that the tourists never came to visit.

It wasn't dangerous like the neighborhood Rafe's halfway house had been in. It was just quietly depressing. These were beach shacks, and on the water they might even have been charming or picturesque. But here, the ocean was more than a mile away. Here, they were just bleak, cheaply constructed boxes that were crumbling around their financially strapped owners.

Felipe pulled the motorcycle up to the curb and braced his feet on either side as they came to a stop. He cut the engine and the sudden silence was a blessing.

Carrie lifted the visor of her helmet and looked around. Whoever this friend was that Felipe was planning to visit, he didn't have much money. It wasn't Jim Keegan, that was for sure. Carrie couldn't picture the daughter of the people who owned that house on Sanibel Island living on this particular street.

Felipe took off his helmet and turned slightly to face her. "We should go inside quickly," he said. "The fewer people who see us, the better."

She climbed stiffly off the motorcycle, and he led the way toward a tiny yellow house. A rusty wire fence surrounded the postage stamp-size yard, and the gate squeaked as he pushed it open. But the yard was clean, the garden filled with beautiful flowers and the house was well kept, with a fresh coat of paint.

Felipe limped up the steps to a small landing and knocked on the screen door.

The inner door swung open and a small, freckled face looked out through the screen.

"Daddy!" a young voice cried, pushing the screen door wide. A little boy launched himself into Felipe's arms.

Daddy?

Carrie stared at Felipe in shock as the door banged shut. He met her eyes for only the briefest of moments over the top of a bright red head. His expression was unreadable.

"Oh my God," another voice said from the darkness behind the screen. "Get inside here, *fast!*"

Felipe's friend wasn't a he. His friend was a *she*.

She was tall, almost as tall as Felipe, with elegant, almost classical features, green eyes and long, wavy red hair. She was obviously the little boy's mother—the same little boy who'd called Felipe Daddy.

Good Lord, was this woman Felipe's *wife?* Carrie stared in shock, realizing that she'd never actually asked Felipe if he was married.

The green-eyed woman pushed open the screen door and pulled Felipe and the boy into the house, leaving Carrie out in the cold—only figuratively, of course, since the sun was beating warmly down on her head.

Still holding the child, Felipe pushed the screen back open. He took Carrie's arm and dragged her inside, shutting both doors tightly behind her.

Green-eyes looked at her with a mixture of curiosity and hostility. Carrie couldn't blame her. *She'd* be hostile, too, if *her* husband brought his lover home.

"What are you doing here?" Green-eyes asked Felipe. Her

voice had the warm sugar-and-spice accent of the Deep South. "Everyone's looking for you. Jim Keegan was by just a few hours ago."

Felipe closed his eyes. "Damn. If only I'd known…"

The young woman was strikingly pretty, with long, pale, slender arms and legs. She was wearing a denim skirt and an off-white tank top with a gently scooped neckline. Her outfit wasn't necessarily feminine, but on her, it looked as delicate as lace. She looked like a dancer, tall and graceful. Next to her, Carrie felt like one of the seven dwarfs.

"I'm sorry," Felipe said. "I know this is awkward. But I didn't know where else to go."

"Phil, so help me God, if you screw up my life—"

"Billy, excuse your mother and me for a moment, please," Felipe said. The little boy slid down out of his arms. He gazed curiously at Carrie as he walked past her and sat down on the living room couch.

Felipe stepped closer to Green-eyes, touching her shoulder, speaking to her in a low, soft voice. Carrie couldn't make out the words, but his tone was soothing, almost seductive.

It was misery, watching him talk to her like that. Carrie stared at the worn floorboards of the living room floor, but she couldn't block the sound of his voice.

I don't really know that much about you, do I?

No, you don't.

Damn straight she didn't. She felt like a fool. She glanced up to find the little redhead watching her. She imagined she could see scorn and disgust in the youngster's eyes.

Carrie heard the answering murmur of Green-eyes's Southern accent, and her attention was drawn back to the other side of the room, where she and Felipe were having their own version of summit peace talks.

Was he touching her face? Had he kept that comforting hand on her shoulder, sliding it down her arm in a gentle, sensuous caress? Was she, right this very moment, lifting her face to his for a kiss.

Carrie couldn't keep from looking over at Felipe. She couldn't stop herself. But as soon as she did, she wished desperately that she hadn't. Because Felipe *was* touching the redheaded woman. He was pushing Green-eyes's wavy hair back from her face. Carrie's heart shriveled inside her as she remembered that he'd touched her that same way mere hours before.

How *could* he have? How could he make love to her the way he had, with his wife and child here in this little house, waiting for him to come home?

Felipe glanced up to find Carrie staring, and she quickly looked away, knowing all her hurt and jealousy were showing in her eyes.

"All right," Green-eyes said, walking across the living room and sitting on the couch next to Little Redhead. "So introduce me to your friend, why don't you?"

"Caroline," Felipe said, moving toward the couch, "meet Jewel and Billy." He didn't sit down but rather stood beside them. It was a charming family portrait. Carrie's head was spinning.

She searched the boy's face for any sign of Felipe's features, any similarities the child might have to his father.

She couldn't see a single one. The red hair, green eyes and freckles came directly from his mother. The nose was entirely the child's own, as was his chin and mouth.

"Daddy, I saw you on the news," Billy said. His small face suddenly looked pinched and nervous. "They say you're a bad man."

"Billy, hush," Green-eyes—Jewel—whispered. Her name suited her.

"No, that's okay," Felipe said. He knelt next to the boy. "You must be pretty upset, huh?"

Billy nodded.

"It's not true," Felipe said. "All that stuff they're saying on TV and in the papers. Someone made a mistake, and I'm being blamed for something that I didn't do."

"You didn't kill those guys?" the boy asked.

"No," Felipe said, "I didn't. And you know I'd never lie to you."

"I know," Billy said. He pressed his lips tightly together and stared down at his hands.

"I'm going to get it all worked out," Felipe said. "Don't worry, okay?"

"Okay." But it was said grudgingly.

"Feel any better?"

Billy shook his head.

Carrie's heart was in her throat. Felipe was gentle with the child, full of soft words and reassurances. It wasn't hard to imagine him talking to her in that same soothing tone. But there wasn't much he could say to make *her* feel any better, either.

"I'm sorry," Felipe murmured, pulling the little boy into his arms. "I wish I could wave a magic wand and make it all disappear, but I can't. I need time. Can you give me some time, Billy? Another week, maybe?"

Billy nodded, on the verge of tears. He wriggled free from Felipe's arms and ran out of the room.

Felipe started after him, but Jewel stood up and stopped him with a hand on his arm. "Let him go," she said. "He doesn't like to cry in front of anyone these days. He's a big boy, nearly seven. He's got enough to worry about—at least spare him the embarrassment."

Felipe looked as if he was about to cry, too. "I'm sorry," he said to Jewel.

"Whoever you're investigating," she said, "you sure got them scared, huh?"

"Yeah," Felipe laughed humorlessly. "We've got them shaking in their shoes, don't we, Caroline?"

She said nothing. What could she say? All she wanted to do was leave. Walk out the door, away from Felipe Salazar, away from his lies and deceit—except he'd never told her that he *wasn't* married. She'd stupidly never asked.

"It said on the news that you'd been shot," Jewel said, pushing her hair back behind her ear. "Are you all right?"

"I'm sore," Felipe said shortly. "I should stay off my leg for another week, but I don't have another week. I don't have enough time."

Jewel smiled wryly. "I know the feeling well. Come on into the kitchen. You can have something to eat while I cut your hair."

Now was Carrie's chance. She'd just stand up and let herself out the same door they'd come in.

Except Felipe took her arm and pulled her with him into the tiny kitchen.

"I need a bathing suit," he said to Jewel as he gently pushed Carrie down into a chair. "And one for Caroline, too." He took out his wallet and handed her a hundred-dollar bill. "Will you run down to Swim City and buy them for me? Caroline's a size five, and I'm still a medium. Get us something funky and young-looking. Something college kids would wear."

"Can I take a spin on that bike you drove up on?" Jewel asked. She filled a spray bottle with warm water from the sink, then dragged one of the kitchen chairs into the middle of the room.

"Sure." Felipe sat down in the chair, and Jewel wrapped a towel around his neck.

"Then it's no problem. I tell you, Phil, it kills me to cut this gorgeous hair off," Jewel said, wetting down his long curls.

"I don't need a bathing suit," Carrie said, finally finding her voice. Her numbness and disbelief were slowly being replaced by anger. That was good. Anger didn't hurt quite so much.

"You need to get out of that dress," Felipe said to her as Jewel combed his wet hair, parting it neatly on the side. "The police have probably issued a description of what you were wearing by now. And besides, we're going down to the beach. If you don't have a bathing suit, you'll stand out."

"*You* might be going to the beach," Carrie said. "But I'm not. I'm out of here."

"Don't be ridiculous—"

"Ridiculous?" she said. "*Ridiculous? This* is ridiculous, Detective. Sitting here like this…"

Jewel took a long, sharp-looking pair of scissors and began cutting Felipe's hair at cheekbone length. Long, dark curls fell on the beige linoleum floor. She glanced up at Carrie. "You got a problem with my kitchen? I admit it *is* kinda ugly.…"

Carrie leaned forward. "I hate to break it to you, sister, but *Phil* here has been unfaithful."

Jewel just kept cutting his hair. "Why, you bad boy, you," she said to him.

"Caroline," Felipe started to say, but she ignored him.

"Don't you care?" Carrie asked Jewel.

Jewel smiled, quickly cutting the hair around Felipe's ears even shorter. "Nope."

"Well, *I* do," Carrie said coolly. "And I'm leaving."

Her chair squeaked as she pushed it back from the table and headed out of the room.

Felipe stood up. "Caroline, wait..."

Jewel put the scissors down. "It seems like this is a good time for me to get those things you wanted from the store."

Carrie spun back to face Felipe as he scrambled after her into the living room and followed her toward the front door. "And by the way," she said, "I have regrets. *Big* regrets. I regret the day I first laid eyes on you."

Felipe had done it. He'd gone and made Caroline ready and willing to walk away from him. Except he hadn't expected her to be quite this angry, quite this upset, quite this willing to walk right *now*.

He had had no idea that she would be so...jealous. *Jealous?* She *was*. She was jealous of Jewel. My God, maybe she cared about him more than she'd let on.

"And," she continued, "I *definitely* regret ever being so foolish as to make love to you, you two-timing *snake!*"

Felipe had been called quite a number of things in his life, but "two-timing snake" wasn't one of them. Out on the street, he heard the roar of Diego's bike as Jewel rode away.

He laughed—he couldn't help it. It was a combination of her words and the giddy way he felt, knowing she was *jealous*.

"Oh, you think it's funny?" she said. "Fine. I'm leaving, and this time you can't stop me."

Felipe stopped laughing. She was dead serious, and the thought of her walking away now was instantly sobering.

"No," he said. "No, it's not— Caroline, I've misled you."

"Damn straight you did, you *bastard*."

"No," he said, pushing his freshly cut hair up and out of his eyes. "I've misled you by letting you believe I have any kind of relationship besides friendship with Jewel."

"No relationship?" she said. "Right. Your *friendship* created a son?"

"He's not my son," he said, talking low and fast as he followed her the last few steps to the door. "He calls me Daddy because he doesn't have anyone else to call that, and because I love him as if he were my son."

Carrie stopped with her hand on the doorknob. She wouldn't look at him, but he knew she was listening. It was a good thing she was listening because there was no way he would let her leave.

"I met Jewel when she was seventeen," Felipe said, talking quickly, quietly. "Billy was nearly three. She'd just come out of rehab, and her uncle was trying to hook her on crack again so he could resume his role as her pimp."

"Lord," Carrie breathed, finally looking up at him. Her eyes were wide and so blue.

"I helped put her uncle in jail," he told Caroline evenly. "She and I became friends. That's all it's ever been—friendship. I've never slept with her—I've never wanted to. I love her, but I'm not in love with her. Do you understand that?"

Caroline's eyes were brimming with tears, but she kept her head turned away. She never wanted him to see her cry. She was so tough, so independent, and at the same time, so damn fragile. She nodded her head. She understood.

"You must think I'm a fool," she said. "A jealous fool."

Jealous. She *was* jealous. Why did that make him so happy? It should worry him, make him wonder if maybe she cared about him too much. "I don't think you're a fool," he said gently.

"Well, that makes one of us," she said and went back into the kitchen.

Felipe briefly closed his eyes. She wasn't going to leave.

Not yet anyway.

"You lovebirds get things ironed out?" Jewel asked Carrie as they sat in the kitchen.

Jewel had returned from the store and finished cutting Felipe's hair. Now Felipe had gone to find Billy, to say goodbye to the little boy.

Carrie was wearing the bathing suit that Jewel had bought at Swim City. It was a bikini of extremely minute dimensions, in a neon orange-and-black zebra-stripe print. Supposedly it made her look like a college student. Over it, she wore a filmy gauze beach cover-up and a pair of overalls dug out of the back of Jewel's closet. The long pants would make riding the motorcycle easier, and help keep her warm if they were out all night.

Carrie shrugged. "It's not love," she said.

"I don't sleep with guys I don't love," Jewel said. She took a sip from the glass of iced tea that sat on the table in front of her. "Not anymore." She looked at Carrie. "And I don't think you do, either."

Carrie was silent, tracing a design on the table with the condensation from her glass.

"How could you not be in love with that man?" Jewel asked.

Carrie looked up into the brilliant green of the younger woman's eyes. "Are you?" she asked.

Jewel laughed. "No," she said. "Well…I used to have a crush on Phil back when we first met, but that was a long time ago." She looked at Carrie from out of the corner of her eye. "However, he *is* the best-looking man on earth."

Carrie had to smile. "Amen to that. But that haircut you gave him makes him look about eighteen years old. I feel like a cradle robber."

"Just push his hair out of his face," Jewel said. "It's only when it's in his eyes that he looks young."

"You're good at cutting hair," Carrie said.

"Thanks," Jewel said almost shyly. "It started out as a temporary career. I'm actually going to school over at the state university. I'm majoring in business, with a minor in Spanish. Although, I like cutting hair so much, I just might stay with it. With the business degree, maybe someday I can own my own salon."

"You speak Spanish?" Carrie asked, leaning forward.

"Nearly like a native of Puerto Rico, or so Mrs. Salazar tells me," Jewel said. Her tone was tongue-in-cheek, but there was some pride there, too.

"Do you know what 'Tay-yamo' means?" Carrie asked.

Jewel nearly dropped her glass of iced tea. She put it carefully down in front of her. "Did Phil say that to you?" she asked, bemused.

Carrie nodded. "When I asked him what it meant, he told me it was too hard to translate."

Jewel laughed. "For Phil, yeah, it'd be really hard to translate. He's got a problem with that particular verb."

"Okay, we better roll," Felipe said, coming into the kitchen. "We've already been here to long."

With his hair cut so that it fell forward past his eyes almost to the tip of his nose, he *did* look much younger. With the combination of his hairstyle and the boldly patterned knee-length bathing suit, the extralarge T-shirt and the cheap beach sandals he was wearing, he looked like he might even pass for a high school student. Provided, of course, that his shirt stayed on to cover the hard, well-developed muscles in his chest and shoulders, and his hair stayed in his face, hiding the mature leanness of his cheeks.

He touched Carrie lightly on the shoulder. His hand was warm through the fabric of her cover-up.

Carrie was still embarrassed about her jealous reaction to Jewel. He'd made it more than clear that she had no claim to his heart. He'd told her that he could only give her here and now, and he may very well have meant their time at the beach house. Come to think of it, that poignant kiss he'd given her before they left, that could very well have been a kiss goodbye.

It was probably over—at least, that part of their relationship was over—yet Carrie had acted like a jealous, spurned lover. Of course, her reaction hadn't been all jealousy. She'd been outraged at the thought that Felipe could make love to her with such little regard for his wife. She'd been shocked and appalled and angry that she had misjudged him so thoroughly. The man she thought she knew wouldn't cheat on his wife. He wouldn't have gotten married in the first place, but if he had, he'd be sure to keep his marriage vows.

Of course, Jewel *wasn't* Felipe's wife. Jewel wasn't even his lover, present *or* past.

So now what?

Carrie had let him see her jealousy and hurt, and now he probably knew that she'd been stupid enough to fall in love with him. He'd probably treat her with the same kindness and gentle compassion he'd shown little Billy.

Terrific.

"We were discussing the translation of interesting Spanish phrases," Jewel said to Felipe. "*Te amo,* for instance."

His hand dropped from Carrie's shoulder. She glanced up to find his gaze fixed on Jewel, his expression suddenly shuttered.

Jewel laughed. "I've always felt that *'te amo'* is one of those things that needs to be explained by the person who says it. The meaning is defined by the situation in which it's spoken." She leaned toward Carrie. "I can't tell you what Felipe meant when he said it. Only he can tell you that."

Chapter 15

"Why exactly are we going to the beach?" Carrie asked as she slipped the motorcycle helmet on her head. Felipe helped her on with a big, unwieldy backpack that held the rest of their clothes and a few beach towels.

"We're going to meet Diego," Felipe said, putting on his own helmet. "He and I used to eat an early dinner at the same sandwich stand on the beach every Wednesday night back when we were partners. I'm hoping that since it's Wednesday he'll show up. I need to talk to him."

"And you're sure that this Diego's not really some gorgeous woman?" Carrie said dryly. "Because if he is, I want to be prepared to go into another jealous snit. I *know* how much you must *love* that."

Felipe grabbed her around the waist and pulled her tightly to him. "I *do* love it when you're jealous," he murmured. If they hadn't been wearing the helmets, he would have kissed her. Instead, he just smiled into her eyes and ran his hands down her back, pulling her hips in closer to him. "But no, Diego's not a woman. You saw him on TV, on that news report, remember?"

Carrie nodded. She remembered. "I'm really sorry about before,'' she said softly. "Seriously, Felipe, I won't behave like that again. I know I don't own you. I know I never will. If I forget, just…remind me.''

She'd been so quick to believe the worst of him. Of course, little Billy had called him Daddy, and she'd simply followed that to its obvious conclusion.

The truth was, she was ready to doubt Felipe Salazar. Was he a killer? She didn't think so. But if the least little bit of evidence showed up that worked against him, she'd probably start to doubt his innocence again.

And yet she loved him. It was a strange and powerful emotion, to be able to overlook the fact that this man *was* wanted by the police for murder.

Felipe started the motorcycle, and Carrie climbed on behind him, wrapping her arms around his waist. He drove slowly toward the beach, careful never to exceed the leisurely speed limit of the side streets.

They approached a patrol car, and Carrie tensed. But Felipe didn't slow, didn't even seem to notice. He was utterly cool, and they passed with no problem. The police officer didn't even glance in their direction.

And then they were at the beach. Felipe parked the motorcycle and they walked toward the food stand.

It was odd, being out in the open. They were in plain sight of anyone who happened to drive by. Except they were surrounded by dozens and dozens of people who looked just like them. Shaggy-haired young men in bright, funky bathing suits and dark glasses. Young women of all shapes and sizes, with all styles and colors of swimsuits, with all lengths and shades of hair. They milled around the sandwich stand. They sat on their towels on the nearby sand, or perched on top of the picnic tables that were scattered across that part of the beach.

It was the perfect place to hide. They were daringly hidden in plain view. No one would think to look for them here.

Except, hopefully, for Jim "Diego" Keegan.

Felipe found an empty picnic table in the shade, near a pay phone. Taking Carrie's hand, he pulled her toward it. He sat on top, not on the bench, and assumed the same relaxed slouch as the other kids. Carrie sat next to him.

"You look tense," he murmured. "Loosen up. And take off your overalls and shirt. You're the only one out here still dressed."

She stood up and slipped out of her pants. She rolled them up and set them next to her on the table. The gauze shirt she unbuttoned, but left on.

"Relax," Felipe said into her ear. "No one's going to look for us here."

She tried to loosen her shoulders, but it didn't seem to help. Felipe looped an arm around her neck, pulling her close. And then he kissed her.

It wasn't a little, polite, out-in-public kind of kiss. It was a huge, devouring, explore-the-tonsils, bone-melting kiss.

He released her, melted bones and all, keeping that possessive arm around her neck. She sagged against him, glad he was holding her up.

No one was watching. No one in this crowd of students had even noticed Felipe kissing her as if the world were coming to an end.

"Much better," he said with a flash of his straight white teeth. "Now you have that same hormone-glazed expression in your eyes that the other kids have."

"I do *not*," she said, insult tingeing her voice, knowing he was right. She pinched him in the side.

He squirmed away, laughing, but still watching the parking lot. "Do, too. You know, you look about sixteen in that bathing suit. It's real heart-attack material."

"Well, *you* look barely old enough to vote, so that makes us even," she said.

He took her hand, lacing his fingers with hers. "I wish I'd known you when you were sixteen," he said, stopping his keen perusal of the parking lot to look searchingly into her eyes. "You were probably one of those really smart, sexy girls. I bet you had every guy in high school following you around."

Carrie laughed. "I was a total nerd. No one followed me anywhere."

"I would have," Felipe said.

She glanced at him. "You would've scared me to death." She laughed. "You *still* scare me to death."

He looked out across the parking lot, squinting into the sunlight as he searched for Jim Keegan's car. "Really?"

Yes, really. Carrie was scared that the part of her heart that Felipe had invaded would never be the same after he left. She was scared that she'd never meet a man who could stand up to her memories of this one. She was scared that she'd love him forever, long after he was gone, long after he'd forgotten her.

And most of all, she was scared that she was wrong about him, that he *had* been involved in the Sandlot Murders.

She didn't answer him. Instead, she looked around in the late-afternoon light at the long, frothy line of water that pulsed and murmured at the edge of the sparkling white expanse of sand.

"I love the beach," she said. "You know, I was eighteen before I ever set eyes on the ocean, but I still loved it. I loved the pictures and the movies and TV shows. 'Hawaii Five-O' repeats. 'Miami Vice.' 'Flipper.' Especially 'Flipper.' Sandy and Bud, remember them? So I came out to Florida to go to college and see the ocean. Mostly to see the ocean."

Felipe was listening to her carefully. He was also looking around, watching the cars that came and went in the parking lot, and gazing at the people passing by on the sidewalk. But every time he glanced at her, she knew from looking into his eyes that he was paying attention to every word she spoke. It was a nice feeling, knowing that someone was honestly listening to her.

"Everyone back home laughed at me because I wanted to be a marine biologist," Carrie told him. "Everyone told me that ranchers' daughters from Montana just didn't become marine biologists."

"Why not?" he asked.

She smiled and reached up to push his hair back from his face. "That's what I asked, too. Why not?" She shrugged. "No one had a good enough answer, so here I am. A marine biologist from Montana."

Felipe took her face between his hands and kissed her. His

mouth was so sweet, his lips so gentle. Carrie's heart lodged in her throat, aching with love for him.

He still held her face after he kissed her, gazing deeply into her eyes.

Suddenly shy, and afraid that her feelings would show, Carrie pulled away. She looked down at her toes.

"Does that help with our cover?" she asked. "Does it make us seem more like college students when you kiss me?"

"That's not why I kissed you," Felipe said. "I kissed you because I wanted to. Because around you, Caroline, I have absolutely no control."

She looked up at him. He wasn't smiling or teasing. His face was dead serious as he gazed at the parking lot.

"No control," he murmured, the muscles working in his jaw.

Carrie gazed at him. No control. Over his body? Or over his emotions?

Hope formed in her stomach like a fragile butterfly. Maybe she *could* make him love her. Maybe...

Felipe was aware he'd given too much away.

Caroline sat next to him, lost in her own thoughts. How long 'til she figured out the control he'd spoken of losing had to do with his heart rather than his hormones?

Of course, her jealousy earlier today had revealed to him that her feelings for him were more than merely casual. And sooner or later, she was going to run into someone who was going to translate *te amo* for her, and then she'd know.

He loved her.

What would happen if he told her? *I love you, but we can't be together because I'd fear for your safety.*

She'd laugh and talk him into ignoring his fears. She'd convince him he was suffering from an overactive imagination.

And then one day, someone like Tommy Walsh would follow him home. And then the next day, Caroline would be dead.

No, he couldn't tell her. He couldn't take that risk.

She shifted slightly and leaned her head against his shoulder. Felipe slipped his arm around her waist, amazed as he always was at how perfectly they fit together.

She rested her hand on his knee, and he felt the sharp stab of desire. Tonight. Tonight she'd be in his arms again.

But they had no place to stay, nowhere to go. God only knows where they'd spend the night. Maybe they could get a room in a cheap motel by paying with cash and signing false names in the registry. But it would mean standing under the watchful eye of the desk clerk as he registered, hoping the guy hadn't seen the papers or the television news.

Of course, his haircut made him look quite a bit different—

Next to them, the public telephone began to ring.

Felipe was up on his feet in an instant. He answered it before it had completed the first ring.

"Yes?"

"Who's the blonde?"

It was Diego—Jim Keegan.

"Oh, man," Felipe said, relief rushing through him. "You don't know how good it is to hear your voice."

"Likewise," Diego said. "I drove by and saw you, but just as I was about to stop, I got this sense that I was being trailed. I don't know. Emily says when she got pregnant, I got paranoid. Maybe she's right. Still, I thought it would be smart to be cautious, you know?"

"Where are you calling from?" Felipe asked, glancing back at Caroline. She was watching him, trying to listen from her seat on the picnic table.

"I'm at a pay phone downtown," Jim Keegan said. "We got us a friendly line, Phil. No taps, no one listening in. So spill it. I know you didn't kill those guys in the sandlot. I got a truckload of questions. Let's start with the girl." He laughed, and Felipe had to smile at the familiar, husky sound. "I drive by, and I see you giving this great-looking blonde mouth-to-mouth. Who is she?"

"Her name is Caroline Brooks," Felipe said, glancing again at the great-looking blonde in question and lowering his voice so she wouldn't hear him. "Do you remember the lady I locked in the trunk of her car at Sea Circus?"

"You're kidding," Jim said. "You used to talk about her so much, Emily was convinced you'd be sending out wedding invitations within the year. How long have you been seeing her? What's going on? Is she helping you hide?''

"I never went back to introduce myself," Felipe admitted. "I haven't been seeing her at all." He told Jim what had happened at Schroedinger's restaurant, how by sheer chance, Caroline had been there that evening, how she had unwittingly blown his cover.

His friend was silent for a moment. "Then she's the same woman you left the restaurant with," he said. "That's why her name sounded familiar. We still don't have a picture of her, but the PR department is working on getting one to release to the press—along with a statement, my friend, that calls her your 'hostage.'"

Felipe swore softly.

"Apparently, the boyfriend's getting ready to tape an impassioned plea to *you,* trying to convince you to let the girl go. It'll be carried by all the local stations—"

"*Boy*friend?" Felipe said.

"Uh-oh," Jim said. "She didn't tell you she has a boyfriend?"

"No." Felipe turned his back to Caroline, afraid that the sudden jealousy that was making his stomach churn would show in his eyes. *Boyfriend?*

"Some ad exec. His name is—hang on a sec." Felipe could hear the sound of pages being turned as Jim skimmed his notes for the man's name. "Robert Penfield. The Third. Lah-di-dah. Big bucks, no brains. The guy's a real load, Phil. He's been doing the circuit of news programs and talk shows, milking the situation. Apparently, he was at the restaurant, when you quote, unquote 'kidnapped' Caroline—"

You two-timing snake… That's what Caroline had called him when she'd thought he was involved with Jewel, too. No way would she have been so vehement if she'd been doing some two-timing of her own, if she'd been hiding a boyfriend from him.

"He's not her boyfriend, this Penfield guy," Felipe said with sudden certainty. "A dinner date, maybe." He turned back to look at Caroline. "Do you know someone named Robert Penfield?" he said to her.

She stared at him blankly.

"The Third...?"

Recognition dawned in her eyes. "I was having dinner with him at Schroedinger's."

"Have you been out with him before?"

"No," she said. "I only met him that afternoon."

"I was right," Felipe said to Jim. "He was her dinner date."

"He's been implying that she's his fiancée," Jim said.

"She didn't even recognize his name at first," Felipe said.

"Maybe that's simply a testament to the overwhelming power you have over women," Jim teased. "When you're around, old what's-his-name's forgotten."

"You got anything else for me, man?" Felipe asked. "Any *good* news?"

"Only bad," Jim said. "*Really* bad."

Felipe braced himself.

"The police just released the ballistics report to the press," Jim continued. "Your police-issue handgun fired the bullets that killed Tony Mareidas and Steve Dupree out in that sandlot."

"Oh, *man*." Felipe closed his eyes. This *was* bad news.

"Was your gun ever taken from you in the past few weeks?" Jim asked. "Was it ever missing for any length of time?"

"No."

"Maybe while you were asleep? Or, um, otherwise preoccupied perhaps...?"

"No. I sleep with it under my pillow," Felipe said. "And I've been sleeping alone." Except for the past few nights, and hopefully again tonight....

"Then I'm right," Jim said. "Richter's got a man inside the St. Simone Police Force—and it's someone with enough rank and power to falsify a ballistics report."

"A captain," Felipe said.

"That's what I figured, too," Jim said.

Felipe told him about the mysterious Captain Rat, Richter's partner. "Last week I got a glimpse of Richter's personal schedule on his computer,'' Felipe said. ''He's got a date to meet with this Captain Rat tomorrow at 3:30.''

''Where?''

Felipe laughed humorlessly. ''That's the catch. I don't know where.''

A fourteen- or fifteen-year-old kid hovered nearby, waiting to use the pay phone. Felipe turned and gave him a steady look, and within moments, the boy nervously walked away.

''Okay, look,'' Jim was saying, ''I'll go and do some more checking around. The bitch about this Richter investigation is that I don't know who the hell knows about it, and who is clueless. And I don't want to ask—I don't want anyone to know that *I* know. Damn, it's complicated. And meanwhile, no one's asking me if *I* know, because they don't want *me* to know what *they* know.'' He swore disgustedly. ''Phil, I'm honestly thinking of just bringing it all out into the light.''

''Not yet, man,'' Felipe said. ''Don't do that yet. Until I know who the man on the inside is, I can't risk coming in. And without me, you've got nothing.''

''I got nothing now,'' Jim said. ''Maybe it's time to shake the hornet's nest, see who gets mad.''

''Not yet,'' Felipe said again. ''Maybe in a few days—''

''I'm worried about you, Phil.''

''I'll get by,'' Felipe said with a quiet confidence that wasn't feigned. At least not entirely. ''Don't do something that will put you—and Emily—in danger.''

Jim Keegan was silent, and Felipe quickly told him about the tape he'd made and left in Rafe's van. ''Just in case,'' he added.

Jim was still silent. Then, finally, he spoke. ''Maybe you should just lie low,'' he said. ''Stay out of sight. Let me nose around a bit more. I've checked out all but two of the police captains, all but Captain Swick and Captain Patterson. Personally, I find it hard to believe Patterson could ever be involved with Richter. He's such a straight arrow. Swick, on the other hand…''

''He's never liked me,'' Felipe said. ''I've overheard him using…derogatory language in reference to…my cultural background, shall we say?''

"He's a bigot," Jim stated bluntly. "But that doesn't automatically make him a criminal."

"He lives down near the water, doesn't he?" Felipe asked. Come to think of it, Donald Swick lived in a very nice house right on the Gulf—a house way too big and expensive for a man who'd been on the police force all his working life.

"Yeah, over on Casa del Sol Avenue," Jim said. "His wife's out of town. He's been putting in quite a few extra hours, working with Chief Earley, trying to track you down. The media's been eating it up. Captain Swick and Chief Earley, the modern Untouchables."

"Man, I got a feeling about Swick," Felipe said. "I'm going to check him out."

"Let me," Jim said. "You stay hidden."

"No, I've got to do *some*thing," Felipe said. "You look into Patterson. I'll check out Swick's house."

"Phil at least find a safe place for Caroline and leave her there."

It was Felipe's turn to be silent. "Can you guarantee that wherever I put her, Tommy Walsh won't find her?" he finally said. "And can you guarantee that if I do find a safe place, she'll stay put?" He shook his head, even though Jim couldn't possibly see him over the telephone line. "No, she's staying with me, Diego. That way I'll *know* she's safe."

For once, Jim didn't argue. He just chuckled quietly. "It happened, huh, Felipe? You finally met your match."

"No—" The word wasn't even out of his mouth before Felipe recognized it was a lie. Diego was right. Caroline was the only woman he wanted, the only woman he'd ever want. After he said goodbye to her, he might as well enter a monastery.

"Oh good, and we're in denial, too." Jim's chuckle got louder. "You poor bastard, you don't stand a chance."

In his native language, Felipe soundly and quietly cursed out his best friend.

But Jim kept on laughing. "Just ask her to marry you and get it over with," he said. "You'll be surprised how much better you'll feel when you just give up the fight."

"I can't, man," Felipe said. "It's not possible. You *know* it's not possible."

"Rule number one," Jim said. "Nothing is impossible. Don't forget that. The first step is to wipe the street clean with Richter's face, bring down his whole organization, including this sonuvabitch on the force. After that, you can work things out with Caroline."

"Sure," Felipe said. Sure, he'd work things out by walking out. It was the only way.

After Jim had been transferred to homicide, Felipe had gotten used to working alone. He found that he *liked* working alone; he liked *being* alone. But the thought of being without Caroline made him feel achingly lonely. He'd never been lonely before, but now he knew he'd never be anything *but* lonely again.

"Remember, if you need transportation, the key to my car is on the right front wheel, where I always leave it. The car's in the lot at the precinct," Jim said. "I'm going to call you at this number same time tomorrow. Try to be here."

"I'll be here," Felipe said. "Or…" He didn't finish the sentence, but they both knew how it ended. He'd be there, or he'd be dead.

Chapter 16

"Whose house is this?" Carrie whispered.

"Don Swick," Felipe said. "He's a captain on the police force."

Carrie nodded. "Nice place," she said.

It was. It was very nice.

It had beachfront, in a section of town where beachfront didn't come cheap. Big and rambling, the single-level house sprawled across a well-manicured lawn with plenty of bushes and shrubbery to keep them hidden.

"You think this Captain Swick is your Captain Rat?" Carrie asked.

Felipe nodded. "Shh," he said, pressing one finger lightly to her lips.

It was hard to be quiet. Carrie was understandably nervous. This was the first time she'd ever broken into a police captain's house. It was the first time she'd broken into *any*one's house.

But Felipe seemed to know what he was doing. He used a tiny penlight he'd taken from the beach house to examine what looked like the access box to a complex security system.

With a Swiss Army knife Carrie didn't even realize he had

been carrying, Felipe set to work. She watched for a moment, then he murmured, "Keep an eye on the street, *cara.* Tell me if a car is coming."

Carrie nodded.

She was scared to death. She was scared that this Captain Swick *was* Richter's partner and that they'd be in danger if they went into his house. And she was scared that he wasn't, that they'd break into his house and still be no closer to clearing Felipe's name.

"Got it," he said quietly.

Carrie turned to see the door swing open.

Gun drawn, Felipe went inside first. He flashed the same penlight around an enormous kitchen. It was nearly twice as big as the kitchen at the beach house.

Carrie shut the door behind them, then followed Felipe out of the kitchen and down a long, carpeted hallway. They passed a dining room and a living room, both vast and quiet and dark and filled with expensive furniture.

It was creepy being in someone else's house like this. True, the beach house had been someone else's, too, but they'd been there with Jim Keegan's unspoken blessing. Here, there wasn't even a hint of an invitation from the owners.

Carrie followed Felipe into an enormous master bedroom suite. His penlight flashed around the room, revealing an unmade bed, clothes draped over the back of several easy chairs, laundry overflowing a hamper. The shades in the windows were all pulled completely down, as if Swick hadn't bothered to open them in the morning.

Felipe went over to the lamp on one of the bedside tables and switched on the light.

There were Chinese food cartons on a TV tray, along with a half-eaten bag of chips and the TV remote control. Books and papers were piled on the half of the bed that Swick hadn't slept in.

"He better clean this up before his wife gets home, huh?" Felipe murmured. "Man, what a mess."

"Where do we start?" Carrie asked.

"We're looking for a calendar or a date book or anything that might mention some kind of meeting tomorrow,'' Felipe said. ''We're looking for any mention of Richter's name, or Walsh, or Mareidas and Dupree—''

''Who?''

''The men who were killed in the sandlot.''

''Oh.'' Carrie nodded. ''How about any mention of the company that's a front for Richter's illegal businesses?''

''L&R Co.,'' Felipe said. ''Good thinking. You'd make a good cop.''

''No thanks,'' Carrie said dryly. ''This is not my idea of fun.''

''You'd rather jump into a tank with a pair of killer whales, right?'' Felipe teased.

''I'd take Biffy and Louise over Lawrence Richter and Tommy Walsh *any* day,'' Carrie said.

''To each his—or her—own,'' Felipe said with a smile. ''Will you be all right in here by yourself? I'd like to go look for Swick's office. He must have a desk or something, where he keeps a calendar.''

''I'll be fine,'' Carrie said, already flipping through the papers on the bed. She looked up. ''Don't go far, though.''

''I won't,'' he said. He moved toward her and kissed her, then disappeared into the darkness of the hall.

Swick's office was a disaster area. His desk was covered by a mountain of papers and files and scraps of envelopes and napkins with notes scribbled on them. Cardboard file boxes were everywhere, even on top of a state-of-the-art stereo system, even on top of a large-screen TV.

Felipe pulled down the shades and closed the curtains and switched on the desk lamp. Well aware of the time, well aware that they couldn't risk staying here too much longer, he grimly set to work, searching for something, *any*thing that would link Swick to Richter's organization.

Swick had a file on his desk for every case he'd worked on in the past—God, it must be the past three years. They seemed to be in no particular order, neither chronological nor alphabetical.

Underneath a two-and-a-half-year-old arson case, Felipe

found a desk calendar. It was mounted on a heavy marble stand, and there was a page devoted to each day of the week. It was open to the page dated January 3, which was more than two weeks ago, and probably the last date Swick had unearthed the calendar in this mess.

Quickly, Felipe flipped to January 20. Tomorrow's date. The date of Richter's meeting with his Captain Rat. There was something written on the calendar.

"Golf," it said. There was no mention of the time or location.

Was it some kind of code, or did it actually mean the game of golf? And if so, there were dozens of golf courses in St. Simone, dozens of possibilities for the game's—and the meeting's—location. Assuming, of course, that Swick was the Captain Rat he was looking for. Assuming that "golf" didn't mean simply golf.

One by one, Felipe opened the drawers of Swick's desk. They were as disorganized as the rest of the room. He quickly rummaged through them, but they appeared to be filled with files and papers even older than the ones on top of the police captain's desk.

He reached down to pull out the lower left drawer but it wouldn't open. He pulled harder, thinking it had jammed, but it still didn't budge. It was locked.

Using a letter opener he'd seen in the top center desk drawer, Felipe tried to jimmy the lock. He slipped the piece of metal in between the drawer and the frame, finally using it as a wedge and the butt of his gun as a hammer to splinter the wood and break the drawer open.

Pay dirt.

A manila envelope at the bottom of the drawer had "Salazar" scribbled across it in black marker.

Felipe took out the envelope and opened it.

An unmarked cassette tape fell into his hands. It was the only thing in the envelope, but Felipe was willing to bet it was all he needed. He quickly cleared the file boxes off the stereo, then popped the cassette into the tape player and turned the power on.

He hit the play button.

There were several moments of silence, then Lawrence Richter's voice came on, smooth and clearly recognizable.

"I've got a problem," he said. "A discipline problem."

"Tony and Steve," said Tommy Walsh's voice. "You want 'em snuffed. That's no problem."

"This is very difficult for me," Richter said. "Alfonse Mareidas has been a friend for a long time."

"Al knew his kid was as good as dead when word came through about the deal he and Dupree were making with the D.A.," Walsh said flatly. "If that had gone through, it would've taken down your entire westside operation. It wouldn't have touched you, but it would've been a mess. Al can't blame you for what you have to do."

"What *you* have to do," Richter said quietly.

"Of course," Walsh said.

"Make it quick and painless," Richter told him. "For Al's sake. But make a statement."

"With pleasure," Walsh said. "Consider Mareidas and Dupree permanently out of the picture."

"Have Julia send flowers to their families," Richter said, and the tape ended.

Yes.

Yes!

This tape was all the evidence Felipe needed to pin the Sandlot Murders on Richter and Walsh, and to clear his name. Now all he had to do was prove Donald Swick was Richter's Captain Rat. That was, unfortunately, easier said than done.

Felipe rewound the cassette tape and took it out of the tape player.

"Felipe!" He looked sharply to see Caroline standing in the doorway. "There's a car pulling into the driveway," she said, her eyes wide. "I saw lights, and—"

He stood up, stashing the tape in the back pocket of his jeans. "Let's get out of here," he said.

"I didn't find anything," she said as they ran down the hallway toward the kitchen door. "I didn't finish looking but—"

"I found a tape," Felipe told her. "A recording of Richter and Walsh planning the Sandlot Murders."

"My *God*," Carrie breathed.

Felipe saw it a fraction of a second too late. A backup laser alarm had come on, probably since the other system had been off-line longer than fifteen or so minutes. Caroline was in front of him, and she reached to pull the door open before he could stop her.

The opening door interrupted the laser beam and all hell broke loose. The alarm shrieked, a high-pitched, keening sound that attempted to shatter their eardrums and announce an attempted break-in to the surrounding square mile.

Felipe grabbed Caroline's hand and pulled her out the door.

Car headlights flashed in his face, blinding him.

"Freeze!" bellowed a voice over the alarm. Swick. It was Swick.

Felipe didn't stop running.

"I said freeze!"

Shielding Caroline with his body, he took her with him as he dived for the bushes.

The booming sound of a gun being fired drowned out for a moment the relentless sound of the alarm.

Then, "God, Chief, you might've hit the girl!" Swick cried.

"Radio for backup," Chief Earley's voice rasped. "We got that son of a bitch cornered now."

Branches and vines slapped at Felipe's arms and legs as he and Caroline scrambled down the slight incline separating Swick's property from his neighbor's yard.

Lights were going on all over the neighborhood.

Felipe tried to stick to the darkness at the edges of the yards. He could hear Caroline breathing hard. He could almost smell her fear. Or maybe it was his own fear he could smell. *Madre de Dios,* she could've been shot. She *still* could be shot.

"Can you swim?" she asked him, straining for air as they hit a stretch of darkened lawn and ran full out.

"Yes," he huffed. He could hear police sirens in the distance, lots of sirens, drawing closer. Man, maybe they *were* cornered....

"Let's head for the water," Caroline gasped. "For the ocean. The tide should be pulling toward the south. We can swim down the coast."

Hope burst like a flare inside him.

"Te amo," he cried. "I *love* you! Caroline, that's brilliant!"

Cutting hard to the left, they ran west, toward the Gulf. Felipe's leg was throbbing, drumming with pain again, but he ignored it. It didn't matter. Nothing else mattered. He could only think of getting Caroline to safety.

Around them, the sound of sirens was growing louder and louder.

Felipe could smell the ocean, see the glimmer of the surf in the darkness. They were close. They were so close. One more road to cross, one more neatly manicured yard and then they'd hit the beach....

With a squeal of tires, a police car pulled onto the street and braked to a stop, cutting them off from the ocean and escape.

Felipe jerked Caroline down with him, hard, into the darkness of some bushes. He could feel her heart racing, hear her ragged breathing.

"I'm in position," the police officer said. "There's no sign of anyone out here. Shall I move on?"

"Stay where you are," the radio speaker crackled. "Keep your weapon loaded and ready. Suspect is armed and dangerous. Repeat, armed and dangerous."

"What now?" Caroline breathed into his ear.

Felipe shifted his weight off his injured leg. "I'm going to surrender," he whispered.

"No!"

"While this guy is busy with me," he said, ignoring her vehement protest, "I want you to sneak across the street and make it down to the water. Are you sure you're a strong enough swimmer?"

"I won't do it," she said tightly. "I won't let you turn yourself in. You said yourself you won't stay alive more than a day in protective custody—"

He kissed her. "I'll find a way," he said. "I'll beat the odds."

"Felipe—"

"Caroline, I won't have them shooting at you!"

"And I won't let you sacrifice yourself for me!"

"Your safety is my priority," he hissed. "Don't make this harder than it has to be."

"If you give yourself up, mister," Caroline said, her head at that determined angle, chin held high, "I'm going in with you. We're sticking together."

She wasn't going to give in. She wouldn't back down.

Felipe swore silently. He was going to have to find another way.

She touched him gently on the face, a whisper of a caress on his cheek. Her blue-green eyes were colorless in the darkness. She looked otherworldly, angelic.

When she spoke, her voice was little more than a whisper. "*Te amo,* too, you know."

Chapter 17

Carrie kept running, holding tightly to Felipe's hand, splashing through the swampy underbrush.

They'd managed to creep away from the police car, crawling back the way they'd come. Carrie had hoped that they would make it to the water by cutting across the road farther down. But other police cars had arrived, their bright headlights slicing through the darkness, lighting both the street and the surrounding yards, herding the fugitives back, away from the ocean.

Dear Lord, let them reach the water.

Then Felipe froze, holding out an arm to stop her, listening hard in the darkness.

Sirens. She could hear sirens and shouting, and...

Dogs. Oh, God, *dogs*. Someone had brought dogs, trained to track by scent alone. They were baying and barking frantically in the distance.

Felipe was drenched with sweat and limping again. His leg had to be hurting. Hers ached from fatigue, and she didn't have a three-day-old bullet wound making things worse.

"Come on," he said, his voice hoarse, and somehow, *somehow*, he started running again.

They didn't make it more than fifty yards before they came up against a twelve-foot-high chain-link fence.

The dogs were getting closer, and Carrie could also hear the throbbing of a helicopter in the distance. She swore. A helicopter with a searchlight would be able to pick them out of the water, no problem.

If they ever made it into the water.

Felipe was thinking the same thing. "When we hit the ocean, we'll have to be ready to swim underwater," he said.

When? *If* was more like it. Carrie could smell the tang of the salt air, but the ocean was somewhere on the other side of this fence that was more than twice her height.

They moved along the fence. It stretched out seemingly forever into the darkness.

Carrie was all turned around. She'd lost her sense of direction. She had no idea where they were, except that the ocean was out of their reach. For all she knew, they'd been running in circles.

"Caroline," Felipe gasped, "do you have the access code to Sea Circus's security system?"

What? "Yeah," she said. "Why?"

And then it hit her. This fence was the fence that surrounded the perimeter of Sea Circus. Lord, she had no clue they'd come this far. If they kept going, kept following the fence, they'd hit one of the park's three entrances. She could punch in the code, open the gates and they'd be inside. There must be a hundred places to hide in the marine park. And the dogs wouldn't be allowed inside—they'd frighten and endanger the wildlife.

And then, there it was, the entrance, one hundred yards farther along the fence. They'd have to cross part of a parking lot to get there, but the lights were out, and in the darkness they wouldn't be seen. At this part of the park, a huge wooden barrier was behind the chain-link security fence. Once they were inside, no one would be able to see them.

A police car passed on the street, going seventy miles an hour, heading up toward Swick's house.

Felipe ran across the lot, bent nearly double. Carrie followed close behind.

She pushed the numbers of the alarm override into the control panel. It flashed green. Thank the Lord! She entered the numbers to unlock the gate, and it swung open with a soft *whoosh*.

Quickly they went in through the open gate, and Carrie keyed in the numbers to close the gate and reactivate the alarm system. The light flashed yellow, then red, then yellow, then red.

What the hell…?

Then all over the park, bright spotlights came on, and sirens began to wail as the alarm went off.

"I did it right!" Carrie cried. "I *know* I did it right! Someone must've changed the access code!"

Felipe grabbed her hand, and again they were running, this time across the brightly lit marine park.

He was heading toward the fence that separated the park from the beach below. He was trying to reach the ocean and the escape it promised, despite the threat of helicopters and their searchlights.

But they weren't even halfway there when Carrie saw a police car skid onto the beach, tires sending showers of sand behind it. Felipe saw it, too, and swerved to the left, going deeper into the park.

All around them, outside the fence, police cars were pulling up, tires squealing. Felipe went around the side of the main aquarium tank and stopped for breath, holding Carrie tightly against him.

"You've got to hide," he said. "This is it, Caroline. They've got me. Let me at least save you—"

"We've been through this once already," Carrie said sharply. "Nothing's changed."

"Yes, it has," he said. "They know where we are. We're trapped."

"You hide with me," she said, "or I don't hide at all."

His hand was shaking as he pushed his hair back from his face. "Dammit, Caroline—"

"I know a place they'll never think to look," she said.

Taking his hand, she pulled him along with her faster and faster across the park. And then she stopped—directly in front of the killer whale tank.

The killer whale tank.

Caroline wanted them to hide in the killer whale tank.

Felipe would've laughed if he had had the time.

Outside the park, Felipe could hear the sound of the police, lots and *lots* of police, so many that he could hear them over the shrieking of the alarm. They were getting ready to come inside. There wasn't any time left.

"This is nuts," he said.

"No, it's not," Carrie said. "There's a place in the tank that can't be seen even from inside the downstairs underwater viewing room. It's a place that's covered by the planks of a walkway. We can stay at the surface, holding on to the edge of the tank. No one will ever find us."

"Except the killer whales," Felipe said, letting her pull him into a door marked Park Personnel Only.

"Move slowly and calmly inside the tank, and everything will be fine," Carrie said, leading him up a set of stairs and through a control room that contained sound equipment and a microphone for the marine show. A small window overlooked the tank. The counter in front of it was covered with piles of cassette tapes. "Biffy and Louise are very gentle."

"Caroline—"

"Trust me," she said, squeezing his hand. "It's your turn to trust *me*."

She pulled him out onto the boardwalk that ran along the edge of the tank. It was slick with water from the waves and foam splashing up onto it. Felipe's eyes widened at the sight of these two enormous beasts who were leaping out of the water, jaws open and big teeth bared.

Gentle? These creatures were *gentle?*

"They're just upset by the noise," Carrie said. "Come on." Sitting down, she dangled her feet in the water, then slipped over the side and into the tank.

Felipe heard the main gate burst open.

Carrie was watching him, holding out her hand to him.

Trust me.

She'd trusted him when he pulled her down into that crawl space at the beach house. She'd trusted him with her life ever since that fateful meeting at the restaurant. If she said the killer whales were gentle, then the killer whales were gentle.

Felipe took the cassette tape from his pocket and held it up so that Caroline could see it. "I can't take this into the water," he said. "I'm going to hide it."

She smiled. "In plain view," she said.

"That's right," he said.

"Hurry."

He hurried. Back inside the control room, he put his tape toward the far end of the counter, on the bottom of one of the piles of tapes.

Caroline was still waiting for him at the edge of the pool. Behind her, the killer whales belly flopped into the water, creating a maelstrom.

"Quickly," she said.

Felipe went into the water, boots and backpack and all. The water was cold, colder than he expected. And his clothes and boots weighed him down.

At least the alarms were muffled under the water. Yet to a marine animal used to quiet stillness, they must have been terribly loud and confusing.

Carrie swam in front of him and he opened his eyes and followed her. With her long, blond hair floating around her, she looked like some sea creature, a mermaid or sea sprite, luring him down to his death.

But that wasn't true. She was luring him *away* from his death and—

Felipe came face-to-face with a killer whale and froze. It opened its mouth as if to snap him in two, yet still he couldn't move. His lungs were bursting from lack of oxygen as he stared at its beady little eye.

And then, suddenly, Caroline was there, next to him.

She touched the *Orca,* gave it some kind of signal, then took Felipe's hand and pulled him toward the surface, safely underneath the boardwalk.

Felipe grabbed the side of the tank and drew in a deep, clean breath, gasping and filling his lungs again and again with precious air. Caroline was there next to him, holding him, pushing his wet hair back from his face, murmuring words of encouragement.

But no sooner had he started to catch his breath than the water in the tank started sloshing around again. Waves slapped him in the face.

"What's going on...?" he gasped.

Carrie pressed her mouth against his ear. "I told Biffy to keep on jumping into the air," she said. "It's one of the moves we've trained them to do. It's featured in the Sea Circus show. It makes them look very ferocious."

"They don't need to *try* to look ferocious," Felipe muttered, shivering as the cool night breeze hit his wet head and face. He looked up at the boardwalk. It wasn't more than eighteen inches overhead, slick and dripping with moisture. It seemed dark and cramped and confining. "This doesn't bother you?" he asked.

Caroline shook her head. "Not as long as I'm in the water," she said. "As long as I have space to move my arms and legs, as long as I don't feel restricted, I'm fine."

Across the park, the alarms were shut off. The sudden silence was odd. It felt heavy and threatening.

"You did the right thing when Biffy approached you," Caroline said almost silently, her mouth against his ear again. "You didn't move quickly or panic."

Felipe had to smile. "I didn't move quickly because I couldn't move at all," he whispered back into her ear. "I believe what I did is called 'being frozen with fear.'"

"You're that afraid," Carrie asked, "yet you'd get into a tank with them?"

"I trust you," Felipe said, pulling back his head to look into her eyes.

Her hair was plastered against her head, and beads of water were caught in her long eyelashes. She looked so beautiful, so delicate, so small and fragile. She was all of those things, yet she was also the toughest, most determined fighter he'd ever met. He would have quit twice already tonight. True, he would have quit purely to save Caroline's life, to give her a chance to get away. But she wouldn't give up; she wouldn't give in.

So here he was, in a killer whale tank, praying harder than he'd prayed in a long time that somehow, some way they'd pull this off.

Caroline's arms were around him, helping him keep his head above the surface. Even though he was holding on to the side of the tank, the water dragged at his jeans and boots and the backpack, pulling him under.

Felipe could feel the muscles in her arms. Man, she *was* strong. She might've been little, but she could more than pull her weight.

She leaned forward to kiss him. Her lips, her nose, her face were cold against his, but her mouth was warm, and he closed his eyes, losing himself in her sweetness.

But then she pulled back, and he heard footsteps on the boardwalk above.

Carrie motioned for him to take a deep breath and sink beneath the water. All he had to do was let go of the side, and he sank nearly to the bottom of the tank. Carrie reached for his hands, and her added buoyancy pulled him back up a bit.

With her hair a cloud of gold around her face, she *did* look like a mermaid. A mermaid in overalls. She smiled at him, and right at that moment, he loved her so much, he could have wept.

Te amo, too, she said. She loved him, too.

Somehow she'd figured out the translation from Spanish to English. Somehow he'd given himself away.

Felipe's lungs started to hurt, to burn, yet still he and Caroline stayed underneath the water. He dragged his gaze away from her face and looked up to the surface of the water. As he watched, the shadowy shapes he could barely see through the slats of the boardwalk moved away.

Carrie was watching, too, and as he looked back at her, she nodded, gesturing with her head toward the surface. She helped pull him up toward the air, and silently, they surfaced.

Felipe could hear Captain Swick's voice as well as Chief

Earley's. He recognized Captain Patterson as well as a number of detectives from the Fourth Precinct.

And then a new voice joined them—Jim Keegan's.

"The dogs have picked up a fresh scent outside the fence, south of the park," he said in his familiar New York accent. "Our theory is that they worked their way around the perimeter, climbing along the chain link of the fence, clinging to it, you know, so the dogs couldn't track them along the ground."

Swick swore long and hard.

"That's why we lost their trail for so long," Jim said. "But the tracker thinks we've picked it up now. We've wasted a lot of time in here, sir. They're out there making good their escape. Shouldn't we get moving?"

"All right," Swick said. "Let's head south. Shut this place down."

The voices moved away.

Felipe turned to find Caroline watching him, her eyes wide. "Someone intentionally led those dogs off the track," she whispered.

"Jim Keegan," Felipe said. "Diego. He came through for me."

"He must really believe in you," Carrie said quietly.

Jim wasn't the only one who believed in him. Caroline believed in him, too.

Jim's loyalty wasn't a surprise—after all, he'd been Felipe's friend for years. But only a few days ago, Caroline had been ready to run away from him, ready to think the worst. Now, not only was she willing to risk her life to help him, but she trusted him enough to let herself fall in love with him.

It was exhilarating, and terrifying.

She loved him.

It was enough to make him feel as if he owned the world—if he lived in the kind of world that could be owned. But he didn't. His world, his life, owned him.

Caroline loved him, but he could give her nothing in return. Nothing but heartache and misery.

As Felipe listened, the police officers left the marine park. The gate was closed, the alarm system reactivated, and one by one, the lights were shut off, leaving only dim security lighting up and running.

Still, he clung to the edge of the killer whale tank, one arm around Caroline, listening and waiting, until they were sure they were alone.

Chapter 18

There were towels in the control room.

Carrie stripped down to her bathing suit and dried herself off. It was chilly tonight. She took an extra towel to dry her hair, shivering slightly at the cold concrete under her feet and the coolness of the air.

Felipe was quietly taking off his own clothes, wringing out his jeans and laying them out to dry with the other things that had been in his backpack.

He glanced at her in the dim light. His eyes were unreadable, but really, what did she expect? They'd just done a triathlon—running, swimming and confessing their innermost feelings. None of it could have been easy for him—certainly not knowing that she'd managed to translate his "untranslatable" Spanish phrase.

Te amo.

She'd suspected its meaning. She'd guessed and she'd hoped, but it wasn't until they were running for their lives that he'd said it again and she'd known.

Te amo. I *love* you.

As Carrie watched, Felipe stripped naked, quickly drying

himself off and tying a towel around his waist. But still he didn't say a single word.

"How's your leg?" she finally asked.

He lifted the edge of the towel, turning to show her the wound. It looked angry and sore. "The salt water from the tank stung," he said. "But I'm okay. I thought maybe the stitches opened up from all that running, but they didn't." He looked over at her again. "Are you all right?"

She nodded. "You probably want to get out of here right away," she said. "We'll need something to wear. My wet suit's hanging by the dolphin tank, but there's probably one in here that'll fit you. George's or Simon's or—"

"No," he said. "No, we're in no hurry. I'd be willing to bet Tommy Walsh and his men are somewhere on the other side of that fence, on the off chance we're still in here. No, we'll stay here tonight and leave in the rush of the crowd tomorrow."

Walsh. Outside the fence, waiting for them. Carrie shivered again, wrapping the towel more tightly around her. "Won't Walsh still be watching for us in the morning?" she asked.

"Yes," Felipe said. "He probably will. And so will the police—particularly after they don't find us tonight."

Carrie was silent, letting his words digest. "So," she finally said, glancing up to find him still watching her, "really, what you're saying is we're not out of danger."

He shook his head. "I'm sorry, but no, we're not." He raked his wet hair back, out of his eyes. "I'm not going to lie to you, Caroline. There's a good chance we won't make it out of this park tomorrow," he said. "If Walsh is smart—and he is—he'll make arrangements for a sharpshooter to be near every entrance. And he'll have people watching for us—for me. It'll be a race to see who spots me first—Walsh's men or the police."

It didn't matter *who* found him first. Either way he'd be dead. He'd be killed immediately if it was Walsh who spotted him first, or he'd be killed later that day or the next if it was the police.

"Caroline." She looked up into the velvet blackness of his eyes. "I want to play that tape for you."

She shook her head. "There's no tape player," she said.

He stared around the room. "All this equipment, and there's no tape deck?"

"It's locked up in the main office," she said. She gestured around the room. "All this other stuff is underwater recording equipment and cameras. It doesn't have a lot of value in the local pawnshops. The tape decks, however, kept walking away."

He swore, then apologized. "I wanted you to hear this tape," he said. "It's a conversation between Lawrence Richter and Tommy Walsh. Richter orders Walsh to kill Mareidas and Dupree. It proves my innocence."

Carrie nodded, gazing steadily into his eyes. "I believe you," she said quietly. "I don't need to hear it."

His eyes filled with tears. He reached for her then, pulling her into his arms and holding her tightly against him.

This time tomorrow, Felipe could very well be dead. That wasn't a crazy, wild thought. It wasn't an extremely unlikely worst-case scenario. It was an honest-to-God possibility.

Carrie felt tears burning her own eyes, and she couldn't stop herself from speaking. She was well aware she might never have another chance.

"I do love you," she said.

She felt him draw in a deep breath as if her words had somehow stung.

"I'm sorry if you don't want to hear that," she whispered, fighting another rush of tears. "But I want you to know how I feel."

"I heard you when you said it the first time," he murmured. He kissed her gently on the lips, then pulled back to look down into her eyes and smile. It was shaky, but it *was* a smile. "Of course, you'd have every right to assume I'd have trouble with the translation."

Carrie stared up at him. He was making a joke. He had somehow found the strength to tease about something that he found so desperately serious and frightening as *love*.

"I'm not asking for anything in return," she told him softly.

He looked away at her words, unable to meet her eyes as she continued in a quiet voice.

"I know when you said you loved me—*te amo*—you probably only meant that you loved me at that moment," Carrie said.

He would've interrupted her, but she stopped him with a gentle finger against his lips.

"That's okay," she said. "It's more than I ever expected. Don't say things you think I want to hear, just because you think you won't be around to keep your promises."

Felipe shook his head. "I'm not going to die tomorrow," he said. "They're not going to catch me, and I'm not going to let them near you. We're going to get out of this park alive."

"Felipe, you just said—"

"That I wasn't going to lie to you. I know, but you've reminded me, *cara*, I've got a powerful reason to stay alive."

His hair had fallen forward over his face again, and Carrie pushed it back. He pressed his cheek into her hand, then reached up and moved her fingers to his mouth, planting a gentle kiss in her palm.

He loved her. Carrie had to believe that he loved her, but he didn't—or couldn't—say the words. Still, she could see it in his eyes as he gazed down at her.

She wanted to believe that they would survive tomorrow simply because Felipe wanted them to. But the real truth was, all they could be absolutely certain of ever having was right here and right now.

"Potato chips, popcorn or pretzels?" Caroline asked.

Felipe stared pensively at the row of vending and gumball machines. "How much change do we have?" he asked.

"Enough for two bags and one can of soda," she said, "with a quarter left over."

Felipe shook his head in disgust. He had nearly three thousand dollars in his wallet—in big bills. The smallest he had was a twenty. The bill changer took nothing larger than a five. "I'm hungry."

"I'm hungry, too. We *could* break into a machine," Carrie suggested.

"And have the police out here first thing to investigate?" Felipe said. "No thanks." He smiled at her. "We're going to have to distract ourselves until the concession stand opens in the morning, no?"

Caroline glanced at him over her shoulder, a small smile playing at the corners of her mouth.

She looked incredible. She was wearing her wet suit—a navy blue, form-fitting unitard that hugged her curves like a second skin. It zipped up the front and she wore it slightly open at the neck. Her hair was nearly dry, and it hung, shiny and blond, around her shoulders, down between her shoulder blades.

She looked capable and in control and utterly, totally feminine.

"Potato chips, popcorn, or pretzels?" Caroline asked patiently.

"I'll have the swordfish steak, grilled in lemon butter, with a baked potato and a house salad," Felipe said. "And I'd like to see the wine list, please."

Carrie laughed. "We have a very nice root beer, dating from December."

"If the lady recommends it, how can I refuse? My goal is to wine and dine her with this gourmet meal in the hopes of finding out exactly what she is wearing underneath that wet suit."

"Aha," Caroline said. "A meal meant to seduce. In that case, pretzels, my favourite."

She put the money into one of the machines and pushed the buttons that made two tiny bags of pretzels fall out.

"Shall we dine alfresco?" she asked, taking the root beer from the soda machine. She handed him the can of soda and the last of their change—a solitary quarter.

Felipe knew exactly what to do with it.

In addition to the snack and soda machines, there was a row of six or eight gumball and candy machines, many of which held inexpensive toys in clear plastic bubbles. One boasted action-hero pencil erasers while another had cartoon-show tattoos. A third contained a collection of cheap plastic rings.

"For such a fine meal, it's only fitting that the lady be properly adorned with fine jewelry," he said solemnly, dropping the quarter into the slot and turning the handle. One of the plastic bubbles dropped down. He flipped up the hatch and took out the bubble. Opening it with a flourish, he presented Caroline with a bright green plastic ring.

It was small, but it fit almost perfectly on her ring finger.

She looked up at him, her sea green eyes wide.

And suddenly, this was no longer a game they were playing. Suddenly, this was real. She was in love with him, and God, he'd just given her a *ring*.

"I'll keep it forever," she whispered.

"It won't last forever," he warned her, so afraid he was going to break her heart. He felt his own heart already start to crack. "The plastic will break."

"Not if I take good care of it," she said. Her chin went up with that determined tilt that was becoming so familiar to him.

"It's not worth the trouble," he said. God, he wished the words he'd spoken weren't true. He wished he had a different life, a life that he could share with her. "It's worth nothing."

"I know what it's worth," she said quietly. "I know exactly what it's worth."

Carrie woke before dawn.

Felipe was still asleep, stretched out on the lumpy sofa bed in the dolphin trainer's room. He stirred and reached for her, wrapping his arms around her, holding her tightly.

Carrie felt safe in his arms, but she knew that that safety was only temporary. It wouldn't be long now before they'd have to wake up, get out of bed and get ready to face this day—and Tommy Walsh and his sharpshooters along with the entire St. Simone Police Department.

Last night, Felipe had called Jewel collect from the pay phones by the concession stand. She'd told Felipe that she had gone to see his brother.

According to what Rafe had heard, Lawrence Richter had

raised the price on Felipe's head to a cool million, and Tommy
Walsh had every available man out and looking for him and
the angel—in other words, Carrie. The scuttlebutt was going
around that things were going to get *really* intense. And word
was spreading—if anyone sees Felipe Salazar, hit the dirt because bullets are gonna be right behind him. Rafe told Jewel
to make sure Felipe knew what he was up against.

What *they* were up against, Carrie thought.

Jewel had talked Rafe into offering his halfway house to
Felipe as a safe haven. That was good to know. That was *very*
good to know.

Felipe hadn't done much more than report the contents of
his conversation to Carrie, but she knew that Rafe's support—
no matter how grudgingly given—was important to him.

Felipe had also told Jewel about the tape that incriminated
Richter and Walsh in the Sandlot Murders, told her he'd hidden
it underneath the sofa bed in the dolphin trainer's room here
at Sea Circus. He'd told her to give this information to Jim
Keegan, to deliver the message in person and written on a piece
of paper so that no one could overhear.

And he'd told her to ask Jim to call him at Rafe's at one
Thursday afternoon—*this* afternoon.

Richter's meeting with Captain Rat was to be at 3:30—two
and a half hours later.

They were running out of time.

Felipe stirred again, and she could tell by the change in his
breathing that he was awake.

"Good morning," she whispered.

"Is it morning?" he asked. It was still dark outside.

"Almost," she said. "It's nearly five."

"What time does the park open?" he murmured, running
one hand lightly along the curve of her hip.

"Nine," she said, closing her eyes. "But the staff starts
showing up around six-thirty or seven."

"Are you hungry?" he asked.

Carrie smiled. "Starved. And it's another four hours 'til the
concession stands open."

"Hmm," he said. "I don't suppose it's any use, trying to distract you...."

Carrie turned to look at him. His eyes were half-closed, the lower part of his face was covered by a day's growth of dark stubble, and his hair was rumpled. He looked deliciously sleepy. He smiled, a slow smile that promised neither of them was even going to *think* about food—at least not for a while.

Chapter 19

There were four uniformed policemen, and God only knows how many plainclothes detectives, at each of Sea Circus's gates. They examined the faces of the people leaving the park, searching for Felipe Salazar—"Rogue Cop."

Felipe checked the clock over the main entrance. Eleven-thirty. Up to this point, there had only been dribs and drabs leaving the marine park. According to Caroline, the bigger groups wouldn't start to leave until after lunch—not much before noon at the earliest.

He scanned the parking lot outside the main entrance. This was definitely the way to leave Sea Circus. Both of the other gates had obvious places outside for a sniper to hide. This gate had only the flatness of the already-crowded parking lot, no trees or bushes or cover of any kind except for the rows of cars.

Of course, that also meant there'd be no place for Felipe and Carrie to hide, either, once they were outside the gate.

Caroline sat near him, cross-legged in the grass, off to the side of the crowded walkways. She was wearing Jewel's over-alls over her bathing suit, with her pants rolled up to just under her knees. She'd put her hair up into a braid rather than the ponytail she usually wore. He'd bought her a pair of sunglasses and a baseball cap at the gift shop—there were quite a few of her co-workers around who could identify her—and she wore them with a certain attitude that made her look like a young teenager.

Watching her, Felipe had an idea.

"Those school buses in the parking lot," he said, sitting down next to her. "Did you happen to notice if any of them carried a group of high school students?"

Caroline bit her lower lip, thinking hard. "I saw some really little kids—first-graders maybe, and some older kids—ten-year-olds." She turned to gaze out through the fence toward the parking lot. "There's an awful lot of buses today—one of them *must* be for a group of high school kids." She looked back at Felipe. "Why?"

"We're going to leave with them," he said.

"If they're not seniors, if they're younger, we'll stand out," Carrie said. He couldn't see her eyes behind her sunglasses, but he knew they were serious.

"Cross your fingers," Felipe said. He leaned forward and kissed her lightly. "So far we've been lucky."

She lay back against him, her head in his lap.

"I'm scared to death," she admitted, peering through her dark glasses to look up at him. "We're sitting out here in the open like this, and I keep thinking someone's going to see me, someone's going to recognize me. Or *you*. Lord, your face has been all over the papers and the TV."

"People see what they expect to see," Felipe said. "They don't expect to see St. Simone's most wanted sitting on the lawn near the main entrance to Sea Circus next to the dolphin trainer. They expect to see some Hispanic kid from the 'hood and his pretty girlfriend sitting around in the shade, wasting time. So that's what they see." He touched the side of her face, stroking her cheek lightly with his knuckles. Her skin was so soft, so delicate.

"Maybe we should separate," Carrie said. "Meet back at Rafe's by one o'clock."

''No.'' The word came out with more force than he'd intended, and he made himself smile to soften its impact. ''We stay together.''

She was quiet, and he intertwined her fingers with his.

''I'm still scared,'' she finally whispered.

Felipe nodded. He was scared, too.

Looking up into the vast blueness of the sky, he prayed. He prayed for Caroline's safety and for his own successful escape. And, failing that, he prayed for the ability to accept his death, to die at peace, knowing he had lived his life as best he possibly could.

But had he?

He couldn't help but wonder how differently his life might've turned out had he gone back to Sea Circus and introduced himself to Caroline Brooks that day after he'd locked her in the trunk of her car.

''Hello, my name is Felipe Salazar and I'm really a detective with the Fourth Precinct. Will you forgive me…and have dinner with me?''

She would have. Maybe not that night, but eventually she would have forgiven him.

And, as surely as she'd done over the past few days, she would have stolen her way into his heart.

And then…

What if…

What if Felipe had said no thank you to the assignment to bring down Richter? What if he had said it was time to take some greatly needed—and greatly earned—vacation time? What if he had spent that time, a month, maybe two, with Caroline, living a regular, *normal* life? What if he'd taken her out to see movies and go dancing? What if he'd moved his toothbrush and an extra change of clothes into her apartment? And what if…what if he had *liked* it?

What if his job had posed no threat, no danger? What if he had stayed away from undercover assignments for a while? What if he had transferred out of vice?

He could imagine this Felipe, this other Felipe, spending much more than twenty-five cents on a ring that was neither green nor plastic. He could imagine this other Felipe taking Caroline Brooks someplace unbearably romantic for dinner, and after sitting down at the small, secluded table, he would take her hand and gaze into her eyes and...

He could imagine their wedding day. Diego would stand up for him, slap him on the back and embrace him, happy that his best friend had also found what he and his wife, Emily, shared.

Felipe could imagine saving their money and buying a house close to Caroline's beloved ocean. He would plant flowers in the yard and bring her one every evening. And every night, he'd make sweet, perfect love to her and sleep with her in his arms.

He could imagine her round and heavy with his child. A familiar flame of fear flickered through him and he squelched it. Small women married tall men all the time. Perhaps the baby would need to be born by cesarean section, but perhaps not. Caroline was strong and tough. Either way, he'd see that she received the best possible medical attention and all the tender loving care she could possibly need.

Time moved faster in his mind, the years blending together, their children growing tall and strong. Sons he could be proud of, daughters with his dark hair and eyes and their mother's beautiful smile. His life became a blur of happiness and love, a blend of passion and tenderness, a mosaic of laughter and song.

Felipe stared up into the blue, blue sky, allowing himself to live that life, the life he had not chosen.

The life he never would have chosen—because he never would have turned down the assignment to put Richter away. He knew damn well that if he hadn't taken on Richter's organization, no one else would have. And he couldn't have lived with himself, knowing that such a man continued to run free, hurting innocent people.

But...

There had been something else, some part of his fantasy...

He closed his eyes, trying to rewind his daydream until at last he touched upon it.

What if he had transferred out of vice?

Felipe sat up suddenly, and Caroline, who'd been dozing, jumped.

"What?" she said. "Is something wrong?"

"No, shh," he said. "It's all right."

But his heart was pounding. What if he transferred out of vice? Not had—*did?* What if he did? Damn, if he lived through this mess, he'd *have* to transfer. There wouldn't be a crime lord or a drug dealer this side of Florida who wouldn't recognize his face. However he looked at it, he was washed up as an undercover detective for the vice squad—unless he moved to another town, another state. And he couldn't see doing that. St. Simone was his home.

He *would* transfer out of vice.

And *what if* he transferred to a less dangerous job, one that would pose less of a threat to Caroline, one where revenge and counterhits weren't part of the norm?

Jim Keegan had done it. He'd left vice and was happy with his new job. He was still making a difference by being a police detective.

Or hell, who said Felipe had to be a detective? He could transfer to youth services, follow in his mentor's, Jorge Gamos's, hard-to-fill footsteps.

The possibilities were endless.

He looked down at Caroline. She was watching him, concern on her face.

What if…? What *if?*

"What's wrong?" she asked.

He didn't know how to answer. He didn't know where to start. But when he opened his mouth, the words that came out were the words that he'd been unable to speak for so long. "I love you," he said simply.

She was quiet, just gazing up at him.

"Do you think…" he started to say. He cleared his throat and began again. "Do you think, after this is over…"

"Yes," she said, no hesitation in her voice.

Felipe had to smile. "You don't even know what I'm asking," he said. "How do you know I wasn't going to ask you to spend four solid weeks with me making mad, passionate love?''

She grinned back at him. ''Well, *that's* an easy yes.''

She took off her sunglasses and he marveled at the love he could see in her beautiful eyes.

''I want to spend time with you after this is over,'' he said quietly, seriously. ''I want to find out if you'll still love me without all the intrigue, without all the danger.''

There was another big if here—an if they both weren't bothering to mention: if, after this was over, Felipe and Caroline were both still alive.

But Caroline was thinking about it. He could see it in her eyes.

Death. His death. Her death.

The possibility was very real.

''Are you asking me to dinner or to move in with you?'' Caroline asked. She was trying desperately to ignore the shadow of the Grim Reaper that was hanging over them.

Her words caught him off guard. Move in with him? His mother would have a heart attack. His father would turn over in his grave. But Felipe hadn't meant dinner, either. What *had* he meant?

Felipe knew what he meant—he just couldn't say the words. But the thought that after today he might not be alive to speak loosened his tongue.

''I'm asking,'' he said slowly, ''for you to think about… considering the possibility of…marrying me. Taking my name, bearing my children.''

God, he wanted that so much. He wanted that life he'd imagined, that sunlight and laughter. He wanted the warmth of Caroline's love forever.

Except…who was he kidding? The odds were that he was going to die. Tommy Walsh, or one of his men, was going to blow a hole in his head and that would be that. No marriage, no children, no laughter.

He'd have the forever—in the form of eternal rest.

And Caroline… God, Walsh would kill her, too.

Felipe closed his eyes, unable to stand the sight of the hope that was blooming on Caroline's face.

God give him the strength to die gracefully.

But Felipe knew with a powerful sense of certainty that if in the course of the next few hours he were to leave this world, he'd go out kicking and screaming and fighting every step of the way.

At seven minutes after twelve, Felipe could hear them coming. At least three busloads of teens, ranging in age from fifteen to eighteen, were heading directly toward the Sea Circus main entrance. He hastily rose to his feet.

Caroline sat up, and he held out a hand to help her up. Still holding on to her, he led her down the sidewalk toward the sound of the shouting, rap music and laughter.

There were nearly a hundred kids, wearing a hundred different, brightly colored shirts and jeans and caps. They were carrying backpacks and purses and listening to boom boxes and Walkman stereos. They were talking—all at once—to each other, at each other.

Felipe stood with Carrie in the middle of the sidewalk and let the teenagers surround them. Like a herd of wild horses, the kids parted and flowed around them.

Then Felipe turned and began walking toward the entrance, in the same direction and at the same pace. It was crowded and someone jostled Carrie. He looped his arm around her, pulling her closer to him.

His mouth was dry and his eyes were drawn to the big clock that hung above the main gate.

Nine minutes after twelve.

Were these the last minutes of his life?

Around them, none of the teens seemed to notice that there were strangers in their midst. And if they noticed, no one cared.

As they approached the gate and the watching policemen, Felipe let his hair fall forward into his eyes. *Please, God, let this work.* He didn't want to die. He didn't want Caroline to die. Without even looking at her, he could feel her fear. She gripped his arm even tighter.

"I love you," he breathed into her ear. "Whatever happens, I love you. Don't forget that."

"My answer is yes," she whispered back.

He glanced at her questioningly.

She explained. "I thought about it, and yes, I'll marry you."

Felipe laughed in disbelief. "Caroline—"

"Stay alive," she said, gazing into his eyes. "Whatever happens, stay alive."

He turned and kissed her on the lips.

Was that their last kiss? Maybe.

She was thinking the same thing; he could see it in her eyes. She clung to him, but he gently pulled away from her to pass through a revolving door made of metal bars. It was a one-way door—exit only. He turned, waiting for her to follow him.

There were police officers ten feet away, staring hard at the back of his neck.

Please, God…

Caroline came through the door and her smile was an explosion of sunshine. "Come on, give me a piggyback ride, Carlos!" she called out, loud enough for the watching police officers to hear. She pulled her cap off her head and shook her hair free from its braid.

Felipe barely had time to brace himself before she launched herself up and onto his back. Laughing, she clung to him, and he forced himself to smile and laugh, too. They were just a couple of kids having some fun.

Caroline leaned her head forward over Felipe's shoulder, and her long, shiny hair covered part of his face. With Caroline on his back, Felipe walked past the officers. They didn't give him a second glance.

And then they were in the parking lot. They were outside of Sea Circus. They were past the police. Now they only had to worry about Tommy Walsh.

Only worry about Walsh. The statement was a paradox.

Felipe felt the hair rise on the back of his neck as he imagined the sight of a long-range rifle aimed at his head. Every one of his senses was on edge.

He could only pray that if he was hit, Caroline would have

the sense to get away from him, to get down, stay out of range and flee to safety.

As the river of teenagers approached the waiting school buses, Felipe pulled Caroline out of the crowd. They ducked down behind a row of cars.

Carrie's eyes were bright and she was breathing hard. "We made it," she said.

"So far," he said, searching the surrounding cars for a model that would be easy to hot-wire.

An ancient white Volkswagen Rabbit bearing the bumper sticker that read I Love Lee had been parked with its windows open. Felipe opened the door and, on a whim, searched under the floor mats. Caroline slipped into the passenger seat.

There was no key under the mats. He'd have to do this the hard way. Or the not-so-hard way, he realized, seeing a set of keys dangling from the ignition.

"Do you think they *want* the car to be stolen?" Carrie asked.

Felipe started the engine, then tried to roll up the windows. It soon became obvious that there were no windows to be rolled up. The driver's-side door didn't even shut properly. It had to be held closed with a piece of wire.

"Could be," he said.

Still, the old car ran smoothly. Felipe pulled it out of the Sea Circus lot and onto the main road.

The cars he could see in his rearview mirror looked innocuous enough. Just the same, he couldn't shake the feeling that Tommy Walsh was out there somewhere, following them.

This had been too easy. Too simple.

And when dealing with Tommy Walsh, nothing was *ever* simple.

Chapter 20

Highboy answered the door at Rafe's halfway house.

He didn't say a word, but he moved impossibly quickly for a man of his girth, throwing wide the door, pulling them both inside and slamming it shut again.

Carrie watched in silence as Highboy fastened every lock and bolt that was on that door. He would have let the alligators loose in the moat and raised the drawbridge if he could have.

When he turned to them, he finally spoke. "I will take you upstairs to Raphael's apartment," he said in an oddly high voice. "The fewer who see you here, the better."

Silently, they followed the heavy man up the stairs. He knocked lightly on the apartment door, and Rafe opened it. He was wearing only a pair of jeans. Carrie tried not to stare at the large dragon tattoo that nearly covered his upper right arm or the ragged scar that sliced across his chest.

"Well, well," Rafe said, "if it isn't the walking million-dollar lottery ticket and the blond angel." He stepped back, so they could come inside. "Come on in. They're talking about you on the news again."

The TV was on, and sure enough, there was a picture of Felipe on the screen behind the news anchor.

"…latest word from the precinct is that the ballistic reports show it was, indeed, Salazar's police-issue handgun that killed Tony Mareidas and Steve Dupree last week in the downtown sandlot. In addition to this late-breaking news, a copy of a videotape that was delivered anonymously to the police several days ago has been released to us. On this tape, which is clearly dated the same evening as the slayings, Detective Salazar can be seen holding Mareidas and Dupree at gunpoint. Let's look at that tape."

Carrie sat down on the sofa, her eyes on the screen. Behind her, Rafe and Felipe were silent as they, too, watched the news report.

The anchor's face disappeared, to be replaced by the grainy footage from a home video camera. The tape showed three men coming out of an unmarked door in an unidentifiable city alleyway.

The television studio had enhanced the videotape, brightening the area around two of the men's faces. Even without the enhancement, it was clear they were Tony Mareidas and Steve Dupree. The videotape was frozen in place, and the station superimposed clear, labeled photos of the two men in the corners of the screen. Yes, those men were definitely Mareidas and Dupree.

Then the tape continued to roll and the third man turned. He had a gun aimed at the two other men, and he was, indeed, Felipe Salazar. The cheekbones, the hair, the set of his shoulders were instantly recognizable. The hard set to his mouth, however, was not. Still, it *was* Felipe.

"What is this videotape?" Rafe demanded, voicing the doubt that was flooding through Carrie. "Man, you said you had nothing to do with these murders."

Felipe shook his head. "This video was taken months ago, back when Mareidas and Dupree first got into trouble. They came to see Richter, but Richter wouldn't even talk to them. I escorted them out of the building. I walked them to their cars, and that was that."

"The date on it says it was made last week," Rafe said, his doubt rapidly turning to disbelief. "Have you *lied* to me, little brother?"

"No." Felipe answered his brother's question, but his eyes were on Carrie, begging her to trust him, imploring her to keep her faith in him. "I didn't kill those men. Tommy Walsh killed them. The proof is on an audiotape I found at Captain Swick's house."

"Where is this tape?" Rafe pressed. "Play it for me."

"It's hidden at Sea Circus," Felipe said.

"Did you hear it?" Rafe asked Carrie.

Wordlessly, she shook her head.

"Perfect," Rafe said sardonically. "There's a tape that clears your name, only you're the only one who's heard it, no? Sounds a little too convenient if you ask me."

"Why do you doubt me?" Felipe asked quietly.

Rafe gestured toward the television. "I see with my own eyes that you were with these men, right before they died."

"That tape was made in October," Felipe said evenly. "I did *not* kill those men."

Carrie moistened her dry lips. "Would you tell us if you had?" she asked. "Us," she'd said, not "me." She was siding with his brother.

He couldn't hide the disappointment in his eyes. "Ah, *cara,* don't *you* believe me?"

"Would you tell us?" she persisted.

He shook his head with a laugh that held not a breath of humor. "Probably not."

"Definitely not," Rafe said, crossing his arms.

A commercial ended and the news anchor reappeared on the screen along with a picture of Carrie.

"To date, there has been no word of Caroline Brooks, the young woman taken hostage by Salazar four days ago at Schroedinger's restaurant," the woman said. The picture changed to that of a familiar-looking man holding a press conference. Carrie leaned closer to the TV. "Despite an impassioned plea from Robert Penfield, Caroline's fiancé, Salazar has not let his hostage go, or even communicated in anyway with the police.''

"So the angel has a name," Rafe said. "*And* a fiancé?"

Robert Penfield? Her *fiancé?* Carrie nearly burst with indignation. "I met this man exactly *once*," she said. "He's *not* my fiancé."

"Are you sure?" Felipe probed, his eyes burning holes into her with their intensity. "After all, don't you believe *every*thing you see on the TV news?"

Good Lord, he had a point. If Penfield could go on the air as her fiancé, then the rest of this so-called news story could also be pure fiction.

"Please," Bobby Penfield III said tearfully into the TV camera, "*please,* Detective Salazar, if you have any sense of decency at all, please let my dear Caroline go."

Oh, blech. And all of Florida actually believed she was going to marry this guy…?

"Despite that plea, there was no response from Felipe Salazar at all," the news anchor said solemnly. "And no word on whether Salazar's hostage is even still alive." She paused for only a split second before continuing. "We now go downtown, where Brett Finland is talking to the newly appointed chief of police, Jack Earley. Brett?"

"Thank you, Mary," the reporter said, and Carrie turned to look at Felipe.

He was standing behind the sofa, watching the screen, listening to the reporter. Surely he felt her eyes on his face, but he didn't so much as glance in her direction. His face was expressionless, but she could see the muscles jumping in his jaw.

She'd hurt and surprised him by not flatly discounting this news report. Hell, she'd surprised herself with how quickly she'd doubted him.

Salazar's hostage. That was as ridiculous a label as Penfield's fiancée.

Wasn't it?

On the television, Chief Earley's wide face looked tired and strained. He seemed distracted and the reporter had to keep repeating his questions.

"It's a hard job, tracking down Felipe Salazar, a man who once was one of St. Simone's finest," Brett Finland said, wrapping up the report. "Jack Earley has clearly lost some sleep over this, his first tough assignment as newly appointed police chief of this city. But Chief Earley, a man who started his law-enforcement career by tracking and trapping the enemy in their hideout tunnels in Vietnam, a man known as one of the marines' legendary 'tunnel rats,' should have no problem finding one rogue cop. This is Brett Finland, reporting live from downtown. Mary?"

"Madre de Dios!" Felipe exclaimed, his eyes still glued to the set. He fired off a rapid stream of Spanish to his brother.

Rafe frowned and shrugged, then answered, also in Spanish. He pointed next to the television. A pile of old newspapers lay there, and Felipe nearly leaped over the sofa to search through them. He scanned the tops, looking, it seemed, for one specific date.

"What?" Carrie said. "What's going on?"

"I need to find the paper that had that article on Chief Earley," Felipe said, still searching the pile.

"Why?" Carrie asked, but he didn't answer.

"Ah! Here it is." He sat down next to her on the sofa, and she moved closer, trying to read over his arm. He folded the paper so they both could see it better.

"Earley served in Vietnam as a *captain*," Felipe said. For some reason, that news really excited him. "Yes!" He looked up into Carrie's eyes. "Don't you get it?"

Puzzled, she shook her head.

He pointed to the text. "Look! It says it right here. Jack Earley served for ten months in Vietnam as an explosives expert. He went down into the tunnels where the Vietcong had been hiding, clearing them of booby traps. 'It was one of the most dangerous jobs in the entire Marine Corps, and not for the faint of heart or claustrophobic,'" he read aloud, glancing over at Carrie for that last bit.

"'Chief Earley and his men were known as the tunnel

rats.'" He smacked the paper with his hand. "Captain Rat! *Earley* is Richter's Captain Rat."

"The police chief?" Carrie was shocked. It couldn't be.

Felipe checked the time on Rafe's VCR. It was a little after one o'clock. "Okay," he said. "Listen, Diego's going to call any minute—"

"No, he's not," Rafe interrupted. "He called about an hour ago—said he was going to be tied up, that he wouldn't get a chance to call without a lot of people listening in."

Felipe swore under his breath. "Man, I really could have used his help. But…all right. I can still do this. We still have time."

"Time for what?" Carrie asked.

"We're going to go down to police headquarters," Felipe said, "and follow Earley to his meeting with Richter." He turned to his brother. "You still want to help me?"

"Even if you killed those guys, I don't want you to die," Rafe said.

"That's not the blazing endorsement I would've liked, but it'll do," Felipe said. "Can you get your hands on some film and a camera? Maybe one of those disposable ones?"

"I got an old Instamatic," Rafe said, crossing to the closet and pulling a box down from the shelf. "It works okay. It's got half a roll of color film already in it."

He fished a small black camera out of the box and handed it to his brother.

Felipe would've turned away, but Rafe caught his arm. "If you killed those men," he said, "you better head for Mexico."

"I didn't kill them."

Rafe ignored him. "If you head for Mexico, I probably won't see you again."

Felipe shook his head. "You'll see me again."

"If I don't," Rafe said, "I just wanted you to know…how sorry I am that I…I let you down all those years, all those times."

Felipe was silent. Carrie could see the tears that had suddenly filled his eyes. She turned away, not wanting to intrude.

"I hope someday you'll forgive me," Rafe said almost inaudibly. "And maybe then, someday, I'll forgive myself, no?"

"Forgive yourself, Raphael," Felipe said, his voice husky with emotion. "I forgave you a long time ago."

"*Gracias,*" Rafe whispered. "Go with God."

Felipe held out his hand, and Rafe took it. The two men, the two brothers, clasped hands, and each gazed into dark brown eyes so like his own.

And then Felipe turned and headed for the door.

"Good luck," Rafe added. "Keep your head down."

Carrie followed Felipe down the stairs. He checked his gun as he went, making sure it was properly loaded. Then he tucked it in the back waistband of his jeans, covering it with the hem of his T-shirt.

"Felipe," she said.

He glanced back at her, but didn't stop. "Yes."

"Please don't be mad at me."

He stopped by the front door then, his hand on the knob. "I'm not mad," he said. "Just…disappointed."

"I'm sorry," she said.

"How can you say that you'll marry me when you don't even trust me?" he asked, then shook his head before she had a chance to speak. "No, don't answer that," he added, rubbing his forehead as if he had a headache. "I honestly don't want to know."

"I keep wondering what if I'm wrong about you," Carrie admitted. "I see all this hard evidence against you and I can't stop thinking what if I've fallen in love with a man who's deceiving me."

Felipe was watching her steadily, his dark brown eyes echoing the disappointment she'd heard in his words.

"I can't help you with that one, Caroline," he said quietly. "It's something you've got to work out on your own. Let me know what you decide, though, okay?"

"Felipe—"

"Right now, we've got to move," he said, opening the door. "Stay close to me. We're getting in the car as quickly as we can."

Felipe took Caroline's arm, and together they went out into the bright afternoon sunlight and down the steps to the sidewalk.

Felipe felt the hair stand up on the back of his neck. Something was wrong. Something was seriously wrong.

Everything looked the same as it had when they'd arrived less than an hour ago. Children still played out in the street. Old men still sat, talking, on their stoops. People sauntered along the sidewalks, moving slowly in the sunshine.

The old white Volkswagen they'd "borrowed" from the Sea Circus parking lot was halfway down the block. Felipe moved quickly toward it, trying to shield Caroline with his body, praying his sixth sense that told him trouble was coming was wrong.

Caroline had thrown him for a loop back in Rafe's apartment. Her admission that she still didn't trust him had hurt even more than he'd let on. She needed time, he reminded himself. In time, she would learn he truly was everything he said he was.

Please, God, give him that time.

Out of the corner of his eye, Felipe saw a shadow move, and instantly, everything kicked into slow motion around him.

He turned his head and looked directly into the cold steel of Tommy Walsh's pale blue eyes.

Tommy had his gun out, hidden under a jacket he was carrying over his arm. It was pointed directly at Caroline.

If Tommy intended to kill them right here in the street, in front of all these people, they'd already be lying there dead. Still, Felipe knew if pushed too hard, Tommy would shoot. The time to move was now, while he was expecting Felipe to hesitate.

But Felipe wasn't going to hesitate. Not with Caroline's life hanging in the balance. No way was he going to let Tommy kill her. No way.

He pushed Caroline behind him and reached for the gun that rested against the small of his back. He drew smoothly, watching Tommy's finger tighten on the trigger at his sudden movement. But Tommy moved in slow motion and Felipe was faster. He aimed and fired.

The noise was incredible, as was the look of total shock on Tommy Walsh's face as the big man fell to the ground, a neat little bullet hole in the center of his forehead.

Stay detached, Felipe ordered himself. That wasn't a man he'd just killed, it was a monster. There'd be enough time later to suffer over the fact that Tommy Walsh might have a mother, maybe even a wife and children, who would mourn him. There'd be enough time—if Felipe could stay cool and concentrate on getting himself and Caroline out of there.

Somebody screamed—maybe it was Caroline—and suddenly the world moved again at its regular speed.

He stepped over Tommy's body and the blood that was pooling on the sidewalk. Stay cool. Don't look at the blood. Don't think. Just get Caroline away.

He wrenched open the door of the Volkswagen and pushed Caroline inside. Vaulting over the hood, he had the key in the ignition and the car in gear and halfway down the street before he even got the driver's-side door closed.

"My God," Carrie gasped. "My *God!* You *killed* him!"

"Fasten your seat belt," Felipe said calmly, as if he hadn't just fired a bullet into another man's head.

He'd killed a man.

An *unarmed* man.

With sickening clarity, Carrie remembered her surprise when Felipe had suddenly grabbed her arm. She could still see that awful, almost inhuman look in his eyes as he drew his gun. They had been filled with a cold, unearthly, unfamiliar savagery that was echoed on his face. His lips had been pulled back from his mouth in a wolfish snarl as he'd violently taken another human's life.

Who was this man, this Felipe Salazar?

Did she really know him at all? Lord knows she had never seen this side of him before—*never.*

Carrie felt sick to her stomach. How could Felipe kill someone and then just…keep going? He'd stepped over the body as if it had been nothing more than a spilled bag of garbage, an inconvenience.

Unless killing was something he'd done before, something he took lightly....

My God, was it possible he'd killed those two men in the sandlot after all?

The police had all that hard evidence against Felipe—a ballistics report that proved his gun was the murder weapon and a videotape of Felipe holding the two victims at gunpoint. Felipe claimed the tape had been made months ago and that the ballistics report was doctored. But ballistics reports were done scientifically. It wouldn't be easy to falsify information....

All her doubts, all her uncertainty came rushing back, hitting her full force in the stomach.

Maybe it was possible that Felipe *had* killed those men. Maybe he *had* been the one who'd shot them in the back of the head execution-style. That savage man she'd had a glimpse of, that man with the deadly flat eyes, had certainly looked capable of such an awful deed.

She took a deep breath, trying to steady her shaking hands, trying to stop the flood of tears that was streaming down her face. She'd been following her heart for the past several days, refusing to allow the cold hard facts to interfere with her feelings for Felipe.

But now those cold hard facts included one very dead man, and she couldn't ignore them any longer.

"Are you all right?" he asked, still in that same quiet, almost unnaturally calm voice.

"No," she said. "I want to get out of the car."

"We will in a minute," Felipe said. He looked into the rear-view mirror. "I just want to be sure that none of Tommy's men are following us. But then we *should* ditch this car. The police will be looking for it."

In the distance, Carrie could hear the sound of police sirens moving toward them, getting louder. A patrol car passed them going sixty miles an hour.

Felipe turned down a side street.

"No," Carrie said again. "You don't understand. I want to get out of the car—*now*."

"Caroline, we can't—"

"Not 'we.' *Me*. I want you to pull over and let *me* get out."

Carrie felt him turn and look at her, *really* look at her. She stared down at her feet, unable to meet his gaze.

"I can't do that," he said quietly.

She did look up at him then. "Can't…or won't?"

The muscles in the side of his jaw were working hard again. This time it was Felipe who wouldn't meet her gaze.

"What difference does it make?" he returned.

"Am I your hostage?" she asked, trying to keep her voice from shaking. "Have I been all along?"

He made a sound that might've been a laugh. "What do *you* think?"

"I don't know." She *didn't* know. Had he been manipulating her right from the start? Were his words of love really empty promises, designed to make her trust him, keep her from running away? And what about her feelings for him? Was this really love she felt, or was it some kind of warped attachment of a hostage for a captor?

"Please," she said softly. "If you care anything for me at all, please let me go."

Felipe was silent as he took a left turn onto McCallister Street. "So," he said, just as quietly, "you've decided not to trust me, huh? That's too bad."

"Please," she said again. "Prove I'm not your hostage, Felipe. Let me go."

"As much as I'd like to prove that to you," he said, "I'd rather you remained alive. As long as there's a threat from Lawrence Richter, you're staying with me."

Carrie gazed out of the window, unable to speak.

"And now you're thinking, 'Ah, I *am* his hostage.'" Felipe's velvet voice surrounded her. "I have to tell you one more time, Caroline, that everything I've ever said to you is God's own truth."

Carrie closed her eyes. "I don't know *what* the truth is anymore." She only knew the facts. She'd seen him kill a man without a second thought. A ballistics report tied him to the murder weapon. A videotape showed that he was with the two men before they died.

As they stopped for a red light, Felipe reached over and picked up her hand, the hand with the green plastic ring he had given her.

"*This* is the truth," he said. "Open your eyes and look. *Look* at me!"

She opened her eyes and looked directly into the eyes of this man that she thought she knew so well, but perhaps didn't know at all. His face was so familiar—high cheekbones, lean, smooth cheeks, long, elegant nose, full lips, dark, mesmerizing eyes. She'd thought she'd seen him in every possible way. She'd seen him relaxed and laughing, tense and worried, cool and calm, thoughtful, angry, unhappy, joyful. But not murderous. At least, not until this afternoon.

Felipe took her hand, the same hand with the ring, and placed it on his chest, over his heart.

"*This* is the truth, Caroline," he whispered. "But if you don't want that truth any longer…"

As she watched, his eyes started to fill with tears, but he blinked them back, forced them away. He returned her hand to her lap.

"It's almost all over," Felipe said, putting the car into gear as the traffic light turned green. "A little bit longer, and then I won't stop you. You'll be free to go."

Chapter 21

Felipe was getting the job done.

He'd ditched the white Volkswagen near the parking lot of the Fourth Precinct. He'd found Jim Keegan's car in the lot. The key was hidden on top of the right front wheel, exactly where Jim had said it would be.

Now he sat outside police headquarters in Jim's gray Taurus, waiting for Chief Earley to leave for his meeting with crime lord, Lawrence Richter.

Yes, he was getting the job done.

He was trying very hard not to think about anything besides the pictures he was going to take of Earley and Richter's meeting. He was trying hard not to think about that small, permanent hole he'd put in Tommy Walsh's head or the nausea he felt as a result. And he was trying desperately not to think about Caroline Brooks.

That wasn't so easy to do, because she was sitting right next to him, and because, while he was busy getting the job done, he was having to take care that she didn't try to run away.

They had come full circle. Apparently, her doubts and suspicions had come out the victor in an emotional wrestling

match. And, apparently, her love for him hadn't stood up to
the test.

That hurt more than he would have believed possible.

So okay. He tried to harden his heart, tried to think about
this practically, tried not to care. So he wouldn't leave the vice
squad. He'd merely leave St. Simone. So what if it was his
home? He hadn't lived here *all* his life. His parents had come
here to make a new start. So now *he'd* go somewhere else to
make his own new start. There were a lot of cities out there
where his face wasn't known. Maybe he'd go up to Diego's
New York, become a New York City cop. Now, *there* would
be a job that was on the edge, that was filled with high risks
and danger. He'd fit right in.

Man, he should be feeling lucky. Here was Caroline, ready
to walk away from him, exactly the way he'd wanted their
affair to end a few days ago. He wasn't going to have to worry
about her safety. He wasn't going to have to deal with the
restrictions that a permanent relationship would bring. Man, he
was getting off easy. He'd had his fun. He'd had a series of
intense sexual experiences with a beautiful, vibrant, passionate
woman. He had the added satisfaction of knowing that he'd
saved her life. He should be more than ready and willing to let
Caroline Brooks simply fade into a fond memory as he continued on with his life as he knew it.

He should, but he couldn't.

Something had happened these past few days. Something
had opened his eyes to the fact that his life wasn't winning any
awards or prizes for Most Fulfilling. Yes, he was making a
difference out on the streets. Yes, he was good at what he did.
And yes, sometimes he even liked it. But he didn't like it all
the time—and lately, he didn't like it at all.

The sorry truth was that the something that had opened his
eyes had been Caroline Brooks. Caroline had shown him firsthand everything he'd been missing. She'd gone and made him
fall in love with her and opened his eyes to a future that was
impossibly joyful.

Impossibly indeed.

She stirred in her seat, and he couldn't keep himself from glancing at her.

She didn't trust him.

He was angry and hurt and even insulted by her mistrust, but the ultimate insult was that these emotions didn't make him stop loving her. He wanted to fall on his knees and beg her to believe him. But pride kept him in his seat.

He wanted to see her smile, hear her husky, sexy laughter. He wanted to know, just from looking in her eyes, that she'd be in his arms again tonight, surrounding him with her warmth and love. But there was not a chance in hell for that.

He wanted to weep for all he'd lost—for the love he'd probably never really had in the first place.

Because how could she have truly loved him without trust?

She was quiet and her face looked pale. She hadn't spoken a word to him since they'd taken Jim's car from the parking lot.

But now she looked up, actually meeting his gaze. The mistrust and trepidation he could see in her eyes burned like acid in his soul. But he didn't look away. He couldn't.

Maybe seeing her looking at him that way would make him love her less. But probably not.

"How many people have you killed?" she asked.

Her question caught him off guard. Of all the things he'd expected her to say to him or ask him, that wasn't one of them.

But he answered honestly. "Five," he said. "Tommy Walsh was the fifth."

"How do you sleep afterward?" she asked. "How do you do it? How do you live your life knowing that you took someone else's?"

Felipe was quiet for a moment, wondering how to answer. But there was really only one way to answer—with the truth.

"You don't sleep," he finally told her. He watched the entrance to the police station as he spoke. "Not at first. You lie in bed going over it and over it in your head. You try to figure out where you went wrong, where you made the mistake, what you could've done instead to make it turn out differently. And then, after about a week of not sleeping, when you feel like hell and you can't handle it anymore, you go visit the counselor—the precinct shrink. And then you start to work through it until you accept the choices that you made—the choices that led you to pull that trigger and take that life.

"You talk to people who were there, who witnessed the shooting," he continued. "You hang out with the person whose life you maybe saved by firing your gun and killing the perpetrator. Or you come face-to-face with the fact that it came down to the guy you killed or yourself. You look at yourself in a mirror and you remind yourself that *he* was the bad guy, not you. If he had been a little faster or a little smarter or a little luckier with his own gun, then it might very well have been *your* family holding that funeral service instead of his.''

"And if he didn't have a gun?'' Carrie whispered.

Felipe shook his head. "They all had guns. Starting with Benny Hammett. He was eighteen years old, just a kid, freaked out on crack. He had his father's handgun and was taking potshots at the children in the playground next to his house. One kid was dead—four years old—and two others were badly wounded. The medical teams couldn't get in to help them. The SWAT team was on its way when Hammett hit a fourth kid who'd been hiding behind some bushes. I was one of the cops who climbed down to his window from the roof and took him down. My bullet killed him.

"Then there was Thomas Freeman, age forty-seven. Took his hunting rifle and went back to where he'd been laid off, killed his boss's secretary and threatened to wipe out the entire office. I went in as a deliveryman, took him out before he killed the mail room clerk.

"Hans Thorne, thirty-eight, escaped convict, tried to hold up a convenience store that Diego and I happened to be in. I stopped him from blowing Diego's head off.

"T. J. Cerrone, twenty-three years old. I believe you had the honor of meeting him at Sea Circus. When we busted him on drug charges, he and his friends decided they'd skip jail and go right to hell. Unfortunately, they took a few of my friends on the force with them. T.J. had access to an Uzi submachine gun when I ended his life with my .45.''

Felipe kept his eyes on the entrance to the police station, but he could feel Caroline watching him.

"And Tommy Walsh?" she probed. "Where was his gun?"

Felipe turned to look at her. "It was aimed at you," he said. He could see the doubt in her eyes. *Madre de Dios,* was it possible she didn't know Tommy had been armed? "You didn't see his gun?"

"No."

"You think I would kill an unarmed man?" His voice rose in disbelief. What kind of monster did Caroline think he was anyway?

"That's what I saw."

Felipe's heart broke into a thousand tiny pieces. "Maybe you saw what you expected to see," he said quietly. "You've already decided I'm guilty, that I'm a killer. But you're wrong, and I'm going to prove that, even if it's the last thing I do."

Numbly, Felipe stared at the door to the police station. He'd lost Caroline. He'd totally lost her trust—if he'd ever even had it in the first place.

Everything around him, his entire life, seemed to be circling the drain.

Everything, *every*thing—his freedom, his reputation, his life—was riding on his conviction that Chief Earley was Lawrence Richter's partner. Everything now depended on his being right about that.

God help him if he was wrong.

Ten minutes after three, and Earley still hadn't left for his alleged 3:30 meeting with Lawrence Richter.

Carrie risked a look at Felipe. He was getting more and more tense by the minute. He muttered something in Spanish, then glanced at Carrie, but didn't bother to translate.

"What if you're wrong?" she asked quietly. "What if Earley's not involved?"

"I drive you to Montana," he said, "then come back and start over again. If Earley's not this Captain Rat, then someone else is. Sooner or later, I'll find him."

He stared across the parking lot at the entrance to police

headquarters. His mouth was set in grim determination and his face was lined with fatigue. His dark eyes were even more unreadable and mysterious than ever.

Where was his gun? she'd asked.

It was aimed at you, he'd said.

Was he lying?

He'd spoken with such conviction, such absolute certainty. There was a gun. She simply hadn't seen it. If he hadn't killed Tommy Walsh, Tommy would've killed her.

What if he was telling the truth? What if all along he'd been telling the truth?

Everything I've ever said to you is God's own truth.

If he *was* telling the truth, then, Lord, how she'd let him down by doubting him.

It was her head versus her heart. Her heart wanted to believe him. But her head couldn't reconcile the cold, hard facts.

And Carrie didn't know what to believe.

Felipe sat forward, gripping the steering wheel tightly in his hands. "My God," he said.

"Is it him?" Carrie tried to see where he was looking. She couldn't see anyone out on the sidewalk who looked like Chief Earley.

"It's Lawrence Richter," Felipe said. "He's going inside." He turned off the engine and unlocked the door. "Come on."

"We're going to *follow* him?" Carrie exclaimed. "Into the *police station?*"

"Yes." Felipe took the paper lunch bag that held Rafe's Instamatic camera, then grabbed her wrist. He pulled her across the bench seat and out the driver's-side door.

"Do you know how many police officers are in there?" Carrie asked in disbelief. "Do you *want* to get caught?"

"I'm not going to get caught," Felipe said shortly, pulling her with him across the parking lot toward the wide stairs that led up to the main doors. "But if anything happens," he added, "get down behind me out of the way. Do you understand?"

Carrie dug her heels into the gravel of the parking lot, and he turned back toward her impatiently.

"Felipe, don't go in there," she said. "Someone's going to recognize you and—"

"How nice that you should care," he said without expression.

"I *do* care—"

He grabbed her shoulders and all the emotion he'd been hiding erupted to the surface. "Then *trust* me, dammit!" he hissed. "Trust me, Caroline, and know that I *have* to go in there if I want this to end."

"I don't want you to die," she whispered, staring into the burning depths of his eyes. "I don't know what you've done or not done, who you've killed or not. I don't know whether or not you've been using me right from the start. I don't know whether you deserve to go to jail or get a medal for bravery, but I *do* know that I don't want you to die."

He touched the side of her face, his hands suddenly gentle, his eyes soft and sad. "I truly have no control when it comes to you," he murmured. "I should despise you for losing your faith in me, but all I want is to kiss you, to touch you. I must be one hell of a fool." He shook his head. "You can help me, Caroline," he added, talking low and fast. "We can get in and out and no one will ever know. I need to do this. I need your help. Please."

Helping him would be aiding and abetting. She could go to jail for that.

"Please," he whispered again, and she nodded. Her reward was a small smile, a mere shadow of Felipe's normal exuberance. "Put your hair under your hat," he said. "Hurry."

She obeyed, stuffing her long blond hair up underneath the baseball cap she was still wearing.

This was crazy. Felipe was crazy. *She* was crazy for going along with this.

He opened the door to the lobby and pulled her inside.

She should scream, run away, do *some*thing to call attention to herself. *Hello, I'm the hostage you've all been looking for all this time!*

Felipe was staring at the elevators.

"Richter got in one going down," he said, pulling her to-

ward a door marked Stairs. "Come on." He pulled her into
the stairwell with him, then started down. "Quickly. I don't
want to lose him," he said, taking the stairs two at a time, all
but swinging Carrie up into his arms to speed her along.

But he stopped running before he pushed open the door on
the basement level. He opened it slowly—just in time to see
Lawrence Richter walk sedately past.

They followed the silver-haired man into a cafeteria that was
open to the general public. And the general public was there
in all their various sizes and shapes. That was good. With these
strange-looking people around, no one would give Felipe a second glance.

Near the door, there was an empty table against the wall,
and Felipe sat down in one of the metal-framed chairs. He
pulled Carrie onto his lap.

She didn't want to sit there. She didn't want to be so close
to him, to be reminded of the way she had let him love her.
She struggled to stand up, but he held her tightly.

"At least *pretend* you like me," he whispered.

Carrie stopped struggling. "Felipe—" she started to say.

"Shh. Richter's got a cup of coffee. He's going to sit down.
Put your arm around me, for God's sake."

Carrie looped her arm around Felipe's neck. She wished she
wasn't sitting here like this, so close to him, touching him. She
wished she were back at Sea Circus or out on her boat, alone
with the sea and sky, or hell, she even wished she were back
in Montana. She wished she were anywhere but here.

Because she also wished that she could kiss him. Her attraction to this man was still there, powerful and strong. Her
love was there, too, even stronger.

Head versus heart, it all boiled down to a matter of trust.
Was he the Sandlot killer? Carrie didn't want to believe that
he was. But wanting simply wasn't enough.

Felipe reached around her to put the lunch bag on the table.
He poked a hole in the bag for the camera lens and aimed it
at the table where Richter was sitting with his coffee.

And then, without any warning, Felipe kissed her.

It was a long, deep, achingly fierce kiss that caught her entirely by surprise. It left her weak and even more off center than she'd been before.

"Sorry." Felipe quietly apologized for the kiss almost before their lips had parted. "I'm sorry—Richter looked this way. I didn't know what else to do."

Oh. That hadn't really been a kiss. It had been a diversion, a form of cover.

"What is Richter doing?" Carrie asked when she finally found her voice. Sitting the way she was, her back was to the man.

"He's picked up a newspaper from the table," Felipe said. He reached out and laid one hand on the paper bag holding the camera and took a picture of Richter. "Put your head against my shoulder and you'll be able to see him. But don't stare. Look past him, not at him."

Carrie turned slightly and leaned back against Felipe. Richter was reading the newspaper. As she watched, he took a sip of his coffee.

Felipe's hand moved on the paper bag. "Did you see that?" he murmured into Carrie's ear. "He just put an envelope in between the pages of the paper."

He did? Carrie hadn't noticed that at all.

"I got it on film," Felipe said. "Now we wait for Earley to show up...ah, he's right on time."

Looking harried, Police Chief Jack Earley, in a white short-sleeved shirt and a loosened tie and carrying his sport jacket over one arm, came into the cafeteria.

Felipe nuzzled Carrie's neck, hiding his face from the man who was leading the statewide intensive search for him.

Earley walked past Felipe and Carrie, past Lawrence Richter—who didn't even glance up—and over to the coffee vending machine. Casually, the police chief put some money into the machine and pressed the buttons for decaf with sugar, no cream.

As the cup was filling with steaming dark coffee, Lawrence Richter stood up, straightened his tie and calmly walked out of the room.

"He left," Carrie whispered to Felipe. "Richter left before the meeting!"

"He didn't take the newspaper," Felipe murmured. "It has that envelope inside it. Just watch. Earley is going to pick it up off the table."

Almost before he stopped speaking, the police chief walked past the table where Richter had been sitting. For a moment, it looked as if the man was simply going to walk on by, but then he stopped, lingering to look down at the headlines of the sports pages.

He glanced at his watch as if in a rush, then took the paper with him, hurrying out of the room.

Felipe hustled Carrie off his lap and grabbed the bag that held the camera. Holding her hand, he pulled her along with him down the hall about fifty feet behind Jack Earley.

Earley stopped in front of the elevator and pushed the button. He took a sip of his coffee, made a face and tossed the cup and its contents into the garbage. The newspaper soon followed.

"Got it," Felipe murmured in her ear, and she realized he was holding the bag with the camera in front of him. "He put the envelope in his jacket pocket."

"I didn't see that," Carrie said.

"That's okay," Felipe said. "I got it on film."

"Now what?" Carrie whispered.

"Now we find a one-hour photo place," Felipe said.

"Holy hell, it *is* you," a voice said loudly. All across the basement lobby, heads turned in their direction. A bald-headed man in an ill-fitting suit fumbled for his sidearm. "Felipe Salazar, *you* are under arrest!"

"Or maybe we'll skip the photo place," Felipe said quietly, pulling Carrie close to him. "Play along."

From around the lobby came a murmur of voices and a wave of movement as civilians backed away and police officers began to draw their weapons.

But Felipe was ahead of them all. His gun was already drawn. He backed up until he hit the wall next to the closed elevator door. "Keep your hands up and guns down," he warned them. "I don't want to have to hurt the girl."

Play along. But was this fantasy or reality? It sure *seemed* like reality. The entire area was frozen like a tableau.

"Come on, Phil," the bald cop said, still trying to get his gun free. "Don't let's do this the hard way. Let me bring you in. I'll see that you get fair treatment."

"Put your hands up, Andy," Felipe said. "And back away."

"Someone get hold of Jim Keegan," the cop named Andy called out, lifting his hands with a sigh. "We got us a hostage situation here." He turned back to Felipe. "Phil, this is a royal pain in the ass."

This was all happening so fast. Carrie could barely breathe. Felipe had his gun pressed against her ribs. *Play along.* She didn't have to pretend to look frightened.

"Tommy Walsh killed Mareidas and Dupree," Felipe told Andy. "Not me. It was on Lawrence Richter's orders. I have proof of this."

"*Richter?*" Andy said, squinting as he tried to place the name. "Isn't he the guy who owns that chain of fish restaurants? My cousin got salmonella from eating there."

"He owns the restaurants—and runs a major crime syndicate," Felipe said. "Guess who else is involved?" He turned to look at Jack Earley. "You get the first guess, Chief."

Chief Earley's face was pale, his mouth a grim line. "Let the girl go, Salazar. You don't really want to see her killed, do you?" He turned to speak to his men. "He's clearly delusional. Get back and clear these civilians out of here."

"You're going down, Captain Rat," Felipe said to Earley. "I have the proof I need. When Jim gets here—"

Next to them, the door of the cargo elevator slid open, and a janitor blinked owlishly out at them from behind a dolly carrying large trash barrels.

Earley made his move. He lunged for Felipe, pulling both him and Caroline back into the big elevator.

"Get out!" he shouted at the janitor, who scrambled out the door. "The man's insane! *Get out!*"

Felipe hit the wall hard and fell to his knees, taking Carrie with him. He fired his gun, and the noise was deafening. She heard herself scream, felt Felipe try to cover her with his body.

Lord, this was it. They were going to die.

Felipe had missed.

He'd had one shot at Earley, but he'd missed. The bullet tore up into the soundproof tile of the elevator ceiling as the door slid closed.

Earley was back behind the cover of the trash barrels in the other corner of the elevator. Felipe tried to shield Caroline from the chief's gun, but it was no use. His body would act as a shield for only so long at this close a range.

"Put your gun down," the chief shouted. "Put it down!"

Slowly, Felipe lowered his gun. He had no choice. Not with Earley aiming his own gun directly at him...and at Caroline.

Earley reached up to the elevator controls and pushed the stop button, halting their journey up to the first floor.

"Heroically, Chief Earley pulled Salazar and his hostage into an empty elevator, risking his own life for the sake of the crowd's safety," Earley said, straightening up and coming out from behind the barrels, his gun aimed levelly at Felipe. "The papers are gonna have a field day with this one. I couldn't've planned it better myself. Put your gun on the floor and kick it over to me."

Felipe set the gun down, but instead of kicking it to Earley, he slid it underneath the dolly that held the trash barrels. Caroline's eyes were wide as she looked from Felipe to Earley and then back.

"It really is a shame when a good cop turns bad," Earley mused, shaking his head.

"You should know," Felipe said. He could see his future in Earley's eyes, and it wasn't going to be a long one. Earley was going to shoot him, and then shoot Caroline with Felipe's gun. And there was nothing Felipe could do about it.

Or was there?

Jim Keegan's Rule Number One: Nothing is impossible.

Felipe's Rule Number One: If you're going to die, die fighting.

The big cargo elevator was about eight feet long by seven feet wide. The dolly holding the barrels cut off one corner of that space.

"Let go of your hostage," Earley said as Felipe slowly rose to his feet, pulling Caroline up with him.

"Te amo," Felipe said to Caroline, brushing the side of her face with his lips. "Get down behind the barrels," he breathed into her ear.

"Very touching," Earley said impatiently. "Now, let her go."

Felipe pushed Caroline hard, away from Earley and toward the trash barrels, as he leaped at Earley. "Get down! Get back!" he shouted again at Caroline.

The gun went off with a roar as he hit Earley in the face. He felt a slap, heard Caroline scream, saw a spray of blood hit the elevator wall.

Felipe had been hit. Where, he couldn't begin to say. All he knew was that the bullet hadn't killed him—he was still alive. And until his heart stopped beating, he was going to fight like the devil himself to save Caroline's life.

He hit Earley again, and the chief's gun flew out of his hand and into the corner.

Earley fought back, trying to get to his gun. He used his hands like a club, striking Felipe hard on the shoulder.

God, he knew now where that bullet had struck him. Earley hit his wounded shoulder again and again and Felipe reeled back in mind-numbing pain. Somehow he managed to kick out at the older man, and his foot connected with Earley's knee. The chief went down with a grunt but scrambled quickly to his feet, assuming a street-fighter's stance.

"Freeze!" Caroline shouted from behind the barrels. "I said *freeze,* dammit!"

She was holding Felipe's gun, and she had Earley's gun behind her on the floor.

Earley straightened up, lifting both his hands as she pointed the gun from him to Felipe and back again.

"Good job, miss," Earley said, starting toward Felipe. "We've got him now."

"Don't you move!" Caroline warned him. He froze.

"You're kidding, right?" Earley said. He gestured toward Felipe. "This man's the known felon. He's the kidnapper, the *murderer*. He's the one who's been holding you hostage all this time."

Caroline's eyes flicked from Earley to Felipe.

Felipe didn't say a word. What could he say? He just looked at her. *Trust me.*

She looked into his eyes, searching for answers, searching for the truth. He hoped she could see it—the truth was clearly there, written permanently in his heart.

Te amo. I love you.

Earley started forward. "Give me the gun, miss."

She turned sharply, pointing the weapon at St. Simone's chief of police.

"Don't come closer, mister, or I'll put a hole in you," she said.

Relief flooded through Felipe. Caroline had followed her heart and trusted him.

He staggered slightly—his knees felt odd, weak. He realized that his shoulder was still bleeding quite heavily. Blood ran down his arm and dripped onto the floor from his fingers.

"You're hurt," Caroline said to Felipe, her eyes still locked on Earley. Her voice shook slightly, but her hands were steady. "Is it bad?"

Felipe shook his head. "I'll live," he said. He moved across the elevator and reached over to take back his gun.

She glanced up at him then. "So will I," she said. "Because of you, I think."

"Hands on your head," Felipe ordered Earley. "Sit down. There, in the corner."

"You're not going to get away with this," Earley said.

"You wanna bet?" Felipe said.

Overhead, an intercom speaker clicked on.

"This is Detective Jim Keegan from the Fourth Precinct," came a familiar voice. "Felipe, are you there? Pick up the telephone in the control panel."

The metal panel swung open with a squawk, and Felipe picked up the red receiver.

"Diego?"

"Phil! *Yes!* I heard a shot and I was afraid—is everyone all right?"

"I've been hit," Felipe said, "but I've cornered my Captain Rat."

"Jack Earley?" Jim said.

"That's right."

"The chief of police."

"Uh-huh."

Jim Keegan laughed. "You got proof?"

"Uh-huh. Photos of him accepting a payoff from Lawrence Richter."

"Well, isn't that dandy," Jim said. "That and the tape you left for me at Sea Circus should just about change your tag from Rogue Cop to Local Hero. I'll have the boys bring in Richter and his pals."

"That's cool, but meanwhile, I've got Andy and the entire police force ready to blow me away when these elevator doors open," Felipe said.

"Go on up to the first floor," Jim's voice said. "Captain Swick will be waiting for you there. Believe it or not, he's one of the good guys. That's why he had that tape of Walsh and Richter planning the Sandlot Murders. He was holding it to clear your name when the time came. He was working *with* you on this case, and he'd suspected Earley for some time now."

Felipe pulled out the stop button and the elevator started with a jerk.

"Keep your hands on your head," Caroline warned Earley.

"This isn't over," Earley hissed.

"Yes," Felipe told him, "it is."

And the elevator doors slid open.

Felipe was sitting on the lobby floor, leaning against the wall by the elevators, waiting for the paramedics to arrive.

A man Carrie recognized as Andy, and several other police

officers, were around Felipe, trying to stem the flow of blood from his shoulder.

Earley had been taken away and reporters were gathering outside for an enormous press conference. In a matter of hours, word would hit the newsstands and TVs that Felipe Salazar was *not* a menace to society. His name would be cleared.

As Carrie watched, Felipe glanced around the lobby, looking for something or someone. Looking for *her*. His eyes landed on her, and he visibly relaxed.

He held her gaze. She could see pain in his dark brown eyes and at the edges of his mouth. His shoulder hurt more than he was letting on. Hell, for all *she* knew, his wounded leg still hurt him, too.

The ambulance was on its way. The paramedics would arrive and take Felipe to the hospital.

What then? Was she simply free to go? Should she just walk out of the police station, hail a taxi and go home to her apartment?

Andy approached her. "Uh, excuse me. You're Caroline, right?"

She nodded.

"Uh, Phil was wondering if you'd mind coming over for a sec before you go," Andy said.

Before you go. Felipe expected her just to walk away, to leave. It was over. All of it. Including any future they might've had together. She'd destroyed that with her doubts and mistrust.

Still, as she walked toward Felipe, she tried to smile.

The other police officers moved tactfully away.

"You trusted me," Felipe said, looking up at her from his seat on the floor. He patted the tile and she sat cross-legged next to him.

"I didn't for a while there," she said. She looked at her hands clasped tightly in her lap, unable to meet his eyes.

"When it came down to the bottom line—" Felipe's soft accent seemed to caress her "—you were there for me."

"No," Carrie said, closing her eyes. "You were there for *me*. All along, you protected me. You risked your life for mine."

"I was glad to," he said simply.

"I let you down," she said. Her voice shook and she couldn't hide it.

"It was hard for you to trust me," he said gently. "The way we started…" He shook his head. "I don't blame you, Caroline."

Carrie nodded. She still couldn't meet his eyes. "I'm so sorry."

"I am, too."

"It could've been really good, couldn't it have?" She risked a glance up at him. His dark eyes were serious and as mysterious as the midnight sky.

He nodded slowly. "Yes," he said. "It could have been remarkably good."

He was just sitting there, watching her. She wanted desperately for him to reach out, to touch her, to pull her into his arms—or at least the one that wasn't hurting. But that wasn't going to happen. Their love affair was over. She'd killed it, smothered it with her mistrust.

"Now what?" she asked quietly.

He held out his hand—his good hand—to her. "Hello. My name is Felipe Salazar," he said, "and I'm a police detective with the Fourth Precinct. I'm with the vice squad right now, but I won't be for much longer. I'm thinking about putting in for an assignment as an urban youth officer." He brought her fingers to his lips and kissed them one at a time. "You've got to be the most intriguing woman I've ever met. Will you have dinner with me tonight?"

Tears flooded Carrie's eyes and hope flooded her heart. "You want to start over?" she whispered.

"I would love to start over," he said. "Will you have dinner with me?"

"Oh, Felipe, can you really forgive me?"

"If we're starting over," he said, with a small smile, "there's nothing to forgive." His eyes were liquid brown and so very warm as he gazed at her. "Even though we've just met, would it be forward of me to ask for a kiss?"

With a trembling smile, Carrie shook her head.

Felipe leaned toward her, careful not to jar his shoulder. Carrie met him halfway in a kiss so sweet, so pure and tender, it brought a fresh rush of tears to her eyes.

"This may be the shortest courtship in the history of the Western Hemisphere," Felipe breathed, desire sparking in his eyes.

"I hope so," Carrie said.

He touched the side of her face as he looked searchingly at her. "Caroline, there *is* a catch to this. I'm about to go into protective custody. As the chief witness against Richter and Earley, I'll have to be kept safe until after the trial. For your own safety, you should come with me. Richter may figure out he can get to me through you. But it's your choice. You don't have to come. If you choose not to, I won't be able to see you until it's over and done. It could be nine or ten months. Longer."

Carrie was silent for a moment. Not see him for nearly a *year?* "I'd have to quit my job," she finally said.

"A leave of absence," Felipe said. Hope lighted his eyes and he leaned forward to kiss her again. "Your position would surely be waiting for you when you returned."

"Returned from where?"

He smiled. "I don't know. Where do you want to go?"

Carrie smiled back at him, her heart exploding with love for Felipe Salazar, who was man enough to give her a second chance. "Someplace where we can go out on a boat," she said. "Someplace near the ocean."

"I know of this great beach house on Sanibel Island," Felipe said. "The owners are friends of mine. Although we may need to go farther away from St. Simone, this beach house might be a good place to start."

Carrie kissed him, closing her eyes and drinking in the softness of his lips, the sweetness of his mouth.

"It would be the perfect place to start."

* * * * *

If you enjoyed this Suzanne Brockmann story,
look out for Letters to Kelly. *Available from*
Silhouette Sensation in January 2004.

The Lady in Red

LINDA TURNER

LINDA TURNER

began reading romances in school and began writing them one night when she had nothing else to read. She's been writing ever since. Single and living in Texas, she travels every chance she gets, scouting locales for her books.

Chapter 1

"What do you mean you don't want me to cover sports?" Blake Nickels demanded in surprise. "I'm a sports reporter, Tom. And a damn good one, too."

"And at one time you were a hell of a news reporter, too," Tom Edwards reminded him as he searched his desk drawers for a stick of gum. He was in the process of giving up smoking after twenty years, and he scowled when he could find nothing but a eucalyptus cough drop to fight his craving. "In fact," he continued as he popped the foul tasting candy into his mouth, "the way I remember it, you won several national awards."

"That was before," he growled.

He didn't have to explain before what—they both knew. Once Blake had been one of the hottest crime reporters in New York City. Then an informant had given him some information that had ended up costing the snitch his life. Devastated, he'd packed up his toys and gotten out of the game, moving from the notoriety he'd earned in New York to the obscurity of covering sports in a town in New Mexico that was no bigger than a pimple on the map. That had been eight years ago. As far as Tom knew, Blake hadn't gone within a hundred miles of a police scanner since.

Which made what he had to ask him all the more difficult. Wishing he had a cigarette, Tom pushed himself to his feet to restlessly prowl the confines of his office. "Lynn Phillips took maternity leave four months early this morning on the advice of her doctor," he said grimly. "If she doesn't get complete bed rest, she could lose the baby."

On the job for only two days, Blake racked his brain for a face to put with the name. "Phillips. The crime beat, right? Oh, no, you don't!"

"Now, Blake, don't go flying off the handle. Just give me a chance to explain—"

"You crafty son of a bitch, there's nothing to explain. I can read you like a book. I know you, remember?"

They'd been best friends since grade school—there wasn't anything that one didn't know about the other, including how the other's mind worked. "You called me up offering my own column on the sports page just to get me over here, didn't you?" Blake demanded, jumping to his feet to glare at Tom. "It was all just a trick."

"You were thinking about leaving Lordsburg anyway. You said so yourself. Ever since Trina ran off with that truck driver and married him when you weren't looking—"

"Leave Trina the hell out of this," he growled. "The woman's name is no longer in my vocabulary."

"Fine," Tom agreed. "Then what about Pop? With your parents going off to France for a year, you know you were worried sick about him being here in San Antonio all by himself. By accepting my job offer, you killed two birds with one stone—you got away from *that woman* in

Lordsburg and you could come home to watch over your grandfather until your parents get back. Instead of yelling at me, you ought to be thanking me, you old goat. I did you a favor.''

"Favor?" Blake choked. If he hadn't been so irritated, he would have laughed. Leave it to Tom to twist things so he looked like a choirboy. "You call manipulating me to get me on the payroll, then assigning me to the crime beat a *favor?* If you'd mentioned what you were planning at the beginning, I never would have left New Mexico."

"I wasn't planning anything. I wasn't," he insisted when Blake merely lifted a dark brow at him. "Oh, I knew Lynn was pregnant, of course, and that she'd be leaving eventually, but I expected to have another four months to fill the position if I couldn't talk you into it. Dammit, Blake, take it, will you? At least for a little while until I can hire somebody else? You're the only one I've got on staff who can give Sabrina Jones some competition."

Blake might not have known Lynn Phillips and most of the rest of the *Times* staff, but he'd only been in town one day when he'd read Sabrina Jones's bylined story on the front page of the San Antonio *Daily Record,* the other major paper in town. She was good, dammit. Good enough to be writing for any major newspaper in the country, which was, no doubt, why Tom was worried. The *Times* and *Daily Record* were in a knock-down-drag-out, no-holds-barred subscription war right now, and the *Times* was going to get its butt kicked without someone who could give the Jones woman a run for her money.

"I'm out of practice," he hedged. "It's been eight years since I've done that beat."

"I don't care if it's been a hundred. You're the best damn reporter I've ever known. That includes sports, crime—hell, even the obits. The second you catch the scent of a story, you'll be off and running, just like old times. It'll be great.''

His expression shuttered, Blake couldn't share his enthusiasm. He wanted to tell him that he didn't care how many murders and sex crimes he covered, it would never be like old times again, but he was afraid Tom was right. He'd really enjoyed covering sports, but nothing had ever challenged him like crime. It was like an addiction that had called to something in his blood—he'd thrived on it. And in the process, he'd lost his objectivity and become obsessed with getting the story. Nothing else had mattered. And because of that single-mindedness, a man had lost his life.

A man who had trusted him, Blake remembered grimly. A man who had seen something he shouldn't have and who should have gone to the police for protection. Blake had sworn not to reveal his identity and he'd stuck by that, but it hadn't done any good. The day after the story hit the paper, the informant had turned up dead, supposedly killed from asphyxiation due to running his car in a closed garage. The police had ruled it a suicide and let it go. Blake had known better. The prominent businessman the informant had exposed as the brains behind an extensive money-laundering and drug-smuggling operation had obviously gotten to him and shut him up for good.

Almost a decade had passed since then, but just thinking about it brought it all back like it was yesterday. He couldn't go through that again. He couldn't put someone at risk just because of a damn story. It wasn't worth it.

So what are you going to do, Nickels? You quit the job in Lordsburg. Remember? You can go back, of course. But what about Pop?

His grandfather, eighty-three and forgetful at times, had no business living alone. Blake could try to convince him to go to New Mexico with him, but the old man could be as stubborn as a mule when he wanted to be. And if he wouldn't go to Paris for a year with Blake's parents, he sure wasn't going to leave his home and everything familiar in San Antonio for Lordsburg.

Stuck between a rock and a hard place, Blake had no choice but to accept the inevitable. "All right." He sighed. "I'll take over for Lynn. For *now*," he stressed when his friend grinned broadly. "So don't go getting any ideas that this is permanent. As soon as you can hire someone to replace Lynn, I'm going back to sports. I mean it, Tom. I see that gleam in your eye—I know what you're up to. You're hoping that once I get a taste of hard news again, you won't be able to pry me away from it with a crowbar, but that's not going to happen. I'm a sports writer, dammit."

Not sure if he was trying to convince him or himself, Tom only grinned. Blake might think he could walk away from investigative reporting twice in a lifetime, but Tom knew better. One good story. That's all it would take for Blake to be hooked.

The woman was young—mid-twenties—pretty, and dead.

Arriving at the murder scene only seconds after the cops themselves, Sabrina got her first look at the victim at the same time that the two officers did. Her eyes wide open, a look of horror etched in her pale, stone-cold face, the dead woman lay just inside the open front door of her house and appeared to have been there all night. Dressed in a lacy white nightgown and negligee stained with her own blood, she'd been shot in the heart, probably seconds after she'd opened the door.

"Jesus," Andy Thompson, the younger of the two cops and a rookie, muttered. "She looks like she was waiting for a lover."

"If that's who popped her, then she was a lousy judge of men," his partner, Victor Rodriguez, said flatly. "I'll call the ME and Detective Kelly. This one's got his name written all over it."

He turned and only just then became aware of Sabrina's presence. An old friend, he scowled disapprovingly. "What the heck do you think you're doing in here, Sabrina? This is a crime scene."

Not the least bit intimidated, she flashed her dimples at him. "No kidding? Then I guess that's why I'm here. C'mon, Vic, gimme a break. Let me look around. I'll be out of here before Kelly arrives, I swear."

"That's what you said the last time, and I got a royal chewing out for it." Blocking her path, he refused to let her peer around his broad shoulders and shooed her outside instead. "You know the rules, Sabrina. You want the particulars, you wait till the detective gets here. He'll tell you everything he thinks you need to know."

"You're all heart, Rodriguez," she grumbled as he escorted her well out into the yard, then blockaded the crime scene with yellow police tape to keep her and the curious out. "Kelly won't tell me squat until he's good and ready, and you know it."

"Wah, wah!" he said, grinning as he mimicked a baby's cry. "Quit your crying, Jones. You'll get your story. You always do."

"That's because I'm good at what I do," she called after him as he turned and disappeared back inside. And because she didn't stand around and wait for someone to hand her a story on a platter.

Her hands on her hips, she surveyed the neighborhood. Quiet and moderately affluent, with neatly trimmed yards and houses that would easily sell for a hundred grand or more, it wasn't the type of place where you expected a shooting, let alone a murder. From the small, unobtrusive signs in the front yards, it was obvious that most of the homes had security systems, including the victim's. Yet a woman had been killed—shot, no less—and no one had noticed anything unusual during the night.

Wondering how that could have happened, she headed for the house next door. When Kelly got there, he wouldn't like it that she'd snooped around before his men had a chance to question possible witnesses. But then again, she thought, mischief flashing in her brown eyes, it wouldn't be the first time she'd skirted the rules to get a story. Kelly had to be used to it by now.

Her chances of finding anyone at home at eleven o'clock in the morning on a weekday were slim to none, so she wasn't surprised when no one answered at the first four doors she knocked on. On the fifth, she got lucky.

The man who opened the door to the house directly across the street from the victim's was thin and balding, with a face full of wrinkles and piercing blue eyes that were as sharp as a hawk's. Peering over the top of his bifocals at her, he scowled in annoyance. "If you're selling something door-to-door, lady, you didn't pick a very good day for it. There's been a murder across the street, and any second now this whole block's going to be crawling with police."

"I know, sir. I'm a reporter. Sabrina Jones, with the *Daily Record.* I was wondering if I might ask you a few questions?"

"I didn't see jack squat," he retorted. "Just her body lying in the doorway when I came outside to get my paper this morning. I take the *Times.*"

Sabrina bit back a smile. Readers, as loyal as fans to their favorite pro team, always seemed to be under the mistaken impression that they couldn't talk to her if they didn't read the *Record.* "It's a good paper," she said easily, her brown eyes twinkling. "But so is the *Daily Record.* Did you know the victim?"

His gaze drifting back to the still figure now draped in a yellow plastic sheet, he nodded somberly. "Her name was Tanya Bishop. She was a sweet girl. And smart. A legal secretary. From what I heard, she made good money, but she didn't blow it. She socked it away and bought that house, and she wasn't even thirty yet."

His loyalty to the *Times* forgotten in his need to talk about the victim, he reminisced about her at length while Sabrina jotted down notes and an image of Tanya Bishop formed in her mind. A young professional woman who was responsible and hardworking, she wasn't the type to make enemies. She didn't drink or smoke or party till all hours of the night. And she was dead…just like Charlene McClintock.

Barely two weeks ago, Charlene had also been found dead. Like Tanya, she'd been young, pretty and professional. Everyone who had known her had loved her. Yet someone had shot her in the heart…just like Tanya Bishop. The similarities between the two murders was not lost on her.

"Were you home all night, Mr.—?"

"Dexter," he replied automatically. "Monroe Dexter. Yeah, I was home. And let me tell you, nobody sleeps lighter than I do. A shift in the wind will wake me up, but I didn't hear anything last night." Emotion suddenly clogging his throat, he swallowed. "What I want to know is how the hell somebody could kill that poor girl without making a sound."

Sabrina was wondering the same thing. After thanking Mr. Dexter for his help, she questioned the two other neighbors that were home, but apparently no one had heard anything during the night, not even a dog barking, or noticed any visitors at the Bishop house. Which was damn odd, Sabrina thought, on a street where the homeowners had formed a neighborhood watch to watch over each other.

Questions buzzing like bees in her brain, she headed back to the crime scene to see if the police had found any more answers than she had. As she crossed Tanya Bishop's front yard, she saw that Detective Kelly and the medical examiner had arrived and were in deep conversation as they examined the body. Anxious to catch what they were saying, she hurried forward and never saw the man who deliberately stepped in front of her until she plowed into him.

"Oh! I'm sorry. I didn't see you—"

"I didn't mean to knock you out of your shoes, ma'am, but you don't want to go in there. It's a pretty gory scene—"

They both spoke at once, each rushing to apologize as they broke apart. Feeling like she'd just run full tilt into a brick wall, Sabrina laughed shakily, intending to take all the blame for not watching where she was going. But the second her eyes lifted to the man in front of her, her mind just seemed to go blank and she couldn't do anything but stare.

He towered over her own five-foot-four frame by a good eight inches and wore a black cowboy hat that only added to his impressive height. In spite of that, he didn't appear to be the type of man who would draw a second glance in passing. His face was too ordinary, too lived-in, like the boy next door who grew up into just an average Joe. But looks, she decided, studying him, were deceptive when it came to this man. His mouth seemed to quirk with perpetual good humor, but his angular jaw looked as unyielding as granite, and deep in the depths of his green eyes was a sharpness that missed little. It was, to say the least, an interesting combination.

Intrigued, Sabrina reminded herself she was there to investigate the city's latest murder, not to drool over a tall, dark stranger who seemed to think she was a little woman who'd faint at the sight of blood. Amused, she said dryly, "I've already been in there, and you're right, it is gory. Now if you'll excuse me, I need to talk to Detective Kelly."

Before she could step around him, however, he moved, lightning-quick, to block her path again. Her patience quickly reaching its limit, Sabrina stopped just shot of plowing into his broad chest again and frowned up at him in growing irritation. "Look, I don't know who you think you are, but I've got work to do and you're in my way. Do you mind?"

"Not at all," he said easily. But he didn't move. His mouth twitching with the promise of a smile, he stared down at her searchingly. "What do you mean, you've already been in there? Are you a cop?"

"No, I'm not. I'm a reporter. Sabrina Jones, with the *Daily Record*. Now, if you'll excuse me…"

Stunned, Blake stared down at her in disbelief. *This* was Sabrina Jones? The pride of the *Daily Record*? The ruthless, go-for-the-throat investigative reporter who would do anything short of murder for a story? The way Tom had talked about her, Blake had pictured her as some type of Amazon with more guts than a Marine and a hide like leather. A pushy broad with a reputation for being as tenacious as a bulldog, she should have been tough, brash, and hard as nails.

But the woman who stood before him was anything but hard. In fact, dressed in a gauzy summer dress that draped her slender figure in a cloud of pale pink and fell to just below her knees, her black hair a mass of curls that tumbled artlessly down her back, she looked as soft as cotton candy. A very delectable, feminine piece of cotton candy, he thought with a frown as his gaze slid over her with an ease that had his jaw clenching on an oath. She was short, her bones delicate, the curves revealed by the gently clinging material of her dress enticing. And she was wearing sandals.

His eyes lingering on her toes, he found himself fighting a smile. This was his competition? This dainty woman who looked like she'd swoon at the sight of blood? Oh, she was a good writer, he admitted to himself. He'd read her stuff. She had a way with words. But so did he. And the day that he couldn't write circles around this slip of femininity was the day he'd pack up his computer and find something else to do for a living.

His green eyes starting to twinkle, he deliberately stepped in front of her again, blocking her way. "So you're Sabrina Jones," he drawled. "I've got to admit, you're not what I expected."

Brought up short, her nose just inches from his broad chest, Sabrina glared at him in growing exasperation. "Look, cowboy, I don't know who or what you are, but I've got work to do, and you're in my way."

"Get used to it," he said, grinning as he watched temper simmer in her brown eyes. "I plan to be in your way a lot more before all is said and done."

Her gaze narrowing dangerously, she arched a brow at him. "And how do you plan to do that, Mr....?"

"Nickels," he supplied, holding out his hand as he grinned down at her. "Blake Nickels. With the *Times*. Lynn Phillips had to take maternity leave early. I'm her replacement."

Sudden understanding dawning, Sabrina eyed his hand warily, amusement flirting with the edges of her mouth. The man had more than his share of cockiness. And charm. But if he thought he could best her in a war of words, he was sadly mistaken. Placing her hand in his for a perfunctory shake, she purred, ''I can't say I've ever read any of your work, Mr. Nickels. Should I be quaking in my shoes?''

''If you know what's good for you.''

She laughed; she couldn't help it. He certainly didn't lack confidence. But then again, neither did she. ''Sorry,'' she said with a chuckle, ''but I don't scare that easily.''

''Maybe you should. I'm good, Ms. Jones. Real good.''

''And modest, too,'' she tossed back, grinning.

Undaunted, he only shrugged, devilment dancing in his eyes. ''No brag, just fact. Check me out, sweetheart. You might be impressed.''

''Maybe on a slow day when I've got nothing better to do,'' she agreed sassily. Her gaze moving past him to the crime scene, she watched the ambulance crew that had arrived with the ME load Tanya Bishop's body onto a stretcher and knew that the police were just about finished with their investigation of the crime scene. ''Right now, I've got work to do. See you around, cowboy.''

She darted around him before he could stop her and quickly ducked under the police tape strung between the trees in the front yard. Swearing, Blake started after her just as a tall, redheaded man in a rumpled suit stepped out of the house and caught sight of Sabrina bearing down on him. ''Why did I know you'd be here, Jones?'' he groaned. ''Every time I turn around, there you are. Are you following me?''

''I got here before you did,'' she reminded him with a cheeky grin. ''So what's going on, Sam? From where I'm standing, this looks an awful lot like the McClintock murder.''

His brows snapping together in a fierce glare, he gave her a hard look that had Back Off written all over it. ''You start a rumor like that, Jones, and I'm going to hold you personally responsible. There's nothing to indicate that the two murders are in any way connected."

Frowning, stuck in the position of playing catch-up and not liking it one little bit, Blake stepped forward. "Blake Nickels, with the *Times*," he told the other man. "What's this about another murder, detective? I'm new in town and this is the first I've heard about it."

Sam Kelly introduced himself, then explained, "Charlene McClintock, one of the city's up-and-coming attorneys, was killed two weeks ago, but there's no connection—"

"Was there any sign of forced entry or signs of a struggle?" Sabrina cut in.

"No, but—"

"Does anything appear to be missing?"

"Not that we can tell at this time," he said patiently, "but we won't know for sure until we can find a friend or neighbor to go through the place. You're beating a dead horse here, Jones. Drop it."

Sabrina, well used to holding her own with Kelly, had no intention of doing any such thing. "I got it from one of the neighbors that Tanya Bishop was a legal secretary, Sam. That means two women, young and pretty and both involved in the legal profession, have been shot to death within a two-week period, apparently by someone they knew. Are you really going to stand there and tell me that they're unrelated incidents? C'mon, Sam, get real!"

"I'm not telling you anything more than I already have until the lab results come back and we have time to look into both murders further," he said curtly. "Until then, I suggest you stick to the facts and not jump to any unwarranted conclusions. Now if you'll excuse me, I've got to question the neighbors, then get back to the station." With a nod to both of them, he stepped past the two reporters.

Staring after him, Blake swore under his breath. So

much for his first day on the job. He'd stood there flat-footed and listened to Sabrina ask questions he hadn't even known to ask, and there hadn't been a damn thing he could do about it. It wouldn't, he promised himself, happen again.

And the sooner Sabrina Jones knew that, the better. Glancing down at her, he found her watching him with brown eyes that were just a little too smug for his liking. Oh, she was something, he thought, fighting a reluctant grin. She thought she had him right where she wanted him, a distant second to her first place in a race in which she had the head start. She was all but crowing and she hadn't even reached the finish line yet. The darn woman didn't realize that he had her right where he wanted her.

"I wouldn't start celebrating just yet if I were you," he warned dryly. "Just because I was unprepared this time doesn't mean I will be again."

Not the least bit worried, she only cocked her head at him and teased playfully, "What's the matter, Nickels? You don't like coming in second to a woman? Get used to it, cowboy. I'm just hitting my stride."

That was the wrong thing to say to a man who thrived on a challenge. "Oh, really?" he drawled. "Well, just for the record, sweetheart, the fact that you're a woman has nothing to do with anything. I don't care if you're purple— I don't like eating your dust. Next time I'll be ready for you."

It was an out-and-out warning, one that only a foolish woman would have ignored. And Sabrina was nobody's fool. Blake Nickels might have been a little out of his depth this time, but as she watched him stalk off to his car, she had a feeling that he was going to be a force to be reckoned with. His eyes had held a sharp intelligence, and then there was that jaw of his—as hard and immovable as concrete, it had had determination written all over it.

Not that she was worried, she quickly assured herself as she turned to her own car. This was her town, her beat. Blake Nickels was the new kid on the block. She knew her own abilities and could handle anything the man could dish out.

She deliberately pushed him from her thoughts, but hours later, when she was back at her desk at the *Daily Record* working on her story about the city's latest murder, it wasn't poor Tanya Bishop's lifeless body that stirred to life in her mind's eye—it was the memory of Blake Nickels' smile. Wicked, teasing, dangerous. No man had a right to look so good just by curling up the edge of his mouth, she decided, trying to work up a good case of irritation. A frown furrowing her brow, she tried to force her attention back to what was sure to be a front-page story, but just thinking about Blake and that grin of his made her lips twitch.

And that worried her. Blake Nickels was full of charm and devilment, and she wouldn't, couldn't, like him. She didn't care if he was the next best thing to sliced bread, he was the opposition, the competition, a male chauvinist who didn't like standing around with his hands in his pockets while she asked all the questions. Given the chance, he'd snitch a story right out from under her nose if she relaxed her guard for so much as a second.

If that wasn't reason enough to avoid him like the plague, the fact that she found herself thinking about him when she had a hot story to write was. She wasn't looking for a man to distract her, or do anything else with her. The women in her family didn't handle relationships well. Between the two of them, her mother and grandmother had been married eight times, and Sabrina had decided at an early age that she wasn't going to follow in their footsteps. Then, three years ago, she'd met Jeff Harper.

She winced at the memory. All her fine resolves had

gone up in smoke the first time he'd kissed her. In spite
of the fact that they'd had absolutely nothing in common,
she'd fallen for him like a ton of bricks. When he'd asked
her to marry him, she'd convinced herself that *she* wasn't
like her mother or grandmother—*she* could make a relationship work. She'd then spent the next two years trying
to do just that, and they'd both been miserable. When
they'd inevitably agreed to divorce last summer, it had
been a relief.

In spite of that, she didn't regret her marriage. She'd
learned the hard way that she, too, like the rest of the
women in her family, had a defective gene when it came
to commitment. Unlike her mother and grandmother, however, she didn't have to go through one divorce after another to learn her lesson. Once was enough. She wasn't
cut out to be anything but single, and that was just fine
with her. As long as she remembered that—and she didn't
plan to forget it—she and Blake Nickels would get along
just fine.

Caught up in trying to find a possible link between
Tanya Bishop and Charlene McClintock's murders, as well
as cover the more interesting stories that came across her
police scanner, she was actually able to forget that the
Times even had a new reporter. Then, just as she was about
to grab something for lunch the next day, news of a bank
robbery in progress had her rushing over to the southside
location. It was just the kind of breaking story she loved,
and normally, she was the first reporter on the scene. Not
this time, though. Blake Nickels was already there, standing in the bank parking lot interviewing a witness, and the
rat was obviously watching for her. The second she pulled
into the lot, he looked up and waved.

Grinning broadly, he pushed his cowboy hat to the back

of his head. "Hey, Jones, what took you so long?" he teased. "You having a slow day, or what?"

Heat flushed her cheeks, the grin that tugged at her mouth impossible to hide. "Put a sock in it, Nickels," she tossed back, trying and failing to maintain a frown. "I know this might come as something of a surprise to you, but some of us actually cover more than one crime a day."

"No kidding? So where were you when I was covering that assault on a nun at Main Plaza this morning?"

"Interviewing a string of restaurant owners who were conned by a homeless lady on the northside. So what have you got to say about that?"

His eyes dancing, he shrugged. "How about I'll show you my notes if you show me yours?"

She wanted the story on the nun, but Fitz, her boss, would have her hide if she so much as shared the time of day with a *Times* reporter. "Not on your life, cowboy," she replied, and turned away to snag a policeman who'd just walked out of the bank.

Turning down Blake's offer, she quickly discovered to her chagrin, proved to be a mistake. Oh, the police were willing to give her the details of the heist and a brief description of the robber, who had escaped with fifty thousand dollars and was last seen racing west on Loop 410 in a white van. But there was only one witness—the teller—and after she'd given the police a statement, the only reporter she'd agree to talk to was Blake.

Unable to believe she'd heard her correctly, Sabrina said, "What do you mean you won't give your story to anyone but Blake Nickels? You talked to the police."

"Oh, I had to tell them," the pretty blonde said airily. "But Blake asked for an exclusive, and I said okay." All innocence, she smiled sweetly. "So you see, I can't go back on my word. It just wouldn't be ethical, now would it?"

Indignant, Sabrina just barely bit back a scathing retort. If the bubblehead of a teller wanted to talk ethics, she never would have let Blake talk her into an exclusive in the first place. And for a darn bank robbery, of all things! She'd never heard of anything so ridiculous in her life. She only wished she'd thought of it.

Frustrated, steam all but coming out of her ears, she forced a smile. "I appreciate your ethics, Ms. Walker, but your boss might not be too pleased when he hears that you're only talking to one reporter. The bank just lost a substantial amount of money that probably won't be recovered—unless word gets out about the robbery and a possible reward." Reaching into her purse, she pulled out a business card and handed it to her. "Think about it. If you change your mind before my deadline, give me a call."

The woman took her card, but Sabrina knew better than to hold out hope that she would use it. You only had to see her staring after Blake like he was the greatest thing since Elvis to know that she was thoroughly smitten. And for some reason she couldn't explain, that irritated Sabrina to no end.

As her gaze followed the teller's to where Blake stood fifty yards away, finishing an interview with one of the first officers on the scene, she told herself he wasn't going to get away with it. He could sweet-talk every woman he saw for all she cared—some people would stoop to any level to get a story—but he wasn't going to stop her from doing her job! Not if she had anything to say about it. Her jaw set, she started toward him.

Thanking the investigating officer, Roger Martinez, for his help, Blake was jotting down notes in the small notebook he never went anywhere without when he looked up to see Sabrina bearing down on him like a ruffled hen with her tail feathers in a twist. So, he thought as a slow grin skimmed his mouth, she'd found out about the exclusive. Now the fur was really going to fly.

"Hey, Jones," he greeted her as she drew near. "You look a little out of sorts. Something wrong?"

Color flying high in her cheeks, she gave him a withering look. "You're damn right something's wrong! You're a yellow-bellied, toad-eating weasel. How dare you!"

Grinning, he chuckled. "Honey, when you get to know me better, you'll find out that I'll dare just about anything. I take it you've been talking to Jennifer Walker."

"If you want to call it that. She wouldn't tell me a darn thing, and you know it. Because *she* promised *you* an exclusive."

Enjoying himself, Blake grinned. "And all I had to do was ask." Leaning closer, his eyes dancing with mischief, he confided, "I think she likes me."

For a moment, he could have sworn he heard her grinding her teeth. "Then the woman has no taste," she snapped in a low voice that didn't carry any further than his ears. "You ought to be ashamed of yourself."

"Why? Because I thought of it before you did? C'mon, Sabrina, admit it. The only reason you're in a snit is because I outfoxed you."

"Don't be ridiculous," she fibbed. "This story is a matter of police record, and I'll get it with or without that blond bimbo teller's cooperation—"

Making no effort to hide his amusement, he cocked a teasing brow at her. "Blond bimbo? Do I detect a little jealousy here? Why, Jones, I didn't know you cared."

Sabrina's lips twitched. Lord, he was outrageous! She'd always liked a man with a quick wit, and if she didn't watch herself with him, she was going to find herself charmed into liking him. And that could be nothing but a disaster.

Somehow managing to look down her nose at him in spite of the fact that he towered over her, she studied him consideringly. "Don't let it go to your head, cowboy. The only thing I care about is the story, and you're throwing up roadblocks. Now, I wonder why that is? You running scared, Nickels, or what?"

"Of you?" He chuckled. "I don't think so. I read your story in this morning's paper, sweetheart." Not batting an eye, he quoted word-for-word from her front-page story on the Bishop murder in the morning edition of the *Daily Record.* "'Tanya Bishop was dressed to meet a lover. A lover who may have killed her.'" Clicking his tongue at her in teasing disapproval, he grinned. "Naughty, naughty, Jones. Of course she was dressed for bed—she was killed during the middle of the night—but that doesn't mean she was expecting a lover. And what's this *may* business? The last I heard, a good reporter stuck to the facts and nothing but the facts, not supposition."

Her cheeks flushed at the gentle criticism. Darn the man, she should have caught that. And when she hadn't, her editor should have! But she'd have eaten worms before admitting it. Instead, she purred silkily, "Why, Nickels, I'm flattered you went to the trouble to memorize my work. Are you one of our new subscribers? You should have told me and I might have been able to get you a discount."

"To the *Record*?" He snorted, amused. "I don't think so. I like my news hard and gritty, and I'll bet your readers do, too. In fact, I'll bet you dinner at the restaurant of your choice that before the month is out, my paper, not yours, is winning the subscription war."

"Watch it, Nickels. I have expensive taste."

"So it's a bet?"

Hesitating, Sabrina reminded herself that he was a man who didn't always play by the rules. And there were some very expensive restaurants in town. If she lost, she'd feel the blow not only in her pride, but in her pocketbook. But she'd never been one to play it safe, and there were some things a woman with daring just couldn't walk away from. And Blake Nickels, she reluctantly admitted, was one of them.

Grinning, she held out her hand and silently prayed she didn't live to regret her impulsiveness. "You're on, Nickels. If I were you, I'd start saving my pennies. This is going to cost you."

Chapter 2

She was running late. Her alarm clock hadn't gone off, and she'd unconsciously taken advantage of it, waking a mere ten minutes before she was due at work. Horrified, Sabrina jumped out of bed and threw on some clothes, but even moving at the speed of sound, it was well after she should have punched in at the paper when she slammed out of her house and dashed to her car. Mumbling reminders to get herself a new clock, she raced down the street, tires squealing, and headed for the freeway three blocks away.

She'd barely shot onto the entrance ramp when she had to hit the brakes. A four-car pileup a half a mile ahead blocked all three lanes, slowing traffic to a virtual crawl. She'd be lucky if she made it in to the paper by noon.

Fitz was not going to be pleased.

Sabrina winced and rubbed at her temples, where a dull pounding started to hammer relentlessly. It was not, she decided, going to be a good morning. As far as bosses went, Fitz was a real gem when it came to letting her run with a story, but he was a real stickler when it came to reporting in in the morning. If you were going to be late, you'd better have a darn good excuse.

Staring up ahead at the whirling lights of at least three patrol cars and two ambulances, Sabrina saw a uniformed officer slap handcuffs on one of the drivers and started to smile. This wasn't evidently one of your average rush-hour fender benders. Things were starting to look up. Fitz wouldn't be nearly as inclined to give her one of his patented speeches about punctuality if she came in with a story. Sending up a silent prayer of thanks for gifts from God, she eased over onto the shoulder of the freeway and raced down it toward the accident scene.

It wasn't noon when she rushed into the *Daily Record*, but it was pretty darn close to it. Glancing at the clock in the lobby, Sabrina winced. Fitz was going to have a hissy. It wouldn't, she thought with an impish grin, be the first one that she'd caused. She seemed to have a talent for it where he was concerned.

"Well, well, well," a familiar, gruff voice drawled sarcastically as she stepped off the elevator and turned to come face-to-face with her boss. "If it isn't our star reporter. And she's actually putting in an appearance at work. Glad you could join us, Ms. Jones. I hope it wasn't too much of an imposition."

Well used to the cutting edge of the old man's tongue, she ignored his sarcasm and gave him a cheeky grin. "Not at all, boss. I'm sorry I'm late, but I knew you wouldn't want me to leave the scene of a story—"

"What story?"

"A four-car pileup on the Loop. It seems that a red van was weaving back and forth between the lanes before it plowed into a car full of college kids from Austin on their

way to the coast. The van driver was drunk as a skunk—
and you'll never guess who it was.''

"Who?" he growled. "And this better be good, Jones.
I've been trying to track you down all morning.''

"I know it, boss, but I was stuck on the freeway with
no way to call you. And it was the mayor's son, Jason
Grimes! He'd been out carousing all night in daddy's car.''

"What? Why the hell didn't you say so?''

Knowing she was forgiven, Sabrina laughed. "I would
have given a hundred bucks to have had a camera. Nobody
was hurt, but those kids from Austin were fighting mad
when it looked like the cops were going to let Jason off
the hook. He's an obnoxious little brat at the best of times,
but when he's drunk, he's an arrogant son of a gun. He
made the mistake of telling one of the kids from Austin
that his daddy would see that he didn't even get a ticket
for reckless driving, let alone arrested for a DWI, and the
kid took a swing at him. He's not quite as pretty as he
used to be.''

Fitz's sharp gray eyes started to twinkle. "Now ain't
that a shame? And he was such a good-looking boy. Write
it up, Jones. Then nose around down at the police station
and see if you can find out what the policy has been in
the past toward young Jason's drunk driving. If he's gotten
special privileges, I want to know about it.''

He started to turn away, only to remember her tardiness.
Glancing over his shoulder, he warned, "And don't be late
again, Jones. Next time, you might not be lucky enough
to have a story fall in your lap the way this one did.''

"No, sir. I mean yes, sir, it won't happen again." Sa-
luting smartly, she dared to wink at him. "I'll get right on
it.''

He scowled like an old Scrooge, but Sabrina caught the
twitch of his lips before he headed for his office. Chuckling

to herself, she turned toward her own desk, her thoughts already jumping ahead to the opening line of her story.

Distracted, she didn't see the note lying right in the middle of her desk until she sat down and started to turn toward her computer monitor. Then she saw it—a single sheet of white, unlined paper folded in half with her name handwritten on the front. Perched precariously on top of some notes from yesterday's bank robbery, it could have been left there by anyone—her co-workers left notes for her all the time. But those were handwritten on little yellow stickies, not typed ones on what looked like fairly expensive textured paper.

Wondering who it was from, she reached for it and had a sudden image of Blake teasing her yesterday about her coverage of the Bishop murder. It would, she thought, unable to hold back a smile, be just like him to take it upon himself to critique another of her stories. Only this time, he'd put it in writing and obviously bribed someone in the lobby to deliver it to her desk, since there was no envelope. She could just imagine what it said.

But when she leaned back in her chair and flipped the note open, her eyes dancing with expectancy, she saw in a single, all-encompassing glance that it wasn't from Blake. Then the typed words registered and a cold chill crept like a winter fog through her bloodstream, chilling her to the bone.

Sabrina,
Tanya Bishop thought she could compete in a man's world, and she was wrong. I tried to tell her differently. Women are the nurturers, the homemakers, the babymakers. They should be home, raising the next generation and saving the world, not having power lunches and taking jobs away from men who can do the work ten times better. It's not right. I told Tanya

that, but she wouldn't listen. She laughed at my warning that she was in danger of upsetting the natural order of things. I didn't want to kill her, but what else could I do? She didn't know her place, so she had to be eliminated. She gave me no other choice.

I know how your mind operates, Sabrina. You think I'm some kind of nut case looking for publicity for a murder I didn't commit. But I really did kill her. We were friends. I hoped we could be more, but she couldn't be what I wanted her to be. *Who* I wanted her to be. So I decided to end it and called to tell her I needed to see her. She was dressed in a white gown and negligee and opened the door to me the second I rang the bell. That's when I shot her. She fell right where she stood in the doorway, and I can't feel bad about it. Other professional women might want to take heed while they still can.

Stunned, her heart starting to pound in her ears, Sabrina stared at the cold, unfeeling words and told herself this was a hoax—one of her fellow reporters was probably watching her right now, grinning like an idiot as he waited for her reaction. But even as she cast a quick look around the city room, she knew deep in her gut that this was no practical joke. The note had a ring of truth to it, a sick logic, that sent goose bumps racing over her skin.

Pale, her fingers not quite steady, she dropped the note as if it were a lit firecracker and reached for her phone, quickly pushing the button for the receptionist's desk in the lobby. "Valerie," she said as soon as the other woman came on the line, "this is Sabrina. Did anyone hand-deliver a note for me late yesterday afternoon or this morning?"

"If they did, this is the first I've heard of it," Valerie replied cheerfully. "Lydia Davidson in classifieds got flowers from her latest heartthrob, but other than that, things have been pretty quiet. Why?''

''No reason,'' Sabrina said quickly. ''I was just wondering. If anyone does come in asking for me, let me know, okay? Thanks.''

She hung up, frowning, refusing to even consider the possibility that Tanya Bishop's killer had hand-delivered a note to her. *If* the thing was even legit, she amended silently. Whoever wrote it must have gotten one of the other staff members to drop it off at her desk. It was the only explanation.

But when she asked around, she got nothing but negative answers. No one had passed a message on to her. No one had seen any strangers or visitors loitering around her desk. For all practical purposes, the note had simply appeared there and no one had a clue how.

Not easily scared, Sabrina told herself she wasn't worried. She could take care of herself—she always had. And if there was a threat in the note, it wasn't meant for her. How could it be? She didn't even know the killer. Whoever he was, he obviously wanted his fifteen minutes of fame, just like everybody else. She could give him that. But first she had to talk to Sam Kelly. Picking up her phone, she punched in the number for the police department.

''C'mon, Kelly, I know you've got the coroner's report—I called the ME's office and asked,'' Blake said with a grin as he lounged in the chair across the desk from the detective. ''What's the big secret? Everyone knows Tanya Bishop was shot in the heart. All I want is the time of death.''

''You'll get it just like everyone else at the press conference this afternoon at three,'' Sam said firmly. ''That gives you plenty of time to make the morning edition.''

In years past, Blake had worked with detectives who hoarded information like misers stockpiling gold, giving it out in beggarly bits and pieces like they were doing the world a favor. Sam Kelly didn't strike him that way. He didn't play games or do anything that might have been considered unethical. He was a strictly by-the-book man, and Blake had to admire that. In a world where whole police departments were as crooked as a dog's hind leg, it was nice to know there were men like Sam Kelly still hanging in there, doing things the right way, fighting the good fight. But it made getting information out of him damn difficult.

"The morning edition's not the problem," he said ruefully, opting for the truth. "It's Sabrina Jones."

His craggy face cracking in a smile, Sam leaned back in his chair and surveyed him knowingly. "So Sabrina's giving you fits already, is she? Somebody should have warned you."

"Somebody did—I just didn't believe him. She's quick, damn quick. And if you tell her I said that, I'll flat out deny it. The woman's already too cocky as it is."

Sam laughed, agreeing. "She never has lacked for confidence. Some men have a hard time handling that. I heard you two have a bet going on—"

Before he could say more, the phone on his desk rang, and with a murmured apology to Blake, he reached over and answered it. Recognizing Sabrina's husky voice, he started to smile. "Well, speak of the devil. I was just talking about you, Sabrina. What's up?"

Snapping to attention at the mention of Sabrina's name, Blake watched Sam's expression turn from teasing to grim in the blink of an eye. All business, the detective reached for a pen and started jotting down notes. "No, don't touch it any more than you already have," he said quickly.

''We'll need to test it for fingerprints, then send it to the lab to see what they can make of it. I'll be right over.''

Impatient, the one-sided conversation giving him few clues to what was going on, Blake started throwing questions at the other man the second he hung up. ''Don't touch what? Is Sabrina in some kind of danger? What are you sending to the lab? Dammit, Sam, what's going on?''

For a moment, he thought the other man wasn't going to tell him anything, but then Sam sighed and said, ''I guess there's no reason to keep it a secret—you're going to find out soon enough anyway. Sabrina got to work late today—just a few minutes ago, in fact—and found a note someone had left on her desk. It appears to be from Tanya Bishop's killer.''

''What?!''

''*Appears* is the operative word here,'' he stressed. ''At this point, we can't be sure it's from the real killer, but Sabrina's not taking it lightly. In fact, she sounded pretty shaken.''

''Well, I would think she damn well would be. Why would the bastard send her a note?''

''The man's a murderer, Blake. He's already killed once, possibly twice, if he offed Charlene McClintock. Who knows what's going on in his head? And he didn't *send* it. Sabrina thinks he hand-delivered it.''

''Son of a bitch! You mean he just walked right into the *Daily Record*?''

''That's the way it looks. I'm heading over there right now to check it out. I'll see you later at the press conference.''

''The hell you will,'' Blake said, rising to his feet. ''I'm going with you.''

Sitting at her desk, her gaze trained unseeingly on her computer monitor, Sabrina tried to focus on her story about the mayor's son and his drunken joyride, but her concentration was shot. She couldn't write a logical sentence to save her life. All she could think about was the series of veiled threats in the note, threats that could have been meant for every professional woman in the city. Including herself.

When the thought had first occurred to her, fear, uncontrollable and unwanted, had surged in her before she could stop it. And she hadn't liked it one little bit. She didn't like being afraid, especially where she worked. This was her desk, her paper, and no murdering wacko was going to waltz in there and scare the bejabbers out of her just because he had a problem with women in power positions!

Giving up any attempt to work, she sat back and glared at the note, a thousand angry questions spinning in her head. Had the writer really killed Tanya? And why had he sent his note to her? Obviously he wanted his message to get out to professional women who were, in his words, "tampering with the world order," but that didn't mean that she was the only reporter who could relay his message for him. Any television station or newspaper in the country would have done the same thing once the note was declared valid by the police. So why her? From the way he sounded, he didn't even like career women, and she'd never claimed to be anything else. What did he want with her, anyway?

Frowning, she was still trying to figure that out when Sam Kelly walked into the city room. And right behind him was Blake Nickels, strolling in as if he was taking a walk in a park!

Stunned, Sabrina couldn't believe her eyes. "What's he doing here?" she asked Sam by way of a greeting.

"Now don't go getting all bent out of shape, Sabrina," he soothed. "He was at the station when you called, sitting right across from me at my desk. What was I supposed to do? Lock him up so he couldn't follow me?''

"It's a thought," she replied, shooting Blake a narrow-eyed look that didn't faze his teasing grin one iota. "You've got a lot of nerve coming here, cowboy. What do you want?''

"A story." Plopping down on a corner of her desk, he tilted his cowboy hat to the back of his head and crossed his arms across his chest as if he planned to stay awhile. "The last I heard, you were it."

Despite the fact that she was still unsettled about the note, she couldn't help but appreciate the vagaries of Fate. Biting back a smile, she asked, "Have you ever heard that old saying 'what goes around, comes around,' Nickels? Well, it looks like it's your turn to get what's coming to you. Yesterday, you had an exclusive. Today, I do. Isn't life funny?"

"Oh, yeah. It's a regular riot," he drawled.

Captivated by the flash of her quick grin, he wondered if she had any idea how tempting she looked, her gaze level with his for once since he was sitting, satisfaction dancing in those expressive brown eyes of hers. A man could be forgiven for kissing a woman under such circumstances, and the sudden need to do just that stunned the hell out of him. Where the devil had that come from?

You've been too long without a woman, his common sense muttered in his ear. *That's the only explanation. Sure, she's a pretty little thing, but she'd just as soon have you for breakfast as look at you. She's the competition. Remember?*

Brought up short by the reminder—and annoyed at the need for it—he scowled and glanced down at her desk. "So where's the note? At least let me take a quick peek at it before you toss me out of here."

Lightning-quick, she grabbed his hand and tried to tug

him to his feet. "Not on your life. You've seen and heard all you're going to, so get. I'm sure Sam has a lot of questions, and I have no intention of answering them in front of you."

"Spoilsport."

Her efforts to move him about as effective as a gnat's, she dropped his hand and squared off in front of him like Sugar Ray Leonard. "Don't make me get tough with you."

"At last she's going to get physical!" he teased, his eyes laughing at her. "Yes, Virginia, there is a Santa Claus."

"Blake—"

When she used that tone, he knew she meant business. "Okay, okay. You win." Though he was left with no choice but to back off, he had no intention of going far. Not until he had some answers. Reluctantly, he pushed himself to his feet. "Enjoy your victory, Jones. The next one may be a long time coming."

Shooting one last, searching look at her desk, he turned away and gave every appearance of leaving as he headed for the exit. But just before he reached it, he glanced back over his shoulder and found Sabrina in a serious discussion with the detective, who was carefully examining a sheet of paper on her desk. That was all the opening Blake needed.

Stopping at the water fountain in the hall to talk to a pretty young copy girl who looked like she was hardly old enough to be out of high school, he shot her his most charming smile, pushed his cowboy hat up off his forehead, and prayed she hadn't heard of him as he introduced himself. "Hi, I'm Blake Nickels. I came with Detective Kelly—"

Her blue eyes bright with shy interest, she said huskily, "I saw you when you came in. Are you a detective, too?"

"Not quite," he hedged, and told himself it wasn't a lie. He hadn't actually misrepresented himself, which would have been unethical—he'd just let her jump to her own conclusions because he had no other choice. If he identified himself as a reporter with the *Times,* she and everyone else in the building would send him packing as fast as Sabrina had. Pulling out his notebook, he said, "I was hoping you could answer some questions for me."

"About the note Sabrina got?"

"You know about it?"

"Oh, sure. The news went through the building like wildfire. The killer just walked in and left the note on her desk."

In the process of reaching for the pen in his shirt pocket, Blake glanced up at her in surprise. "Someone saw him?"

She hesitated, then had the grace to blush. "Well, no, not exactly. But how else could it have gotten there if he didn't deliver it in person? All the employees have been questioned, and no one knows a thing about it."

She had a point, one that Blake didn't like one little bit. Tanya Bishop's killer was no stumbling novice. The man—he'd heard of no evidence that pointed to the sex of the murderer, but his gut was telling him it had to be a man—had been smart and cunning enough to surprise her, then kill her without leaving a single clue. Just the thought of him walking into the *Daily Record* and finding Sabrina's desk without anyone being the wiser turned Blake's blood cold. If the bastard could track her down so easily at work, what was to stop him from following her home?

His expression darkening at the thought, he said tersely, "That must have been a hell of a note, if he was willing to take that kind of risk to deliver it. Any idea what was in it? I haven't seen it yet."

The girl nodded, indignation sparkling in her blue eyes. "It was a bunch of garbage about women not knowing their place and taking jobs away from men. Supposedly, that's why Tanya Bishop was killed. She was warned to stay home where she belonged and she laughed in the jerk's face.''

His pen flying over the pages of his notebook in his own brand of shorthand, Blake took down every word and could already see the headlines. But the elation he should have felt at outsmarting Sabrina in her own backyard just wasn't there. Not when she had drawn the attention of a murderer. He tried to tell himself that he would have been disturbed by the thought of any colleague receiving what sounded like a threatening note—it was nothing personal. But this felt distinctly, disturbingly, personal.

"Did I say something wrong? You look awful mad all of a sudden."

Glancing up from his notes, he found the copy girl staring at him with a puzzled frown. "No," he said quietly, forcing a crooked smile that didn't come as easily as it usually did. "You didn't say anything wrong. My mind just wandered for a second. Is that the gist of the note?"

She nodded. "Pretty much. Except that it was a warning to other professional women that the same thing could happen to them if they're not careful."

To Blake, that sounded more like a threat than a warning, one directed right at Sabrina. And if she didn't have the sense to recognize that, she wasn't as smart as he thought she was. Thanking the copy girl for her help, he returned to the city room to find Sabrina pounding out a story on her computer while Detective Kelly questioned the other *Record* staff members.

Crossing the room in four long strides, Blake came up behind her and boldly began to read the opening paragraph on her monitor. "That'd better not be what I think it is, Jones."

Startled, she whirled in her chair, her hand flying to her

throat. "Damn you, Nickels! You scared the stuffing out of me! What are you doing here? I thought I told you to leave."

He grinned, but there was little humor in his eyes when he said, "Nobody scares me off a story that easy, honey, especially a shrimp like you." Dropping with lazy grace into the chair positioned across from her desk, he nodded to her computer monitor, where the opening lines of her story were still clearly visible. "You're not really going to print the contents of that note, are you?"

"Not print it?" she choked, swivelling the monitor so he could no longer see the screen. "Are you out of your mind? Of course I'm going to print it!"

"Don't you think that's a mistake? What if it's bogus? You'll come off looking like a fool."

"I'd rather risk that than not let the professional women of this city know that there's a psychopath out there with a vendetta against them. This man, whoever he is, doesn't live in a vacuum, Blake. Somebody out there knows him, and when they read his note in the paper, they just might come forward. Anyway, the note's not bogus. If you don't believe me, ask Sam."

Dammit, he didn't have to ask Sam. He'd heard enough from the copy girl to know that she was right. And that's what worried him. "Then that's just one more reason not to print it," he said stubbornly. "If the killer really wrote it, he didn't send it to you because he wanted to be friends or give you the scoop of the century. It was a threat to you and every other career woman out there, and you'll only encourage him if you print it."

"Don't be ridiculous," she scoffed. "You're just ticked because I've got the inside track on the best story to hit this town in years. You know you're going to lose our bet and it's driving you up the wall." Daring to smile at him, she goaded sweetly, "Better save your pennies, cowboy. You're going to need them, and then some."

Frustrated, his hands curling into fists to keep from reaching across her desk to shake the stuffing out of her, Blake couldn't for the life of him understand why he was so burned. He didn't want to see her or anyone else get hurt, but the lady meant nothing to him. Oh, he liked her well enough, but he'd always been a sap for smart, independent women. He liked bran, too, but he knew better than to overindulge. And Sabrina Jones was definitely an indulgence he wanted no part of, especially after Trina had made a fool out of him. He was concerned, just as he would be for any other woman who was standing on the edge of disaster and didn't know it.

Still, she could obviously take care of herself. She might look as soft as a powder puff, but underneath that cloud of silky black curls and the soft blouses and skirts that emphasized her femininity was a woman who had a reputation for being tough when it came to her work. If she wasn't worried about developing a tenuous relationship with the killer, why should he be?

Because two other career women had no doubt once thought they could take care of themselves, too. And now they were dead.

"This has nothing to do with the damn bet," he said curtly, pushing to his feet. "I was just concerned for your safety, but I guess that's not my problem, is it?" Not waiting for an answer, he headed for the door.

He walked away from Sabrina because she hadn't given much choice, but there was no way in hell he was walking away from the story, he decided as he pulled out of the *Record*'s parking lot a few minutes later. There was a reason the killer had sent it to Sabrina, and he meant to find out what it was—with or without her cooperation.

And there was no better place to start his investigation

than with the lady herself. When she found out about it, she was going to be madder than a wet hen. Grinning at the thought, he stopped at a convenience store and borrowed a phone book to look up her address. Seconds later, he was headed for the near north side.

She lived off St. Mary's Street in an older neighborhood that had once been quite nice but had declined as the city grew. Most of the homes were wood-framed, with wide porches, many of them sagging and sad-looking. More often than not, graffiti marked fences and walls, a by-product of the gangs that had taken over the area and claimed it as their own. It went without saying that crime was high.

There were pockets of hope, though, Blake noted. A cluster of homes here and there, even a whole block where homeowners were trying to reclaim their neighborhood. Here, the homes were painted and restored, the yards mowed. And it was here that Sabrina lived.

Parking at the curb in front of her house, Blake found himself smiling at the sight of it. Somehow, out of all the houses on the street, he would have known without asking that this one was Sabrina's. The winding walk that led from the curb to her front porch was bracketed with flower beds that were bursting with wildflowers, and on the porch itself were bright pots of geraniums and begonias that were as thick as thieves. Every yard on the street seemed to have flower beds, but while the others were neatly trimmed and organized, Sabrina's were wild and free and bold with color. Just like the woman herself, he thought with a frown. And it was that boldness that was going to get her into trouble if she wasn't careful.

But that wasn't why he was there, he reminded himself grimly. The killer had made Sabrina a part of his story when he'd delivered that note to her. Until the murderer was identified and caught, Sabrina was the only living tie to the man that anyone was aware of, and Blake meant to find out why. What it was about her that attracted the killer's attention?

Studying the homes of her neighbors, he decided to check the one on the left, where there were two cars in the driveway. The old lady who answered the door was round and jolly, with a double chin and inquisitive blue eyes that twinkled behind the lenses of her glasses. Lifting a delicately arched brow at him, she said, "Yes? May I help you?"

"I certainly hope so, ma'am." Introducing himself, he pulled his wallet out of his back pocket and showed her his credentials. "I'm Blake Nickels, with the *Times*. I wonder if I could ask you a few questions about your neighbor, Sabrina Jones?"

Alarmed, her easy smile faltered. "Why? Has something happened to her?"

"No, she's fine," Blake quickly assured her. "In fact, I just left her a few minutes ago at the *Daily Record*." Knowing there was no way he was going to find anything out about Sabrina without her friends' cooperation, he quickly told the older woman about the note. "The police are aware of the situation and are checking out the note in the hopes that it will lead them to Tanya Bishop's murderer, but I'm more inclined to check out Sabrina. The killer didn't just pick her name out of a hat. He chose her for a reason. I was hoping you or one of the other neighbors might be able to tell me why by giving me some information about her background."

For a moment, Blake thought she was going to turn him down flat. Not committing herself one way or the other, she studied him through the screen door, then nodded as if coming to a silent decision and pushed open the door. "I'm Martha Anderson. Come on in. If Sabrina's in trouble, I want to help."

Blake only meant to ask her a few questions, but the old lady was obviously lonely and hungry for visitors. After settling him at her kitchen table, she fixed them each a glass of iced tea, then settled into the chair across from him, eager to talk.

"Sabrina's such a wonderful girl," she confided. "And everybody around here is just crazy about her. It's such a shame about her husband—"

"Husband?" Blake echoed, sitting up straighter. "I didn't know she was married."

"She's not…now," Martha replied. "How that girl could be so smart and make such a huge mistake, God only knows. Anyone with eyes could see that Jeff Harper was about as wrong for her as a bad case of the flu, but she was infatuated and just threw caution to the wind. She's like that, you know," she added, leaning closer as if she was confiding a secret. "Impulsive. Lord, that girl's impulsive! I swear she doesn't have a self-protective bone in her body, but you won't find a better friend or neighbor in this city. When I broke my hip last year, she was over here just about every evening to cook supper for me. And then when Louis— Louis Vanderbilt, he lives on the other side of Sabrina—had to have his dog put to sleep last summer, Sabrina went out and bought him another one. I cried myself, just seeing how moved he was."

"What about this Jeff Harper character?" Blake asked with a frown. "Where's he? And how does he feel about her dating again?"

"Well, that's just it, dear," the old lady replied. "She doesn't date. Ever. As far as I've been able to tell, she hasn't been out a single time since she and Jeff split. Not that he would care. He's already remarried and got a baby on the way. As far as I know, Sabrina hasn't seen him in over a year."

Intrigued, Blake found that hard to believe. Whether he

wanted to admit it or not, Sabrina Jones was a beautiful woman with a sassy personality that any man with blood in his veins would find hard to resist. She had a job that took her all over the city and gave her plenty of opportunities to meet people. So what was wrong with the men in San Antonio? Were they blind, or what?

"So she doesn't date and there's no men in her life," he said thoughtfully. That ruled out the possibility of the killer being someone she'd been involved with romantically. "What about enemies?"

"Enemies?" Martha laughed, her blue eyes fairly sparkling behind the lenses of her glasses. "You obviously don't know Sabrina very well or you wouldn't even ask that. She can be as nosy as an old woman when she's after a story, but she's just doing her job. Nobody holds it against her."

Obviously extremely fond of Sabrina, she drew a tantalizing picture of her that Blake found thoroughly captivating. But she didn't tell him anything that even hinted at why Tanya Bishop's killer had turned his sights on Sabrina. Thanking the old lady for her help, he went looking for more answers from the other neighbors.

Since most of Sabrina's neighbors were retired, he didn't have any trouble finding someone to talk to. Unfortunately, he didn't get the information he was hoping for. All of them knew and liked Sabrina and had their own stories to tell about her, but none could think of a single reason why a killer would send her a threatening note. Except for Louis Vanderbilt.

A quiet, unassuming man who was out walking the now-grown Labrador that Sabrina had given him as a puppy, he paled when he stopped to talk to Blake and was told about the note. "Sabrina did a special series last year about sexual discrimination in the workplace," he said quietly. "It was excellent. In fact, I think she won several awards for it. But one of the editors at her own paper quit over allegations that she stirred up, and from what I heard from Sabrina, he vowed to get even. But that was months ago. Sabrina probably forgot all about him. Do you think he could be the one who sent her the note?''

Blake didn't know, but it was definitely worth checking out and mentioning to the police. Feeling like he was finally getting somewhere, he quickly jotted down notes. ''What was the man's name? Do you have any idea what happened to him after he quit the *Record*?''

A thin, balding man with wire-rimmed glasses and the kind of ageless face that didn't show the passage of time, Louis murmured to the Lab, who was impatient to resume his walk, and tried to remember. ''It seems like it was Saunders or Sanders or something like that. Carl, I think. Yeah, that was it. Carl Sanders.''

Shaking his head, he whistled softly as the facts came rushing back to him. ''He was a nasty sort. If I'm remembering correctly, he was arrested for punching his wife about a week after he lost his job. She later dropped the charges and he sort of faded from sight after that. Which isn't surprising considering the fact that all the TV stations in town picked up the story,'' he added. ''After all the negative publicity, he'd have been lucky to get a job as a dogcatcher, which was no more than he deserved.''

''Did he ever contact Sabrina? Ever show up here at her home and harass her or send her any kind of threatening letters?''

Shocked, the older man said, ''Oh, no! Not that I know of. Sabrina never mentioned any kind of letters, and I know for a fact that he never came around here. This is a very close-knit neighborhood, Mr. Nickels. We're all friends and watch out for each other. Sabrina and only a handful of others work—the rest of us are retired—so there's always someone home on the block. If Carl Sanders or anyone else had tried to get to Sabrina, you can bet one of us would have seen him.

"Of course," he added with a rueful smile, "we can't do much to protect her when she's out on the streets. She does tend to take chances."

Blake snorted at that, his lips twitching into a grin. "She's a regular daredevil, Mr. Vanderbilt." Holding out his hand, he said, "Thanks for the information. You've been a big help. If you remember anything else that might be important, would you give me a call at the *Times*? I'd really appreciate it."

A twinkle glinting in his eye, the older man hesitated, then nodded as he returned the handshake. "Sabrina won't like me helping the competition, but if it'll help keep her safe, I'll be glad to do it." The Lab tugged on her leash again, and with a murmur of apology, the man continued his walk.

Staring after him, Blake grinned. Whether he knew it or not, Louis Vanderbilt hadn't just helped the competition. He'd given him enough information that would—if it proved reliable after further research—blow Sabrina and the *Daily Record* right out of the water. It was, he decided, picturing the huge steak he was going to let her buy him next month, his lucky day.

Chapter 3

An hour later, Blake hung up the phone at his desk at the *Times* with a muttered curse. Louis Vanderbilt's story had checked out—to a point. Carl Sanders *had* lost his job at the *Daily Record* after Sabrina did a series of stories on sexual harassment. And in the single, bitter exclusive interview he'd given the *Times* after his abrupt resignation, he had placed all the blame on Sabrina. There was no question that the man was a chauvinist of the worst kind and that he had the mind-set and motive to at least be considered a suspect. The only problem was that less than a month after he quit the *Record,* he had apparently moved to Billings, Montana. A check with information and a short call to a C. Sanders there had verified that he was still there and wanted nothing to do with anyone from San Antonio.

Considering that, and the fact that he couldn't stroll into his old workplace without being recognized, the odds were slim that he'd threatened Sabrina, let alone killed Tanya

Bishop or Charlene McClintock. So he was back to square
one, Blake thought in disgust.

"Problems?"

Looking up from his musings to find Tom grinning at
him, he growled, "No, thanks. I've got enough of my own.
One, in fact, that you're probably not going to like."

"Let's hear it and I'll let you know," his friend and
boss said as pulled up a chair. "Lay it on me."

"Tanya Bishop's killer sent a threatening note to Sabrina Jones." He filled him in on his conversation with
the copy girl at the *Record* and his canvasing of Sabrina's
neighbors. "This Carl Sanders character sounded like just
the type of lowlife who would do something like this, but
with him out of the picture, there aren't any other suspects.
So the only story I've got is a note I haven't actually seen.
I know its general contents, but not any specifics I can
quote. And even if I did, I don't like the idea of encour-
aging the jerk."

Tom frowned. "If you're suggesting we don't print the
story at all, I can't go along with that. Two women have
died in two weeks, Blake. The whole city's abuzz about
it, and just this morning, I heard on the radio that a record
number of women are buying guns to protect themselves.
Any developments in the case have to be reported—even
if it concerns a reporter for the competition."

"But the killer wants recognition," Blake argued.
"Why else would he have sent the note to Sabrina? If we
give him that recognition, not only do we chance turning
this into a media circus, but we'll be giving him what he
wants. He could get a real taste for this type of thing."

"And kill more?" Tom asked shrewdly. "I doubt it. He
didn't need any encouragement for the first two. I can't
see why he would now."

"But—"

"This isn't anything like the situation in New York

eight years ago, Blake," he cut in quietly. "You don't have information that's going to get someone killed. If anything, letting everyone know what kind of threats this jerk is making could save lives. Exposure and the knowledge that most of the city is on the lookout for him may be the only things that keep him in check."

Put that way, Blake had to agree. Still, he didn't like the idea of publicizing the jerk's sudden interest in Sabrina. Who was he? What did he want with her? And why was he—Blake—so concerned about her safety when she could obviously take care of herself? She wasn't his problem. Why did he have such a hard time remembering that?

It was nearly dark when Blake finally left the paper and made his way home. When he'd first moved to town two weeks ago, he'd planned to move in with his grandfather so he could keep an eye on him, but the old man had let him know that first day that he didn't need a baby-sitter, despite what Blake's mother thought. Amused, Blake hadn't pushed the issue. Pop had always been an independent cuss, and arguing with him only made him dig in his heels. So Blake had assured him that he'd moved to San Antonio for a job, not to watch over him, and backed off.

He'd had, however, no intention of leaving the old man to his own devices. Finding himself an apartment several blocks away from the house his grandfather had lived in for over sixty years, Blake had planned to come up with an excuse to check on him every day. So far, that hadn't been necessary. If his grandfather didn't call him around supper time every day, he was invariably waiting for him when he got home. After the first few days of finding him waiting on the landing outside his second-story apartment, Blake had given him a key.

Now, as he climbed the stairs, he caught the scent of chicken frying and had to grin. The rest of the world might be cutting back on cholesterol, but Pop didn't have much use for what he considered a conspiracy dreamed up by a bunch of quack scientists who wanted to control the world. A cook in the navy, he'd been eating bacon and eggs and fried foods all his life, and at eighty-three, he was still going strong. Why the devil would he want to change his diet at this late date?

Letting himself in, Blake followed his nose to the apartment's small kitchen just in time to see the old man slip a pan of homemade biscuits into the oven. Propping a shoulder against the doorjamb, he teased, "You'd make some old woman a great husband, Pop. Want me to place a personal ad for you?"

The old man only snorted, his grin a mirror image of Blake's. "What makes you think I could only get an old one? In case you didn't know it, I'm a damn fine catch. I've got all of my own teeth—"

"And most of your hair," Blake added, chuckling.

"You're damn right," his grandfather agreed, playfully patting the cloud of wavy white hair that was his only vanity. "And you're going to look just like me. If I were you, I'd be thanking my lucky stars you got your looks from the Finnigans, boy. Your daddy's bald head shines in the moonlight."

"Only when he polishes it," Blake retorted, repeating one of his father's favorite jokes about his lack of hair. Pushing away from the doorjamb, he strode over to the stove and started lifting lids. "You making gravy, Pop? I can't remember the last time I had your gravy."

With pretended fierceness, the older man swatted at him, shoving him away from his cooking. "Get out of there before I forget you're my favorite grandson."

"I'm your only grandson." Blake laughed, snatching a green bean before he stepped back. "When do we eat?"

"When you set the table. I can smell those biscuits, son. Get moving."

His stomach grumbling, Blake didn't have to be told twice. Grabbing plates and silverware, he quickly set the table, then moved to help his grandfather dish up the food. Five minutes later, they sat down to a feast that would have fed a small army.

Filling his plate, the old man, as usual, asked about work. "So how'd it go today? You run into that Jones woman today?"

The question was smoothly, casually added, almost as an afterthought, but Blake wasn't the least bit fooled by his grandfather's attempt at subtlety. He'd made the mistake of telling the old man about Sabrina that day he'd met her at the scene of Tanya Bishop's murder, and ever since then, Pop had been convinced that Blake was interested in her. A day didn't go by that he didn't ask about her.

Shooting him a hard look, he warned, "There's nothing going on between Sabrina and me, Pop, so don't start getting any ideas."

As innocent as a choirboy, he arched a craggy brow. "Did I say there was? All I asked was if you ran into her today. If you read more into that, then it seems to me that you're awfully sensitive where that girl's concerned."

"I'm not sensitive," he began defensively, then caught the gleam in the old coot's eye. "You old rascal, I know what game you're playing and it's not going to work," he warned, grinning. "Just because Sabrina and I run into each other covering the same stories—"

"So you did see her!"

"Yes, but—"

"I knew it!" he cackled gleefully. "You just can't stay away from her. So tell me about her. Is she pretty? How old is she? I know she's got spunk—you can tell it from her writing. I always did like a girl with spunk.''

Amused in spite of himself, Blake said patiently, ''Yes, she's pretty, but that's got nothing to do with anything. She got a threatening letter from Tanya Bishop's killer, and I went over to the *Daily Record* to cover the story. That's all there was to it.''

The old man snorted, unconvinced. ''You went over there to make sure she was okay and you know it. That's good. A man should protect the woman he cares about— even if she can take care of herself. So why haven't you asked her out?'' he demanded, pointing a chicken leg at him. ''A girl like that won't stay single for long.''

''I don't know about that,'' he said dryly. ''According to one of her neighbors, her ex-husband burned her bad and she doesn't even date. Anyway, even if I was interested—which I'm not saying I am—I can't ask her out. She works for the competition.''

''So? What's that got to do with anything? Your grandmother's family didn't even talk to mine, but Sadie was the prettiest thing I'd ever seen. And she had just as much spunk as your Sabrina. I'm telling you, boy, you'd better snap her up while you can. Women like her don't come along every day of the week. Believe me, I know. Why do you think I never married again after your grandma died? A good woman is hard to find.''

Giving up in defeat, Blake laughed. ''Okay, okay! I'll think about it.''

Pleased, the old man passed the platter of chicken to him and grinned. ''If you're going to get mixed up with a woman like that, you're going to need to keep up your strength. Here. Eat.''

Tired, a nagging headache throbbing at her temples, Sabrina pulled into her driveway at twenty minutes to seven and sighed in relief. Finally! It had been a long, disturbing day, and all she wanted to do was collapse into bed, pull the covers over her head, and forget the world. Tomorrow would be soon enough to worry about the two women who had been murdered and the note personally delivered to her from their killer.

But as she cut the engine and stepped from her car, she found herself wondering if the killer who had dared to track her down at work had made it his business to find out where she lived. A first-grader could have done it— she was in the book, under S. Jones. There were three others, but that wouldn't present much of a problem for a man who had committed two murders without leaving behind a single clue that could be used by the police to identify him. All he would have to do was scout out the others or follow her home from work.

A cold chill slithering down her spine in spite of the fact that the heat of the day had yet to ease much, she whirled, her heart thumping, and searched the street in both directions. But the neighborhood was blessedly normal, and there wasn't a stranger in sight. Louis was washing his car next door, and across the street, the Garzas' oldest son, Chris, was mowing the lawn. Other than that, the street was quiet and deserted.

"You're being paranoid, Sabrina," she chided herself as she waved to Louis and Chris, then turned back to unlock the front door. "And that's just what the killer wants. Why else do you think he sent you that damn note? He's trying to scare you and you're letting him. What's the matter with you? You're not the type to jump at your own shadow. Straighten up, for God's sake! No one's been here, so quit looking over your shoulder and get inside. You're perfectly safe."

Her chin up, she hurried inside and did something she rarely did except at night when she went to bed—she shot the dead bolt into place. The click it made was loud in the silence, and she couldn't help but smile sheepishly at her own foolishness. "You're losing it, Jones," she chided herself, and turned toward the kitchen to see about supper.

She'd barely taken two steps when there was a sudden knock at the door. Startled, she jumped, then cursed herself for being so skittish.

It was probably just Chris wanting to know if he could mow her lawn, she decided. He was saving for a car and did chores for her and everyone else in the neighborhood whenever he got a chance.

But when she opened the front door, it was Mrs. Anderson who stood there smiling gaily, a plate of just-baked brownies in her hand. "Hi, sweetie. I saw you drive up and thought I'd bring you some dessert for after supper." Not the kind to stand on ceremony, she didn't wait to be invited in, but simply swept inside and headed straight for the kitchen. "I won't stay long—you look a little tired. Did you have a rough day?"

If she hadn't been so drained, Sabrina might have laughed. "Don't ask." She caught the scent of warm chocolate then and lifted her nose to the air. "Mmm. That smells heavenly. How did you know I needed a chocolate fix, Mrs. A.?" she asked as she followed her down the entrance hall to the kitchen at the back of the house. "I didn't even know it myself."

"That isn't surprising, considering the day you've had," the older woman said as she set the brownies down on the table and waved her into a seat. "Sit down and dig in, honey, while I get you a glass of milk. My mama always said nothing tasted better than something sweet from the oven after a bad day. What do the police say about that nasty note you got? I hope they're doing something about it. Just imagine, a cold-blooded killer waltzing into that paper and leaving you something like that! All I can say is, if I was in charge, I'd string him up by his thumbs the second I got my hands on him."

In the process of bringing a nice thick square of brownie to her mouth, Sabrina stopped halfway. "You know about the note?" she asked in surprise.

Her faded blue eyes dancing, Martha Anderson sank down in the chair across from her and leaned close to confide, "That nice Mr. Nickels came by asking about you earlier and told me the whole story. I tell you, I was shocked, dear!"

"Blake was here? Asking about me?"

"Oh, yes. And he was very concerned." Helping herself to one of her own brownies, she took a healthy bite and frowned. "I think these need a little more sugar. My sister gave me the recipe, and this is the first time I've made them. What do you think? Should they be a little sweeter?"

Struggling for patience, Sabrina assured her they were delicious just the way they were. "But what about Blake? Just what kind of questions was he asking?"

"Oh, the usual thing," she said airily. "I think he thought the killer might be someone you know, so he wanted to know about your background, if you had any enemies or former boyfriends who might have a grudge against you, that sort of thing. I laughed, of course. I just can't imagine you having any enemies. Why, you even managed to stay friends with Jeff after you two split, and how many people can say that?"

"You told him about Jeff?"

She nodded and rattled happily on. "It just came up when I mentioned that you didn't date much. Then Mr. Nickels just naturally assumed that there must be some bad blood between the two of you, so I had to set him straight."

Suddenly realizing for the first time that she might have

let her tongue get away with her, she frowned worriedly. "You're not mad because I told him about the divorce, are you? I really didn't mean to tell tales out of turn, but he was so nice. And he seemed genuinely concerned that you were in danger. I just wanted to help. If something happened to you because I kept a vital piece of information to myself, I'd never forgive myself."

Knowing the way Mrs. A dearly loved to gossip, Sabrina knew that was never going to happen, but she only smiled and patted her hand. "Nothing's going to happen to me," she assured her. "And no, I'm not mad." At least not at her. But Blake Nickels was another matter. Temper starting to simmer in her eyes, she said, "You did the right thing, Martha. I'm just surprised that Blake felt the need to question you and the rest of the neighbors. I saw him this afternoon at the paper, and he never said a word about his plans to check me out."

"Well, you work for opposing newspapers," she pointed out with a mischievous grin. "Maybe he wanted to outscoop you on your own turf."

"He wouldn't dare," Sabrina began, only to hear his teasing words ring in her ears as clearly as if he were standing beside her.

Honey, when you get to know me better, you'll find out that I'll dare just about anything.

"Oh, I'd like to see him try," she seethed. "That note was delivered to me, not him, so that makes it my story. He's not going to come in through the back door and snatch it right out from under me. Just wait till I see him again—he's going to get an earful."

Martha laughed gaily at that and rose to her feet. "Just don't be too hard on him, sweetie. He's such a nice-looking young man. And he wasn't wearing a ring," she added with twinkling eyes. "Who knows what might develop if you give him a chance?"

A snowball had a better chance in hell, Sabrina thought with a snort, but there was no use telling Martha that. A hopeless romantic, she had been trying to find Sabrina a man ever since she and Jeff had split. In spite of Sabrina's insistence that she wasn't looking for a man, Martha refused to believe that she was perfectly happy going through life alone.

"The only thing that's going to develop between me and Blake Nickels is an all-out war if he doesn't quit trying to muscle in on my turf," she replied as the older woman turned to leave. "But thanks for the brownies—they were just what I needed."

Wandering back to the kitchen after she'd shown Martha out, Sabrina couldn't shake the image of Blake canvasing her neighborhood, questioning the neighbors about each other and her friends. And the more she thought about it, the more indignant she got. Talk about nerve! The man had it in spades. Who the heck did he think he was, anyway? She wasn't the story here—the note and whoever wrote it were, and if Blake didn't realize that, maybe it was high time she told him.

Steaming, she walked over to the kitchen wall phone, snatched it up, and punched in the number for information. Seconds later, she had his phone number and address. Scowling down at them, she started to call him, only to hang up before she completed the call. No, she thought, her brown eyes narrowing dangerously. Some things were better said in person. Not giving herself time to question the wisdom of her actions, she grabbed her purse and car keys and headed for the door.

Blake and his grandfather were in the middle of watching a baseball game and arguing over which was the better team when the doorbell rang. Seconds later, someone pounded angrily on the front door. The old man arched a brow and said dryly, "Somebody sounds madder than a hornet. You expecting company?"

"Nope. Not that I know of." Pushing to his feet, Blake strode over to the apartment's front door and peeked through the peephole. At the sight of Sabrina standing there, glaring up at him as if she could see him through the door, he started to grin. Evidently, she'd found out that he'd been asking around about her, and she was more than a little ticked about it. He could practically see the steam pouring from her ears.

Pulling open the door, he made no attempt to hide his grin. "Well, well," he drawled. "If it isn't Ms. Jones. And to what do I owe the honor of this visit?"

Giving him a look that should have turned him to stone where he stood, she didn't wait for an invitation to come inside, but simply stepped around him and whirled to let him have it with both barrels. "All I can say for you, Nickels, is you've got a hell of a nerve. How dare you badger my neighbors and friends about me and pretend to be concerned about my safety when all you were really after was a damn story! Of all the low-down, underhanded, despicable—"

"You tell him, missy," an unfamiliar gravelly voice said encouragingly from behind her. "He ought to be ashamed of himself, and if he wasn't too big to take a switch to, I'd do it for you."

Startled, Sabrina jerked around to find an old man seated in a rocker in front of the television and obviously enjoying her tirade. Mortified, she blushed all the way to her toes. Driving over there, all she'd been able to think about was what she was going to say to Blake when she saw him, and like an idiot, she hadn't even stopped to make sure they were alone.

Wishing she had a hole to climb into, she said stiffly, "I'm sorry. I didn't see you sitting there."

"That's all right." He chuckled, rising to his feet. "It's been a while since I've heard a woman give a man a piece of her mind. I enjoyed it." Offering his hand, he stared down at her with sparkling green eyes that reminded her of Blake's. "I'm Damon Finnigan, Blake's grandfather. Most people call me Pop. You must be Sabrina Jones. I've read your stuff. It's good."

Surprised, Sabrina blinked. "You read the *Daily Record*?"

"He likes to keep up with my competition," Blake confided as he shut the front door and strolled over to join them. "He's one of your biggest cheerleaders."

"You're damn right," the old man agreed, giving Sabrina a playful wink. "If I was just a little bit younger, I'd give this young rascal here a run for his money."

"Pop—"

"A run for his money?" Sabrina echoed in confusion, frowning. "What—"

"Pop likes to tease," Blake said, shooting the old man a hard look that should have shut him up. It didn't.

Unrepentant, his grin daring, his grandfather only laughed. "It's one of my better talents, but I know a pretty woman when I see one. And so does Blake. He told me you were pretty, and he was right."

Swallowing a groan, Blake wanted to strangle him, but Pop had had his say and was obviously content to leave while he was ahead. "Well, I guess I'd better get out of here and let you two talk," he said cheerfully, heading for the door. "I need to get home anyway. I don't like to drive after dark."

"It was nice meeting you, Mr. Finnigan," Sabrina called after him.

"You, too, missy. And it's Pop. Mr. Finnigan's that old man that used to be my granddad."

With a promise to call Blake later, he shut the door on

his way out, leaving behind a silence that all but hummed. Her temper now under control, Sabrina let the silence stretch a full minute before she said coolly, "I like your grandfather. He's sweet. Too bad you don't take after him more."

A dimple in his cheek flashing, Blake chuckled. "Actually, I've been told I'm just like him. I guess you'll have to get to know us both better, though, before you see the similarities."

"Fat chance, Nickels," she retorted. "In case you haven't figured it out yet, I didn't come here to be sociable. Especially with a rat like you."

Instead of insulting him, her hostility only seemed to amuse him. "No kidding? Now why doesn't that surprise me?"

"You are the most aggravating—"

"Guilty as charged."

"Sneaky—"

"I know," he agreed cheerfully. "It's deplorable, isn't it? But my mother swears that once you get used to it, it's one of my more endearing qualities."

Her lips pressed tightly together, Sabrina swore she wasn't going to laugh. Damn the man, how was she supposed to tell him off when he agreed with everything she said? Stiffening her spine, she said through her teeth, "If that's an invitation, thanks but no thanks. I'd just as soon cozy up to a snake. Any man who would go behind my back and grill my neighbors about me and the men in my life is a—"

"Damn good reporter," he finished for her easily. "Of course, I could have come to you for that information, but somehow I don't think you would have told me that you spend your Saturday nights in bed with a good book."

"You're darn right I wouldn't have! Because it's none of your business. And who said that about me, anyway?"

she demanded huffily. "I have lots of friends and go some-where almost every weekend."

"We're not talking about friends here, sweetheart, but boyfriends. You know...men? Those good-looking, supe-rior creatures who take a woman out, wine her and dine her, and sometimes want something more than a peck on the cheek in return? If you had any contact in the past with the pushy sort and offended him, he just might be the kind to hold a grudge and go after you and all the other women who gave him the cold shoulder over the years."

"That's ridiculous! *I* am not the story here."

"Aren't you?" he asked quietly. "Think about it. If any other woman but you had gotten the letter, you would be asking the same questions of her neighbors that I asked of yours. There's got to be a personal link. If all the killer wanted was a forum to express his view, he could have sent the note to the editor for the letters column. But he didn't. As far as we know, he hand-delivered it to you personally. There's got to be a reason for that."

He had a point, one that made her more than a little nervous and irritated her at one and the same time. Tamp-ing down the uneasiness that stirred in her stomach, she turned away to pace restlessly. "This is all just conjecture. It has to be. Don't you think I would know if someone I knew was capable of murder?"

"Maybe. Maybe not," he said with a shrug. "Psycho-paths are damn clever."

"But I don't know any psychopaths."

"Not that you know of, anyway."

"Dammit, Blake, stop that! I know what you're doing, and it's not going to work."

"Oh, really? And what am I doing?"

"You're trying to distract me from the real issue here, which is *you* poking *your* nose into my life. It's got to stop."

His eyes searching hers, Blake couldn't believe she was serious, but there was no doubting her sincerity. She actually expected him to walk away from what could be the story of the decade because she asked him to. Roguish humor tugging up the corners of his mouth, he said, "Sorry, sweetheart. No can do."

"What do you mean...*no can do?* Of course you can! If you really want to find the murderer, go talk to the friends and family of those poor dead girls. That's where the story is."

"Bull. *You're* the story, Sabrina. We both know it—you just don't want to admit it because it scares you to death."

"That's not true! I've never been afraid of anything in my life."

"Well, you'd better be," he growled, stepping toward her. "Because a little healthy fear keeps people like you and me alive. Whether you want to admit it or not, someone out there means you harm. Until I find out why the killer sent you that note and who he is, everything about you is my business."

"The hell it is!"

"And if you don't like it, that's just too damn bad. Get used to it. I'm a hell of a good investigative reporter, so if you've got a secret, I'll warn you right now that I mean to find out what it is. By the time I get through with checking you out, honey, there won't be a panhandler on the street you've given a dollar to that I won't know about."

She swore at him then, highly imaginative curses that didn't include a single curse word but put him in his place, nonetheless. Against his will, he couldn't help but notice that she was something to see when she had her dander up. Temper blazed in her dark eyes, and twin flags of color burned in her cheeks. Dressed in a red dress that would have looked like a sack on another woman but somehow seemed to emphasize her every curve, she looked soft and feminine and full of fire. And he couldn't remember the last time he had wanted a woman so badly.

The thought caught him off guard, killing the grin that curled his lips. This wasn't the time to even think about getting romantic with a woman. Especially this woman, he told himself firmly. She wasn't in the mood. Hell, she was practically spitting daggers at him and would probably scratch his eyes out if he so much as touched her.

But even as he ordered himself to back away from her, he was eliminating the distance between them, as drawn to her as a moth to the scorching heat of a candle. And something of his intent must have gotten through to her because she faltered suddenly, her eyes wide, as he reached for her. ''What are you doing?''

''Giving in to temptation,'' he said with a devilish grin, and hauled her into his arms. Before she could do anything but stiffen and gasp in outrage, his mouth was hot and hungry on hers.

He'd only meant to catch her by surprise and steal a kiss that would shut her up, but the second his lips touched hers, there was a spark of heat, a flash of desire that caught fire like a gasoline spill, and in the next instant, he felt like he was going up in flames. Burning for more than just a taste of her, he could have no more stepped away from her than he could have cut off his right arm. Her name a prayer, a curse, on his lips, he dragged her closer and gave in to the need that had the blood roaring in his ears.

Stunned, her head spinning and her knees threatening to buckle at any second, Sabrina clutched at him like a drowning woman going under for the last time. Trying to hang on to her common sense, she told herself that they had been headed for this from the second they met. Every time their eyes met, the attraction was there like a tiger hiding in the shadows, waiting to spring. She could handle it. She could handle *him*. Or so she'd tried to tell herself.

But now, caught tight against him, every nerve ending she had throbbing from his closeness, she felt as giddy as a young girl being kissed, *really kissed,* for the first time. All her senses were attuned to him…his hardness, the feel of his heart slamming against hers, the underlying tenderness of his kiss, the rush of his hands over her. And with every slow, intoxicating rub of his tongue against hers, the craving that he stirred in her grew stronger, hotter. Her lungs straining, something deep inside her just seeming to melt, she crowded closer, aching for more.

How long they stood there, lost in each other's arms, she couldn't have said. Magic engulfed them, holding the world at bay, and she was entranced. But it couldn't last. His breathing as hard as hers, he wrenched his mouth from hers, glazed eyes sharpened, and suddenly they were both staring at each other in disbelief as reality returned with a painful jolt.

Dear God, what was she doing? This was Blake Nickels, her adversary, the man who could irritate her faster than anyone else she'd ever known, and she'd kissed him like an old maid who'd been given one shot at Prince Charming.

Stunned, her cheeks on fire, she never remembered moving, but suddenly half the distance of the room was between them and it wasn't nearly enough. She had a horrible feeling that putting the entire state of Texas between them wouldn't have been enough. She could still taste him, still feel him against her, still draw in the spicy male scent of him with every breath she took.

And that frightened her more than a dozen notes from a killer. "I don't know what you think you were doing, but if you ever do that again, you're liable to lose a lip, not to mention a finger or two."

As shaken as she, Blake knew he should have taken the warning to heart and gotten the hell out of there while he still could. But the lady had just thrown down a gauntlet that no man with any blood in his veins could walk away from.

His green eyes alight with wicked laughter, he took a step toward her. "I don't know about you, sweetheart, but that sounds like a dare to me."

"Dammit, Blake, you stay away from me!"

"Make me," he said softly, and reached for her.

Ready for him, she made a break for the front door, but she never made it. On the television, the baseball game was interrupted by a special report, and they both instinctively turned to catch it.

"We interrupt scheduled programming for this breaking news story," the local ABC anchorman announced somberly. "There has been another murder of a young professional woman. The police are still investigating the scene in the four-hundred block of San Pedro, but preliminary reports indicate that the murder appears to be similar to that of Tanya Bishop and Charlene McClintock. We hope to have more details at ten. At this time, we return to regularly scheduled programming."

Stunned, Blake and Sabrina stared at each other. A split second later, they were running for the door.

Chapter 4

Her name was Elizabeth Reagan. She was a twenty-eight-year-old loan officer for one of the city's oldest and most successful banks. She made good money, had a lot of friends, and had a reputation for giving the shirt off her back to anyone in need. And she was dead, killed by a single bullet to the heart in her own living room while "Chicago Hope" played on the TV.

Standing on the edge of the crowd that had gathered in the front yard to watch from a distance as the police investigated the crime scene, Blake questioned shaken neighbors and crying friends, but just as with the other two murders, no one had seen or heard anything. All the neighbors had apparently been home at the time, in their homes on a summer evening with their windows and doors shut and the air-conditioning on, totally oblivious to what was going on at Elizabeth's house. Apparently, someone had walked in and shot her and not even a dog had barked a warning. She might have lain there for hours, staring glassy-eyed at her living-room ceiling, if the elderly woman across the street, a Mrs. Novack, hadn't let her cat out and noticed Elizabeth's front door standing wide open, all the lights on in the house, and her car missing from her driveway. She'd immediately called the police. It was a young rookie who'd been on the job barely a week who had made the grisly discovery and called for backup and Detective Kelly.

Frustrated, unable to believe that three murders could take place in three weeks, apparently by the same killer, without anyone seeing anything, Blake slowly made his way through the crowd, asking the same questions over and over again. Did Ms. Reagan have any known enemies? Any old boyfriends who might hold a grudge? Any acquaintances that she'd recently argued with? And always the answer was the same. No. No. No. She was a sweet girl. Everybody loved her. Her killer couldn't have possibly known her. It all had to be a tragic mistake—she must have surprised a burglar, who killed her and took her car.

Kelly and the rest of the investigative team was still inside, but there was no sign of a break-in or forced entry, and nothing but the car seemed to be missing. Blake had barely finished questioning Mrs. Novack about whether or not the vehicle had been there at all that evening when a pale and drawn teenager pushed his way through the crowd and announced to the police that he was Elizabeth's brother. He'd borrowed her car for a date after she got home from work and was, apparently, the last person who'd seen her alive. He, like everyone else, didn't have a clue as to who could have killed her.

Frowning, Blake searched the crowd of neighbors for Sabrina and finally found her talking to a young mother who was standing in the shadows under a magnolia tree, a curly-haired toddler clutched protectively in her arms. Throwing questions at her, Sabrina obviously wasn't hav-

ing any better luck than he was. The woman just kept
shaking her head and wiping at the tears that trailed down
her ashen cheeks. As he watched, Sabrina touched her arm
in sympathy, but when she turned away, her jaw was
clenched with frustration. He knew just exactly how she
felt.

Reading over the few facts he'd been able to gather, he
swore. There just wasn't much to go on. And what little
he had been able to find out, he didn't like the sound of.
It went without saying that the victim was a young, single
professional woman. She was also, according to the neighbors, petite and slender, with a cloud of black, curly hair
that cascaded down her back. From her physical appearance alone, he could have been describing Sabrina.

His expression grim, he tried to tell himself that he was
letting his imagination get the better of him. Just because
the killer had left her one damn note didn't mean he'd
started picking victims who looked like her. It was just a
coincidence. But Blake was a man who didn't believe in
coincidence…especially when it came to murder.

His gut knotting at the thought, he was just wondering
if Kelly had made the connection when the man himself
appeared at the entrance to the cordoned-off house and
spoke to the uniformed officer standing guard there. A few
seconds later, the man ducked under the yellow crime tape
that blocked the doorway and slipped into the crowd.
When he returned, he had Sabrina with him.

Pale and shaken, Sabrina stood in the dead woman's
kitchen and stared in disbelief at the note found by the
evidence team on the kitchen table. It was already stored
in an evidence bag, but through the clear plastic, she could
see that the handwriting was the same as that on the note
she'd found on her desk at the *Daily Record* earlier in the
day. And like that one, it was addressed to her.

"I can't believe this is happening," she told Sam. "It has to be some kind of sick joke. Who would do this?"

"I was hoping you could tell me that," Kelly said. "I don't have to tell you that all kinds of weirdos come out of the woodwork on a case like this—you've covered the police beat long enough to know that some people get a real kick out of the thought of being connected to something like this. We could be dealing with that here, but I don't think so."

"You don't? Then who—"

"This particular weirdo knows you, Sabrina."

"No!" Denial instantly springing to her lips, she took a quick step back. "Don't start with me, Sam. You sound just like Blake—"

She started to say more, but there was a commotion at the front door, and they both turned to see Blake trying to talk his way past the junior officer stationed there. With a nod to the rookie, Sam allowed him access, then said curtly, "Since you were in on this earlier, you might as well hear the latest. I'm going to have to make a statement to the press later, anyway." Holding up the bagged note, he showed him Sabrina's name on the front. "We found this on the kitchen table. I was just telling Sabrina that there's a good likelihood that the killer is someone she knows. Apparently, you agree."

Blake nodded, his eyes on Sabrina. "She doesn't want to believe it. What's in it?"

"Basically, it's pretty much a replay of the other one," Kelly replied. "The perp wanted to make sure that Sabrina got the message this time. *'Learn your place,'*" he quoted. "He doesn't want to see her end up like Elizabeth and all the others."

"So why doesn't he just leave me alone?" she demanded. "That'll solve that problem easily enough."

"Because you're the one he's been trying to kill from

the very beginning,'' Blake said flatly. ''Dammit, haven't you noticed?''

Confused, she frowned. ''That's ridiculous. He hasn't come anywhere near *me*. Except to leave the notes, of course, and I wasn't anywhere in the vicinity when he did that.''

''But every time he kills, he's striking out at you. Look at the victims. If you put their descriptions and yours in a box and picked one out, they would all be the same. A young, single, professional woman who lives alone and has a slender build and dark, curly hair.''

Kelly, looking more dour than Sabrina had ever seen him, nodded in agreement. ''This guy, whoever the hell he is, is too methodical and careful to do anything by chance, Sabrina. He chose his victims for a reason, and considering these damn notes, I've got to agree with Blake. The killer seems to be obsessed with you and is working up the courage to come after you.''

Apprehension clawing at her, she shook her head, immediately rejecting the idea even as it struck a chord deep inside her. ''None of this makes any sense. Why me?''

Blake shrugged. ''Who knows? You're in the public eye. You're a fighter. You live off the St. Mary's strip and look great in red. There's no telling what's going on in this guy's head. But he knows where you work and there's a good possibility he knows where you live since he's getting closer to your front door with every killing. The McClintock woman lived ten miles away from you, Tanya Bishop only four. And this one's practically right around the corner.''

It was, in fact, a little over a mile and a half from her place to Elizabeth Reagan's, but that was still too close for comfort. ''That could just be coincidence,'' she began desperately.

Blake swore in frustration, wanting to shake her.

"C'mon, Sabrina, you don't believe that anymore than I do! This crackpot's after you and he's going to get you if you don't do something to protect yourself. Dammit, Kelly, talk to her before she gets herself killed!"

Raising a brow at the sudden tension crackling between the two reporters, the detective watched them glare at each other and forced back a smile. "I hate to sound like a parrot, but he is right, Sabrina," he told her. "For your own protection, you might consider letting someone else cover the murders until we can catch the jerk. Preferably a man."

"And let that murdering slimeball dictate to me how I can live my life?" she gasped. "Never in a million years! Would you expect a man to do that?"

"You wouldn't be in this fix if you were a man," Blake answered for him. "But that's okay. You go ahead and risk your pretty little neck just to prove a point to a madman. When we plant you six feet under, we'll have it carved on your tombstone that you went to your grave a martyr for women's rights."

"I'm not proving a point—I'm just doing my job." Exasperated, she turned to Sam. "Is there anything else we need to discuss? If not, I need to get to the paper and get this written up so it'll make the morning edition."

He hesitated, obviously wanting to add his two cents to Blake's comments, but he only sighed and gave in in defeat. "No, go on. But I want to see you down at the station first thing in the morning with the names of everyone you ever knew who might have a grudge against you. I don't care if it was some jerk in college who didn't like working with you on the school paper—I want his name. Got it?"

She nodded. "I'll come up with a list tonight." Not sparing Blake a glance, she turned on her heel, stepped outside and headed for her car.

Blake almost let her get away with it. Then he remembered a kiss that just over an hour ago had rocked him back on his heels. The lady might think she could take care of herself, but he'd held her in his arms and knew just how delicate and vulnerable she was. He didn't even want to think about what a bullet shot at point-blank range from the gun of a crazy could do to her. His jaw hard with resolve, he started after her.

He caught up with her just past the outer fringes of the grim-faced, silent crowd that still stood on the perimeter of the front yard. "Wait just a damn minute, Jones," he growled as the shadows of the night swallowed them whole. "I've got a bone to pick with you."

She didn't even slow her pace. "I've already said all I have to say to you, Nickels. Don't even think about getting in my way."

With two quick strides, he was not only in her way, he was blocking it. "You're either crazy as a loon or you've got a death wish—I haven't decided which," he muttered. "Stand still, will you?"

"I'm in a hurry, Blake. Unlike you, I seem to be the only one around here concerned with a deadline."

"Oh, I'm aware of it, all right. It's just that some things are a little bit more important than making the morning edition."

"Like what?"

"Your life."

"We've been all over this, Nickels," she said, letting her breath out in a huff. "There's nothing left to say."

"Maybe not," he agreed, surprising her, "but I'm going to say it anyway. For what it's worth, Jones, I used to be like you, obsessed with a story—"

"I'm not obsessed!"

"Then a snitch got killed because of something he told me," he continued as if she hadn't spoken. "It was my fault."

Stunned, she gasped, her eyes wide with instant sympathy. "Blake, no! You shouldn't blame yourself. You're not responsible."

"I lost my objectivity," he said simply, making no excuses for himself. "I was so determined to get the story that I didn't even realize I was putting that kid in danger. I don't want you to do the same thing."

"But this is different."

"Is it?" he asked sardonically. "Think about it."

"It isn't just the story," she said earnestly. "It's the principle of the thing. You wouldn't let a murdering piece of trash scare you off a story and I can't either. Because if I do, the word'll be all over the street that all you have to do is threaten Sabrina Jones when she gets too close to a story and she'll fold like a deck of cards. I might as well go back to obits because they're the only stories I'll be able to dig up."

He winced at the play on words, but he didn't smile. Not about this. "You won't dig up any stories with a bullet in your heart, either. Have you thought about that?"

"That's a chance I'll have to take."

"Dammit, Sabrina, you take chances at the horse races, not with your life. I don't like the idea of you traipsing all over the city with a killer on your tail."

"I don't like it, either," she said. "But it's not going to stop me from doing what I have to do." Suddenly suspicious, she studied him through narrowed eyes. "You're not getting all bent out of shape over this because of that kiss, are you? It was just a kiss, Blake. Nothing else. It didn't give you any rights where I'm concerned, so don't start getting any ideas."

Normally, Blake would have agreed with her and thanked God that she was being so levelheaded over what he'd intended as nothing more than an impulsive kiss. But somewhere between his intentions and the execution of the

kiss itself, things had gotten out of hand. Her response had
nearly blown the top of his head off, and her casual dis-
missal of that irritated him to no end. If she hadn't wanted
him to get any ideas, she damn sure shouldn't have kissed
him the way she had!

"That wasn't *just* a kiss and you damn well know it,"
he said huskily, his green eyes dark with temper. "You
forgot what planet you were on, and so did I."

"I did not!"

"Little liar," he retorted softly, taking a step toward her.
"Shall I prove it to you?"

He would have done it, right then and there, but she
never gave him the chance. Lightning-quick, she shied out
of reach. "Oh, no, you don't! You stay away from me,
Blake Nickels!" she warned, throwing up a hand to hold
him at bay as she walked backwards away from him. "Do
you hear me? You just keep your distance, and we'll both
get along fine. I've got a job to do, and so do you, and
we're not going to complicate the situation by getting involved. So just stay away from me."

She reached her car then, and darted around it like the
devil himself was after her. Letting her go, Blake watched
her climb inside and drive away and didn't know whether
to laugh or curse. Didn't she know that he'd tried staying
away from her from the very beginning? He wasn't looking for the entanglement of a relationship any more than
she apparently was. Fate, however, seemed to have other
ideas.

The note left at Sabrina's desk was splashed across the
front page of the *Daily Record* the next day, and the
phones at the police station were swamped with calls from
people who were sure they knew who the murderer was.
Two days after that, the report on the note found at the
scene of Elizabeth Reagan's murder came back from the

lab and confirmed what everyone had already suspected—
it was exactly like the one found at the *Record*. Written
on paper that could have been bought at any one of a
hundred or more office-supply stores in the city, it was
wiped clean of fingerprints and any clues that might have
led to the identity of its author.

With no murder weapon, no witnesses, and none of the
phone calls to the police panning out, Blake did what he
did best—he went looking for leads. And he started with
the victims. Figuring there had to be some kind of connection between the three women, he checked out their
hobbies, any clubs or associations they belonged to, even
their churches. And everywhere he turned, he reached a
dead end. Frustrated, he was left with no choice but to hit
the streets and start making friends with snitches and other
lowlifes that were in a position to know what was going
down in the city.

He didn't like it. Even though he knew that the chances
that the past would repeat itself were slim to none, he
wanted nothing to do with informants. That, unfortunately,
was a luxury he didn't have—not if he wanted to keep up
with Sabrina.

The lady really was incredible. And as much as he hated
to admit it, she kept him on his toes and pushed him to
do his best work. She covered the city like a blanket, digging up stories on everything from a drug ring and money-
laundering scheme on the west side to embezzlement at
city hall. He couldn't go anywhere without running into
her or hearing that she'd already been there and gone. He
found himself looking for her everywhere he went and
reading his own work with a critical eye, comparing it to
hers. Their styles were different—who could say whose
was better? His was grittier, yet hers was just as compel-
ling. With a simplicity that he couldn't help but admire,

she pulled the reader into a story and didn't let him go until he reached the end.

If she hadn't worked for the competition, Blake would have subscribed to the *Daily Record* just to read her stuff. As it was, he couldn't do that without helping her win their bet, and that was something he was determined not to do. So he had to be content with picking up the *Record* in coffee shops whenever he could and sneaking a peak at her work so he could tease her about it when he saw her.

And he did see her, in spite of her best efforts to avoid him. In the week after Elizabeth Reagan died, they ran into each other often, but Sabrina was as wary as a kitten with a thorn in its paw. If she saw him first, she cut a wide swath around him and left just as soon as she could. If he surprised her and approached her before she knew he was anywhere within a ten-mile area, she kept the conversation strictly professional and just dared him to bring up the subject of a certain kiss. He didn't. But the knowledge was there between them every time their eyes met.

Grinning at the memory, Blake dragged his attention back to the grumblings of the snitch who'd insisted on meeting him at an out-of-the-way bar on the east side. The place was a dive and smelled like it. Blake wouldn't have touched a drink there if his life had depended on it, but the bar's other occupants weren't nearly as particular.

Watching Jimmy, his snitch, pour rotgut down his throat, Blake wondered how the man had any lining left in his stomach. "Okay, spill your guts, man. What's the word on the street?"

"Nothing," Jimmy claimed, wiping his mouth with the back of his hand. "Honest. Whoever's knocking off those broads is doing it with a clean piece. I've talked to everybody I know and no one sold a hot shooter to the nut case. He already had it or he bought it legit."

Blake swore. He'd figured as much, but with a serial

killer on the loose, you couldn't take anything for granted. Jimmy had connections in most of the hellholes in the city. If someone out there had sold a stolen gun to the killer, he would have heard about it. "That's what I was afraid of, but thanks for asking around. If you hear anything—I mean anything—let me know. And get yourself something to eat. You're skinnier than a fence post."

Taking the bill Blake slid him, he grinned, exposing crooked yellow teeth, and snatched at the money as if he was afraid it was going to disappear any second. "Sure thing, man. Later."

He was gone, slipping away and into the shadows of the bar between one instant and the next. Shaking his head over the man's ability to fade into the woodwork, Blake did a disappearing act of his own and headed outside to his car.

His thoughts still on the gun, he was heading back to the paper when the crackling report on his police scanner finally penetrated his concentration. Someone had called in a mugging at an ATM machine. Normally, he wouldn't have bothered to cover such a minor crime, but it wasn't the crime itself that interested him—it was the location. It was just a couple of miles from where Sabrina lived.

Later, he would have sworn he never made a conscious decision to check it out, but he turned right instead of left at the next intersection and found himself heading for the near northside. It only took him minutes to get there, but the police were already there, blocking the parking lot where the ATM was located, leaving him no choice but to find a spot around the corner to park. Not surprisingly, Sabrina's red Honda was already there.

The minute his gaze landed on the sporty little car, he knew he was in trouble. Because it wasn't, as it should have been, the story that had brought him to that part of town. It was the possibility of seeing Sabrina Jones.

* * *

In the process of interviewing the victim, Thelma Walters, an elderly neighbor who was surprised by the mugger when she stopped at the ATM to get money for groceries, Sabrina glanced up and felt her heart constrict at the sight of Blake slowly walking toward her. The smile that usually flirted with his mouth was noticeably absent, and in his eyes was something—a heat, a dark intensity—that was aimed right at her. Her mouth suddenly dry, she couldn't remember what she was going to ask next.

"Is something wrong, sweetie?" Mrs. Walters asked suddenly, reaching out to feel her forehead. "You're awfully flushed all of a sudden. Are you feeling all right? Maybe you've been out in the sun too long."

Her blush deepening, Sabrina blinked her friend back into focus. "Sorry," she said, forcing a laugh. "I guess I just drifted off. It must be this heat. It is awfully hot today." Fanning herself, she struggled to concentrate. "Now, about the mugger. I understand you caught him all by yourself after he took off running with your purse. The police said you threw a rock and hit him in the head?"

Pleased with herself, Thelma Walters laughed gaily. "It was more like a pebble than a rock, but yes, I beaned him one in the noggin. He glanced over his shoulder to see what had hit him and ran right into a security officer from the apartments across the street who heard my cries for help." Grinning, she confided, "I used to be a softball pitcher in high school, but it's been fifty years since I threw a ball. I guess I've still got it, huh?"

"You can be on my team any day of the week," Sabrina said, chuckling. "You did get your money back, didn't you?"

"Every penny," the older woman said proudly. "The next time that young man decides to go after a senior citizen, he'd better think twice about it. We're not all old fogies sitting around waiting to die."

Her lips twitching, Sabrina promised to include that little tidbit of information in the story. "Well, that's a wrap, Thelma. Thanks. You want me to call someone to come and get you? I know you weren't hurt, but finding yourself face-to-face with a mugger would shake up just about anyone. Maybe you shouldn't drive."

Her eyes crinkling, the older woman held out her hand to show her she was steady as a rock. "I'm fine, sweetie," she confided, "but if you don't mind, I'm going to see if I can talk one of those good-looking policemen to take me home. I noticed the blonde wasn't wearing a wedding ring, and my niece, Jenny, is looking for a good man."

"Well, then, hey, don't let me get in your way." Sabrina laughed as she stepped back and motioned for her to proceed her. "Go get him, girl."

She was still grinning when Blake strolled over and joined her. Her heart, remembering a kiss she had tried her damndest to forget, knocked out an irregular rhythm in greeting. Annoyed with herself, she lifted a brow at him and gave him a smile guaranteed to set his teeth on edge. "You having a slow day or what, cowboy? These types of stories are usually beneath a superstar like you."

His eyes glinting in appreciation of the dig, he shoved his hands in his pants pockets and rocked back on his heels. "That's funny. I was just about to say the same thing about you, sweetheart. And the last I heard, you were the only superstar around here. When I first came here, all anyone ever talked about was the great Sabrina Jones. For a while there, you really had me shaking in my shoes."

She might have been pleased if he hadn't begun the admission with a qualifying phrase. "For a while," she repeated, her smile tightening ever so slightly. "But not now?"

Delighted that she'd asked, he grinned. "Do I look like I'm worried?"

No, he didn't, she had to admit, irked. In fact, she'd never seen a man who appeared less worried. Loose-limbed and relaxed in jeans and a polo shirt, his dark hair windswept by the afternoon breeze, he looked as if he didn't have a care in the world. If he was concerned about losing their bet at the end of the month, he certainly didn't show it.

Perversely irritated, she said, "For your information, Nickels, I happen to know the victim. She called me right after she called the police. Now that we know why I'm here, what's *your* excuse?"

Opting for the truth, knowing she wouldn't believe him, he teased, "I figured you'd be here, since it was so close to where you live, and I couldn't pass up the chance to see you again. We haven't talked much the last week. Did you miss me?"

"Like a dog misses a flea," she tossed back, not batting an eye. "Why don't you do us both a favor and go back to sports? This town's not big enough for the two of us to both cover crime."

"Then we've got a problem," he said with a chuckle, "because I'm not going anywhere. Anyway, I kind of like running into you just about everywhere I go." Her words suddenly registering, his grin broadened. "Why, Jones, you had me checked out! I'm touched."

She laughed, she couldn't help it, and cursed her slip of the tongue. Damn the man, did he have to be so charming? Lifting her chin, she said, "Don't go jumping to conclusions. Of course I checked you out. I'm a reporter. That's what I do for a living."

She might as well have saved her breath. "Yeah, yeah," he teased. "That's what they all say. Why don't you just admit it, honey? You're crazy about me."

"Me and half the female population of S.A.," she retorted, going along with him. "I bet you can't go anywhere without beating the women off with a stick."

His green eyes dancing, he shrugged modestly. "It's rough, Jones, but I somehow manage to make time for all of them. Shall I pencil you in for Saturday night? It's the only night I've got free this week."

"And I'm busy. Darn! Isn't that the pits?"

"Yeah," Blake drawled, enjoying himself. "I can see you're real broke up about it."

"Oh, I am," she claimed with mock seriousness that was ruined by the smile that tugged insistently at her lips. "I just don't know how I'll get through the rest of the day."

"Oh, I'm sure you'll manage. You can always bury yourself in your work."

"True," she agreed. "And speaking of work, I guess I'd better get back to it." Reaching up, impish mischief sparkling in her eyes, she dared to pat him on the cheek. "See you around, Nickels."

Letting her go, Blake grinned. Little witch. It would serve her right if he snatched her up and laid a kiss on that beautiful mouth of hers. But the next time he kissed the lady—and there would be a next time; he had no doubts about it—he wanted her all to himself, preferably in a dark, secluded place where he could take his time with her. Then they'd see just who was crazy about whom. But for now, there was work to do.

It didn't take him long to get Thelma Walters's side of the story—thoroughly enjoying the attention, she was only too eager to talk about the mugging. Her attacker, however, was a little more tight-lipped; the arresting officer had to supply the thug's name and the information that he had a long record.

Armed with that, Blake had all he needed. And so, apparently, did Sabrina. He saw her heading for her car, which was parked around the corner near his, and fell into step beside her. "Now that we're through with that," he said easily as they rounded the corner, "why don't we grab something to eat? I know this great little Chinese place right down the street."

"Sorry, Nickels. I can't. I—"

Whatever she was going to say next seemed to stick in her throat. Puzzled, Blake frowned down at her. "You okay, Jones? You're looking a little strange around the gills."

Strangling on a laugh, she said, "I'm sorry. I know I shouldn't laugh. It's really *not* funny—"

"What?"

Unable to manage another word, she only shook her head and pointed down the street. His eyes following the direction of her finger, Blake didn't see anything at first to explain her amusement. Then his gaze landed on his pickup.

Someone had set it up on blocks and stolen the two rear tires.

"Dammit to hell!"

Sabrina tried, she really did, to summon up some sympathy, but she was fighting a losing battle. Muffled laughter bubbling up inside her like a spring, she bent over at the waist and buried her face in her hands, whooping for all she was worth. "I'm sorry," she choked, giggling as she wiped at the tears that streamed from her eyes. "Really, I am! But if you could just see your face..."

He scowled at her, and that set her off again. "Stop it, Blake. You're killing me!"

"I ought to kill you," he retorted, his lips twitching in spite of his best efforts to appear stern. "What kind of neighborhood is this, anyway? Those were brand-new tires!"

"Well, I should hope so." She laughed. "What's the

point of stealing old ones? Dammit, Blake, don't you know better than to drive a new truck into this part of town?''

''Apparently not,'' he said dryly. ''I guess I'll have to get an old clunker like yours.''

Smirking, she retorted, ''At least I don't get my tires stolen in the middle of the day. C'mon, I'll give you a ride to my place and you can call a wrecker from there. It looks like you're going to need one.''

She'd only meant to offer a helping hand to make up for laughing, but the minute Blake followed her inside her house, she knew she'd made a mistake in bringing him there. The small two-bedroom home her grandmother had given her when she'd married husband number five was her personal space, a retreat from work and crime and the senseless violence she made a living from in the streets. As she watched Blake look around the living room with interest, she knew she would see him there long after he left.

Panic hit her then, right in the heart, shaking her. Lord, what was wrong with her? He had kissed her one stinking time—*one time*—and she hadn't been able to get him out of her head since. She had to stop this, dammit! She wasn't the type to moon over a man, especially one like Blake Nickels, and she wasn't going to start now. Still, she couldn't help noticing how right he looked in her house.

You're losing it, Sabrina. Really losing it. Shaking her head over her own fanciful thoughts, she motioned to the old-fashioned, Forties-style rotary on the small table at the far end of the couch. ''The phone's right there. It'll probably take a tow truck a while to get here. Would you like some iced tea while you're waiting?''

''Oh, don't go to any bother,'' Blake began, but he might as well have saved his breath. She was already gone, heading for the kitchen as if the hounds of hell were after her. Staring after her, his lips twitched into a smile. He'd never seen her nervous before, but she was showing definite signs of it now. And he had to ask himself why. If he'd been the conceited type, he might have wondered if it had something to do with him.

Grinning at the thought, he strode over to the phone and called information for the number to the garage down the street from his apartment. Placing the call, it took him only minutes to explain the situation and request a tow truck.

Sabrina was still in the kitchen when he hung up, and he couldn't resist the urge to look around. Reasoning that he wasn't going to go through her drawers or anything, he found himself wandering over to the photographs that covered nearly all of one wall. Most of them were wedding pictures taken over the course of what looked like half a century, if the style of dress of the wedding guests was anything to go by.

"They're something else, aren't they?" Sabrina said as she returned to the living room with a glass of iced tea in each hand. Strolling over to him, she handed him his glass and nodded at the picture of a beaming older couple he was studying. Standing on the deck of a ship before a judge, they were dressed in full scuba gear, complete with masks. "That's Grandma and Grandpa Bill," she said, smiling fondly. "Number four."

"Number four?" Blake repeated, lifting a brow in inquiry. "Number four what?"

"Husband number four," she explained. "Grandma likes to get around."

His brow climbed higher at that. "Your grandmother's been married *four* times?"

"No, actually it was five at last count. Well, six, if you count Grandpa Mason," she amended. "She married him twice."

Amazed, Blake turned back to the wedding pictures and

frowned, unconsciously counting them. "But there's more than six wedding pictures here."

"Oh, not all of those are Grandma." She laughed. "The rest are Mama. She favors Grandma a great deal, don't you think? In fact, Grandpa Harry said the two of them looked so much alike that they could have passed for twins if they'd been closer in age. It's a shame he and Grandma didn't stay together. I really liked him. But he had this daughter who couldn't stand Grandma, so that was the end of that."

"He divorced her?"

She nodded. "Six months after they married. Grandma was heartbroken until Chester came along."

"Then why is his picture still with the rest? I would have thought she'd have tossed it out."

"Oh, Grandma doesn't hold grudges. Once your picture goes up on the wall, you're up there for life."

Blake almost laughed. She had to be kidding. But there was no question that the wedding pictures were legit. Frowning, he said, "Just for the record, how many times have your mother and grandmother been married?"

Sabrina didn't even have to count. "Eight and holding—if you don't count Grandpa Mason twice. Of, course, things could change at any time. Mom's in Alaska with Hank right now, and Grandma's touring the country with Grandpa George, and I haven't heard from any of them in a while. If there's a shift in the wind, who knows what can happen?"

It wasn't something to brag about, but Sabrina had learned a long time ago not to apologize for it, either. Her mother and grandmother were what they were, and there was nothing she could do to change that. At this late date, she wouldn't even try, but there were times, like now, when she could use their atrocious number of divorces to make a point.

"The women in my family are very good at saying 'I do,'" she said quietly. "They're just lousy at commitment, and it's not even something they can help. It's a defective gene, and the only cure for it is not to get married."

Her tone was light, amused, almost facetious, but as she watched Blake frown, she knew he'd gotten the message. If he was looking for a relationship, he could look somewhere else. She wasn't interested.

Chapter 5

She should have been pleased that she'd made her point and he didn't give her an argument about it. But long after Blake left with the tow-truck driver who stopped by to give him a ride to the garage where he would take his pickup, Sabrina stood in her front yard, frowning as she stared down the street after him. She felt sure he wouldn't try to kiss her again. Why didn't that bring the relief she'd expected it to?

"Somebody having trouble?" Louis asked as he passed by on the sidewalk with his Lab, Lady. "I thought I saw a tow truck stop here."

Jerking out of her musings, Sabrina summoned a smile. "Oh, hi, Louis. Yeah, there was a wrecker here. Mrs. Walters was mugged at the ATM on McCullough when a mugger tried to rob her. While Blake and I were covering the story, somebody stole the back tires off his pickup."

"In broad daylight?" Louis exclaimed. "And no one saw anything?"

"Well, I don't know about that," Sabrina said dryly. "A mockingbird can't land on the back fence without old lady Charleston seeing it two blocks over, so I thought I'd ask around and see what I could find out. If you happen to see two slightly used Michelins lying around while you're walking Lady, let me know, will you?"

"I'll keep my eyes open," he promised. "But if I were you, I'd check first with that Gomez kid down on the corner. From what I've seen, he's a little thug. The police have already questioned him a number of times about several robberies in the area. Stealing tires sounds like something that'd be right up his alley."

Sabrina nodded. She'd been thinking the same thing herself. "You might be right. I think I'll check him out right now."

"Be careful," he warned as Lady grew impatient and started to tug him farther down the street. "With someone like that, you never can be sure of what he's capable of."

That might have been true of someone else, but Sabrina had known Joe Gomez since he'd been in grade school. Despite the fact that he was a gang member with a reputation for stealing just for the heck of it, he had a twisted code of ethics when it came to robbing his own neighbors. He just didn't do it. But that didn't mean he wouldn't know who did.

Heading up the street, she approached the Gomez house cautiously, more out of respect for Killer, the Rottweiler that was usually chained to the tree in the front yard, than because of any fear of Joe. The dog, however, was nowhere in sight. Relieved, she strode boldly up onto the front porch and knocked on the weathered siding next to the wrought-iron grillwork that covered the front door.

Deep in the bowels of the old wood-frame house, she heard Killer's fierce growl and a terse command to knock it off. Then Joe was opening the door and looking at her as if he'd just found his favorite centerfold on his threshold. Seventeen and full of himself, he propped a shoulder against the doorjamb and looked her up and down with wicked, dancing eyes. "If you've come to borrow a cup of sugar, I'm the only sweet thing in the house." Grinning, he held his arms wide. "Take me. I'm yours."

Sabrina laughed and shook her head at him. It was an old joke between them, his flirting with her, and she never took him seriously. She liked his sense of humor and enjoyed jawing with him, but even if he hadn't been ten years her junior, she wouldn't have been interested in Joe. The teenage girls that followed him around like puppies might be impressed with his flagrant macho antics, but Sabrina didn't find them the least attractive and would have never stood for them from any man, young or old.

"Sorry, Joe, but I'm on a diet. No sweets allowed."

"Well, hell, honey, don't let that stop you. Cheat."

"I don't think so," she said, grinning. "Anyway, that's not why I'm here."

Just that quickly, his smile vanished. "Oh, boy, here it comes," he groaned. "The third degree about that mugging over on McCullough." Glancing over his shoulder to make sure his grandmother had heard nothing of the conversation, he quickly stepped outside and shut the door behind him. "You think I had something to do with it, don't you? Just because I knew old lady Walters stopped there every Monday to get money for her bratty grandson doesn't mean I told anyone about it."

Amused, Sabrina lifted a brow at him. "You sound just the teensiest bit defensive, Joe. Did I accuse you of anything?"

"No, but—"

"*Should* I be accusing you of anything?"

"No!"

"Then what's the problem? The mugger was caught. I just wanted to talk to you about some tires."

"Tires?" he echoed, frowning. "Now what would I know about tires?"

Another reporter might have been fooled by the scowl and innocent tone he adopted in the blink of an eye, but Sabrina had known him too long to be taken in by such a display. Grinning in appreciation of the act, though, she said lightly, "Oh, nothing. I just thought you might put the word out for me that two Michelins taken off a certain black, 4X4 Chevy pickup belonged to a friend of mine."

"No kidding? You talking about that tall dude that was down here earlier in the day? Somebody stole his tires?"

"Apparently so. And I'd really appreciate it if they were returned."

Slipping his hands into the back pockets of his tattered jeans, he rocked back and forth on his heels, considering the matter with a twinkle in his eye. "I don't know anyone who's into that kind of thing, you understand," he finally confided, "but I can see how tempting two new tires would be to someone running around on retreads. Life's tough, you know."

Sabrina just barely managed to hold back a smile. "And two new tires don't come rolling by every day. You think if I offered a reward it might convince whoever took them to give them up?"

At first, she thought he was going to jump at that, but after careful thought, he shook his head. "Nope, that'd only encourage whoever did this to try it again. Just sit tight. I'll drop a hint in a few ears."

That was all Sabrina could ask for. Beaming, she said, "Thanks, Joe. I knew I could count on you."

"Yeah, yeah," he snorted. "I'm a regular prince."

"That's what all the young girls around here say," she

said with a laugh as she took the porch steps. "'Bye, Joe. Behave yourself.''

He wouldn't—the kid just didn't seem to have it in him—but he would do as he promised. And that was all Sabrina could ask for.

When she came home from work late the following afternoon, the tires were sitting on her front porch with a big red bow on them. And suddenly a day that hadn't been all that good got better. Pulling into her driveway, Sabrina laughed. Glancing down to the corner, she thought she saw a movement in an upstairs window at Joe's grandmother's house. It was Joe, of course, but she knew he wouldn't come out for her thanks, or even admit that he was the one responsible for getting the tires back—that would clash with his bad-boy image. But without his help, those tires would be on the back of somebody's low-rider, and they both knew it. Waving gaily, she saw the curtain swish again and grinned.

Five minutes later, she was headed for Blake's place with the tires loaded in the trunk of her Honda. She'd leave them by his front door, she decided, and let him wonder how they had gotten there. It would drive him nuts. Her eyes starting to sparkle at the thought, she turned into his apartment complex and found a parking spot within a few feet of the stairs to his second-floor apartment. Seconds later, she was rolling the first tire up the steps.

As quiet as a mouse, she propped it against the doorjamb, then went back to her car for the second. She would have sworn she didn't make a sound, but just as she leaned the second tire against the first one, the door was suddenly jerked open and both tires fell across the threshold with a soft thud. Caught red-handed, she glanced up, a quick explanation already forming on her tongue, only to find herself face-to-face with Blake's grandfather.

"Oh! Mr. Finnigan! You startled me. I didn't think any-one was here."

"Pop," he automatically corrected her. "I thought you were Blake." His green eyes, so like his grandson's, lit with mischief as his gaze slid from her to the tires and back again. "You know, in my day, I had a few women surprise me with a cake or two, but I don't believe one ever showed up on my doorstep with a load of tires. Have you got a car hidden somewhere to go with those?"

Sabrina laughed. "No, but Blake does. These are his—the ones stolen off his truck yesterday. They sort of showed up on my doorstep."

"Just like that?" he asked, arching a brow at her. "Why do I have a feeling you're leaving something out?"

"Well, I did sort of feel responsible since it happened in my neighborhood," she admitted. "So I put the word out that Blake was a friend and I'd like them back. But I'd prefer that he didn't know that," she added quickly.

"Didn't know what? That you consider him a friend or that you're the one who got his tires back for him?"

He was, Sabrina thought, fighting a blush, altogether too sharp for her peace of mind. "Let's just say this is our little secret," she suggested with a smile. "I wouldn't want Blake to feel beholden or anything. Especially since we're both usually fighting for the same stories. He might feel like he has to step back and let me have an exclusive, and that's not what I want."

"You want to beat him fair and square at his own game." It wasn't a question, but a statement from a man who obviously read her like a book. Grinning, he pulled the door wider. "I like your style, missy. Since Blake's not going to be able to thank you for the tires, the least I can do is offer you a drink after you carted those dirty things up the stairs in this heat. Come on in."

"Oh, that's not necessary," she began.

"Then humor an old man," he said with a shrug, blatantly playing on her sympathies. "I don't get a chance to talk to a pretty girl very often. Blake doesn't bring too many home, and when he does, they're not interested in jawing with an old geezer like me."

The pitiful look might have worked on somebody else, but Sabrina wasn't buying it. "Nice try, Finnigan, but somehow you don't strike me as a lonely old man who roams around an empty house talking to himself all day. You've lived here all your life, haven't you? You probably know more people than God."

Laughter deepening the wrinkles lining his weathered face, he nodded. "Probably. But most of them are on the downhill side of seventy, and all they want to talk about is aches and pains and where they've got their money invested. I bet you can tell some stories that are a sight more interesting than that. So, you coming in or not?"

She should have said "Thanks, but no thanks," then come up with a quick excuse to get out of there. She already knew all she wanted to know about Blake Nickels—he kissed like something out of one of her dreams—and the less she saw of him and his family, the better. But she really did like his grandfather, and what harm could a few minutes do?

"Well, it is hot, and I would like to wash my hands," she said, finding more excuses than she needed to ignore her common sense. "But I can't stay long."

Thirty minutes later, she was still there. Sitting at Blake's kitchen table and on her second glass of iced tea, she couldn't remember the last time she'd enjoyed herself more. Pop Finnigan had a real gift for storytelling, and more than once, she laughed so hard, she cried. He told her outlandish tales about his stint in the navy as a cook and his travels around the world, stories, she was sure, that he'd carefully edited for her delicate ears. She could have told him that there wasn't much she hadn't heard covering crime in some of the city's worst neighborhoods, but she appreciated his old-fashioned courtliness. He was a wonderful old man and Blake was lucky to have him for a grandfather.

He was also sneaky as a fox. Without Sabrina quite realizing how it happened, he cunningly shifted the focus of the conversation to Blake. One minute he was telling her about shore leave in Italy, and the next, he was confiding that as a child, Blake had traveled all over the world with his parents, who were career diplomats.

"That kid had a ball," he said with a grin. "He could speak French and German fluently by the time he was eight and knew Rome like the back of his hand when he was fourteen. Karen—that's my daughter—really thought he would go into politics." Laughing softly at the thought, he shook his head. "She'd better thank her lucky stars he didn't. Blake always did have a nose for secrets. With all the intrigue in international politics, he would have asked questions he had no business asking and ended up starting a war or something by now. The kid's a born reporter."

"I'll give him his due," Sabrina said, eyeing him knowingly. "He does seem to know what he's doing."

"You're darn right he does," the old man agreed promptly. "He always knew what he wanted and went after it. Of course, his mother still thinks this writing stuff is an act of rebellion on his part, but you won't find a better man anywhere. When Karen and Richard got assigned to France for a year, she had this crazy notion that I was too old to live alone. I told her I was just fine, thank you very much, but you know how daughters are. She worried, so Blake quit his job in New Mexico and moved here to watch over me. I told him I didn't need a babysitter, but he still checks in with me every day. I know what he's doing, of course, but I don't say anything because I don't want Karen to worry.''

Fighting a smile, Sabrina nodded solemnly. "Of course. I'm sure your daughter sleeps a lot easier at night knowing Blake is here to watch over you.''

"Sure she does. She'd sleep a lot better, though, if he'd settle down with a wife and a couple of kids. A man his age needs a good woman in his life, don't you think?''

A blatant matchmaker, he winked at her, just daring her to disagree with him, and it was all Sabrina could do not to laugh.

Lord, he was outrageous—and as bold as his grandson! She didn't have the heart to tell him that he was talking to the wrong woman. "Mr. Finnigan—''

"Pop," he corrected her, flashing his dimples at her.

"Pop," she repeated with a smile. "Blake's marital status is really none of my business—''

"It could be.''

"Stop that!" Sabrina laughed. "If Blake wanted a wife and children, I'm sure he'd have them. You said yourself that he always knew what he wanted and went after it. Anyway, that has nothing to do with me. I just came over to deliver his tires. And now that I've done that, I really do need to get out of here.''

He tried to talk her into staying a little longer, but she was adamant. Thanking him for the tea and the entertaining conversation, she headed for the door. But she'd waited too long. The sound of a key in the lock stopped her in her tracks. A split second later, Blake pushed open the door with his shoulder and stepped into the apartment carrying the two tires she'd left on his doorstep.

Surprised, he lifted a brow at the sight of her as a slow smile stretched across his face. "Well, look who's here. And you came bearing gifts. At least I assume I have you to thank for these,'' he said, dropping the Michelins on the floor next to the door. ''And I didn't think you cared, Jones. That just goes to show you how wrong a man can be about a woman.''

''Don't let it go to your head, cowboy,'' Sabrina returned sweetly. ''I just didn't want you to have an excuse when I won our bet.''

Pop, watching them with a broad grin, stepped into the conversation at that. ''Bet? What bet?''

''We have a little wager over who can bring in the most new subscribers by the end of the month,'' Blake informed him without ever taking his eyes off Sabrina. ''Right now, I'd say it's a dead heat.''

''In your dreams,'' Sabrina snorted. ''I just checked the numbers this morning, and I've got nothing to worry about where you're concerned, Nickels. I'm so far ahead of you, you'll never catch up.''

Not the last bit concerned, he only grinned. ''I'm a patient man, sweetheart. And the month's not over with yet. With a little luck, you just might have to eat those words, not to mention buy me the thickest steak in town.''

''Speaking of which,'' his grandfather cut in smoothly, ''I think I smell my roast cooking. How about staying for dinner, Sabrina? There's plenty.''

''Oh, no,'' she began. ''I couldn't.''

''What's the matter?'' Blake teased. ''Scared of breaking bread with the competition?''

''No, of course not!''

''Maybe she has another date,'' his grandfather supplied.

''No—''

''Then there's no reason why you can't stay,'' Blake said easily. ''After all, feeding you is the least I can do after you got my tires back for me.''

Put that way, there was no way she could gracefully refuse, and he knew it. ''All right, all right,'' she said, laughing. "I'll stay. I just feel guilty about showing up here at suppertime without an invitation. I should have waited until later."

"That's okay," Blake assured her, his smile crooked. "If it'll make you feel any better, we'll make you work for it. You can do the dishes."

The meal that followed was one that Sabrina knew she would remember until her dying day. The food was delicious, but it was the company that was superb. Unlike most men she knew, who were reluctant to show their emotions, Blake made no attempt to hide his affection for his grandfather. And the old man was just as affectionate with Blake. They teased and cut up and traded stories about each other until Sabrina could hardly eat for laughing. Long after the meal was finished and the roast was just a memory, they sat at the table talking and reminiscing about old times, fascinating Sabrina. Enthralled, she could have sat there for hours and just listened to them talk.

Which was, in fact, what she did. No one was more surprised than she when she glanced at her watch and saw how late it was. "Oh, my God, it's going on ten o'clock! And I still haven't done the dishes yet."

"You don't have to do that," Pop said when she jumped up and started collecting the dirty plates. "Blake was just teasing."

"Oh, but it's the least I can do," she argued. "I can't remember the last time I had such a wonderful meal. It was delicious, Pop."

Pleased, he grinned. "I'm glad you liked it. You'll have to come again. Won't she, Blake?"

Blake, recognizing the mischievous glint in his grandfather's eyes, shot him a quelling look behind Sabrina's back, and said easily, "Sure. Maybe next time, you can make that stuffed-pig dish you learned to make in Fiji."

"I don't know," the old man said. "That sort of smokes up the house. And I wouldn't want to go to all that trouble when you never know when you're going to be called out on a story. Maybe you should just take her out instead."

"Oh, no, that's not necessary—"

"Pop—"

Ignoring Sabrina's automatic refusal and his grandson's warning tone, the old man said innocently, "Weren't you looking for someone to go with you to the awards ceremony at the National Newspaper Convention next weekend? Sabrina's probably going, too, so why don't you go together? It seems kind of dumb to go in two cars."

Under ordinary circumstances, Blake would have agreed. If he and Sabrina had just been rivals, he wouldn't have hesitated to suggest the same thing. Just because they worked for competitive papers didn't mean they couldn't be friends. But there was nothing friendly about that kiss they'd shared or the way the memory of it made him ache in the middle of the night. He was having a damn difficult time getting her out of his head, and taking her out, even to an awards ceremony, would only make the situation worse.

But before he could think of an acceptable reason to sidestep his grandfather's suggestion, Sabrina came up with one for him. "Thanks for the offer, Pop, but I wasn't even planning on going. I don't get much out of those kind of things, and even if I did go, I'd sit with the *Daily Record* staff. Arriving with Blake could be…awkward."

As far as excuses went, it was a good one, and Blake knew he should have been thanking his lucky stars for it. But she'd come up with it damn quick. And what the hell did she mean…arriving with him could be *awkward?* He was no Cary Grant, but he wasn't some homeless guy off the street, either. He knew a lot of women who would jump at the chance to go out with him!

Perversely irritated, his ego bruised, he should have let it go. But a man had his pride, dammit, and she'd just stepped all over his. "Why don't you tell him the real reason you don't want to go with me?" he challenged her. "This has nothing to do with work or your boss and co-workers seeing you with me. You're chicken."

It was the wrong thing to say to a woman who prided herself on being gutsy. Gasping as if he'd slapped her, she carefully set the dirty plates she'd collected back on the table, drew herself up to her full five foot four inches, and planted her hands on her hips. "Let me get this straight, Nickels. You think I'm afraid? Of *you?*"

His grandfather's presence forgotten, he nodded. "You got it, sweetheart. You can't take the heat."

"I can take anything you can dish out."

"Then prove it. Go to the awards banquet with me."

"I told you—I can't sit with you!"

"That's okay. I'll pick you up and take you home. Is seven o'clock okay?"

He knew the exact moment she realized she'd walked into a trap. Her brown eyes widened slightly with panic, then in the next instant, snapped with fire. If she could have gotten her hands around his throat, she probably would have squeezed the life out of him, but she apparently had more self-control than that. Her nostrils flaring as she drew in a calming breath, she nodded curtly. "Seven will be fine."

For the span of ten seconds, Blake savored the victory and started to grin. Then it hit him. Sabrina wasn't the only one who'd walked into a trap. He'd sworn the last thing he was going to do was ask her out, then he'd turned around and done just that. And it was all his grandfather's fault! Turning to glare at the old man, he found him watching the two of them with glee dancing in his eyes. If Blake hadn't been so disgusted with himself, he might have laughed. Lord, he was going to have to watch Pop. If he wasn't careful, he'd have him married with children before he even knew what hit him!

She had to be out of her mind.

Standing in front of the mirror on the back of her bedroom door, Sabrina stared at her image and, for the fifth time in as many minutes, gave serious thought to calling Blake and claiming that she was too sick to go anywhere. It wouldn't be a lie. Her stomach was in a turmoil, her nerves jumpy, and she was definitely sick in the head. She had to be. Why else would she be standing here decked out in a new dress wondering if Blake would find her pretty?

Dear God, what was she doing?

Turning away from the sight of herself in a red silk dress that showed more skin than she'd ever showed in her life, she nervously paced the length of her bedroom. This was crazy. *She* was crazy! She didn't even know how she had gotten talked into this madness. She didn't like these kinds of shindigs, even if she was up for one of the most prestigious awards in the business. And she didn't go out with men who made her heart skip in her chest. It just wasn't smart when she had no intention of getting emotionally involved.

Turning back toward the mirror, she caught sight of herself again and winced. What had ever possessed her to wear red? It made her look...hot. Lord, she had to change!

But before she could even think about going through her closet for something more subdued, the doorbell rang and time ran out. Her heart jumping into her throat, she froze, every instinct she possessed urging her to run.

Why don't you tell him the real reason you don't want to go with me? You're chicken.

She stiffened, heat spilling into her cheeks. What was

she doing? she wondered, disgusted with herself. She wasn't afraid of Blake Nickels or the feelings he stirred in her. After all, it wasn't as if they were even going out on a real date. For most of the evening, they would be seated at separate tables and she wouldn't even have to look at him if she didn't want to. So what was she getting into such a stew for? He was basically giving her a ride, nothing more. She could handle that—and him—with one hand tied behind her back.

Or so she thought until she opened the front door and caught sight of Blake Nickels in a tux.

No man had a right to look so mouth-wateringly good in formal wear. Or so comfortable. He should have been pulling at his collar or at the very least grimacing at the fit of the rented tux, but instead, he looked like he'd just stepped off the cover of *GQ*. Relaxed, one hand casually buried in the pocket of his black slacks, he grinned down at her with that familiar devilish sparkle in his green eyes and had no idea what he did to her heart rate. Stunned, Sabrina knew she was staring, but she couldn't take her eyes off him. How could she have ever thought this man was just an average Joe?

His grin suddenly tilting boyishly, he glanced down at himself and patted his bow tie. "What? Have I got this thing on crooked, or what?"

"No, I..." Unable to stop herself, she reached up and straightened his tie. When her eyes lifted to his, something passed between them, something hot and intimate and private. A wise woman would have stepped back then and run for cover, but she couldn't seem to make herself move. Her pulse was skipping, her legs less than steady. And he hadn't even touched her.

Her breath lodging in her throat, she struggled for a light tone, but her voice was revealingly husky when she said,

"You know, Nickels, you clean up real good when you put your mind to it."

He should have come back at her with a smart remark that would have eased the tension sizzling in the air between them, but his brain was in a fog and had been ever since she opened the door to him. He'd expected her to be dressed up—formal wear was required for the banquet— but nothing could have prepared him for the sight of her in that dress. There was nothing the least bit risqué about it, but it made him think of satin sheets and candlelight and touching her everywhere.

She'd put her hair up, confining her usually wild curls in a sophisticated, provocative style so that only a few wisps tumbled down to sweep the nape of her bare neck. Lord, how he envied those curls! His fingers curling into fists to keep from reaching for them, he dragged his eyes away from her hair and immediately regretted it. Her skin was like the silk of her dress, soft and smooth. The rich fabric hugged her breasts and waist, revealing every curve before flaring out to a full, flirty skirt that fell to just below her knees. A man could spend hours just wondering what she had on underneath it.

His mouth suddenly as dry as west Texas, he said hoarsely, "Thanks. You don't look half bad yourself. Ready to go?"

She nodded. "Just let me get my purse and lock up."

He waited for her on the porch, then escorted her to where he'd parked his pickup at the curb. When he opened the passenger door for her, Sabrina stopped in surprise, her eyes impish as they lifted to his. "Why, Blake, I didn't know you had it in you."

"There's a lot about me you don't know," he retorted, flashing a wicked smile at her. "You ain't seen nothing yet, sweetheart."

They were both grinning when he closed the door and

walked around to the front of the truck to climb behind
the wheel. But the second he slid in beside her and started
the motor, their smiles faded. In the close confines of the
pickup cab, they weren't touching, but they might as well
have been. Scents, tantalizing and sexy, mingled and
teased, and every time one of them moved, the other felt
it deep inside. It was only five miles to the convention
center, but it seemed like a hundred.

Breathless, her palms damp and every nerve ending attuned to Blake's nearness, Sabrina should have been relieved when they finally reached the banquet hall. The
place was already packed, crowded with reporters and
newspaper publishers from all over the country. And somewhere in the mass of humanity, her boss and the rest of
the *Daily Record* staff were waiting for her to join them.
But instead of hurrying off when it was time for them to
part, she found herself reluctant to leave Blake.

"Well," he said as she hesitated at the entrance, "I
guess this is it. I'll meet you here after this shindig's
over." Suddenly noticing her silence, he frowned down at
her. "Hey, you okay?"

Forcing a smile, she moved closer to him as the crush
of people coming through the doorway jostled them. "I
just don't care for this sort of thing. In fact, I wouldn't be
here now if you hadn't dared me."

"Don't blame me." He chuckled. "It's not my fault you
rose to the bait like a trout after a fly. Anyway, what are
you worried about? I know the guys you're up against for
the best crime story, and they can't hold a candle to you."

Surprised, she smiled. "My, my, Nickels, that sounds
an awful lot like a compliment. Are you sure *you're* feeling
all right? You must be coming down with something."

He grinned in appreciation and caught her hand before
she could feel his forehead for a temperature. "Don't let
it go to your head. You'll win. *This* year. Next year's a

different matter. Then you'll be competing against me, and
I'll warn you right now, I like to win.'' Giving her hand
a squeeze, he dropped it and urged gruffly, "Go on and
find your table before your boss sees you standing here
holding my hand. I'll see you back here in a couple of
hours.''

Sabrina could have pointed out that *he* was the one
who'd been holding *her* hand, but honesty forced her to
admit that she'd started it by trying to touch him first. And
she wanted to do it again. Color stealing into her cheeks,
she stepped away from him while she still could. "Okay,
okay. But we're going to talk about this later, Nickels.
You're not the only one who likes to win."

She found the *Daily Record* staff at a large table near
the stage at the far end of the room and wasn't surprised
when her attire drew a few friendly wolf whistles. Most
of the crew had never seen her in anything more sensuous
than a business suit, and she took their ribbing in her stride.
Then the master of ceremonies, a well-known television
news journalist, stepped up onto the stage, and the awards
ceremony began.

He was an entertaining speaker, but the awards were
what everyone was waiting for, so he quickly got to them.
Reporters from all over the country were nominated for
everything from the best entertainment column to best obit,
with each category divided into subcategories based on the
size of the newspaper. With nominations restricted to work
done over the course of the past year, Blake was up for
sports coverage he'd done for the *Hidalgo County Gazette*
in Lordsburg, New Mexico, while Sabrina competed with
other police-beat reporters from larger papers.

She hadn't lied when she'd told him she didn't care for
awards. It was the tracking down of stories and the writing
itself she enjoyed, not the accolades of her peers, but when
Blake's category came up and he was announced as the

winner, she was thrilled for him. Sitting back in her seat, she found herself smiling as he strolled up to the microphone with an easy grace she couldn't help but admire. Relaxed and at ease, he joked with the crowd, then eloquently thanked the association for the honor.

Then it was her turn. Just as Blake had predicted, she was the winner. Unlike her *date,* she didn't shine at public speaking, so she kept her thanks short and sweet and got off the stage as quickly as she could. Back at her table, Fitz and the other reporters from the *Record* gave her high-fives and hugs, then it was time to party.

She should have stayed right where she was and celebrated with her friends until it was time to leave—but the only person she wanted to celebrate with was Blake. Later, she knew that was going to worry her, but for now, all she could think of was finding him in the crowd.

With the ceremony itself over, people were milling about, renewing old friendships, congratulating winners and commiserating with losers, and it seemed like everywhere she turned, someone wanted to talk to her. Struggling to hang on to her patience, she finally reached the *Times* table, but he was nowhere in sight.

Seeing her frustration, Vivian Berger, a crusty old gossip columnist who made a healthy living out of knowing who was seeing whom around town, grinned at her knowingly. "Well, hello, Ms. Jones. You looking for Blake?"

Sabrina didn't ask her how she knew—the woman had eyes in the back of her head and had probably seen them come in together. Cursing the color that spilled into her cheeks, she said casually, "As a matter of fact, I was. I thought I'd congratulate him on his win."

"Then you're going to have to get in line," the old lady said with a cackle, gesturing behind her. "He's right over there."

Turning, Sabrina expected to see him accepting the backslaps and handshakes of the other sports writers he'd beat out for the award. Instead, she found him in the arms of another woman.

Chapter 6

She wasn't the possessive type. She never had been. When it came to men, she didn't get jealous or catty; it just wasn't in her. She'd caught Jeff talking to attractive women dozen of times during their short-lived marriage, and she'd never even lifted a brow—not because she hadn't cared, she'd assured herself at the time, but because she'd trusted him. But the man hugging the pretty redhead across the room wasn't Jeff. It was Blake, and for some reason she didn't want to examine too closely, that made all the difference. Something that felt an awful lot like jealousy slammed into her, knotting her gut and heating her blood, stunning her. This wasn't even a date; she was hardly entitled to an explanation, she reminded herself. But that didn't stop her from taking a step toward them anyway.

Before she reached them, however, someone in the crowd stepped around her, jostling her and bringing her back to earth with a thud. Mortified, she stopped in her tracks. What in the world was she doing? She had no claim to Blake and didn't want one. He was a free agent and could hug a dozen women for all she cared—it was nothing to her.

Then why are your eyes green right now, Sabrina? a mocking voice whispered in her head. *You'd like to scratch that woman's eyes out and you know it.*

God, she had to get out of there!

But before she could turn away, Blake looked over the woman's shoulder and saw her. He grinned broadly, murmured something to his companion, then he was hurrying toward Sabrina. "There you are! I was just going to come look for you." Surprising her, he swept her into a bear hug. "Congratulations, Jones. I knew you could do it."

He was so exuberant, she couldn't help but smile. With his arms tight around her, squeezing her close, all she could think of was how good it felt to be held by him again. Then she caught the faint scent of perfume that clung to his tux jacket—perfume that belonged to the redhead he'd hugged just seconds ago. Unable to stop herself, she stiffened.

"Congratulations to you, too." Suddenly needing to get out of there, to think, she quickly drew back. "The party looks like it's going to drag on awhile and you probably have a lot of friends you want to talk to—"

"Yeah, I do," he cut in, grinning down at her. "The whole gang's here from New Mexico, and I didn't even know they were coming. C'mon, I want you to meet them." Not giving her a chance to object, he grabbed her hand and dragged her through the crowd after him.

And before Sabrina was quite ready for it, she found herself face-to-face with the redhead. Up close and personal, she was just as beautiful as Sabrina had feared. Dressed in a pale mint-green sheath of a dress that showed off her petite figure to perfection, she was positively glowing. And she didn't seem to mind in the least that Blake had left her to return with another woman. Her smile friendly, her big blue eyes alight with expectation, she waited patiently for him to make the introductions.

"Sabrina, this is Sydney O'Keefe Cassidy. We used to work together at the *Gazette* in Lordsburg," Blake confided with a grin.

"Actually, he used to pester the *H* out of me," Sydney corrected, her blue eyes dancing as she shook hands with Sabrina.

"I was just keeping you in line until Dillon came along," Blake retorted, and nodded to the tall, lean man who stood behind Sydney, towering protectively over her. "The big guy there is Dillon Cassidy, Sydney's husband," he told Sabrina. "God only knows why, but he's crazy about her."

A slow smile stretched across Dillon's square-cut, good-looking face. "I think it's the red hair—"

Huffing, Sydney said, "It's not red—"

"It's strawberry blond," her husband and Blake said together, laughing. "Anyway, it's nice to meet you, Sabrina," Dillon said, smiling down at her. "I don't know what plans you two have for the rest of the evening, but we were talking about getting out of here and partying on the River Walk. I hope you'll come with us."

"Hey, that's a great idea," Blake said, grinning. "Let's go."

Sabrina hesitated, wanting to go, but knowing she didn't dare. Not after the jealousy that had sunk its claws into her. And over a married woman, too—a friend who was obviously very much in love with her husband. How, dear God, had this happened? When had she begun to think of Blake as hers? She had to be out of her mind!

Hanging back, she immediately drew a frown from Blake. "You go ahead," she told him huskily. "I'm sure

the three of you have a lot to catch up on, and I've got to
be at work early in the morning. I'll just call a cab—''

"Don't be ridiculous!" Blake said. "I'll get you home
before midnight. I promise." The matter settled, he linked
his fingers with hers and pulled her outside after him.

It was a beautiful night. The heat of the day had passed,
and a lover's moon lit up a clear sky filled with stars. Not
surprisingly, the River Walk was packed with summer
tourists and locals who were drawn to the music and lights
and the cooling breeze that rippled over the slow-moving
water of the San Antonio River as it wound its way
through downtown.

Walking hand in hand with Blake, Sabrina felt as if
she'd stepped into a dream and any second now, she was
going to wake up. She hadn't even planned to go out with
him, yet here she was on what was virtually a double date
with him and the Cassidys. And in spite of the voice murmuring in her ear that she was going to regret this, she
was having too much fun to even think about calling it a
night.

Any reservations she had about Sydney had died the
second her husband stepped forward to claim her, and it
hadn't taken Sabrina long to realize that she and the other
woman had a great deal in common. Sydney, too, was an
investigative reporter who, according to her husband and
Blake, didn't know the meaning of the word fear. She had
once worked in Chicago, covering the crime beat, as Sabrina did in San Antonio, and had some fascinating tales
to tell. Chatting like old friends, they could have talked
for hours if the men hadn't interfered.

"No shoptalk," Dillon said as they finally got a table
at the Hard Rock Cafe, which was packed to the rafters.
"This isn't a night for blood and guts."

"Dillon's right," Blake agreed. "We came here to party. C'mon, Jones, I want to dance."

And with no more warning than that, he pulled her out onto the dance floor. Chagrined, Sabrina stood flat-footed in front of him and felt like a duck out of water as the crowd gyrated around them to the heavy beat of the ten-year-old hit blaring on the speakers. There were a lot of things she could do well, but dancing wasn't one of them. She loved music, but she just couldn't loosen up enough to move in time with it.

But Lord, she hated to admit it. Especially to someone who appeared to dance as well as Blake. His body already starting to languidly move in time to the beat, he looked as if he didn't have a bone in his body. Just watching him made her mouth go dry. Embarrassed color stinging her cheeks, she reached up to slip a hand behind his neck and pull his head down so he could hear her over the throb of the music. "There's something you should know about me, Nickels."

Casually draping his arms around her, he smiled down into her eyes. "What's that, Jones?"

"I've got two left feet."

His gaze, sparkling with amusement, dropped to her feet. "No, you don't. You've got a lefty and a righty just like everybody else."

She grinned, she couldn't help it, and struggled to give him a stern look. It wasn't easy when his mouth was only scant inches away from hers and he was so close that she could almost feel his body swaying against hers. "Blake, I'm trying to be serious."

"Don't," he growled low in his throat as his arms tightened around her to pull her more fully against him. "You can be serious tomorrow. Tonight, let's just…dance."

"But I can't!"

"Sweetheart, nobody who moves like you do has two left feet. Trust me. You're doing fine."

She wasn't—they both knew it—but when his voice turned all rough and deep and seemed to reach out and physically stroke her, warming the dark, secret recesses of her being, she found it impossible to care that she was a step behind everyone else on the dance floor. She was in his arms, her cheek pressed against his chest, with his heart knocking out its own erotic rhythm in her ear, and nothing else mattered. Like Cinderella, she was at the ball with a make-believe prince and it would all come crashing to a close at the stroke of twelve. For now, at least, she intended to enjoy herself.

Midnight, however, came and went and she never noticed the passage of time. They left the Hard Rock and checked out Planet Hollywood, then stopped in at a little jazz place where the music was as low as the lights. When they weren't dancing, the four of them were talking and laughing and trading stories about everything from high school to first dates to their most embarrassing moments. By the time they called it a night, it was going on three in the morning.

She'd talked all evening without once having to search her brain for a topic of conversation, but the second she and Blake were alone in his pickup and headed for her house, silence slipped into the truck with them. For the life of her, she couldn't think of a single thing to say to break it. Downtown was left behind, the odometer clicked off the miles, and the quiet, accompanied by a growing tension, thickened.

Desperate, she broke it just as Blake turned down her street. "I liked your friends. They were fun."

His smile flashed in the darkness. "They liked you, too. Dillon doesn't open up like that for everyone, you know. When he and Sydney first met, he was pretty much a loner, and wanted to stay that way. She's brought him out of it, but I've never heard him tell stories about his days in the DEA like he did tonight.''

Breaking to a stop in front of her house, he cut the engine and turned to her. She'd left the porch light on, but it hardly touched the shadows filling the truck. ''He must have really been taken with you,'' he said huskily. ''I can't say I blame him. Did I tell you what a knockout you are in that dress?''

He didn't move so much as an eyelash, but Sabrina could feel his touch as surely as if he'd reached out and trailed his fingers across her bare neck. Between one breath and the next, her heart was hammering and the temperature in the cab seemed to have risen ten degrees.

Blindly, she fumbled for the release to her seat belt. ''Not in so many words, but I sort of got the general idea, thanks,'' she said in a voice she hardly recognized as her own. ''I'd better go. It's late.''

''Wait! I'll walk you to the door.''

She opened her mouth to tell him that wasn't necessary, but she was too late. He was out of the pickup like a shot and walking around to open her door for her before she could tell him that was the last thing she wanted. Left with no choice, she stepped out and joined him on the sidewalk.

The walk to her front porch had never taken so long. With the neighborhood quiet, asleep, they could have been the only two people in the world. Her pulse skipping every other beat, Sabrina half expected him to take her hand, but he seemed content to shorten his strides to match hers and walk along beside her without touching her. Then they reached the porch.

''Thank you for a wonderful—''

''I had a great—''

They both spoke at the same time as they turned to face each other. Normally, Sabrina would have laughed, but in the glare of the porch light, there was nothing comical about the heat in his eyes. It stole her breath and weakened her knees and set off alarm bells in her head. He was going to kiss her. She knew it as surely as she knew her own name, and if she had a single ounce of self-preservation, she'd get inside while she still wanted to.

But she just stood there, her heart knocking against her ribs so loudly that he had to hear it, and waited. In the quiet of the night, it seemed like an eternity, but something of her need must have shown in her eyes because in the next instant, he was reaching for her and she, God help her, was stepping into his arms. "Blake…"

All she said was his name. Just that. She didn't use his first name often, and had no idea what it did to him when she called to him in quite that way. He considered himself a civilized man who could easily control his passions, but she'd been driving him crazy for hours. They'd laughed and talked and casually touched and all he'd been able to think of was this moment, when he'd take her home and finally have her all to himself. He'd been so sure that he would sweep her up into his arms and ravage that beautiful mouth of hers the first chance that he got, but the hunger he heard in the simple calling of his name—and the trepidation she couldn't quite conceal—echoed the confusing mix of emotions churning in his own gut. God, he wanted her, even when she scared the hell out of him. He should back off and give his head time to clear, but he couldn't, not when she was this close.

Silently cursing himself, aching for her in a way he had for no other woman, he found himself murmuring reassurances as he gathered her closer. "It's okay, honey. It's just a kiss."

But the second his mouth settled on hers, nothing was quite that simple. Not with Sabrina. Not since that first kiss that had tied him in knots and left him wanting for days now. Did she know how soft her mouth was? How hot? How giving? He could have spent days just learning the taste and texture of her, and still it wouldn't have been enough. Not when she was flush against him like a heat rash, her arms climbing around his neck, her tongue sweetly welcoming his in the liquid heat of her mouth. If he never kissed her again, a month from now, a year, he would still be able to taste her.

That thought alone should have brought him to his senses, but at that moment, every sense he had was occupied with the woman in his arms. His blood rushing through his veins, need like a fist in his gut, he wanted her. In his bed. Under him. Her arms and legs and body surrounding him, taking him in, holding him like she would never let him go. Uncaring that they were standing under her porch light in full view of anyone who cared to look, he slanted his mouth across hers to take the kiss deeper.

Her head spinning, Sabrina clung to him as if he was the only solid thing in a world that had suddenly turned topsy-turvy. All her life, she'd promised herself she would never lead with her heart the way her mother and grandmother had. She just wouldn't let herself be that weak. But Blake was a man who could shatter convictions she would have sworn were carved in stone. If she hadn't known that before, she knew it now, when he kissed her as if she was something infinitely precious that he needed more than he needed his next breath. That alone should have had her fighting her way out of his arms, but his hands seduced, even while his mouth wooed her, and her mind blurred. As if from a distance, she heard the whisper of silk as he blindly caressed her, then his fingers were closing over her breast, his thumb searching out her nipple. Lightning, sweet and warm, streaked through her, and with a soft moan, she melted against him.

For long, breathless moments, she held on tight as their kisses turned hot and wild and desperate. She couldn't think and didn't want to. Then his hands slid to her hips and pulled her against him, trapping his arousal between them. Urgency firing her blood, she whimpered.

At that moment, she would have given just about anything to be the type of woman who could enjoy the moment for the pure sake of pleasure and not ruin it by thinking too much. But she couldn't. She just couldn't.

She never remembered moving, but suddenly she was pushing out of his arms. "No! I can't do this!"

Stunned, Blake instinctively tried to pull her back into his arms. "Sweetheart, wait—"

"It's late," she said huskily, gliding out of reach as she fumbled for her keys. "You should be going."

The only place he wanted to go was inside with her, but when he ducked his head to get a look at her face, he knew that wasn't going to happen. She was pale except for the wild color that fluctuated in her cheeks, and her eyes were dark with what looked an awful lot like panic as she tried to avoid his gaze. His desire-fogged brain abruptly clearing, he frowned. "In a minute. First I think we should talk about what just happened here."

"There's nothing to talk about," she said curtly, turning away. "You kissed me. I kissed you back. End of story."

End of story?! She'd just knocked him loop-legged in front of God and any of her neighbors who cared to look at that hour of the night, and she thought that was the end of the story? The hell it was!

Wanting to strangle her, he followed her across the porch to her front door. "If you really think that, then maybe I should kiss you again because that sure didn't feel like it was the end of the story to me, honey. In fact, it damn well felt like the beginning. Dammit, Sabrina, will you at least look at me?" he fumed.

She didn't even bother to answer him. Her back to him and ramrod straight, she just stood there, staring at something in front of her. Frowning, he stepped around her and swore when he saw that she was as white as a sheet. "What is it? What's wrong? What are you looking at?"

"The door," she whispered, her gaze focused on the latch. "It's unlocked."

His eyes following hers, Blake saw that not only was it unlocked, but it was slightly ajar, pulled to, but not quite closed. "Are you sure you locked it when we left? We were both distracted. Maybe you just thought you pulled it shut."

Shaking her head, she hugged herself, suddenly chilled. "No, I know I locked it. This isn't the kind of neighborhood where you can leave your doors unlocked. I always check it twice just to be sure."

"Then someone's been here." His face grim, Blake moved between her and the door. "And for all we know, they could still be in there. Stay out here while I check it out."

It was the wrong thing to say to a woman who made her living covering crime. "Not on your life, Nickels," she said quietly. "In case you've forgotten, this is my house. If someone's still in there, they're damn well going to have to answer to me!"

Ignoring his muttered curses, she was right behind him as he stepped into the entrance hall and soundlessly switched on the light. Tension scraping against his nerve endings like a jagged piece of glass, Blake cocked his head and listened for sounds of an intruder, but nothing moved. The old house, in fact, seemed to be holding its breath and didn't even creak. Whoever had been there was, in all probability, long gone.

Still, he had no intention of bumbling through the house like an idiot in search of trouble. His pace slow and mea-

sured, his eyes watchful as he moved from room to room
with Sabrina just a half step behind him, he flipped on
lights and patiently waited for her to inspect the contents
of each room and take a quick inventory. Nothing had been
moved, let alone stolen.

By the time they reached the kitchen, Sabrina was beginning to wonder if maybe she *had* forgotten to lock the
door. Considering how nervous she'd been about going out
with Blake, it was a logical explanation. She'd taken one
look at Blake in his tux, and evidently everything else had
gone right out of her head, including locking the door.
Granted, she'd never done such a thing before, but that
made more sense than a thief breaking into the house and
leaving without taking anything.

An invisible weight lifting from her shoulders, she almost laughed at her own foolishness. Then her gaze drifted
to the kitchen table and a piece of paper that hadn't been
there when she'd left. A piece of paper that was folded in
half with her name scrawled on the outside.

She froze, her blood chilling in her veins at the sight of
that familiar jagged handwriting. She'd only seen it twice
before, but she would have recognized it in the depths of
hell. "Blake…there's a note.…"

He followed her gaze to the table and swore, reaching
it in two strides. Touching only one corner, he flicked the
unlined piece of paper open and quickly, silently, scanned
the typed message inside. When he finally looked up, his
face was set in harsh lines. "I think you'd better call the
police."

Her heart in her throat, she stepped closer. "What does
it say?"

"It doesn't matter," he retorted grimly, moving to block
her path. "Call Kelly."

Ignoring him, Sabrina tried to move around him, but he
anticipated her and once again stepped in front of her.

Scared and hating it, she knew what he was doing and couldn't even be angry with him. "You can't protect me from this, Blake," she said gravely. "Whoever wrote that damn thing was in my house! He knows where I work, where I live, where I go and when. Do you have any idea how that makes me feel, knowing he's out there somewhere, watching my every move? He's a sicko, a murderer, and I've got a right to know what kind of threats he's making, especially when they're made in my house."

Hesitating, he stood his ground. "It's just trash. Not worth worrying about."

"I deal with garbage every day on the streets," she retorted. "I can handle it. Just because I'm wearing silk tonight doesn't mean I'm soft."

He didn't like it, but she saw something flare in his eyes and knew she had won. "All right," he said with a sigh. "Read the damn thing if you insist. I'm calling Kelly." Striding across the room, he picked up the phone.

For all of ten seconds, Sabrina almost reconsidered. But if she could be intimidated by a simple note, how could she ever look herself in the mirror again? She was a reporter, and if the innocent-looking paper on the table really was from the murderer, which it certainly appeared to be, then it was news. And she didn't cower behind anyone when it came to covering a story.

Squaring her shoulders, she approached the table as if it was a nesting ground for rattlers and cautiously lifted the same corner of the note Blake had, careful not to put any more of her prints on the paper than she had to. The pounding of her heart loud in her ears, she braced herself and began to read.

You slut! I thought you were different, that you cared, but you're just like all the rest. You got your story and your headlines—headlines I gave you!—but it was him you went out with. And it should have been me, damn you! It should have been me you dressed up for in that pretty red dress, but you couldn't see anyone but him. Did you sleep with him when you got home? Just thinking about the two of you together made me sick to my stomach. I won't allow it! Do you understand? You're mine! That's why I killed her, the girl in the red dress like yours. Now you have another story to write, and you don't have to think of anyone but me. Just me. I'll kill them all if I have to to make you happy.

Horrified, Sabrina dropped the note, snatching her hand back as if she'd been burned. "No!" she said hoarsely. "It isn't true! He couldn't have killed someone else just because I went out. That's crazy!"

Finished with his call, Blake hung up and said, "Of course he's crazy! Why do you think I didn't want you to read the damn thing? He's a sicko who doesn't know reality from a hole in the ground. For all we know, he could be making the whole thing up."

"But what if it's true?" she whispered, stricken. "What if he really did go out and kill a girl in a red dress because he was angry with me? You read the note. Some poor girl could have died tonight because I went out with you."

"Bull!" he growled. Placing his hands on her shoulders, he swore at the guilt he saw already darkening her eyes and gave her a shake. "Don't you dare blame yourself for this, Jones! You didn't do anything wrong. If the bastard really did kill again tonight, he did it because he wanted to, not because of anything you did. Dammit, Sabrina, he's a loony tune! This isn't your fault."

Deep down inside, she knew that, but that didn't make her feel any better. The killer had been there tonight, not only in her home, but watching her from the shadows somewhere like a panther waiting to spring. He could have been anywhere…hiding in the bushes in some neighbor's yard, mingling with the crowd on the River Walk, following her all night and growing angrier by the second as he'd watched her laugh and dance with Blake and his friends. And she hadn't even known it.

Damn him, who was he? And what did he want from her?

"It might not technically be my fault, but I can't help but feel that I should know who this jerk is."

"What about the list you came up with for Kelly?" he asked as she kicked off her high heels and began to pace in her stocking feet.

She laughed, but there was little humor to the sound. "Believe it or not, the list wasn't that big. And somehow I can't see the guy I turned down for the senior prom in high school doing something like this ten years later. It's got to be somebody else, but who? He's leaving clues all over the place, just daring me to figure out who he is. Why can't I put it all together and come up with a name?"

"Because he's just playing with you the way a cat does with a mouse, Jones," he said flatly. "He hasn't given you that much information, just enough to tease you and drive you crazy. If you let yourself, you'll spend hours just thinking about him, and that's what he wants…your total attention. Don't let him win that kind of head game with you."

Sam Kelly arrived then with two uniformed officers. While the officers searched the house for signs of a break-in that would explain how the killer got into the house, Sam read the note, his expression stony, then silently slid it into an evidence bag. "Since you're both dressed fit to kill, you obviously went out tonight," he said as he dropped the bag on the table with a grimace of distaste and pulled out a chair. "Tell me about it. When you left, where you went, when you got back. Everything."

Unable to sit, Sabrina roamed around the kitchen, her words jerky as she began to recount the events of the evening. "It didn't start out as a date. Since Blake and I were both going to the awards banquet for the National Newspaper Association, we decided to go together. Blake picked me up—"

"What time?" Sam asked sharply.

"Seven," Blake said, answering for her. "It was still light out. A man down the street was mowing his lawn, and a couple of ladies two houses up were gossiping over the fence between their yards. There was a jogger passing the house just as I drove up, but I didn't get a look at his face. He was about six foot, a hundred and seventy pounds, with blond hair."

Jotting down notes, Sam nodded. "I'll check it out. Go on."

Amazed that Blake had noticed such things when all she'd been able to see was him, Sabrina told the detective about their arrival at the convention center, where they'd parted company until after the awards ceremony. "The banquet hall was full," she added. "But everyone seemed to belong there. If someone was watching either one of us, I didn't see them."

"From there we went to the River Walk," Blake told him, picking up the story. He gave him a list of every night spot they hit, including the Hard Rock Cafe and Planet Hollywood. "We were with friends until about three," he concluded. "Then I brought Sabrina home. She didn't notice the front door was unlatched until she started to unlock it."

His expression shuttered, Sam scribbled notes, then made them both go over the details again, questioning them sharply about who might have seen them leave together, then followed them. Unfortunately, Blake wasn't familiar enough with Sabrina's neighbors to know if there'd been any strange cars parked within view of the house, and Sabrina hadn't paid attention. If anyone had followed them—and someone obviously had—they'd been damn discreet about it.

They appeared to be back at square one again, with no clues but the note itself, when one of the uniformed officers stepped into the kitchen and informed Sam quietly, "There seems to be no sign of a break-in. All the screens and windows are securely latched, and neither the front or back doors were jimmied."

"What are you saying?" Sabrina asked sharply. "That whoever left the note had a key? That's impossible!"

Sam shrugged. "Maybe. Maybe not. Have you had your car worked on recently or loaned it to anyone who might have had the opportunity to have a copy of your house keys made?"

"No. Nothing. I haven't even had the oil changed, though God knows it needs it."

"What about a spare key to the front door?" Blake asked. "Do you keep one hidden somewhere in case you lose your keys?"

"Well, yes, but nobody would be able to find it without knowing where it was."

That was all Sam needed to hear. "Show me," he said, and pushed to his feet.

Obediently, Sabrina lead the way to the front porch. "It's here," she said. "Behind the mailbox. The box is loose, but you can't tell from just looking at it. So I put a small magnet on the back of the box and just stuck the key to it."

She started to show him, but the detective quickly stopped her, grabbing her hand before she could touch the small metal box that was attached to the wall right next to the front door. "Don't touch it," he said curtly. "I want to dust it for prints first."

Stepping around her, he examined the black mailbox in the light of the front porch light, then dusted the entire area for prints. "Most of these are probably yours and the mailman's," he said when the task was complete, "but we can't take any chances. Now, where's the key?"

It was just where Sabrina had said it would be, held in place by a small magnet that was about the size and thickness of a dime. Relieved, she let out the breath she hadn't even known she was holding and smiled shakily. "See, I told you no one could find it."

Sam wasn't so sure. "Not necessarily. Whoever left the note for you could have put the key back to make you think he didn't know where it was or he could have already had himself one made at another time. Either way, we can't assume that your locks are secure. You need to get a locksmith over here in the morning to change them for you."

"Then see about having a security system installed," Blake added, his face carved with harsh lines in the glare of the porch light. "In fact, you should have already done that. Dammit, Sabrina, this neighborhood isn't safe! Especially for a woman living alone."

Put on the defensive, she frowned. "Crime happens everywhere. You know that. And at least here, I know my neighbors, which probably wouldn't be the case if I moved into some newer, fancier subdivision where people don't even talk to each other." Wound up, she would have said more, but she suddenly spied the circle of neighbors that had collected in her front yard, drawn there by the flashing lights of the patrol cars. "See?" she told Blake triumphantly. "Everybody cares about each other here. I'm perfectly safe."

"Sabrina? Is there a problem?" Martha Anderson called

worriedly. Her iron-gray hair in rollers and a hot-pink cotton robe wrapped around her rounded figure, she hugged herself and stepped closer to the porch. "When I saw the police lights, I came running as soon as I could. What's wrong?"

"It's nothing," Sabrina assured her. "Just a break-in. Nothing was taken."

"A break-in! Oh, my!"

"Did any of you see anyone lurking around Ms. Jones's house this evening between seven and three-thirty?" Sam asked the group as he moved to join them.

"No, but I did hear a dog barking around eleven-thirty," Martha said. "I thought it was Louis's, but I didn't get up to check. When he quieted down after only a few minutes, I just thought he was after a cat or something."

"It was a jogger," Louis said quietly, pushing up his wire-rimmed glasses from where they'd slid down his thin nose. "I had just turned out the lights to go to bed when Lady starting throwing a fit. I thought it was a cat, too— she really hates them—but when I looked out the front window, all I saw was a jogger trotting down the street."

Blake lifted a dark brow at that. "At eleven-thirty at night? Do you usually have people running through the neighborhood at that hour of the night?"

Suddenly chilled, Sabrina felt goose bumps ripple down her bare arms. "No, of course not. Can you describe the man, Louis? And which way was he running? Toward my house or away from it?"

"Away," he said reluctantly. "And I'm sorry to say I didn't have my glasses on, so I didn't get a very good look at him in the dark. He was tall, with sort of a lanky build and dark hair. Sort of like Jeff."

"Jeff?" Blake repeated sharply. "Jeff Harper, her ex-husband?"

"I'm sure it wasn't him, dear," Martha told Sabrina

when Louis nodded reluctantly. "I know you two had your differences, but I can't see him breaking into your house. Not after all this time."

Sabrina didn't think so either, but when she saw Blake and the detective exchange speculative looks, she had no choice but to come to Jeff's defense. "Louis didn't say it *was* Jeff, just that the jogger was built like him. There must be hundreds of men in San Antonio who fit the same description. And it was dark, and Louis didn't have his glasses on. It could have been anyone."

"She's right about that," the older man agreed. "I'm the first to admit that I'm blind as a bat without my glasses. Anything more than three feet away tends to be rather blurry. I guess that doesn't do you much good, does it?"

"I wouldn't go so far as to say that," Sam Kelly said with a smile as he closed his notebook. "You've given us a general description of the man and the approximate time of the break-in. If you or any of the rest of you think of anything else, I'd appreciate it if you'd call me at the station."

They all promised to do just that, then reluctantly returned to their homes. Sam conferred with the two uniformed officers, then sent them on their way. When he turned back to Sabrina, his face was set in somber lines. "Considering the circumstances, I think you'd better find some place else to stay for a while. At this point, we have to conclude that that note is from the same person who killed Charlene McClintock and the others, and if he's to be believed, he killed again tonight. We can't be sure until a body's found, but one thing is for sure—he's furious with you. For your own safety, you need to get away from here for a while."

Blake couldn't have agreed more. "She can stay at my place until the bastard's caught. No one will bother her there."

"Oh, no! I couldn't!"

Sabrina's response was automatic and held more than a trace of panic. Watching the color come and go in her pale cheeks, Blake could understand her reservations. He didn't have to read her mind to know that her thoughts, like his, were on the kisses they'd shared on that very porch less than an hour ago. He wanted her. More than he should, considering the painful lessons Trina had taught him. And Sabrina, in spite of her claims to the contrary, wasn't exactly indifferent to him. Together, the two of them could set a forest ablaze, they were that hot. Living with her, even for a day or two, and keeping his hands to himself, would be impossible.

"Yes, you can," he said, throwing caution to the wind. "I'll stay with my grandfather, and you'll have the whole place to yourself. No one will know you're there but me and Sam and Pop. You'll be perfectly safe as long as you make sure no one follows you there after work every evening."

Safe. Just thinking about it made her want to jump at the chance to get away, but she'd never been one to run from a threat before, and she couldn't start now. "I appreciate the offer, Blake, but you haven't talked to your grandfather. He told me himself how independent he was. He may not want you to move in with him."

He laughed at that, his grin rueful. "Are you kidding? He'd do just about anything for you, even put up with me for a couple of weeks."

"But it could take longer than that," she argued. "And I don't like the idea of letting this monster, whoever he is, drive me out of my own house."

"What's more important?" he tossed back. "Your life or your pride?"

Put that way, she had no argument. Left with little choice, she gave in. "All right, you win. Give me a minute to pack some clothes, then we can leave."

Chapter 7

It was nearly four-thirty when Blake unlocked the door to his apartment and waited for Sabrina to precede him inside. Tired, her nerves frayed from an evening that had had more emotional highs and lows than a roller coaster, she stepped over the threshold and could have sworn she heard her heart pounding in the dark, intimate silence that engulfed the place. Moving past her, his shoulder just barely brushing hers, Blake switched on a light, but it didn't help ease the sudden tension. Standing just inside the door, she stopped, her mouth dust-dry. This was a mistake. A terrible mistake.

What was she doing here? she wondered, hugging herself. It wasn't as if she were destitute or friendless. She could have gone to a hotel. And any one of her co-workers would have been happy to put her up for as long as necessary.

She stopped short at the thought. She couldn't drag her friends into this mess, any more than she could afford to go to a hotel for an extended stay. And with the police not even close to making an arrest in the case, it could be weeks, months, before it might be safe for her to go home again. She couldn't impose on even the best of friends for that long.

So she was stuck, left with no choice but to be beholden to Blake. And there didn't seem to be a darn thing she could do about it, either. She'd tried to explain to him before they'd left her place that she couldn't, in good conscience, put him out of his apartment indefinitely, but the stubborn man had flatly refused to listen. He'd hustled her into her car, warned her that he was going to take a circuitous route to make sure they weren't being followed, and like a lamb to the slaughter, she'd followed him.

She shouldn't do this. She couldn't! She was already having trouble handling the emotions he stirred in her. How was she going to put the man out of her head when she would be living among his things—sleeping in his bed, for heaven's sake!—for God only knew how long? She had to be out of her mind.

But if Blake noticed her sudden trepidation or was the least bit shaken at the thought of her living among his things, he gave no sign of it. Striding toward the short hall that opened off the far end of the living room, he opened one of the two doors there and set her suitcase inside. "The bedroom's through here, and the bathroom's right across the hall," he told her. "There's a laundry room off the kitchen, and clean sheets and towels in the linen closet in the bathroom. Feel free to use whatever you need."

She shouldn't, she was already taking advantage of him—but she hadn't thought to bring her own sheets and towels. Nodding, she whispered, in no mood to argue with him tonight, "Thank you."

"Well, then, I guess I'd better pack some things, then get out of here if either one of us is going to get any sleep tonight. Another couple of hours, and it'll be time to get up.''

Sabrina could have told him she didn't expect to sleep much anyway, but he'd already disappeared into the bedroom. When he returned to the living room a few minutes later, all he carried was a single duffel bag. ''This'll do me for now,'' he told her as he headed for the front door. ''I'll drop by in a couple of days for the rest.''

Her throat tight, she forced a smile that wasn't nearly as breezy as she would have liked as she followed him across the living room. ''It's your apartment. Drop by whenever you like.''

Stopping just short of the front door, Blake barely stifled a groan at the suggestion. No, he thought as he stared down at her, he wouldn't be dropping by, not without a damn good reason. Not if he had a brain in his head, which at this point was doubtful. She looked damn good there. The only place she would look better was in his bed.

Images hit him then, hot and intimate and seductive. His teeth grinding on a curse, he told himself to get the hell out of there while he still could. His blood pressure was already through the roof, his fingers itching to reach for her and haul her close. But even as his head ordered his feet to move, he came up with reasons to linger.

''Are you sure you're not going to be scared here?'' he asked in a voice that was as rough as sandpaper. ''I know we weren't followed, but it is a strange place and you don't know any of the neighbors.''

Her face lifted to his, her eyes meeting his in the shadows near the door, she murmured, ''I'll be fine, Nickels. Really. You don't have to worry about me.''

She might as well have asked him not to breathe. Like it or not, he was worried, and he didn't like leaving her. He hadn't realized how much until just now. ''If you have any problems, you can reach me at Pop's. The number's in the directory by the phone in the bedroom.''

She nodded, her voice as hushed as his. ''I don't think that's going to be necessary, but thanks.''

Seconds passed, long moments of silence that seemed to hum and throb with expectation. Fumbling for his keys, he held them out to her. ''The silver one is for the dead bolt, the other one for the main lock. Make sure you use them both.''

Her gaze never leaving his, she reached for them and, in the process, brushed her fingers against his. It was an innocent touch, over in the blink of an eye, but he felt the warmth of it all the way to the soles of his feet. And she was just as stirred by it as he. He watched her eyes darken, heard her nearly silent gasp as her breath caught in her lungs, and keeping his hands to himself was almost more than he could stand. With no conscious decision on his part, he started to reach for her, only to let his arm fall back to his side. He couldn't. She was a guest in his home, there because he'd promised her she'd be safe and have the place all to herself. If he kissed her now as he longed to, as his body cried out for him to, he'd never be able to walk away from her.

Cursing himself for being a man of scruples, he had to content himself with cupping her cheek in his hand and rubbing his thumb with painstaking slowness across her bottom lip. ''Lock the door behind me,'' he said thickly. When she nodded, dazed, he gave in to temptation and brushed his thumb across her sweet mouth one more time. A split second later, he was gone, quietly shutting the door after him.

For what seemed like an eternity, Sabrina just stood there, the thunder of her racing heart roaring in her ears. She never remembered reaching for the dead bolt, but suddenly her hand was on the latch, shooting it home. From the other side of the door, she heard Blake whisper a husky good-night, then the fading sound of his footsteps as he walked away.

She *almost* called him back. Her hand was on the dead bolt, the words already trembling on her tongue, when she realized what she was doing. Muttering a curse, she snatched her hand back as if she'd been burned. Dear God, dear God, dear God! What was she doing?

"Sabrina Jones, stop this!" she said out loud to the empty apartment as she whirled away from the door. "You're not here to drool over the man, so just get him out of your head right here and now."

It was sound advice, but she soon found that it was almost impossible to follow. Too wired to even think about going to bed, she wandered around the apartment and saw Blake everywhere she turned. The refrigerator was filled with hot dogs and Twinkies and enough cholesterol to choke a horse. With no effort whatsoever, she could picture him drinking directly from a half-gallon carton of whole milk, then flashing a grin at her as he wiped his mouth with the back of his hand. And then there was the bathroom. His shampoo was there…and his cologne. She didn't open it, but she didn't have to. She only had to close her eyes and he was holding her again, kissing her again, the clean, spicy, sexy scent of him surrounding her as surely as his arms.

"Don't start, Sabrina," she muttered, heading for the bedroom. "Don't you dare start."

She should have gone to bed, but she unpacked her suitcase instead, which meant she had to go through Blake's dresser and closet to find space for her things. Touching his clothes was like touching him. Shaken, she felt like she was peering into his soul. There were some things, she decided, that a woman had no business knowing about a man she'd claimed she wanted nothing to do with. Like the way he arranged his sock and underwear drawer.

Lord, she needed to get out of there. But there was no place to go except to bed. She told herself she was tired— she would be more in control of her thoughts tomorrow. But when she pulled on a sleeveless cotton gown a few minutes later, turned out the lights, and crawled into Blake's queen-size bed, she knew she wasn't going to get any sleep in the remaining few hours that were left of the night. Not when his scent clung to the sheets, making it impossible to think of anything but him.

Her heart thumping crazily, she couldn't stop herself from clutching at his pillow, muttering curses all the while. Tomorrow, she promised herself, she was going to wash every sheet and towel in the place with her own laundry detergent. Maybe then she'd be able to at least bathe and sleep without her senses clamoring for a man who wasn't there.

How long she lay there like that, she couldn't have said. The deep, dark silence of predawn enveloped her, surrounding her like a blanket, weighing her down. Exhaustion pulling at her, she should have slept, but her mind was too busy, her pulse too erratic. Restless, she couldn't even seem to lie still. She was all over the bed, searching for a comfortable spot that just wasn't there. Finally giving up in defeat, she rolled over with a disgusted sigh and stared up at the darkened ceiling. Maybe she should just forget the whole thing and get up.

When the phone on the bedside table suddenly rang, shattering the silence, she nearly jumped out of her skin. Instinctively, she reached for it without turning on a light, her heart slamming against her ribs. It was nearly five o'clock. Who could possibly be calling Blake at that hour of the morning? "Hullo?"

"Did I wake you?"

Blake's deep, rough voice rumbled softly in her ear, as clear as if he was there in the bed beside her. With a will of its own, her heart slowly turned over and picked up speed. Just that quickly, she was smiling and couldn't for the life of her say why. "Do you make a habit of calling women at five o'clock in the morning, Nickels?" she teased softly.

"Only ones who are sleeping in my bed when I'm not there," he countered smoothly, chuckling. "You are in my bed, aren't you?"

She should have said no, that she'd decided to just stay up the rest of what was left of the night, but the truth popped out in the most provocative way. "Yes, cowboy, I'm in your bed," she murmured huskily. "I've been hugging your pillow for the last fifteen minutes trying to get to sleep."

He groaned and admitted thickly, "I don't think I needed to know that part, Jones. Now *I* won't be able to sleep."

She laughed, not the least bit repentant. "Don't expect any sympathy from me. You're the one who insisted on giving up your bed for me."

"Only because I was worried about you. Are you okay?"

"I'm fine. Really," she assured him. "Anyway, if you want to worry about someone, you'd better worry about yourself. Once word gets out on the street that you've got a knight-in-shining-armor complex, you're going to have damsels in distress from all over the city beating a path to your door. If I were you, I'd get out of town while I still could."

His chuckle vibrated in her ear, warming her inside and out. "I'll have you know I don't pull out the armor for just anyone. Only a particularly feisty female reporter I have a bet with."

"A bet you're going to lose," she reminded him sweetly.

"Time will tell. Speaking of time," he said gruffly, "I guess I should get off of here and let you try to get some sleep. You know where I am if you need me, Jones."

She should have made some lighthearted, breezy comment, but his raspy words seemed to reach right through the phone line to squeeze her heart. Her smile faltered, and emotions, thick and warm, clogged her throat. "I know," she whispered. "Good night, Blake."

His soft good-night echoing in her ear, she hung up and hugged their conversation to her breast as fiercely as she did his pillow. It was a long, long time before she finally fell asleep.

The morning sun was bright and cheerful, and if he'd had a shotgun, Blake would have shot it out of the sky. Slamming his eyes shut against the glare, he cursed long and low, damning his throbbing head, the too-small twin bed in his grandfather's guest room, the hot, sensuous dreams of Sabrina that had haunted the few hours of sleep he'd finally been able to snatch from what was left of the night.

In spite of his best efforts, a reluctant smile propped up one corner of his mouth as he thought of their whispered phone conversation while most of the rest of the world slept. It was, he realized, a good thing that they'd been almost two miles apart, or he would have had a damn difficult time keeping his hands off of her. God, what was he going to do about her?

She was tying him in knots, taking over his thoughts, his dreams, haunting him. And that didn't even begin to touch the emotions that gripped him every time he thought of the note that had been left for her on her kitchen table. Just the thought of some sleazeball following her, watching her every move, wanting her, enraged him. She was in danger, more than she seemed to realize, and every instinct he had urged him to lock her up somewhere safe, out of harm's way, until the bastard was in custody.

Slinging an arm over his eyes to blot out the sun, he rolled to his back and tried to laugh at the thought of anyone trying to protect Sabrina Jones when she didn't want to be protected. She'd take his head off if he even suggested such a thing. The lady was a fighter, with more guts than any woman he knew. He didn't doubt for a minute that in most circumstances, she could take care of herself, but that gave him little comfort. There was nothing ordinary about her current situation. She had a serial killer on her tail, and that wasn't something she or any other woman should have to deal with alone.

And *that* was something he could do something about. Rolling over onto his side, he reached for the phone. A few seconds later, he grinned as a familiar voice drawled, "Alamo City Investigations. This is Adam Martin. May I help you?"

"Well, that depends. How much is it going to cost me?"

"Blake?" his friend said, shocked. "Is that you? Son of a gun! I tried calling you last week in Lordsburg, but your number had been disconnected. Where the hell are you?"

"Some P.I. you are," Blake teased, his green eyes twinkling. "I'm right here in town. I've been working at the *Times* ever since the beginning of August."

"Hey, man, I've been working my tail off. Who's got time to read the paper?" An old college friend, Adam gave him a hard time about not calling sooner, then proceeded to catch up on the latest news. "So what's going on?" he asked finally. "And don't tell me you need a P.I. I told you before if you ever wanted to give up reporting, I'd hire you in a second. I've got employees with ten years' experience who can't hold a candle to you when it comes to investigating. Say the word, and you've got a job.''

Blake's smile faded. "Actually, I do need your services," he said seriously. "I want you to watch Sabrina Jones for me."

"Sabrina Jones, the reporter for the *Daily Record*?" he asked in surprise. "Why? Is she stealing your stories or what?"

"I can hold my own with the lady when it comes to reporting. This is something else. I guess you've heard about the serial killer going around town killing professional women?"

"Of course. Every woman I know is as jumpy as a scalded cat, and I can't say I blame them. What's that got to do with Sabrina Jones?"

"The killer's become fixated on her. The bastard's sending her notes, threatening her. Last night, she came home to find one on her kitchen table. The police think he has a key."

"Damn! And she doesn't have a clue who he is?"

"No. Detective Kelly and I finally convinced her that she needed to stay someplace else until the son of a bitch is caught, so she's taking over my place until it's safe for her to go home. I'm staying at Pop's."

"So she's still alone at night and roaming all over the city during the day," Adam concluded. "If the jerk really wants to get her, she's an easy target, Blake."

"I know. That's where you come in. I want you to watch her night and day and not let her out of your sight."

"And the lady's agreeable to this?"

"Are you kidding?" Blake laughed. "She'd be all over my case in a heartbeat if she suspected that I was even talking to you about her, let alone hiring you. So you're going to have to be damn discreet. She's no dummy."

"Hey, discreet's my middle name," Adam joked.

"Give me all the particulars, and I'll put someone on her right away. And don't worry. She'll never suspect a thing."

Relieved, Blake gave him a detailed description of Sabrina, his address, and the license-plate number of her red Honda. When he hung up a few minutes later, a worry that he hadn't allowed himself to acknowledge lifted from his shoulders. She'd be furious if she ever found out he'd put a tail on her, but for the first time in what felt like days, he knew she was safe. Maybe now he could get her out of his head and sleep at night.

Her head sluggish from what amounted to a little over an hour of sleep, her eyes bloodshot, and her stomach rolling at the mere thought of food, Sabrina reported to work on time, but God only knew how. She didn't remember dressing, or for that matter, actually driving to work. And things only went downhill from there. On a day when she would have liked nothing better than to trade places with someone on the obit desk, Fitz sent her all over town, chasing one breaking story after another. By three in the afternoon, all she wanted to do was drag herself back to Blake's apartment, crawl into bed, and not move for another twenty-four hours.

"Jones, get over to Comanche Courts," Fitz yelled across the city room at her. "There's been a drive-by shooting. Go see what you can get on it."

She groaned, but she went, hanging on to the thought that in another couple of hours, she could call it a day. Just two more hours. Surely she could get through that.

Comanche Courts was a housing project on the near east side of downtown, mere blocks from the River Walk and Alamo and the hundreds of thousands of tourists who visited the city every year. Since it was so well-known to her, Sabrina could have driven there with her eyes closed. A hotbed of poverty and crime, the courts had, over the years, been the site of more drug busts, murders and shootings than Sabrina could hope to remember. And she'd covered almost all of them.

It was not a place where you dropped your guard, but Sabrina had never been scared there. As usual, the police were present in intimidating force, the lights on top of their patrol cars silently whirling as they questioned possible witnesses. No one had been hurt—this time—but too many times before, she'd arrived to find an innocent victim lying in his own blood while his family screamed and wailed, helpless to save him.

Making her way through the crowd, Sabrina started questioning people, but if anyone had seen anything, they weren't willing to talk about it. Then she found herself next to a young girl who couldn't have been older than twelve. An innocent with dimples, she looked like a baby—until you got a look at her eyes. Dark and knowing and *old*, they had obviously seen things that no twelve-year-old should have even dreamed about, let alone witnessed firsthand.

"It was the Demons," she said in a voice so low that Sabrina had to bend her head to hear her. "They were after Joshua Cruz because they think he joined a rival gang."

At the mention of one of the most dangerous gangs in the city, Sabrina arched a brow. "I thought the Demons stuck to the west side."

"Not anymore. They declared war on the Devils."

"So this is the start of a gang war?" Sabrina asked in surprise, jotting down notes. "Is the Cruz boy a member of the Devils?"

Hugging herself, goose bumps rippling across her skin in spite of the heat of the afternoon, the younger girl shook her head, tears of frustration gathering in her dark eyes. "No, but they don't care. Franco Hernandez is a bully and a killer. He doesn't care who he hurts as long as it makes him look tough.''

Studying her, Sabrina asked quietly, ''Are you saying you saw the shooting? Was Franco the shooter?''

For a minute, she could almost see the word *yes* hovering on the girl's tongue. Then fear crept into her eyes and she clammed up. ''I'm sorry. I can't say any more.'' And before Sabrina could even ask her her name, she disappeared into the crowd.

''Damn!'' Muttering curses under her breath, Sabrina knew her one shot at getting anyone to talk to her had probably just slipped through her fingers. The people in the courts had their own brand of justice that had nothing to do with the legal system, and that, unfortunately, led to more shootings, more deaths, a catch-22 without end.

Still, she couldn't give up. Not when there was a chance that someone among the fifty or so people milling around might give her a little more information. And she still needed to question the officers investigating the shooting.

All her concentration focused on pulling information from witnesses who wanted nothing to do with her, it was a long time before Sabrina felt the touch of someone's eyes on her. Frowning, she turned, half-expecting to find Blake watching her with a mocking grin, but he was nowhere in sight. And no one else seemed to be paying the least attention to her. In fact, no one even made eye contact with her.

''You're losing it, Jones,'' she muttered to herself. ''That's what happens when you only get an hour of sleep. Chill out.''

She tried, but when she turned back to the rookie officer she'd just started to question, the fine hairs at the back of her neck rose in warning. Suddenly chilled, her heart lurching in her breast, she fought the need to glance over her shoulder.

"Something wrong, ma'am? If you don't mind me saying so, you look a little green around the gills."

Sabrina winced at that *ma'am*. She must look more haggard than she realized, she thought with a groan. She couldn't be five years older than the fresh-faced officer, and he was treating her like his grandmother.

Forcing a smile, she said, "Actually, I'm fine, just a little paranoid at the moment. You're going to think I'm crazy, but could you do me a favor?"

"Sure, if I can. What is it?"

"Just casually look behind me at the crowd. Do you see anyone watching us?"

Rubbing the back of his neck, he glanced around with a nonchalance that would have done an Academy Award winner proud, then shrugged, his smile crooked, as he turned his attention back to Sabrina. "People always stare when the police show up, but I don't see any suspicious characters if that's what you mean. Why? Has someone been bothering you?"

"Not bothering me exactly. Just…watching me." Unable to explain the disquiet that had her pulse jumping in her veins, she laughed shakily. "Just forget I said anything. I didn't get much sleep last night—I guess it's catching up with me. If you hear anything else about the shooter, I'd appreciate it if you'd give me a call."

She gave him her card, then drove back to the paper, double-checking her rearview mirror every couple of blocks. The traffic shifted and flowed normally enough around her, giving her no reason to think that she was being followed, but her gut was churning, the back of her head itching in awareness, and nothing she could say would reason her growing uneasiness away. Her fingers curling tightly around the steering wheel, she hit the gas, zipped around the car in front of her, and made a sharp right turn at the next corner without bothering to use a signal. Horns honked and someone threw an obscene gesture at her, but she didn't care. The *Daily Record*'s fenced-in parking lot was a half a block away, the security guard clearly within sight. Sending up a silent prayer of thanks, she raced into the lot like the devil himself was after her.

It wasn't until she braked to a stop and cut the engine, however, that she realized she was shaking like a leaf. Laying her head back weakly against the headrest, she let her breath out in a rush. "This isn't like you, Jones," she lectured herself in a voice that wasn't nearly as firm as she would have liked. "You don't jump at every shadow like a 'fraidy-cat. Those notes must really be getting to you. Maybe you really should think about taking a long vacation and letting someone else deal with this for a while."

It sounded good, but she knew she wasn't going anywhere. Whoever had left those notes for her could threaten her as much as he wanted, stand in the dark and stare at her, try to follow her if he thought he could keep up with her, but it wasn't going to do him any good. She was scared—only a fool wouldn't be—but there was no way she was letting a sniveling coward of a murderer scare her off the story of a lifetime.

The matter settled, she strode into the city room of the *Daily Record* with her chin at a confident angle. If her knees still had a tendency to knock and her heartbeat wasn't as slow and steady as she would have liked, no one knew that but her.

"Hey, Jones," Fitz called out the minute she stepped into the city room. "Did ya get the skinny on that drive-by?"

She nodded, holding up her notebook. "Got it right here, boss. Give me a few minutes to transcribe my notes, and I'll have it to you by five."

"Atta girl! Now if I can just light a fire under the rest

of the bums around here, we just might be able to put out a paper tomorrow.''

Sinking down into the chair at her desk, Sabrina grinned at the old man's familiar litany. He'd been with the paper for nearly forty years, and as far as she knew, he'd never yet missed a morning edition. But he still worried like an old woman, pacing and grumbling and fretting until the paper was put to bed every night. That kind of stress might have eaten away the lining of someone else's stomach years ago, but Fitz seemed to thrive on it. It was, she knew, what made him so good at his job.

The city room was, as usual, mayhem, with her co-workers coming and going and putting the last finishing touches on stories for tomorrow's edition. Flipping open her notebook to her notes, Sabrina hardly noticed. With the ease of years of practice, she blocked out everything but her thoughts and started to pound out the story on her computer keyboard.

Concentrating, she couldn't have said when she first became aware of the fact that someone had stalked into the city room and crossed directly to her desk, where he stopped and glared down at her, waiting for her to notice him. Her gaze trained on her computer monitor, she caught sight of movement from the corner of her eye and figured it was one of the copyboys. ''Just a minute,'' she said absently. ''I'll be right with you.''

Frowning, she closed her eyes, searching for the ending to her article, and suddenly there it was. Her fingers flew over the keys. Saving it, she smiled in satisfaction. ''There! Now, what can I do—''

Her eyes widened, the words dying on her tongue as she looked up into her ex-husband's furious face. ''Jeff!'' Straightening in shock, she blurted out, ''What are you doing here?''

"Looking for you," he said through his teeth. "I want to talk to you."

Taken aback by his hostile tone, Sabrina blinked in surprise. Jeff was a man who prided himself on his self-control. He didn't get angry—he just got very very quiet, and his gray eyes took on a coldness that chilled you to the bone. But something had his shorts in a twist. From the looks of the hot, red flush staining his cheeks and throat, he was more interested in yelling at her than talking, but she wisely kept that thought to herself. One wrong word just might push him over the edge and she had no intention of doing that while they were the object of at least a dozen curious pairs of eyes.

Rising to her feet, she forced a smile. "Why don't we talk outside? Would you like a Coke or something from the break room?"

"No."

So much for good manners. "Okay. Let's go."

Her curiosity killing her, she led him through the maze of corridors to the rear door that opened onto the parking lot, where they wouldn't be disturbed. Before it had even closed behind them, she was demanding some answers. "Okay, Jeff, let's have it. What's going on?"

"What's going on?" he echoed, outraged. "Don't you dare stand there and pretend to be Miss Innocent! You know damn well what's going on. You told the police that I was threatening you!"

"What?"

"You heard me," he growled. "A Detective Kelly showed up at the office this morning asking questions about my whereabouts last night." A pained expression crossed his thin face just at the memory of it. "I don't have to tell you what Mr. Druthers thought of that. I spent two hours in his office trying to explain myself, and I don't

even know what this is about. If this costs me a partnership…"

The phrase was an old familiar one that left Sabrina
cold. A partnership. It was all he'd ever thought of when
they were married, all he'd ever wanted. A lawyer with
one of the oldest, most prestigious firms in the city, Jeff
would have sold his own mother to get in the firm if he
thought Mr. Druthers and the other partners wouldn't have
severely disapproved.

"I'm sorry you were inconvenienced," she said coolly.

His eyes glacial, he sniffed, "'Inconvenienced' doesn't
begin to describe what you did to me."

"*I* didn't do anything. Louis was the one who mentioned your name to the police, but only because someone
had broken into my house and he saw someone in the
neighborhood who favored you."

She tried to tell him that she had become the unwitting
target of a serial killer, but as usual, he wasn't interested
in anyone but himself. He didn't even hear her.

"Wasn't it convenient that you had an ex-husband to
blame?" he said snidely. "So what can I expect next, Sabrina? The police showing up at my house? Searching it?
Just because you've gotten mixed up with a sick character
who'll do anything to get his name in the paper? I don't
think so. I won't have it. Do you hear me? Whatever your
problems are, you keep me out of them."

For a man who never broke a sweat if he didn't have
to, he stormed off with an amazing amount of energy.
Watching him disappear around the corner, Sabrina could
only shake her head. She'd actually been married to that
pompous ass for two years. What had she ever seen in
him?

Her temples starting to throb, she headed back inside
and told herself to forget him. She could not, however,
forget what had brought him back into her life. The killer.

For all she knew, he could be watching the parking-lot exit, waiting for her to leave. He would follow her, of course, all the way to Blake's if she wasn't careful.

Sick, her nerves jumpy at the thought of playing cat and mouse with a man she couldn't name or put a face to, she considered the idea of working late. But what good would it do? She would have to leave eventually. It would be better to do that now than after dark when she couldn't see who might be watching her, tailing her, from a distance.

Still, that didn't make driving out of the secured parking lot any easier. Her heart in her throat, she turned left instead of right, away from Blake's apartment, then spent the next half hour trying to make her way unobtrusively back to it. It was nerve-racking business. By the time she finally pulled into the apartment complex and pulled the door down on Blake's private garage, hiding her car from prying eyes, she was shaking.

Deep down inside, she found herself hoping that Blake would be waiting for her in the apartment. She hadn't seen him all day, not even when she'd gone to Comanche Courts to cover the drive-by, and as much as she hated to admit it, she'd missed him. She wanted to see that crooked grin of his, that spark of devilment in his eyes, and, just for a minute, walk into his arms and feel them close around her. Later, she would deny it, but for now she just needed to be held.

But when she unlocked both locks and pushed open the door, she knew before she ever stepped over the threshold that he wasn't there. The apartment was too quiet, the air too stale. She'd turned off the air-conditioning when she'd left that morning, and the place was like an oven. Disappointed, she shut the door and shot the dead bolt home and tried to find comfort in the sound of it clicking into place.

Instead, all she felt was lonely, and that horrified her. Flipping on the air conditioner, she told herself to knock it off. Just that afternoon, she'd had an excellent reminder of why she didn't need a man in her life. She was just like her mother and grandmother when it came to the male of the species—she was a lousy judge of character. If she didn't want to be married a zillion times like they had been, then she was going to have to resign herself to living alone. That didn't mean she couldn't be attracted to Blake or enjoy his kisses. She had the same needs as any other woman. She just had to be on guard and make sure her romantic heart didn't trick her into thinking there was anything more between them than physical attraction.

Satisfied that she'd finally resolved that issue, she headed for the bathroom and a cool shower in the hopes that it would wash her nagging headache down the drain. It didn't. She knew it was just a combination of exhaustion and tension, but she found it impossible to relax. For her own safety, she was virtually a prisoner here until the following morning, and the walls were already beginning to close in on her.

Outside, the sudden yapping of what sounded like a terrier broke the quiet. Figuring it belonged to one of Blake's neighbors, who was no doubt walking the dog after it had been locked up in the apartment all day, she strolled over to the window and looked out. The dog was nowhere in sight, and at first glance, the street outside the apartment seemed to be deserted except for tenants on their way home from work. Then she saw the man blending into the shadows beneath an Arizona ash tree across the street.

He was just standing there, during the hottest part of the day, watching her.

Chapter 8

"You ought to go check on that girl and make sure she's okay."

Hardly tasting the meat loaf his grandfather had made for supper, Blake only grunted. Pop had been hounding him about Sabrina from the moment he stepped in the front door from work, blatantly playing matchmaker, and had no idea how close to success he was. Over the course of the day, he'd had to force himself to stay away from her, to let someone else cover stories where he knew he might run into her. Knowing Adam or one of his men was watching over her had eased his mind considerably, but not enough. He wanted to see her with his own two eyes, touch her, pull her into his arms and assure himself that she really was okay.

Which was why he was staying the hell away from her.

His jaw set, he pushed the food around on his plate, his appetite nonexistent. It was that late-night phone call that had done him in, he decided, and knew he had no one to blame but himself. He'd lain on that torture device that was disguised as a bed in Pop's guest room and listened to her murmur in his ear, his body hard and aching and hurting. Given the chance, he'd have done it again in a heartbeat.

And that was what had him worried. She'd gotten under his skin, into his head, and was in danger of worming her way into his heart, and he couldn't just stand by and let it happen. He'd learned the hard way that you never really knew a woman, no matter how good a friend or lover you thought she was, and that wasn't a lesson he had to learn twice.

So he was staying well away from Sabrina Jones. He'd done what he could to make her safe; that was all he could do. From here on out, she was on her own. If he couldn't sleep for thinking about her, well, that was just too damn bad.

"I just don't understand you," his grandfather complained. "In my day, when a lady was in trouble, a man didn't leave her to fend for herself. Have you even talked to her today? How do you know she's not lying dead in a ditch somewhere?"

"She's fine, Pop."

"You don't know that. What if that bastard who's leaving her all those notes found out she was staying at your place? He could have surprised her like he surprised those other women."

Knowing how his grandfather would jump to all the wrong conclusions, he hadn't meant to tell him about his arrangement with Adam, but if he didn't, he'd hound him until he finally gave in and gave Sabrina a call. "That's not going to happen, Pop—"

Scowling at him, he growled, "And just how the heck do you know that? She's a gutsy girl—"

"Too gutsy for her own good sometimes," Blake agreed. "Which is why I called Adam Martin today."

His mouth already open to argue, his grandfather snapped it shut as his green eyes started to twinkle. "You put a P.I. on her? Oh, boy, are you going to be in hot water when she finds out!"

"Hopefully, she'll never know," Blake said just as the phone rang. Glancing at his grandfather, he lifted a brow. "You want me to get that?"

"Yeah, it's probably your mother. She calls just about every day at this time to remind me to take my blood-pressure medicine. You'd think I was a senile old man or something," he grumbled.

"You?" Blake laughed as he rose from the table. "You'll be as sharp as a tack when you're a hundred, and you know it." Snatching up the phone, he said, "Finnigan residence."

"Blake, is that you?"

Recognizing Sam Kelly's voice, he stiffened. "Yeah, Sam, it's me. What's up?"

"I thought you'd want to know that Sabrina just placed a 911 call from your place. Evidently she spied someone watching her from across the street. I'm heading over there right now."

Blake's heart stopped in midbeat. "I'll meet you there." Hanging up, he hurriedly told his grandfather what was going on, then headed for the door. "I don't know when I'll be back."

He drove like a madman, breaking every posted speed limit without a thought, just daring a cop to try and stop him. But if there were any black-and-whites in the vicinity, he didn't see them. Within three minutes of rushing out of his grandfather's house, he braked to a rough stop in front of his apartment.

In spite of the fact that he'd made the short drive in

record time, Sam Kelly was already there. His unmarked car was parked at the curb across the street, the portable red light he'd slapped on the roof whirling. He was standing in the shade of an Arizona ash talking to a man who was dressed like a jogger in T-shirt, shorts and running shoes. One look at him and Blake knew the fat was in the fire. It was Adam Martin.

"Well, damn!" Muttering curses, he got out of his pickup and crossed the street, a sheepish grin curling the corners of his mouth as he approached the two men. "I guess I don't have to introduce you two. Dammit, Adam, you weren't supposed to let Sabrina see you!"

"I know," he said with a grimace. "I blew it. But I wasn't expecting her to be staring out the window. I was just going to sit under the tree and pretend I was catching my breath, but she caught me looking. The next thing I knew, the police were driving up. I'm sorry, Blake. I guess you're going to have to tell her now, huh?"

"If he doesn't, I will," Sam said, shooting Blake a reproving look. "You should have told her the minute you put somebody on her tail."

"I didn't think it would be necessary. Anyway, she never would have agreed to it." Glancing up to the apartment's living-room window, he wasn't surprised to see Sabrina standing there, a worried frown furrowing her brow. "Who's on the next shift, Adam?"

"Mitch Hawkins, then Don Sanchez," he said, then gave him a description of both men. "I take it you're not going to pull them?"

"Hell, no. She's not going to like it—in fact, I can pretty much guarantee she's going to read me the riot act—but that's just too damn bad. She'll be safe, and that's all that matters. Well, I'd better get this over with."

Amused, Sam drawled, "If she tosses you out the window, at least there'll be a witness to call for an ambulance. Keep up the good work, Adam.''

Blake's mouth twitched, but he wasn't smiling when he crossed the street and took the stairs to his second-floor apartment. If all she did was toss him out the window, he'd be damn lucky.

Standing at the window, watching the three men laugh, Sabrina frowned as Blake crossed the street toward the apartment complex. When she'd seen Sam drive up, she'd expected him to immediately arrest the man across the street posing as a jogger, not chat with him like this was old home week. Couldn't he see the man was definitely stalking her? What in the world was going on?

Troubled, she was seriously considering going down there to find out for herself when there was a knock at the door. She didn't have to check through the peephole to know that it was Blake. Crossing to the door, she snatched it open. ''Thank God you're here! I was just going down there,'' she said as she pulled him inside. ''Who is that man? I couldn't believe it when I looked out the window and saw him watching me. Why isn't Sam arresting him?''

''It's all right. It's not what you think—''

Turning back toward the window, she hardly heard him. ''I've had this feeling all day that someone was following me. It was like an itch at the back of my neck. I thought I was going crazy, then suddenly, there he was. He never tried to get into the apartment, but he scared me to death.''

''I'm sorry about that. I should have told you—''

Frustrated, she cried, ''What does he want? He just stands there....'' His words suddenly registering, she whirled back to face him. ''What do you mean, you should have told me? Told me what?''

He hesitated, and when he did, a flush started at his throat and slowly worked its way up to his face. Sabrina didn't like the suspicions suddenly stirring in her head. Her eyes narrowing dangerously, she stepped toward him. "What have you done, Nickels? What do you know about that man down there?"

There was no help for it—he had to tell her. "He's a friend," he began reluctantly.

"A friend!"

"His name's Adam Martin. We went to college together."

"College," she repeated, sounding like a broken record. "You went to college with a stalker?"

Here it came. Bracing himself, he said bluntly, "He's not a stalker. He's a P.I. I hired him to watch you."

"You *what?!*"

"I hired him—"

She waved him off, not needing to hear the words again.

Stunned, outrage and confusion warring in her eyes, she just stared at him. "Why? Why would you do such a thing? Who gave you the right?"

"No one, but—"

"You're damn right no one did!" Working herself up into a fine temper, she started to pace, muttering half to herself. "God, I can't believe you did this! Jeff, yes—he didn't think I had the sense to get off the tracks when a train was coming. But I do the same work you do, go to the same sleazy places in this town that you do. I've never been hurt, never been shot at, never even been scared. But you think I need a bodyguard."

Blake told himself to keep a tight rein on his own temper. She was entitled to her anger. He just had to let it blow itself out. But damn, he didn't like being compared to her jerk of an ex-husband in any way, shape or form. "You never had a serial killer after you before, either," he pointed out tersely.

"Whether I have or haven't isn't the point. *You had no right!*"

"I don't see it that way," he said flatly. "Three women are dead. Three women who were probably just as independent as you are. Right or wrong, I wasn't going to stand around flat-footed while you became the fourth, so I did something about it."

Her hands on her hips, she glared at him. "Without so much as a by your leave."

It wasn't a question, but an accusation, and he didn't flinch from it. "You're damn right. It was easier that way. You would have just given me a hard time about it when there was nothing left to discuss. I hired the tail and I'm the only one who can fire him."

Too late, Blake realized he probably should have found a more diplomatic way to put that. It was nothing less than the truth, but he didn't have to rub her nose in it. She started to sputter, her brown eyes sparking fire. He should have been backpedaling, trying to soothe her ruffled feathers, but instead, he found himself perversely struck by the humor of the situation. Grinning, he said, "Go ahead and blow a gasket, but if you're going to get mad, get mad at the right person. This is all your fault."

That stopped her in her tracks. "*My* fault? How the heck do you figure that? You were the one who took it upon yourself to hire that man," she snapped, motioning in the general direction of the street. "I didn't do anything."

"Except bring out the caveman in me."

The admission came out of nowhere to steal her breath. Caught off-guard, her heart lurching in her breast, Sabrina blinked, sure she must have heard him wrong. "I beg your pardon?"

Wry humor glinted in his eyes. "You heard me. I've never considered myself a chauvinist, but there's something about you that just seems to bring out the caveman in me. Logically, I know you can take care of yourself, but this doesn't have a whole hell of a lot to do with logic.''

''Blake—''

''I know, it's crazy, but there it is. So if it'll make you feel any better, I didn't hire Adam for you—I hired him for me. So I don't have to worry about you when I'm not around.''

Not sure what he was admitting to, Sabrina couldn't seem to drag her gaze away from his. He was still smiling, but there was something in his eyes, an emotion that drizzled through her like honey, warming her to her soul and alarming her at one and the same time. With no effort whatsoever, he was slowly, bit by bit, carving a place for himself in her life, in her heart. She'd only known him for a matter of weeks, yet she was already living in his apartment, sleeping in his bed. Granted, he wasn't in there with her, but for how long? How long before she lost her head, then her heart?

Dismayed, she shook her head. ''No,'' she whispered hoarsely. ''I appreciate your concern, but you aren't responsible for my welfare. If you're getting ideas about me just because I'm staying here, you can forget it right now. I can find somewhere else to stay.''

She started to brush past him, but he grabbed her, hauling her in front of him. ''Oh, no you don't,'' he grated. ''You're not going anywhere until we get this settled.''

''There's nothing to settle!'' she insisted, tugging at her arm. ''Let me go, Blake. I've got to get out of here.''

That should have gained her her release. Instead, he drew her inexorably closer. ''I don't think so,'' he murmured. ''You can't walk away from this any more than I can. Not this time.''

Her spine ramrod straight, she didn't bother to tug at her arm again. ''Did I ever tell you that I've never cared much for Neanderthals?'' she purred. ''You might remember that.''

He *almost* laughed. Lord, she was something! He watched her try to stare him down and couldn't for the life of him look away. Or let her go. Not when he had her this close and he was aching to kiss her again. She was probably going to be furious with him, but he'd just have to risk it. Murmuring her name, he leaned down and took her mouth with his.

Half braced for a struggle, he felt her stiffen, felt every muscle go perfectly still as her breath seemed to catch in her lungs. Her palms were flat against his chest, wedged there to push him away—with the slightest pressure, she could have won her release. Because as much as he wanted her, he would have never forced her. But instead of shoving him away, her fingers curled into the material of his shirt. It was just a faint movement, a caress that she probably wasn't even aware of. But it told him far more about what was going on in her body than she knew.

She couldn't fight the attraction between them any more than he could.

A wise man would have stopped there, content with the small victory. But the emotions raging within him had nothing to do with contentment, and there was no way in hell he could stop now. His mouth gentling, softening, cajoling, he planted tiny, nibbling kisses at the corners of her mouth, the curve of her cheek, the sweet, sensitive hollow at the base of her throat. ''God, I want you, Jones,'' he breathed huskily into her ear. ''Can't you feel how much? Tell me I'm not the only one going crazy here.''

''No,'' she whispered, but even as she denied it, her mouth lifted to his.

''Yes,'' he insisted in a rough growl. Swooping down, he pressed her lips open with his, seducing her with his tongue in a series of long, slow, drugging kisses that were guaranteed to drive her quietly out of her mind. He was the one, however, who felt his control slipping. His breathing ragged, he tore his mouth from hers, but he didn't let her go. He simply couldn't. His arms tightening around her, he held her close, his eyes locked with hers. "Tell me, honey."

Dizzy, the thunder of her heart loud in her ears, she couldn't for the life of her look into those forest-green eyes of his and deny what he did to her. Not when her pulse was all over the chart and her knees had long since lost the ability to support her.

Her arms tightening around his neck, she muttered, "Damn you, Nickels, I don't know how you keep doing this to me. I can't think when you kiss me like that."

She didn't know another man she would have trusted enough to make that admission to. One more kiss, and he could have turned her to putty in his arms, but he didn't take advantage. A half smile curling one corner of his mouth, he lifted a hand to her cheek and admitted thickly, "I seem to be having that problem myself. What do you think we should do about it?"

Her senses beginning to cloud, she leaned into his hand. "Talk about it later," she murmured, pulling his mouth down to hers. "I can't think right now."

Later would be too late. She didn't give her heart lightly, and instinctively she knew that Blake could hurt her in ways Jeff never had. But they had, by fits and starts, been racing toward and fighting this moment from that first day when he'd stepped in her path and tried to protect her from something she didn't need protection from. She couldn't deny it any longer. Couldn't fight it any more. She wanted him. Here. Now. In every way a woman could want a man. Just once, she promised herself dreamily as she gave herself up to his kisses. She would have him just this once and get him out of her system. Maybe then she could sleep at night without reaching for him in her dreams.

But if she thought they were just going to have sex, she soon discovered how wrong she was. Nothing that they stirred in each other was that simple, that uncomplicated. His hands moved slowly over her, charting every dip and curve with a touch she somehow knew as well as the beat of her own heart, and intimacy was there between them, strong and sweet and sure. The world was just outside the apartment, waiting to intrude, but all she heard was the sigh of his breath, the thunder of his heart, the whisper of their clothes as they strained against each other, wanting more as need coiled tight between them.

"Blake—"

His name was all she could manage, the only thought in her head. How long had she been waiting for this, for him? He scared and thrilled her and shook her with the way he seemed to know her better than she knew herself. He nuzzled her ear and smiled softly when her breathing changed. And there were her breasts. She never said a word, never indicated by so much as a gasp how sensitive her breasts were to the play of his fingers even through the cotton of her shirt and bra, but he knew. Gently, tenderly, he trailed a finger around the crest of her nipple, circling, circling with infinite slowness, until all her attention was focused just there.

Shuddering, throbbing deep inside, she held her breath, waiting. Then, just when she thought she couldn't stand the torture any longer, he brushed against the tight bead he had created with a touch that was as soft as the brush of an angel's wing and heat streaked like an arrow straight to the core of her. Moaning, she turned into his hand, her breast filling his palm. Nothing had ever felt so good.

Holding her, caressing her, Blake told himself he'd been waiting too long for this moment to rush it. But, God, she made it difficult! She was so sweet, so responsive, that it was all he could do not to strip her clothes from her, drag her down to the living-room floor and take her like the caveman she so easily turned him into.

Tearing his mouth from hers, struggling for the control that was suddenly as elusive as a snowflake on a hot summer day, he forced himself to release her breast, but only so he could lock his arms around her and mold every soft, beautiful inch of her to him. But that, too, was agonizing. Snuggling close, her arms trapped between them, she plucked at the buttons of his shirt, undoing them one by one. Then she was touching him, running her hands under his shirt, stroking him like a cat and kissing him wherever she could reach, and in ten seconds flat, he was hotter than a two-dollar pistol.

Even then, he might have found the strength to stop. But when he burrowed his fingers in her dark, wild hair and turned her face up to his to ask her if she had any idea what she was doing to him, her brown eyes were nearly black with passion and lit from within by a fire that burned just for him. Staring down at her, he felt something shift in the region of his heart, something he couldn't control, something that swamped him with emotion and stole the breath from his lungs. His control going up in flames, he swept her up in his arms and carried her to his bed.

The last rays of the setting sun were streaming through the blinds at the window, striping the sheets with bars of golden light, but all he saw when he laid her on the bed and came down next to her was Sabrina. Her lips slightly swollen from his kisses, her cheeks flushed, her hair spread out across his pillow, she looked like something out of a fantasy, the answer to a lonely man's dreams.

He hadn't realized just how lonely he had been for her until then.

Urgency filling him, tearing at him, he fought out of his

shirt and jeans. Before they even hit the floor, he was reaching for the buttons to her blouse. He couldn't remember the last time he'd fumbled with any kind of fastenings on a woman's clothing, but suddenly his fingers were shaking. That should have stopped him cold, set him back on his heels, made him think, but he wanted her too badly. Swearing, he tugged at her blouse, then her hands were there to help him, as impatient as his, and in seconds, she was bare and reaching for him.

She was beautiful. Another time, he could have spent hours just looking at her, touching her, delighting in her small, perfect breasts and slim hips and the impossible softness of her skin, but not now. Not when she pulled him into her arms, nipped at his ear and rasped softly, "Hurry."

As the day aged, the light shifted and mellowed and the shadows grew long. Outside, the sound of laughter from the apartment pool floated on the early evening air, but in the bedroom, the only sound was of Sabrina's soft, fractured moan as he slipped into her. Then her legs were closing around him, her wet, hot heat welcoming him, and his mind blurred. He moved, and she was there with him, catching his rhythm, taking him deeper. And as he took her like a man possessed, and she started to come apart in his arms, his name a keening cry on her lips, his only thought was that he had finally come home.

In the silence afterwards, their breathing was rough, the racing of their pounding hearts slowly easing. His face buried against her neck, feeling more satisfied than he'd ever felt in his life, Blake held her close and couldn't seem to make himself let her go. Not yet. Not when he could still feel the little aftershocks that rippled through her. He was crushing her, but even when he managed to roll to his side, he took her with him, his arms twin bands of steel around her. He couldn't stop touching her, caressing her, assuring himself she was real.

It had been a while for him, he told himself. It was just chemistry. And loneliness. Trina had been a part of his life for a long time, and he hadn't even looked at another woman until Sabrina had crossed his path and the sparks had flown between them. After such a long dry spell, it hadn't taken much to light a fire. But now that they'd made love, he could get her out of his head.

But even as he tried desperately to believe that, she stirred in his arms and dropped a kiss to his chest, and just that quickly, he wanted her again. More than before, in a hundred different ways. Shaken, he drew in the scent of her and knew he could have spent hours just exploring her, learning her secrets, loving her again and again and again, until they were both too tired to move.

Dear God, what had she done to him? he wondered as the light outside gradually darkened with twilight. When Trina ran off with that trucker the night before he'd planned to ask her to marry him, she'd ripped his heart out by the roots. Like a damn fool, he hadn't known that she was even seeing anyone else. And it had hurt, dammit!

Never again, he'd promised himself. He was never going to open himself up to that kind of pain again. Especially with a woman who had made it clear that she wasn't interested in anything that even hinted at long-term commitment. If he was going to get involved—and he still wasn't sure that he was—he wouldn't settle for anything less than the long haul.

Even as his hands trailed over her, loving the feel of her, he knew he had to get out of there. Now, while he still could. He had to think, figure out where he was going, where the hell *they* were going, if anywhere.

But leaving her wasn't nearly as easy as he would have liked. His arms didn't want to release her. His jaw clenched on an oath, he rubbed his cheek against the top of her head and said quietly, "I've got to go. I rushed over here like a madman when Kelly called, and Pop is probably worried sick by now thinking you've been murdered. You going to be okay by yourself?"

His hard, sinewy body pressed close from shoulder to thigh, Sabrina nodded, dazed. "Mm-hmm."

What in the world had just happened here? She'd been married, divorced; she'd made love more than enough times to know what to expect. But nothing and no one had ever swept the ground right out from under her the way Blake just had. For the first time in her life, she'd actually felt the earth move and she didn't know if she wanted to call AP with the news or run for cover.

Something of her inner agitation must have shown because Blake was suddenly pulling back to get a better look at her face, a frown worrying his brow as his eyes searched hers. "You're awfully quiet."

Heat burning her cheeks, she ducked away from that all-too-discerning gaze of his, afraid he could read her like a book. "Actually, I was just about to doze off," she said with forced lightness. "You make a nice pillow, Nickels."

His mouth quirked, but he didn't smile. "My pleasure," he said gruffly. "About what just happened—"

"We're both consenting adults," she said hurriedly, cutting him off. "There's nothing more to discuss."

She moved then before he could stop her, dragging the covers up to her breast as she turned to face him with half the width of the bed between them. Her smile breezy, she prayed that he couldn't see how fake it was in the gathering twilight. "Go on now, get out of here. It's getting late. Your grandfather will be worried."

He should have been pleased, she thought. After all, didn't most men worry about a woman getting the wrong idea after sex? He wanted out and she was making it easy for him, but instead of acting grateful, he was looking at her as if she'd just insulted him.

"All right, all right," he said stiffly. "I'm going."

Throwing off the covers, he rose naked from the bed and had no idea what the sight of him did to her. Her mouth dry, her heart skipping every other beat, she watched as he tugged on his clothes, the frown that wrinkled his brow growing darker with every article of clothing he pulled on. By the time he was completely dressed, he was positively scowling at her. "We're going to talk about this tomorrow," he warned, then stalked out.

The second the front door slammed behind his stiff back, Sabrina wilted like a week-old rose, the need to call him back almost more than she could bear. She wanted him to hold her, to reassure her that she wasn't the only one who'd been shattered by their loving. And that alone terrified her. What if he, too, had experienced the same free fall through space and he was just as thrown by it as she? What then? Where did they go from here?

The possible answers shook her to the core.

Her heart slamming against her ribs, she climbed out of bed and grabbed a robe, chiding herself not to lose her head. It was just lust. It had to be. Simple, basic desire. The kind that made fools of the women in her family and caused them to make all the wrong decisions about men and love and life. She wouldn't, couldn't get caught up in the wonder of it. Her mother and grandmother might love walking down the aisle so much that they were willing to risk the divorce that inevitably followed, but she couldn't handle it. Once was enough. Some people just weren't cut out for marriage, and she was one of them.

Not that Blake had asked her to marry him, or was even thinking about doing such an outrageous thing, she quickly assured herself. He wasn't the type of man to get caught up in the emotion of the moment and lose his head. But he also wasn't, she decided, the kind of philandering low-life who jumped from woman to woman, bed to bed. According to his grandfather, his family had high expectations for him in politics and that meant nothing short of marriage to the right woman would ever be acceptable. She was not, and never would be, that woman.

Still, there was a part of her, deep in the heart of her, that remembered his loving and cried out for more. He'd touched something in her that no one else had, stirred something in her that she'd dreamed of without even realizing it until now. She didn't want to lose that. Didn't want to lose *him*. God, what was she going to do?

Torn, she spent the rest of the evening prowling around the apartment in search of a distraction from her own thoughts. But everywhere she turned, she was reminded of Blake. She tried reading, even television, but nothing seemed to help. She couldn't even look out the window without being reminded that there was a man out there, watching the apartment for Blake, keeping her safe. Her head told her that her safety wasn't his responsibility—her heart whispered that he cared.

Frustrated, exhausted, she finally went to bed, and though she slept, she didn't really rest. She couldn't. Not when her heart and mind spent the hours between midnight and dawn arguing like a couple of eight-year-olds. By the time the alarm went off at seven, she knew she had to go back home. Blake wouldn't be happy about it and neither, for that matter, would Sam Kelly, but she needed her own things around her—if only for a little while—to remind her of who and what she was.

She called in to work and asked for a couple of hours off, then headed to her place an hour later. Not surprisingly, Blake's hired gun followed her the whole way, never letting more than one car get between them during the drive, not even on the freeway. Scowling at him in her rearview mirror, Sabrina recognized him from Blake's description as Mitch Hawkins—a blond surfer-type who looked like he had more brawn than brain. He'd smiled and nodded at her when she'd first emerged from the apartment, but she hadn't made the mistake of thinking that he took his job lightly. Before coming to work for Adam, he'd been a border-patrol agent and could, according to Blake, track a scorpion across solid rock.

Not surprisingly, he didn't follow her into her driveway, but parked at the curb two houses down and across the street. By the time she stepped out of her car, he had already shut off his motor and slumped down in his seat. If she hadn't known he was there, she would have never seen him.

"Hey, gorgeous! Where you been hiding out? I ain't seen you in a while."

At Joe Gomez's sexily growled greeting, Sabrina turned to find him pushing a battered Harley toward her down the street, his brown eyes, as usual, sparkling with devilment. As far as Sabrina knew, he didn't own a motorcycle, and there was a good possibility he'd burrowed this one from a friend without asking, but he looked so refreshingly normal that she wanted to hug him. Restraining herself, she grinned fondly at him. "Hey, yourself," she said, striding down the driveway toward him. "What do you mean, hiding out? I've been around."

"Yeah, right. And I'm the Easter bunny." Hurt, he gave her a chiding look, his eyes, for once, dead serious. "Do I look like I'm stupid or what? In all the years I've known you, you've always come home at night. The word on the street is that dude killing all those women has got it in for you."

Alarmed, Sabrina stiffened. "Where'd you hear that?"

"I've got my sources, don't you worry about it. And they're right, aren't they? You're in deep—"

"Joe!"

At her sharp warning tone, he widened his eyes innocently. "What? All I was going to say was you were in deep trouble."

"Sure you were."

He grinned. "I don't know why everyone jumps to the conclusion that my mind is in the gutter...."

He would have said more, but before he could, a black Chevy pickup came roaring around the corner at the end of the street and slammed to a stop in front Sabrina's house. A split second later, Blake was striding toward where they stood talking, so angry steam was practically pouring from his ears. Sabrina took one look at him and felt her heart start to knock in her breast. She didn't have to ask how he'd found her—her watchdog had obviously called Adam Martin, who had reported to Blake.

"If you've come to chew me out, you can save your breath," she began quickly.

That was as far as she got. "There's been another murder," he said tersely. "Apparently the killer made good on his promise to you in his note. The body was found less than three blocks from here."

Chapter 9

The murder scene was a particularly gruesome one. The victim, Denise Green, a florist who had just opened her own shop and was still struggling to get the business off the ground, had been shot in the head and the heart in her own kitchen and had died immediately. Then the killer, going on a rampage, had ransacked her house with a viciousness that he'd made no attempt to hide. In his rage, he had paid particular attention to the bedroom, ripping the sheets and mattress with a kitchen knife, then shredding every piece of clothing in the room.

There was no note, but none was necessary. Denise Green's general description was the same as Sabrina's…she was slender and petite, with curly black hair and brown eyes. And the similarities didn't stop there. Not only did she live in the same neighborhood in a house that was almost identical in style to Sabrina's, she also, as a florist, loved flowers. Her yard and front porch, like Sabrina's, were overflowing with them. And though her body had only just been found, she had, apparently, been dead for several days. Her neighbors thought she had gone to a floral convention in Phoenix and only started to wonder if something was wrong when they noticed that her dog was still in the backyard instead of at the kennel.

The police wouldn't know for sure until they got the report from the medical examiner, but she appeared to have died the night Sabrina went with Blake to the awards ceremony at the convention center. The same night the killer had slipped into Sabrina's house and left that note on her kitchen table. He had, to put it mildly, had a busy evening.

Stricken, Sabrina stood in Denise Green's bedroom with Blake and Sam and stared at the bed, at the ruined clothes, and felt the rage that had been directed squarely at her. Chilled to the bone, she hugged herself, nausea backing up in her throat. It should have been her, she thought numbly. As much as she wanted to deny it, she couldn't miss what was right there in front of her eyes. She should have been the one lying stone-cold dead in her own kitchen with two bullets lodged in her head and her heart. She was the one the killer had been furious with, the one he'd struck out at, the one he would have killed if he could have gotten his hands on her. But she hadn't been available, so he'd gone out and murdered an innocent woman instead just because she'd had the misfortune to remind him of Sabrina.

Dear God, when would this end?

"We're still going through the house for prints," Sam said, breaking the shocked silence that had fallen over them at the sight of the bedroom. "The perp's been damn careful up to this point, but it looks like he lost it when he did this. If we're lucky, he slipped up and made a mistake."

And if they weren't, there would be more deaths, more

of the same, before the killer was caught. "What about the neighbors?" Sabrina asked stiffly. "Did any of them see or hear anything? Whoever did this didn't do it quietly."

"Not that we've been able to discover so far, but the body wasn't found until after most people had already gone to work. We should know more later in the day."

Noting the condition of the bedroom in his notebook, Blake glanced up with a frown. "What about signs of forced entry? Whoever this bastard is, he can't have keys to all these women's houses."

"No, there was no key this time," the detective said flatly, leading them back to the kitchen. The body had already been removed and taken to the morgue, but there was still dried blood everywhere. Motioning toward a bouquet of wildflowers on the counter, he said, "We think that was how he got in."

"You mean the flowers?" Sabrina asked in surprise. "Like a delivery boy?"

He nodded. "The card was still on the flowers, unopened, and the body was found right by the counter. She was still clutching her open purse...."

"Digging for a tip while he shot her right between the eyes," Blake concluded, creating an image of the murder that they could all see with sickening clarity. "God, that's cold."

Sabrina shuddered. "If he had to use a delivery to get in the door, then he didn't know her."

"Probably not," Sam agreed. "Which means he's changed his M.O. slightly, and I don't like the sound of that. Up until now, he's taken out his rage with you on women he appears to have known who remind him of you—that makes it personal. Now he's killed a stranger, someone he knows nothing about and really can't pretend is you, and that can't give him nearly as much satisfaction.

That's only going to increase his rage, which might be what he needs to finally work up the nerve to come after you. For your own safety, you really do need to get out of town for a while.''

As the last of the blood drained from her cheeks, Sabrina had to give him credit. When he issued a warning, he shot straight from the hip and didn't pull any punches. ''Believe me, Sam, nobody would like to do that any more than I would, but I just can't afford to walk away from my job and hide out somewhere until this weirdo is caught. Anyway, you said yourself it's me he wants. I'm the one he really wants to kill. If I just disappear, he might go underground until I show up again.''

''If you're thinking of offering yourself up as a decoy, you can just forget it,'' Blake said harshly before the detective could so much as open his mouth. ''It's not going to happen.''

Just days ago, she would have bristled at his tone, but the loving they'd shared last night had changed her, and to her horror, she couldn't stop her heart from lurching at the possessive, protective glint in his eyes. What had he done to her? She should have been setting him straight on the fact that only one person was in control of her life and it wasn't him, but all she wanted to do at that moment was walk into his arms.

Instead, she said huskily, ''Nobody said anything about being a decoy.''

''Good. Just so we understand each other.''

His eyes, as green as a high-mountain forest, snared hers and held them captive, setting the pulse at her throat jumping crazily. The rest of the world faded from her consciousness, and for a split second in time, it was just the two of them, alone and needy.

Clearing his throat, Sam said dryly, ''Now that we've got that cleared up, we still have the problem of keeping

Sabrina safe. Considering how reckless this bastard's getting, I think he's ready to snap. I wouldn't put it past him to go after her in broad daylight.''

"That's not going to be a problem," Blake said, never taking his gaze from Sabrina. "From now on, I don't intend to let her out of my sight."

"What?" she exclaimed. "What are you talking about?"

"You heard me. You're not going anywhere from now on without me."

"But you've already hired a P.I.—"

"And he's doing a good job," he replied. "But he can't watch over you the way I can."

His lips twitching, Sam glanced from the grim resolve in Blake's eyes to the sudden flush stinging Sabrina's cheeks and had the good sense to cut and run. "Well, I can see you two need to discuss this. I'll just get out of your hair and let you at it."

Blake never spared him a glance. "There's nothing to discuss," he told Sabrina flatly once they were alone, "so don't even think about arguing with me."

"The hell I won't," she hissed, keeping her voice deliberately low so it wouldn't carry to the policemen in the other rooms of the house. "Dammit, Blake, have you lost your mind? You can't go with me everywhere I go!"

"I don't know why I can't. Who's going to stop me?"

"Well, my boss, for one," she snapped. "What are you going to do when I report to work in the morning? Go with me?"

Not the least daunted by the idea, he nodded. "Every morning until the creep who's after you is behind bars."

"But that could be weeks! Months! Do you honestly think Fitz is going to sit back meekly and let me bring someone from the *Times* into the city room when we're in the middle of the biggest subscription war ever? He'll have a fit!"

Grinning, he pushed away from the counter to sling a friendly arm around her shoulder. "Better watch it, Jones," he teased. "Anybody hearing you just might think you're worried about me." When she only sniffed at that, he chuckled and steered her out the door. "I can take care of myself and you, too, sweetheart. Are you through around here? Good. So am I. Let's get back to work."

He followed her back to his apartment, left her car there, then drove her downtown to the ninety-year-old building that housed the *Daily Record.* In spite of that and his claims at the murder scene, Sabrina still didn't expect him to go inside with her...until he got out of the truck and started to follow her toward the employee entrance, his hand riding protectively at the bow of her back.

Fighting the sudden need to melt back into his touch, she stopped in her tracks. "Blake, this is crazy! Even if you can somehow get Fitz to agree to this, what about when you need to report in at the *Times*? Your editor's not going to be exactly pleased to see me, you know."

"Don't worry about Tom. He's an old friend. I'll square it with him."

"But what if you can't?"

His green eyes twinkling with devilment, he teased, "In the words of a talented writer I happen to have the good fortune to know, 'We're in the middle of the biggest subscription war ever.' Do you really think your boss or mine is going to fire either one of us when we're the two best reporters they've got?"

"Well, no, but—"

"I rest my case." Reaching past her shoulder, he pulled open the heavy steel door for her and waited for her to precede him. "Let's go."

Stepping inside, she was sure that they'd be stopped any second for an explanation. But Blake's presence didn't raise so much as an eyebrow. The few reporters that they did encounter who recognized Blake only nodded and went on about their business, and those in the city room didn't even glance up from their computers. Relieved, Sabrina dropped into her desk chair and sighed like a woman who had just made it through an obstacle course.

Chuckling, Blake took the chair opposite her desk, out of sight of her monitor, and pulled his notebook out of his pocket. "Go ahead and work, honey," he said, shooting her a smile that would have made her grandmother's heart jump in her breast. "I'm going to organize my notes. Then when you're finished here, we'll go over to the *Times* so I can write my piece."

Sure she wouldn't be able to write a word with him sitting right there, Sabrina cast him a suspicious look, but he was frowning at his notes and never noticed. Turning her attention back to her computer screen, she didn't even have to close her eyes to find herself back in Denise Green's bedroom, the carnage there sickening her. Suddenly, her fingers were flying over her keyboard as the words just flowed.

Lost in her own thoughts, Sabrina never saw her boss walk into the city room, but suddenly he was standing three feet away from her desk and scowling from her to Blake and back again. "You want to tell me what the hell is going on here, Jones?" he growled.

She jumped, her heart in her throat, and sent a line of *S*s running across her computer screen. "Fitz! You scared the life out of me! This is Blake—"

"I know who it is," he said curtly. "What I want to know is what's he doing here?"

"He's with me—"

"I can see that. Any particular reason why? And this better be damn good."

He had that look on his weathered face, the one that warned Sabrina that he had already made up his mind not to like what he was about to hear, and it was all she could do not to shake him. "Now don't go getting your back up before you've even heard what's going on, Fitzy. I know this looks odd, but I can explain everything if you'll just give me a chance—"

"I didn't give her a choice in the matter," Blake cut in, pushing to his feet to tower over the elderly editor. Quickly and concisely, he filled the other man in on the latest developments. "The psycho's obviously after her and I'm not letting her out of my sight until he's caught. So you'd better get used to seeing me around, Fitz," he warned with a cocky grin. "You're going to be seeing a lot of me. From now on, Sabrina and I will be going everywhere together."

Known more for his bluster than his bite, the editor scowled. "Let me get this straight, Nickels. You're telling me you're going to waltz into my paper whenever you feel like it and I'm supposed to get used to it?"

Even to his own ears, it sounded damn arrogant, but Blake had no intention of backing down to Fitz or anyone else when it came to Sabrina and her safety. His jaw set like stone, he nodded. "You are if you expect Sabrina to come in personally to file her stories. Otherwise, she can call them in from my place. The choice is yours."

His cheeks flushing with temper, Fitz opened his mouth to tell him exactly what he could do with those choices, but something in the depths of Blake's eyes must have warned him he was making no idle threat. Closing his mouth with an audible snap, he expelled his breath in a huff. "You really think she's in that kind of danger?" he asked gruffly.

"Yes, sir, I do," Blake replied quietly. "Detective Kelly

asked her to leave town but she refused because she knows how you need her right now.''

Sabrina sniffed at that, frowning. "You don't have to make me sound like a martyr, Nickels. I had other reasons for staying besides that—like the fact that I happen to need this job. And no coward of a murderer is going to run me out of my town.''

She might as well have saved her breath. Neither man spared her a glance. "I don't like the idea of anyone from the *Times* walking in and out of here like they own the place, but if I've got to put up with one of Edwards' crew, I guess I'd just as soon it be you. I can trust you not to use any insider information you pick up while you're here against us.''

It wasn't a question, but Blake treated it as one anyway. Lifting his hand to his heart, he said solemnly, "On my word as a Boy Scout.''

The old man nodded. "Good enough. Jones, don't take any more chances than you have to. That's an order.''

Giving her one last stern look to make sure she got the message, he strode off, leaving Sabrina staring after him in amazement. He'd practically given Blake carte blanche to come and go as he pleased. She never would have believed it if she hadn't heard it with her own ears.

Shaking her head, she frowned up at Blake. "Were you really a Boy Scout?''

Shrugging, he grinned. "What do you think?''

Over the course of the day, they covered a robbery involving a tourist near the River Walk, a bank hold-up, investigated the rise of gang activity in one of the city's more affluent high schools and looked into a money laundering scheme among some businesses near Fort Sam Houston. Half expecting Blake to hover over her like an overprotective parent, Sabrina was pleasantly surprised at the first crime scene when he gave her plenty of space to do her job. Interviewing the investigating officers while she spoke to the victim, he kept an eye on her, but never got close enough to overhear her questions.

Walking back to his truck with him when they were both finished, she couldn't help but tease him as he opened the passenger door for her. "You know, Nickels, I think there really must be some truth to this Boy Scout stuff. I gotta tell you—I'm impressed. I didn't think you had it in you."

Playfully tugging on her hair, he grinned. "Don't let it go to your head, Jones. I still plan on winning our bet— this is just a temporary lull in competition. Once things are back to normal, you'd better watch out. I'm going to eat your lunch."

"Oh, yeah?" she tossed back, her own eyes starting to sparkle. "You and whose army? You're good, cowboy, I'll give you that. But I'm better and you know it. I guess it's a man thing."

Confused by the sudden shift in her reasoning, he frowned. "What?"

"Not being able to accept when you're beaten," she said sweetly. Flashing her dimples at him, she dared to reach out and pat him on the cheek. "Poor baby. Men have such fragile egos."

Lightning-quick, his fingers trapped hers against his face, and suddenly, neither one of them was smiling. His blood starting to warm in his veins, Blake deliberately reminded himself that he'd sworn not to touch her again. Not after he'd gone up in flames with her and come damn close to losing his soul to her. After he'd forced himself to leave her last night, he'd lain in his narrow bed at his grandfather's and spent what was left of the night convincing himself that he'd blown their lovemaking all out of proportion. It was just good sex, nothing more. His emotions weren't involved. They couldn't be. Then he'd heard about the fourth murder and called Adam to find out where Sabrina was. When he'd learned that she'd gone back home, his heart had stopped in his chest.

He'd broken all speed limits to get to her, and ever since then, he'd been fighting the need to snatch her close. Damn, she tied him in knots! He wanted her—she didn't want commitment. So where the hell did that leave them? Until he had the answer to that, he had no business touching her. But he couldn't seem to stop himself.

Holding her hand to his jaw, he said in a voice that was sandpaper rough, "My ego's just fine, thank you very much. And I wouldn't count my chickens before they hatch, honey. You just might end up with egg on your face."

Her eyes darkened, and becoming color stole into her cheeks. "I can handle whatever you dish out, Nickels," she promised huskily. "And don't you forget it."

Staring down at her, his heart beginning to knock against his ribs, Blake told himself they were talking about the bet, nothing more. But as he slammed her door and walked around the hood of his truck to slide in beside her, all he could think about was that she could handle him, all right. Anytime she damn well pleased, better than any woman ever had before. All she had to do was say where and when and he'd be there.

Awareness humming on the air between them, they both gave a start as Blake's police radio crackled to life and a disembodied voice called all available patrol cars within the vicinity of Loop 410 and Broadway to Texas State Bank for a hostage situation. With a muttered curse, Blake started the motor and pulled away from the curb with a squeal of tires. Seconds later, they were racing across town, each of them sending up silent prayers of thanks for the distraction of work.

* * *

When they ended up at the *Times* right before quitting time, Sabrina couldn't believe how well things had gone. After Sam Kelly's grim warning earlier that morning, she'd expected to spend the day looking over her shoulder, wondering when the killer was going to make his presence known. But it was usually Blake her eyes found whenever she looked around, and he didn't give her time to wonder about anything. When he wasn't discussing the stories they'd just investigated, he was distracting her with some tall tale that invariably made her laugh.

For a woman who valued her independence, she should have been more than a little exasperated with him—after all, he hadn't given her any choice when he'd designated himself her personal bodyguard, and she wasn't used to a man just taking over her life that way without so much as a by-your-leave. But he hadn't crowded or pushed or in any way interfered with the way she worked. He'd just been there, a protective shadow who worked alongside her as if he did it every day of the week. And as much as her head hated to admit it to her heart, she'd liked having him there. He was a man a woman could get used to having underfoot.

When they'd first walked into the *Times,* she'd expected his boss to demand an explanation once he discovered her identity, but Tom Edwards only lifted a brow in surprise, told her that something big had to be in the works if Blake was conspiring with the competition, then offered her a job if she ever decided to jump ship and come work for a real paper. She'd liked him on the spot.

Seated at the chair Blake had drawn up for her at his desk, she watched him pound out three stories in record time and couldn't help but be fascinated. He used two fingers—just two—and never looked at his computer screen until he was finished. And even then, he only made a few changes before he flipped to his notes for the next story.

Unabashedly reading over his shoulder, Sabrina had to admit the man was darn good at what he did. She could knock out a story in record time when she had to, but it always took her a few stops and starts before her writing really got going and she got out of the way of her own muse. Blake seemed to have no such problem. What came off the top of his head was pretty much what he turned in as his finished work, and there was a grittiness to it that reached out and grabbed her with the first word. She couldn't help but be impressed, and knew that long after he was out of her life, she would carry in her heart a picture of him sitting at his desk, his forehead wrinkled with concentration and his eyes intently focused on something she couldn't see, hammering out a story.

Then, as quickly as he had begun, he was finished. Turning to her with that wicked grin of his that never failed to jump-start her heart, he said, "Now that you've seen a master at work, what d'ya say we blow this joint and get out of here, Jones? I don't know about you, but I'm starving."

Feeling a little hungry herself, she started to agree with him, only to frown with mock indignation. "Hold it right there, Nickels. What was that crack about a master at work?"

His eyes crinkling with amusement, he rose to his feet and reached down to pull her from her chair. "The truth hurts sometimes, Jones. But hey, look at it this way—now that you've seen me in action, maybe some of my genius will rub off on you. Of course, some things you just have to be born with—"

Laughing, she playfully punched him in the gut. "Yeah. Like modesty and talent and true greatness. When I get my Pulitzer, you can say you knew me when."

Enjoying himself, he only snorted and hauled her after him toward the nearest exit. "I've been meaning to have a serious talk with you, honey, about these delusions of grandeur you've been having," he teased. "I know this good doctor—"

Glancing over his shoulder to laugh down into her eyes, he pushed open the outside door and never noticed that while they'd been inside, the sky had turned dark and threatening and the wind had picked up. The minute they stepped outside, the rain that had been forecast all day started to fall with just a scattering of drops.

Surprised, Blake glanced up as thunder rumbled threateningly overhead. "Uh-ho. Better hurry. We're in for it."

Well used to summer storms that could blow up out of nowhere, Sabrina knew better than to linger. Practically running to keep up with Blake's long stride, she dodged raindrops like bullets and rushed across the parking lot. They were halfway to Blake's truck when the heavens opened up like a floodgate. By the time they threw themselves into the pickup's cab, they were both soaked to the skin.

Laughing, Sabrina shook her wet hair out of her face and turned to Blake, intending to make a crack about not having to wash her clothes when she got home, but the words died unspoken on her tongue. His shoulder almost rubbing hers, Blake sat as if turned to stone behind the steering wheel, totally oblivious of his wet clothes as he stared down at her, his green eyes hot and intense and devouring as they moved over her.

The thud of her heartbeat, along with the dancing of the rain on the roof of the truck, was suddenly loud in her ears. Sabrina automatically glanced down...and gasped. Drenched by the rain, her thin, white cotton blouse, normally sedate enough for church, was nearly transparent and molded her breasts like a wet T-shirt. Embarrassed color firing her cheeks, she hastily moved to cover herself.

Blake, however, was faster. Reaching behind the seat, he pulled out a lightweight cotton jacket. "Here. This'll help." His voice as rough as a gravel road, he draped it around her shoulders, then couldn't seem to stop touching her as he adjusted the collar and pulled it snugger around her. "Are you cold? I can turn on the heater."

Cold? Sabrina thought shakily, swallowing a moan of laughter. Even if it hadn't been a sticky ninety or more degrees, the brush of his hands would have warmed her if it'd been thirty below. Everywhere he innocently touched—and a few places he didn't—she burned.

"No," she choked. "I'm fine. Really. Just embarrassed to death."

"Don't be," he growled, lifting her chin so that she was forced to meet his gaze. "You're beautiful. And no one saw you but me."

And he had already seen all of her there was to see. The knowledge was there in his eyes, in the tension that curled between them like a lick of fire, in the breathlessness that suddenly seized them both. His hand slid from her chin to her throat in a slow glide, and just that quickly, they were back in his apartment, in his bed, and she was aching for another kiss.

His own need was just as fierce—she could see it in his eyes, feel it in his hands, which weren't quite steady as he moved to draw her closer, his head already lowering to hers. Then, on the street that ran in front of the *Times*'s parking lot, they heard the blare of a horn and the sudden screech of tires as a BMW, going too fast on the wet streets, narrowly missed a van that pulled out right in front of it.

Stiffening, Blake drew back abruptly and swore, remembering nearly too late that they were sitting in a public parking lot in full view of anyone who cared to look. "Let's get out of here," he muttered. A muscle ticking along his clenched jaw, he started the motor with a sharp twist of his wrist.

They didn't speak all the way home.

There was no question that he was staying the night. Or that he was sleeping in his own bed...with her. Neither one of them said anything, but the knowledge was there in his eyes, in the accelerated thump of her heart, in the expectation that filled the air like a gathering storm.

Restless, all her senses attuned to his every move as he followed her into the apartment, Sabrina knew that making love with him again could be nothing but a mistake. He was coming to mean too much to her. He made her want things she knew she couldn't have. When he touched her, kissed her, took her into his arms, she felt that anything was possible, that together they could single-handedly defeat the curse that made it impossible for the women of her family to find lifelong happiness with one man. He made her ache to believe in fairy tales and happily-ever-after and the love of a good man.

Wrapped close to his heart, it was so easy to believe that anything could happen, that he would be with her forever and grow old with her. She hadn't realized until now how desperately she wanted that, ached for that. She knew, though, that was just her emotions crying out to her. With nothing more than a heart-stopping grin, he stirred the romance in her soul. In her family, romance didn't last. Deep down inside, she knew that. But still, she couldn't send him away.

"You need to get out of those wet things," he said gruffly from behind her, shattering the silence that engulfed them. "Why don't you climb into the shower, and I'll start supper?"

His jacket still around her shoulders, she nodded, hugging herself as a blast of air from the air conditioner hit her, raising goose bumps on her damp skin. "I think I will. With the rain and everything, I am kind of cold."

"Then I'll put on some soup. Take your time. It'll be ready when you are."

If he'd touched her—just once—she wouldn't have needed soup or a shower to warm her, but he turned toward the kitchen and didn't see her need. So she headed for the bedroom to collect clean clothes, then stepped across the hall to the bathroom. She'd just started the shower and was adjusting the water temperature when there was a soft tap at the door. Her heart starting to knock like an out-of-balance washing machine, she called huskily, "Come in."

Without a sound, the door glided open to reveal Blake standing on the threshold, his expression solemn as his eyes met hers. "Sorry to interrupt, but I just remembered the city has a serious water shortage, what with the drought and everything."

Caught off guard, Sabrina almost smiled. The mayor had asked all citizens to practice voluntary conservation methods, just as he did every summer, but the water supply wasn't close to critical and they were hardly in a drought, especially considering the fact that it was currently pouring outside and showed no signs of letting up.

"A water shortage," she repeated in bemusement. "I hadn't realized the problem was that bad." Struggling to keep her expression as serious as his, she felt her heart shift into a heavy, primitive rhythm and could do nothing to quiet it. "What do you suggest we do about it?"

Without a word, he crossed the threshold and shut the door. A half step was all it took to leave only a few inches between them. Slowly, giving her time to object, he lifted his hands to the jacket she still wore and began to ease it from her shoulders. "We both need to take a shower," he said hoarsely. "If we took one together, think of the water we'd save."

Her eyes locked with his, she felt the jacket slide to the floor and found herself holding her breath, waiting for his eyes to drop to her wet blouse, but his gaze never left hers. He didn't touch her again, but simply stood there, waiting as the bathroom filled with steam. The next move, if there was going to be another one, was clearly hers.

A wise woman would have taken a moment to step back and give herself time to think. A smart one would have insisted on it. But right from the beginning, she hadn't been wise or smart when it came to this man. He tempted her past all bearing, confused her, haunted her, made her long for the impossible. And in the end, he was going to hurt her. Oh, he wouldn't do it intentionally, but she knew him well enough now to know that there would come a time that he would want to talk of the future. And they didn't have one.

Still, she couldn't deny herself—deny them—these precious moments stolen out of a lifetime of being alone. Swallowing the lump that had risen to her throat, she lifted fingers that were far from steady to the top button of his shirt. "I suppose, then," she murmured, "that you could say it's our civic duty."

He nodded, a whisper of that wicked, wicked smile of his flirting with his mouth as his hands copied hers and reached for the top button of her blouse. Between one heartbeat and the next, he slid it free. "No question about it," he agreed huskily, turning his attention to the next button. "It's the only right thing to do. We save time…" His hands still busy with her buttons, he leaned down and nuzzled her ear. "And water. And—"

"Soap," she finished for him softly as her head fell weakly back and her eyes grew heavy with desire. "I could rub it on you. Then you could rub against me.…"

She didn't finish the suggestion, but she didn't have to. He growled in approval, his hands fisting in her partially opened blouse as he pulled back to stare hungrily down into her eyes. "Is this one of your favorite blouses?"

Thrown by the sudden shift in conversation, she frowned. "Not particularly. Why?"

"I'll never forget it, but right now it's in the way." His fingers tightening in the material, he gave a quick jerk of his hands and sent the remaining buttons flying.

"Blake!"

He grinned. "There. That's much better. Do you mind?"

How could she mind when he was looking at her as if he'd just gotten three wishes for his birthday and all of them were her? His eyes scorched her, his hands worshiped her, and his mouth…she couldn't even think when he stripped her bra from her and kissed his way down to a nipple that pouted for his possession. Her cry of pleasure echoing above the drumming of the shower, she clutched his head to her breast and felt her bones melt one by one.

When he finally kissed his way back up to her mouth, she couldn't even remember her own name. Giving her a quick, hard kiss, he tore at his own clothes and what remained of hers until they were both naked. His green eyes dark and intense in the mist that shrouded them, he pulled her into the shower with him, laughing as the warm spray immediately soaked them both. Then he was pulling her in front of him, his back to the shower head, blocking the water from hitting her in the face. "Now what was that you were saying about soap?"

His eyes sparkled with a dare; his grin said she flat-out didn't have the nerve. He should have known better. With him, her heart was quickly discovering, she would dare just about anything. Happiness bubbling up in her like the clear, laughing water of a spring, she picked up the bar of soap from its holder on the side of the shower stall and slowly lathered it between her hands, her smile hot and sultry and wicked. "It seems to me," she murmured huskily, "that I mentioned something about rubbing...."

His grin broadening, he spread his hands wide, the outrageous man not the least bit self-conscious when it came to his body. "Start anywhere you like, honey. I'm all yours."

She could have started with his very obvious arousal and brought him to his knees, and she knew he wouldn't have offered a word of complaint. Instead, she reached for his hand—his left—and folded it between her palms.

"I like your hands," she said simply. Hugging his wrist to her bare breast, she gently transferred the soap on her hands to his, and all the while she talked. "Sometimes at night when I'm sleeping, I picture them touching me, undressing me, then slowly driving me out of my mind." Rubbing her fingers over the back of his hand in slow-moving circles, she looked up and asked in a sexy rasp, "Have you ever done that? Pushed a woman right over the edge with nothing but your hands? Stroking? Caressing? Everywhere?"

Staring down at her, her fingers lighting a slow burn deep in his gut, Blake could only nod. Did the little minx know what she was doing to him? She had to—he certainly had no way of hiding it from her—and all she was doing was soaping his hand! And seducing him with the kind of love talk that no man with any blood in his veins could resist. With infinite care she took his other hand, giving it the same attention to detail as she confided how she liked his hands on her breasts and sliding down her belly.

There was no doubt that she knew exactly what she was doing—her eyes were alight with naughtiness as she lathered her hands again, then carefully soaped each arm all the way to his shoulders, all the while telling him how safe she felt with his arms around her, how she knew nothing and no one could hurt her as long as he was holding her.

He'd thought he was a strong man, but with nothing more than that, she broke him. Groaning, he reached for her. "Come here, witch."

"Wait." She laughed as he hauled her against his chest where she belonged. "Don't you want me to wash your back?"

"Later," he rasped, kissing her senseless. "Much later."

On fire for her, he gave her no time to tease or argue or even catch her breath. Pushing her up against the shower wall, he tried to hang on to patience, tenderness, but he was beyond that. His hands were shaking—*shaking!*—his lungs straining. He could feel the fire in her, the need, and by God, he ached. Then her hands were on him, right where he'd wanted them, and something in him just seemed to snap. Sweeping her up, her urged her legs around his hips.

"Blake! What—"

"I've got you, sweetheart," he said thickly, surging into her before she could do anything but gasp. "I won't let anything happen to you."

He wanted to say more—that he hoped to God she hadn't been teasing when she'd said how safe she felt in his arms—but she moved, clutching him tighter, taking him deeper, and his entire universe shrank to the wet, hot heat of her surrounding him, her breasts slippery with soap as she slid against him, her name a chant, a promise, that called to him in his head. The world could have stopped and started turning the other way, but, lost in the wonder of her, he never would have noticed. There was nothing except Sabrina, pulling him toward paradise, taking him as he'd never been taken in his life.

Chapter 10

Too spent afterwards to do much more than clumsily drag a towel over both of them, Blake carried her to bed and crawled in beside her in the dark, dragging the sheet and bedspread up around them as the cool air from the air conditioner brushed over their still-damp bodies. Shivering slightly, Sabrina scooted back against him, her soft sigh a whisper in the night as he draped an arm around her waist and anchored her close. Outside, the rain drummed against the roof and dripped from the eaves, and occasionally, thunder rumbled far off to the east. Sated, content, they slept.

They turned to each other again in the night as naturally as if they'd been doing it for years, lazily exploring each other with slow hands and drugging kisses. The white-hot flash of heat that had driven them before was now a glowing ember that warmed instead of burned. This time, they had the patience to linger, to stroke, to pleasure each other until they were weak with the wonder of it. And when he swept her under him and she welcomed him with a soft moan, they looked into each other's eyes in the dark and couldn't seem to stop smiling. Whatever happened in the future, they had now, tonight, and nothing could ever take that away from them.

Still buried deep inside her, unable to let her go, Blake drifted back to sleep with her in his arms. Exhausted, replete, more relaxed than he'd ever been in his life, he never heard the rain stop or the nurse who lived next door come home after working the three-to-eleven shift. Not wanting anything to disturb this night with Sabrina, he'd remembered to shut off the phone on the nightstand after they'd made love in the shower, so he never heard the one in the kitchen ring around two in the morning. Ten rings later, it finally stopped, but his face was buried in Sabrina's hair, his dreams filled with her, and the rest of the world had long since ceased to exist.

When someone pounded on the front door at three, he frowned in his sleep, fighting wakefulness. It was thunder, he told himself groggily. Another storm had rolled in—it would blow itself out in a little while and be gone by morning. But the pounding continued, and he came awake with a start to realize that someone was hammering at his front door loud enough to wake the dead. Muttering a curse, he eased away from Sabrina, careful not to wake her, and reached for his jeans.

"Hold your horses," he grumbled as he quietly shut the bedroom door and hurried barefoot across the living room. "I'm coming, dammit! And this damn well better be good."

His jeans zipped but not buttoned, he glanced through the peephole and lifted a brow in surprise at the sight of the uniformed policeman standing there pounding on his

door as if he intended to do so for the rest of the night if
he had to, to wake him up. "What the hell!"

Turning the dead bolt, he jerked open the door and
scowled at the fresh-faced cop who looked like he was
hardly old enough to shave. "You want to tell me what
the hell you're doing, Officer?" he growled. "Besides
waking up everybody in the complex. Dammit, it's three
o'clock in the morning!"

Flushing, the younger man said stiffly, "I know that, sir.
I'm sorry to disturb you, but I'm just following orders. Are
you Blake Nickels?"

"Yes, I am," he retorted, scowling. "Whose orders?"

"Detective Kelly's, sir. When he couldn't reach you on
the telephone, he told me to hammer the door down if I
had to to wake you up. There's been an arrest in the serial-
killer murders, and he was sure you would want to know
about it as soon as possible."

"An arrest!" Surprised, Blake cast a quick look over
his shoulder to make sure the bedroom door was still shut,
then stepped outside onto the open cement balcony that
connected all of the second-floor apartments to the garden
patio below. The gutters still dripped, splashing raindrops
on his bare toes, but he never noticed. "I had no idea Kelly
was that close to making an arrest. Who is the bastard?"

"His name's Jeff Harper. He was picked up a little over
an hour ago at his home on the north side—"

"Jeff Harper!" Blake exclaimed, stiffening. "Are you
sure about that?"

"Yes, sir," he said grimly. "He's downtown right now
being booked, and he didn't come easily. From what I
heard, he fought like the devil. It took four officers to bring
him in."

Stunned, Blake couldn't believe it. Jeff Harper. Granted,
he didn't like the son of a bitch or the thought of him

coming anywhere near Sabrina, but she had trusted him
once, loved him enough to risk marrying him in spite of
her family history. She might not love him any longer—
she couldn't, dammit!—but she didn't hate him, either.
Harper had disillusioned her and hurt her, but finding out
that he was the one who had stalked and terrorized her
while she had defended him to the police was going to
tear her apart.

God, how was he going to tell her?

She would have to know, of course. And then there was
the story to write. They had to get downtown, find out
what the hell had happened to break the case wide open
tonight, and get some answers from Sam. "Thanks for the
information, Officer Johnson," he said, noting his name
tag. "Sabrina and I'll get downtown as soon as we can. Is
Kelly at the station?"

"The last I saw him, he was at the suspect's house su-
pervising the collection of evidence," the other man said.
"But he expected to be back at the station within the hour.
I can check if you like."

"That's okay," Blake said. "I'll find him. Thanks for
your help."

His mind already jumping ahead to what he was going
to tell Sabrina, he stepped back into the apartment and shut
the door behind him and never saw her standing in the
darkened living room until he started toward the bedroom
and she switched on a light. She'd pulled on a robe and
stood hugging herself as if it was the middle of winter, her
brown eyes huge and haunted in her pale face, and he
knew she knew.

"I woke up and you weren't there," she said huskily.
"When I couldn't find you, I noticed the front door was
ajar...."

So she'd heard it all, every damning word. Watching

the hurt darken her eyes, he would have given just about anything short of his first-born child to have five minutes alone with Jeff Harper in a dark alley. Stepping toward her, he reached for her and hauled her into his arms. ''Honey, I'm sorry.''

''I can't believe it,'' she said against his chest, clutching at him. ''Not Jeff. There has to be a mistake.''

He shouldn't have been surprised by her defense of the bastard—even when his car had been spotted near her house and her neighbor had given a description of a jogger that had sounded like the twin of her ex, she'd still refused to believe that Jeff could be involved—but it still twisted in his gut like a rusty knife. Stiffening, he said, ''Why? Because you still care about him and you can't believe that someone you have feelings for would want you dead?''

''No, of course not,'' she began, only to suddenly become aware of his coolness. Drawing back, she looked up and gaped in amazement at the rigid set of his jaw. ''You're jealous!''

''I am not! Don't be ridiculous.''

He scowled, glaring at her, just daring her to repeat such nonsense, but she only laughed, not the least bit intimidated, and stood on tiptoe to loop her arms around his stiff neck. ''If I weren't so surprised by the idea of you being jealous of anyone, I just might be insulted, Nickels. Do you really think I could have done what I did in that shower with you if I cared two cents about another man?''

His lips twitched, but he stood unbending before her, softening only when she melted against him, giving him an excuse to hold her again. ''You were awful damn quick to defend him,'' he grumbled, stroking her hair as if he couldn't help himself.

''Only because I thought I knew him,'' she said quietly,

sobering. Her heart suddenly aching, she laid her cheek against the hollow of his bare shoulder and fought the crazy need to cry. "Try to understand," she said softly. "It wasn't all that long ago that I was married to him, Blake. For two years, I slept with him, cooked for him, even washed his damn underwear. How could I have been so close to him and never sensed the violence in him? Was I that blind? Or just insensitive? What did I do to make him hate me so?"

"You didn't do anything," he said roughly, tightening his arms around her. "You aren't the one with the problem, honey. He is. The man's sick. He has to be. And you aren't the only one he fooled. He has friends, family, people that have known and worked with him a heck of a lot longer than you have. If none of them saw this coming, how could you?"

"But the Jeff Harper I knew couldn't even take a sick dog to the vet. How could someone like that kill four women and terrorize me?"

He shrugged. "People change."

"But not that much. There's been a lot of pressure on the police to make an arrest. Maybe someone made a mistake—"

He drew back, his hand cupping her chin to lift her gaze to his. "You know better than that. Kelly was the one who made the collar, and he never would have done that without a hell of a lot of evidence. You know how careful he is. Especially where this case is concerned. The whole state's watching, not to mention his superiors. He wants a conviction too badly to risk making a mistake."

He was right, but that didn't make it any easier to accept. Jeff. Dear God, how could it be Jeff? She hadn't lied when she'd told Blake that she didn't care two cents about him, but he was still the first man she'd ever loved, the first man she'd ever given her heart and body to. They hadn't parted friends, but she hadn't thought they were enemies, either. Obviously, she'd been wrong.

"I know," she said thickly, forcing a halfhearted smile that did nothing to conceal the pain squeezing her heart. "It just makes no sense. Why would he do such a thing now? If he was going to try to kill me, why didn't he do it when I divorced him?"

As short on answers as she, Blake shrugged. "I don't know, sweetheart. I wish I did. Who knows what pushes somebody over the edge? It might not have had anything to do with you at all—he could have just been looking for somebody to strike out at about something and your name came to mind. You know yourself that these types of crimes don't always make a lot of sense."

"Do you think Kelly will let me talk to him?"

Blake stiffened at that. No! Now that they knew Harper was responsible for terrorizing her, he didn't want her anywhere near the man. But she was the intended victim here, and he knew her well enough by now to know that this would eat at her like a cancer until she got some answers.

Still, his first inclination was to lock her up in the bedroom until Harper was tried and convicted and behind bars for a good, long stretch. She'd fight him on that, however, and he couldn't say he'd blame her. She had a right to know what was going on in Harper's head. But if she was hurting now, that could damn well rip her apart, and there wasn't anything he could do to protect her from that kind of pain. Except be there for her.

Slinging an arm around her shoulder, he turned her toward the bedroom. "Let's get dressed and go downtown and find out."

By the time they rushed into the central station downtown, it was going on four. Normally at that hour of the morning, the only ones about were cops and the lowlifes of society—drunks and brawlers and an occasional scumbag who got his kicks punching the woman in his life. But not tonight. Somehow, the word had already gotten out that there'd been an arrest in the serial killings, and the place was crawling with press. There were at least three field reporters from the local television stations, complete with camera crews, hassling the officer at the front desk for the story, not to mention radio and print reporters from every town within a fifty-mile radius. By dawn, there'd probably be some from Dallas and Houston as well.

Swearing at the sight of them, Blake shouldered his way through the crowd, pulling Sabrina after him. Finally reaching the front desk, he flashed his press badge at the scowling sergeant and said, "We need to see Detective Kelly."

"So does half the world," he drawled. "You're going to have to wait just like everybody else. He's called a press conference for seven. You can ask him anything you like then." Suddenly spying Sabrina where she was half-hidden behind Blake, his weathered face cracked into a smile. "Hey, Jones! What are you doing down here? The last time you covered the graveyard shift, you were still writing obits."

Sabrina grinned, affection lifting the heavy boulder that seemed to be sitting on her heart. Stoney Griffen had been sitting at that desk the first time she walked into the police station as a nervous cub reporter. He could have made things hard for her, but he'd gruffly taught her the ropes and had been a friend ever since.

"There's not a whole lot of things I'd crawl out of bed for at this hour of the night, Stoney, but this is one of them."

Suddenly remembering who the suspect was they had in the lockup, his teasing smile faded. "Aw, jeez, Sabrina, I'm sorry." Snapping at the other reporters to back off, he waited until they'd stepped back a couple of paces before he confided quietly, "I don't know what I was thinking of. Of course you'd be here. Are you okay?"

"Well, I can't pretend it hasn't been a shock, but I'm dealing with it." Introducing Blake to him, she said, "We really need to talk to Sam, Stoney. Isn't there some way we could see him before the press conference?"

Sighing heavily, the older man shook his head. "Sorry, darlin'. He's not even here right now. He's still over at Harper's house with the evidence guys. And I wouldn't go over there if I was you, either—he won't have time to talk to you. The last I heard, they were taking the place apart brick by brick."

"Then when he gets back—"

"He's got a meeting lined up with the chief. There ain't no way in hell I'm interfering with that."

"He's meeting with Travelino at this hour of the morning?"

The older man nodded. "The chief's been keeping a close eye on this one. In fact, Kelly hasn't made a move without letting him know about it. The old man wants to go over the evidence the minute Kelly walks through the door."

Blake swore. "It looks like we're going to have to wait just like everyone else."

If it had been any other night, any other case, Sabrina would have been more than willing to do just that. But questions hammered at her, nagged at her, pulled at her like a persistent child who refused to be silenced. Given the least encouragement from Stoney, she would have been out of there like a shot and racing for Jeff's house. But she knew police procedure as well as he did, and even though Kelly had notified her about Jeff's arrest, there was no way he was going to give her special treatment at a crime scene of this importance. Not when Travelino was waiting for him back at the station.

Reluctantly accepting defeat, she sighed. "Great. So what are we supposed to do for the next three hours?"

"Eat," Blake growled as he steered her away from the front desk and headed for the nearest exit. "In case you've forgotten, we missed supper. I'm starving. Let's go over to Mi Tierra and grab a George's Special."

She hadn't forgotten anything, least of all *why* they hadn't eaten. And in the few minutes it took for them to walk down the street to the all-night Mexican restaurant that was the heart and soul of Market Square, find a booth, and order their food, all she could think of was those moments in the shower, then later in his bed. He was coming to mean too much to her. Even as her heart swelled with joy at the thought, her head insisted that she take steps to do something about it now that she was safe again and Jeff was behind bars—

Just that quickly, her thoughts were dragged back to the murders, the notes left for her, the deliberate attempt to terrorize her, the threats to kill her. What little appetite she had vanished.

Seated across from her, Blake knew the minute he'd lost her. One second, her eyes were all dreamy, a sexy little smile playing with her mouth, and the next, her cheeks didn't have any color and she'd withdrawn into herself. And it didn't take an Einstein to figure out that her mind was back at the police station with that murdering ex-husband of hers.

And he *was* jealous. He wasn't happy about it, but he couldn't avoid the truth when it slapped him right in the face. Somehow, without quite knowing how it had happened, he had come to think of her as his.

God, he had to get this caveman stuff under control, he told himself. But even as he lectured himself to get a grip, he pushed his iced tea and place setting across the table. When Sabrina blinked in surprise, he grinned crookedly and moved around to slide in next to her on her side of the booth. "You look a little lonely over here all by yourself, Jones. Mind if I join you?"

Since he already had, she could do nothing but laugh. "Don't mind me, Nickels. Make yourself at home."

"Thanks. I think I will." Slipping an arm around her shoulders, he drew her flush against his side, unmindful of who might be watching. It wasn't until then that he realized just how badly he'd needed to have her back in his arms. "You know, Jones," he confided huskily as he trailed his fingers up and down her arm, "I could get used to holding you. You're real...touchable."

Watching her, he caught a wisp of a smile, then he felt it, that softening that always seemed to steal his breath when she leaned against him, letting him take her weight. "We're supposed to be working, Nickels."

Her tone was gently reproving—but she didn't pull away. Encouraged, Blake blatantly caressed her. "I am, sweetheart. I'm working real hard at controlling myself."

"Blake!"

"I just love it when you cry out my name that way," he growled outrageously. "Do it again."

She laughed, she couldn't help herself. "Stop that!" She giggled, casting a quick look around. "I swear, I just can't take you anywhere. We're in a public restaurant, for heaven's sake!"

Unrepentant, he leaned down to nuzzle her neck. "There's not another soul within twenty feet, and he's half-asleep. Which is what we would *not* be doing if we were back in my bed,'' he muttered roughly for her ears alone.

Telling her exactly what he would do to her if they were back in his apartment, he watched in growing satisfaction as the color flowed back into her pale cheeks, and her eyes lost that haunted look. And while she might have been chilled by her own thoughts only a few moments ago, the lady definitely wasn't cold now. Leaning more fully against him, she was warm and soft and responsive, and she never even flinched when the waiter brought their food, then quickly left them alone.

If he thought he was pulling a fast one on her, however, she quickly set him straight once the waiter was out of earshot. Capturing the hand that had dropped to her knee, she gave his fingers a warning squeeze. ''You think you're pretty tricky, don't you, Nickels?''

''Who? Me? I don't know what you're talking about.''

''You can cut the innocent act, cowboy. It's not working. The day you're innocent is the day the Alamo becomes the next Disneyland. You're not the type to seduce a woman in a public place. You're trying to take my mind off Jeff.''

Amusement glinting in his eyes, he leaned down and brushed a kiss across her mouth. ''So how am I doing?''

Surprised that he even had to ask, she grinned. ''I'll let you know later—when we're alone.'' When he groaned, she only laughed and pulled his arm from around her shoulder. ''Eat, Nickels, before your food gets cold.''

For the next twenty minutes, by unspoken agreement, they avoided any mention of Jeff or the murders or the evidence that Sam Kelly was even now collecting against her former husband. Concentrating instead on their food, they enjoyed each other's company as if they didn't have

a care in the world. They traded stories about their child-
hoods and colleges and every boss they'd ever had, then
argued good-naturedly over their favorite movies. By the
time they stopped to catch a breath, their plates were clean
and they were both more relaxed than when they had
walked in.

That couldn't last, however. As they headed back to the
police station, Blake shifted the conversation to the
weirdest stories they'd ever covered, but Sabrina couldn't
concentrate. Tension crawled along her nerves, wiring her,
and her steps unconsciously slowed as the station grew
closer and closer. For the first time in her life, she actually
dreaded a press conference.

"You start stiffening up again and I'm going to have to
kiss you right here on the street in front of God and everyone," Blake warned as he laced his fingers with hers.
"You'll get through this, Jones. Just don't beat yourself
up over it. None of it was your fault."

She could have told him it was too late for that—somehow, she should have seen this coming—but they'd
reached the front steps of the station by then and it was
time to go back to work. Resisting the sudden childish
need to cling to his hand, she gave his fingers a quick
squeeze, then dropped them, squared her shoulders, and
marched up the steps.

When Sam Kelly presented himself to the press at seven
in the morning, he didn't look as though he'd been up all
night. Clean-shaven and neatly dressed in a gray suit and
white shirt that didn't show a single wrinkle, he walked
into the media room with a confident step and took the
podium like a man who was well used to taking control.
All business, he greeted the crowd with a brisk good-

morning and, without bothering to glance at his notes, began to relate the details of the arrest of Jeff Harper.

"Mr. Harper was taken into custody at 2:23 this morning at his home on O'Connor Road. He initially resisted arrest, but there were four uniformed officers on the scene and he was quickly subdued. Presently, he is being charged with the murders of Charlene McClintock, Tanya Bishop, and Elizabeth Reagan."

"Why not Denise Green?" Jason McQuire, a reporter for the local ABC affiliate, called out. "Are you saying that Harper didn't kill her?"

"No," he said carefully, "I'm saying that he's not currently being charged with that murder. The M.O. in Ms. Green's murder was slightly different, and we're not booking anyone until we've had a chance to sift through the evidence more thoroughly."

Seated next to Sabrina at the rear of the room, Blake spoke up. "When did Jeff Harper become a suspect?"

His expression grim, Sam said, "Right after Sabrina Jones got the first note about Tanya Bishop's murder. We knew the murderer was somehow linked to her—it was just a matter of finding out how. As most of you may or may not know, the suspect is Ms. Jones's ex-husband."

"Did you find physical evidence linking him to the crimes?" a reporter from Austin asked. "Is that why you were at his house so long?"

Automatically taking notes, Sabrina listened as Sam described the extensive evidence found at Jeff's home. A gun—an unregistered .38 wiped clean of fingerprints—and a stash of bullets were found in the garage, wedged up in the rafters behind a box full of Christmas ornaments. They wouldn't know for sure until ballistics tests were done, but Sam and his men were pretty sure it was the same .38 used to kill the four women. The fact that it had been wrapped in various items of clothing that were believed to have belonged to the victims and were taken by the killer as trophies only added to the conviction that the gun was the murder weapon.

A radio reporter from the nearby town of Seguin said, "So the evidence you have presently is circumstantial?"

His mouth tightening, Sam nodded. "Obviously, we'd like an eyewitness or a confession, but given what we've got, we're sure we have the right man. The gun and clothes didn't just walk into Harper's garage by themselves and hide. And we have three witnesses who will testify to seeing a car matching the suspect's in the area at the time two of the murders were committed."

"What about an alibi?" Blake asked.

"Mr. Harper claims he was at home with his wife at the time of all four murders, but when we questioned the wife, she couldn't corroborate that because she was asleep each time and couldn't guarantee that he was in the house or not."

Stricken, her hand flying across her notebook as she jotted down notes, Sabrina wanted to cry out that this was all a terrible mistake. It had to be. But even as she tried to find an explanation for the facts that Kelly had so clearly laid out before them, her own professional objectivity forced her to admit that the evidence was damning. If it had pointed to the guilt of any other man but Jeff, she would have believed it in a heartbeat.

Sick at the thought, she had to force herself to concentrate on the task at hand. "What broke the case for you?" she asked Sam. "It couldn't have been the recovery of the murder weapon. You didn't find it until you went in to make the arrest, did you?"

"No, but we knew it was on the property some-where—"

''How?''

''We got an anonymous tip around seven-thirty last night,'' he admitted. ''And before you all start throwing questions at me, there's not a lot I can tell you about that,'' he said quickly when most of the inhabitants of the room perked up in interest. ''The call came in over a 911 line from a pay phone across the street from the Alamo. As you know, that area is usually crowded with tourists, especially in the middle of the summer, and no one noticed anything. We do know the caller was male, but that's about it. He claimed he preferred not to give his name because he's a neighbor of Harper's and has to live on the same block with him. If he was mistaken in what he had seen, he didn't want the suspect to know that he was the one who had turned him in. That's all I can tell you.''

The roomful of reporters had no intention of letting the matter drop with that, and started firing questions at him. There was, however, little else he could add. If he had any other information, it wasn't for public consumption until the trial, which wouldn't be for months. Minutes later, the press conference broke up.

They rode back to the *Daily Record* in silence. His attention divided between his driving and Sabrina's withdrawn figure, Blake ground a curse between his teeth. He'd watched her all during the press conference, watched her agitation as she jerkily scribbled notes, watched her almost visibly flinch as Kelly gave an accounting of the evidence. She hurt, and it was all he could do to stop himself from reaching for her. She hurt, and he hated that.

For the life of him, he couldn't understand how she could have any kind of feelings for the bastard who'd had her looking over her shoulder every time she stepped outside. Harper had threatened to kill her, for God's sake! For no other reason than that, Blake would have liked to hang him up by his thumbs and leave him to twist in the wind. That, however, wasn't going to make Sabrina feel any better, and that was his only concern right now.

Braking to a stop at the curb in front of the *Daily Record,* he frowned. She was safe now. It was all right for him to let her out of his sight. The rational part of his brain knew that he could let her go back to her life and not worry about some sleazeball stalking her like a hunter after his next big kill. The nightmare was over, the danger past. He no longer had to feel responsible for her.

But even as he silently acknowledged that, he was reluctant to let her go. They needed to talk. But they couldn't do it now, not when they each had to get back to their papers and write their accounts of the night's events. Over the course of the next twelve hours, there would be recaps of each murder to do and interviews with Harper's friends and neighbors. And one with Harper himself if he could get it, he silently acknowledged.

Just the thought of that should have had him making his excuses so he could get to the jail and convince the man to give him an exclusive. Instead, he said, "Do you want me to come in with you? I can wait while you write your story, then take you home so you can get your car."

Sabrina hesitated, wanting to jump at the offer, but she knew she couldn't. He had his own story to write, and she couldn't take advantage of him that way. But Lord, how she wanted to! For the first time in her career, she dreaded writing a breaking story. Just thinking about Jeff and the hatred he must feel for her made her want to jump into Blake's arms. But she was no longer in danger—she no longer needed his protection. Her heart ached at the thought of going back to an adversarial relationship with him, but she was the one who had insisted only a few weeks ago that there was no place in her future for him or any other man. She couldn't cling to him now.

Reluctantly, she shook her head. "Thanks, but that's not necessary. I don't know how long it's going to take me, and you've got your own work to do. I'll get a ride."

He wanted to argue—she could see the struggle going on his eyes—but she didn't give him the chance. Reaching for the door handle, she said huskily, "I've got to go."

He made no move to stop her, but just as she stepped out of his truck, he warned, "You haven't seen the last of me, Jones. When things calm down a little, we're going to talk."

His words carried the hint of a promise—and a threat. Her heart doing a flip-flop in her chest, Sabrina watched him drive away and bit her tongue to keep from calling him back.

Fitz told her later that her piece about Jeff's arrest was one of the best she had ever written, but Sabrina took little pleasure in the compliment. She'd tried to divorce herself both physically and emotionally from it and write it as she would any other story, but she just couldn't do it. By the time she finally finished, she was drained. Her head ached and her eyes burned, and all she wanted to do was go home and sleep around the clock.

But in spite of the fact that she had started work before four that morning, her day had hardly begun. She had a whole string of interviews she had to conduct, starting with the crime scene investigators who had uncovered the evidence at Jeff's house and continuing right down to the snow-cone seller at Alamo Plaza who might have caught a glimpse of whoever had made the anonymous phone call about Jeff to the police. But first, she had to have wheels.

When one of the sports reporters heard she was afoot,

he volunteered to give her a ride home since he was headed in that direction. She jumped at the offer, and a few minutes later, had him drop her off at the corner half a block from her house. At barely ten in the morning, it was already hot, but she didn't care. She just wanted to walk down her own street without feeling that someone was watching her.

It was heaven.

Martha Anderson was, as usual, outside in her front yard gossiping over the hedge with Gwen Richards, the widow who lived on her west side. The two were fast friends who kept an eagle eye on the neighborhood—a leaf couldn't fall without them knowing about it. Reassured that some things remained consistent, Sabrina waved gaily at them, then hurried up the porch steps to her front door. Both women waved back and continued to talk to each other as if they didn't have a care in the world, but Sabrina wasn't fooled by their nonchalance. They weren't called "the Newspapers" by the rest of the neighbors for nothing. The minute Sabrina was safely inside her house, the two old ladies would call everyone on the block to let them know she was home.

Grinning at the thought, she let herself inside. Silence closed around her immediately, clammy and thick, intimidating. Unable to stop herself, she shivered, the pleasure she expected to feel when she walked through her front door just not there. She wanted to forget Jeff and the sick murders he had committed, but all too easily, she found herself remembering the night after the awards banquet when she'd come home with Blake to find her front door unlocked and the threatening note waiting for her on her kitchen table.

She shouldn't have come here, she thought. Not yet. She wasn't ready for the memories or the nagging silence of her own thoughts. She should have just grabbed her car keys and gotten the hell out of there. But it seemed like ages since she'd been home. Her plants needed watering, and there was mail to go through. She could take a few minutes to see to those things, then grab a quick shower. Maybe then she'd be able to get through the rest of the day without going quietly out of her mind.

She had just started to water the ivy in the kitchen when there was a knock at the front door. Not really surprised, Sabrina's lips twitched. If her calculations were right, it had taken Martha all of two minutes and twenty-five seconds to get away from Gwen and make her way over there to find out where she'd been for the last two nights. That had to be a record even for her.

Her eyes starting to twinkle, she turned back to the front door. But it wasn't Martha standing on her porch, or even Gwen. It was Louis, and he looked extremely upset.

Chapter 11

"My dear, I'd just heard about Jeff's arrest on the radio when I saw you walk up. I know you're divorced and all, but you must be devastated. Is there anything I can do?"

Sabrina appreciated his concern, but she couldn't take any sympathy right now, not when her emotions felt as though they'd just been put through a food processor. He was, however, only being kind. Her smile forced, she said, "Well, it was something of a shock, but I'm coming to grips with it. And I don't have to be afraid anymore."

"That's the important thing," he agreed gruffly. "He's behind bars now and he can't hurt you. You probably have a million things to do, but I just wanted you to know that if you needed to talk, I've been told I'm a good listener."

The throbbing of her head intensifying, Sabrina reminded herself that he'd been a good neighbor to her over the years, and she couldn't be rude just because the last six hours had been rough ones. "I've got to get back to work in about an hour, but I've got a little time now. Why don't you take a seat on the porch swing and I'll fix us something cold to drink," she suggested. "I'll be right back."

Leaving him on the porch, she hurried back to the kitchen, trying to remember what she had in the house to serve him. She knew he didn't like sodas, so that left iced tea or lemonade and she wasn't sure she had the makings for either. Of course, there was always water, but—

Lost in her thoughts and wishing she could have put this off until later, she was checking to see how much sugar she had when she heard a noise behind her. Startled, she whirled and nearly dropped the sugar canister when she spotted Louis standing in the kitchen doorway. "Oh!" she laughed shakily, her heart hammering against her ribs. "You scared me."

Contrite, he immediately apologized. "I should have said something, but I thought you heard me come in. Are you all right?"

"I guess I'm still a little jumpy." Replacing the sugar canister on the counter, she decided to brew tea and moved to the sink to fill the teakettle with water. "The last week has been pretty hairy," she admitted as she crossed to the stove. "Not knowing who was threatening me was the worst. I was constantly looking over my shoulder. Then to find out it was Jeff…" She shuddered. "I still can't believe it."

His expression suddenly hard and cold, Louis nodded. "I know. I'm sure he fooled a lot of people, but there's no question that the man is a first-class bastard, dear. I hope he gets the book thrown at him. It's no more than he deserves for hurting you."

His vehemence surprised her. She knew Louis was as protective of her as an older uncle, but he'd always seemed to like Jeff, even after she divorced him. In fact, she'd never heard him say a harsh word against him. "I really think he has to be sick, Louis. Or he's on drugs or something. It's the only explanation. Four women are dead. The Jeff I was married to would have to be out of his mind to do something like that."

"I don't care if he's crazy as a loon. He hurt you, and he's going to pay for that."

Confused, she frowned. "He scared me, but he never touched me physically. It's those poor women who are the real victims—"

"They didn't suffer like you did," he said flatly, dismissing their deaths with a careless wave of his hand. "You were the one who constantly tried to please a man who couldn't be pleased. I stood by and watched you try to make that son of a bitch happy, and it made me sick to my stomach. He didn't deserve you."

Stunned, Sabrina could only stare at him. She'd never heard Louis talk like this, hadn't a clue, in fact, that he'd ever felt that way about Jeff. And how could he dismiss the death of those four women so easily, without an ounce of compassion? She'd always thought he was such a kind and gentle man, but there was a barely controlled rage in his eyes now that was more than a little scary.

Suddenly aware of the way he stood in the doorway, blocking it, she told herself to remain calm. There was no reason to get all paranoid. Obviously, something was going on here that she didn't understand. She would get him outside and they would talk about it.

The teakettle whistled then, and relief almost weakened her knees. "The tea will be ready in just a second," she said brightly. Her smile felt like it would crack her face, but it was the best she could manage under the circumstances. "Why don't you go on out to the front porch and

I'll be right there?'' she suggested. ''I think I've got some cookies around here somewhere—''

''No.''

She jumped at his sharp response, her smile slipping. ''Okay, fine,'' she said carefully, watching him warily. ''Then we'll just have the tea.''

Never budging from the doorway, he only looked at her, his pale eyes suddenly coolly amused behind the lenses of his wire-rimmed glasses. ''You just don't get it, do you, Sabrina? You're not going anywhere.''

Her heart jumped into her throat, but she only laughed shakily. ''Of course I am. I told you, I have to get back to work—''

''I've been watching you for a long time, you know. Years, in fact,'' he said casually, not even hearing her as he leaned against the doorjamb. ''The first day the two of you moved in here, I knew Jeff was all wrong for you. Anybody with eyes could see that he was a selfish bastard who didn't deserve you, but you tried your damndest to make it work. Do you know how hard it was for me to stand back and watch you do that?''

Transfixed, she could do nothing but mutely shake her head.

''No, of course you didn't,'' he said bitterly. ''You never even knew I was alive. And I couldn't blame you. You were married and you should have had eyes for no one but your husband, even if he didn't deserve you. But then you divorced him, and I thought I might finally have a chance. Surely you would see then how much I loved you. But you never looked twice at me.''

Shocked, Sabrina couldn't believe what she was hearing. He *loved* her? As a man loves a woman? Surely she must have misunderstood. But even as she tried to convince herself otherwise, she looked into his eyes and knew she hadn't made a mistake. He made no attempt to hide his pain—or resentment. Remorse stabbing her in the heart, Sabrina wanted to defend herself, but there was nothing she could say that wouldn't make him feel worse. He was right—she hadn't noticed, but he was over thirty years older than she was. He'd always been friendly when they spotted each other in the yard, but she'd never dreamed that he was romantically interested in her. Why would she? He was old enough to be her father!

"Louis, I'm sorry. I never realized."

"No, you didn't," he retorted, not making things easy for her. "You were young and pretty and you didn't have time for an old man. So I looked around and found myself someone else. She was a lot like you, a professional woman who knew what she wanted out of life. Unfortunately, she wasn't you."

Becoming more uncomfortable by the moment, Sabrina really didn't want to hear about his love life, but he hadn't budged from the doorway, and she knew he wasn't letting her out of there until he'd said everything he had to say. "That doesn't mean she wasn't right for you," she said earnestly, trying to reassure him. "Maybe you need to give her another chance."

"I can't. She's dead."

"Oh, I'm sorry!"

"I killed her."

He said it so easily, in the same casual tone he might use to mention that he'd mowed the grass, that, at first, the confession didn't register. Then her startled eyes met his and there was no question that he'd said exactly what she thought he'd said. Her heart starting to slam in her chest, she paled. "If this is some kind of a joke, I don't think it's very funny."

"Oh, it's no joke," he assured her seriously. "I tried to

make her into you—the same perfume and hairstyle, but she kept fighting me. She said I was old-fashioned and domineering and no man was going to dictate to her what she could and couldn't wear. She didn't know her place, so I shot her.''

Horrified, Sabrina realized she must have made a strangled sound of protest because he pushed away from the doorjamb, the smile that played about his mouth rueful and twisted and deranged. ''Don't worry, she didn't suffer. None of them did.''

A restless hand flew to Sabrina's suddenly tight throat. ''None of them?''

''There were others,'' he said simply. ''But they didn't work out, either''

''How many others?''

''Three more. I knew you would put two and two together, after the first two, and you did. Finally, you noticed me!'' A pleased smile bloomed across his face. ''It was wonderful. So I killed again. Then once more because I couldn't help myself. *You* made me mad.'' Suddenly noticing her ashen complexion, he frowned. ''You should sit down. You're awfully pale all of a sudden.''

Her blood roaring in her ears, Sabrina almost choked on a hysterical laugh. He'd just admitted to killing four women and he was concerned that she was a little pale?

It hit her then—*four* women. He'd claimed he'd killed four women, and the only murders she'd written about recently were those committed by the serial killer.

The logical part of her mind immediately rejected the idea. The police had arrested Jeff; they were sure they had the right man. He had motive and opportunity, not to mention a garage full of incriminating evidence and no alibi. They couldn't have made a mistake. Could they?

Dread clutching her heart, she stepped around the table

before he could help her into a chair. "I don't need to sit down, but I would like to hear more about these murders," she said quickly. "When did all of this happen? And who were these women? Did you know them personally or just pick them by chance?"

Amused that she even had to ask, he chided softly, "Surely you've guessed by now, Sabrina. I can't think of anyone in San Antonio who wouldn't know their names. Charlene McClintock, Tanya Bishop—"

"But Jeff was arrested for those murders. The police found evidence—"

"That I planted," he said quite proudly. "How do you think they even knew to look for it, dear? I called in the tip."

He was serious. Even though a smile still clung to his thin lips and he spoke in a tone that was warm with affection, there was a feral gleam in his eye that a blind woman couldn't have missed. "Why?" she choked out hoarsely. "Why are you telling me this?"

In the blink of an eye, his smile vanished. "Because I love you!" he raged. "I've loved you forever, but you couldn't see it. You couldn't see *me!*" he snarled, hitting himself hard in the chest with a clenched fist. "It was your work, always your work that got in my way. Then when I finally figured out a way to get your attention there, you couldn't see anybody but *him!*"

Agitated, his mouth twisting with contempt, he turned suddenly and swept all the canisters from the counter. "Damn you, you're in love with Blake Nickels, aren't you? Don't try to deny it. Don't you dare! Do you think just because I'm an old man I can't see what's right in front of my eyes? *I saw you!*"

Startled, more frightened than she'd ever been in her

life, Sabrina took a step back. "When? What are you talking about?"

"At that damn newspaper party when you couldn't keep your hands off each other. And then later on the porch when you kissed him like a slut. You left with him that night, after you found my note on the table. You left and went to his apartment, didn't you? You made love with him."

"No. Not then—"

"Don't lie to me!" he roared, jerking a very small, very ugly little revolver out of his pocket. "I won't stand for it. Do you hear me? I've killed for you, and by God, you'll love me or you'll love no one."

Trapped, caught between the locked back door and where he stood blocking the doorway to the rest of the house, Sabrina knew real fear for the first time in her life. He was going to kill her—there wasn't a doubt in her mind. If she didn't find a way to reason with him, he'd snuff her out as easily as he had Tanya Bishop and all the others. The police would know then that Jeff was innocent, but they wouldn't suspect Louis in a million years. They would look for someone with an obvious grudge, not an elderly neighbor who had never had a cross word with her.

Never taking her eyes from the gun, she slowly pulled out a chair at the table and sank down into it. Every instinct she had was screaming at her to run, but that was probably what he was hoping for, so he would have the pleasure of gunning her down. "Please," she pleaded shakily, "put the gun down and let's talk. Surely there's some way we can work this out...."

Staring at his computer screen, Blake quickly read over his story about Jeff Harper's arrest. It was good, he silently acknowledged. Damn good. The kind of thing that just might win him another award. And he didn't like it at all.

Scowling, ignoring the commotion of the *Times'* city room, he dropped his hands from the keyboard and sat back, wondering what the devil was wrong. He'd checked all his facts twice, arranged and rearranged them, and started over more times than he had on any other story in the last six months. And he still couldn't shake the niggling feeling that something wasn't quite right.

The facts just didn't add up, dammit!

Tapping a pencil against the edge of his desk, he told himself he was getting as bad as Sabrina. She'd tried every way she could to find an excuse for the incriminating evidence found in her ex's garage, and now he found himself doing the same thing. And not because he cared two cents about Jeff Harper. He didn't like the man. But if he was a serial killer, then Blake was Al Capone.

Oh, all the facts pointed to Harper's guilt; there was no doubt about that. *If* you just took them collectively and didn't ask any questions. Like who called in the anonymous tip. How had the caller known there was enough evidence in Harper's garage to choke a horse? And why would a man of Harper's obvious intelligence keep damning evidence on his property just days after he'd been questioned about the murders by the police? He had to know he was a suspect and the police could return at any time. And then there was the car. If Harper really was the killer and the same man who had left those notes for Sabrina, why would he use his own car in a neighborhood where it was known and he was sure to be recognized? Only an idiot would do that.

Or someone who was trying to frame Harper.

Instinctively, he tried to dismiss the idea. Kelly was an

experienced detective—he would have smelled a setup like that in a heartbeat.

But he'd also been under a lot of pressure to make an arrest in the case, a voice in his head pointed out. *Harper made it easy for him by publicly confronting Sabrina and acting like an ass. With the evidence that was found in that damn garage, what else could Kelly do but arrest him? That doesn't necessarily mean Harper actually killed anyone.*

And if he didn't, then the real killer was still out there, still after Sabrina.

His blood running cold at the thought, Blake snatched up his phone and punched out the number for the *Daily Record.* "Let me speak to Sabrina Jones," he snapped the minute someone answered in the other paper's city room.

"Hold on a minute," a disembodied, bored feminine voice said. "I think she just stepped out for a second. Let me see if I can find her."

Blake winced as the receiver was thrown down on a desk, every instinct he possessed urging him to hurry. Too late, he realized he should have told the woman that it was an emergency, but he'd expected Sabrina to be right there. Dammit, where the hell was she?

Twenty seconds ticked by on the clock on the wall at the far end of the city room, then another thirty, before the phone was picked up again and the same feminine voice said, "Sorry, she's not here. She left about twenty minutes ago to go home and pick up her car. You want to leave a message?"

Blake felt his heart stop in his chest. Home? She'd gone *home?* Swearing, he growled, "Yeah. This is Blake Nickels. If she shows up there, tell her not to leave again without talking to me first. You got that? Don't let her leave!"

Slamming the phone down, he jerked it up immediately

and called Sabrina's home number. But if she was there, she didn't answer, and with every ring, the muscles in his gut tightened. "Dammit!"

She hadn't gotten there yet, he told himself, and prayed it was true. If somebody at the *Record* gave her a ride, they could have had some errands to run before they could drop her off. If he hurried, he could beat her there. Hanging up, he ran for the door.

Her eyes locked in fascinated horror on the gun that Louis held on her with icy determination, Sabrina jumped when there was a sudden pounding on her front door. Before she could even think about screaming for help, Louis was around the table and pressing the revolver to her temple.

"One word," he snarled in a low voice, "and it'll be your last."

Her gasp quickly stifled, she nodded and felt the cold steel of the gun's barrel slide against her skin. Nausea churned in her stomach, backing up into her throat.

"Sabrina? Are you in there?"

At the first sound of Blake's voice, she bit her lip to keep from crying out, the need to call out to him almost more than she could bear. He'd come for her. Somehow she'd known deep inside that he would, even though he couldn't possibly have known that she was in trouble. He would take care of Louis. All she had to do was scream—

"I'll kill him," Louis grated, reading her mind. "I swear to God I'll kill him if he doesn't get away from that door."

"No!" Horror choking her, she ignored the revolver at her temple and turned to him with pleading eyes. "He must have called the *Record* and found out I got a ride home. Let me talk to him. I can convince him to leave.''

''Yeah, right,'' he drawled sarcastically. ''Before or after you tell him to call the police?''

''I won't. I swear!'' she promised. ''You can stand right there behind the door and listen the whole time. We had a fight yesterday,'' she lied in growing desperation. ''I'll tell him I'm still mad at him and make him leave. Please. If you shoot him, the neighbors will hear and then what will you do?''

He hesitated, clearly not trusting her, the look in his eyes wild and panicky. Whatever was going on in that twisted head of his, he obviously hadn't anticipated this kind of kink in his plans. ''All right,'' he muttered. ''But you say one wrong word, you even look at him funny, and I'll shoot you both. Get up.''

Jerking her to her feet, he jammed the gun in her back and pushed her through the kitchen door into the central hall that ran all the way to the front of the house. His breath hot against the back of her neck, he stopped her three feet from the front door simply by curling his fingers into her arm until she winced. ''Remember what I said. One wrong move and you won't have time to regret it. I'll make sure of it.''

Her knees quaking, her heart pounding so hard she could hardly catch her breath, she nodded stiffly and took two shaky steps toward the door just as Blake knocked again. Out of sight behind the door itself, Louis thrust the revolver into her ribs. ''Put the chain on and keep it on,'' he said between his teeth in a nearly soundless whisper.

Her fingers far from steady, Sabrina did as ordered, then waited for his nod for her to open the door. When he grudgingly gave it, she braced herself. Her heart in her throat, the cold, hard barrel of the revolver pressing threateningly into her ribs, she opened the door as far as the chain would allow, all of four inches.

"Thank God!" Blake breathed. "I was beginning to think you weren't here."

"I was in the middle of something," she said coldly, and nearly snatched the words back when she saw his eyes narrow in surprise. Please, please, let him understand, she prayed, then demanded, "What do you want?"

He took a step toward her, only to stop, his dark brows snapping together when she didn't release the chain. "I need to talk to you. Can I come in?"

"No," she said curtly. "Everything we had to say to each other was said last night. I told you then to leave me alone and I meant it. Now, if you'll excuse me, I'm going to take a bath and go to bed. Alone." Without another word, she shut the door in his face and shot the dead bolt home. Stunned, Blake stared at the closed door in disbelief. She'd slammed it in his face. As if he was some kind of door-to-door salesman who didn't know when to take a hint, he thought in growing fury. So she wanted to be left alone, did she? Well, by God, she didn't have to tell him twice. He didn't push himself on any woman.

Fury and hurt clouding his judgment, he stalked down the porch steps to the curb and climbed into his pickup without once looking back. With a savage twist, he turned the key in the ignition and tore off down the street with an angry squeal of tires. What the hell did she mean, whatever they'd had to say to each other was said last night? He'd made love to her until they were both too weak to move and he hadn't heard a single word of complaint out of her. In fact, he would have sworn she was as caught up in their loving as he was. Dammit to hell, how could he have been so wrong about her?

Scowling, he was already turning the corner, intending

to head back to the *Times,* when he realized that nothing she'd said had made sense. They hadn't exchanged cross words last night. In fact the only thing they'd come close to arguing about was Jeff, and that was only because she hadn't wanted to believe that he was capable of murder. She'd been upset, but not with him. So why was she acting now like she couldn't stand the sight of him? What the hell was going on?

Replaying the entire conversation in his head a second time, he still couldn't make any sense of it. She hadn't even taken the safety chain off! She'd stood there, pale and nervous, and stared up at him through that damn crack in the door as though he was some kind of rapist who was going to force his way in and drag her down to the floor. If he hadn't known better, he would have sworn she was scared to death. But why would she be scared of him? She had to know he wouldn't harm a hair on her head—

But the bastard who had killed four women and promised her she would be his next victim would.

His hands clenched on the wheel at the thought. No! He couldn't have gotten to her so quickly. He was just being paranoid. If she'd been in trouble, she would have said something, given him some kind of sign.

Everything we had to say to each other we said last night. I told you then to leave me alone and I meant it.

Her words echoed in his head, haunting him, chilling his blood. She'd never told him to leave her alone. Never! So why would she say that unless she was trying to relay some sort of message to him, a message she couldn't just spit out because someone else was there, listening? He hadn't seen him or heard so much as a whisper of movement from the other side of the door, but suddenly he knew in his gut that she hadn't been alone and she was terrified.

God, how could he have been so blind? Swearing, fear

clutching him by the throat, he jammed down on the accelerator, uncaring that he was fairly flying down a residential street as he circled the block, his only thought to get to her before it was too late. He'd kill him, he raged. He didn't care who the son of a bitch was, if he so much as touched a hair on her head, he'd kill him with his bare hands.

Caught up in the fury burning like the fires of hell deep inside him, he turned back onto her street, just in time to see her step outside onto her front porch. With Louis Vanderbilt.

''What the hell!''

Stunned, he whipped over to the curb and jerked to a stop behind a parked car six houses from her place, unable to believe his eyes. Louis Vanderbilt was her stalker? The man who had shot four women in their own homes, then walked away and left them to bleed to death? *He* was the one who was in love with Sabrina and planned to kill her because she didn't know he existed?

Dazed, he shook his head. This case was driving him nuts and twisting his thinking. Louis Vanderbilt was an old man who wouldn't hurt a flea, let alone kill anyone. Especially Sabrina. He was clearly fond or her and watched over her with an eagle eye. He would never do anything to harm her, he assured himself.

Then he saw the gun.

He only caught a flash of it, a glint of metal in the morning sun before Louis crowded close to her, concealing the small pistol between their two bodies as he urged her toward where her Honda was parked in the driveway. Then he was pushing her through the passenger door and making her scoot over the center console to the driver's seat. Seconds later, her face as pale as death, she backed out of the driveway and drove off in the opposite direction from where Blake was parked at the curb.

He swore and just barely stopped himself from racing after her. He couldn't do that, dammit, not without taking a chance that the old man would recognize his pickup behind them and shoot her on the spot. But, God, he couldn't just sit there! Snatching up his cellular phone, he quickly called Sam Kelly, his gaze never leaving Sabrina's red Honda as it moved slowly down the street.

The unfamiliar voice that came on the line, however, didn't belong to Sam. It was a secretary who informed him that the detective was currently out of the office but expected back at any moment. Swearing, Blake identified himself. "I can't wait for him to get back. Page him if you have to, but track him down. The wrong man was arrested for the serial killings." Rattling off his cellular number, he barked, "Have him call me the second you find him. And hurry, dammit! There's not much time."

At the end of the street, Sabrina turned right, and within seconds, her Honda disappeared from view around the corner. Muttering a curse, Blake pushed the end button, tossed the phone into the passenger seat and pulled away from the curb in one smooth, quick movement. It seemed to take forever just to reach the corner.

The cross street was a main thoroughfare that ran due north and was usually busy at that hour of the day. Several cars zoomed past before it was clear enough for him to turn right as Sabrina had, and he found himself holding his breath, afraid he'd lost her. But when he turned the corner, making sure to stay a healthy distance behind the car in front of him, Sabrina was nearly a half a mile down the road, but well within sight. Sending up a silent prayer of thanks, he started after her.

His cellular rang nearly ten minutes later, cutting like a

fire alarm through the tense silence that filled the cab of his truck. Never taking his eyes from the red Honda in the distance, he snatched it up.

"What the hell's going on, Blake?" Kelly demanded in his ear. "I was in a meeting with the chief when I got your message, and it was kind of hard for me to explain to him how we could have arrested the wrong man when I don't know what the devil you're talking about. What—"

"Just listen," Blake cut in, swearing as Sabrina turned at the next light and headed west. Where the hell was she going? "Jeff Harper didn't have anything to do with killing those women—he was set up by Louis Vanderbilt."

"Louis Vanderbilt?" the other man repeated in confusion. "Sabrina's neighbor? C'mon, Blake, he's old enough to be her father!"

"I don't care if he's older than dirt," Blake snapped. "Right now, he's holding a gun on her in her car and forcing her to drive west on Hildebrand."

"*What?* Hell!" Throwing questions at him, the detective determined his location, then growled, "I've got three units on the way, Blake. As soon as they get there, I want you to back off and let them handle the situation. And don't give me a hard time about this," he added quickly, anticipating an argument. "You're unarmed and a civilian. Let my men do their job and Sabrina won't get hurt."

Silence his only answer, Blake wasn't making promises he had no intention of keeping. If the bastard hurt Sabrina, he was going to tear him limb from limb. "They're turning right on State Avenue," he retorted. "It looks like they're headed for Crocker Park. Get your men over there, Kelly. Now!"

"Dammit, Blake, don't you dare go rushing in there like John Wayne—"

For an answer, Blake pushed the button to end the call

and tossed the phone back into the passenger seat. When it immediately rang again, he ignored it, his gut tightening as he, too, reached the intersection with State Avenue and turned right. Crocker Park lay less than a mile down the road. A popular recreation spot for families on the weekends, it wasn't nearly as savory a place during the middle of a workday. Occasionally, you might come across a mother with young children playing on the swings, but more often than not, the only occupants of the park were people who, for whatever reason, didn't want to be seen. They sat in isolated parts of the parking lot in cars with darkened windows, doing God knows what. Drivers using State Avenue to cut through the park seldom spared them a second glance, nobody but an occasional park ranger took an interest in what was going on, and no one seemed to care.

Wishing there were more than two cars between him and Sabrina, Blake followed cautiously, checking his rearview mirror every few seconds for the police, but there was no sign of them. Dammit to hell, where were they? Any second now, Sabrina was going to be in even deeper trouble than she was now, and the only thing he had that resembled a weapon was a tire iron. And while he'd like nothing better than to brain Vanderbilt with it, it wasn't going to do a whole hell of a lot of good against a gun.

Racking his brain for a plan, he abruptly ran out of time ten seconds later. Sabrina turned into the park entrance, and there was no way he could follow her. With so little traffic, Vanderbilt would spy him immediately. Swearing, he had no choice but to drive on past the entrance.

Daring to slow to a crawl, he cast a quick look through the park entrance as he passed and saw the red Honda disappear into some low-hanging bushes near the creek that marked the park's western boundary. When he was a teenager, it had been a popular necking spot for teenagers. Now it was deserted, with the nearest car nearly a hundred yards away. Vanderbilt could do anything he liked to Sabrina there, out of sight of prying eyes, and the few other occupants of the park wouldn't notice a thing.

God, he had to do something! The police were never going to get there in time if he didn't.

His heart slamming against his ribs, he waited until he reached the far end of the park and pulled into the parking lot of the church across the street. The need to hurry ate at him from the inside out, but this was no time to go rushing blindly in like a fool. He had to think! Grabbing the tire iron from behind his seat, he was just stepping from the truck when his cellular rang again. Muttering a curse, he almost ignored it. He had to get to Sabrina, dammit! But if it was Kelly, he needed to let him know exactly where Vanderbilt was holding her.

Answering it, he said, "Kelly? I'm at the church parking lot at the end of the park. Do you know where the old lover's lane is?"

"At the south end of the park?" the other man asked. "Opposite the main entrance?"

"Yeah, that's the one. Vanderbilt's got Sabrina back there in the bushes. I'm going in."

"Dammit, Blake, I told you to sit tight!" Kelly snapped. "My men'll be there any second. You rush in there now, you just might get Sabrina killed."

"And if I don't, that just might get her killed, too. Don't ask me to sit on my hands on this, Sam. I can't. I'm going in, and there's not a damn thing you can do to stop me."

"The hell I can't. I'll arrest your ass—"

Without another word, Blake ended the call and shut off the phone's power. Stepping out of his truck, the tire iron clutched in his hand, he soundlessly eased the door shut.

Across the street, the park was deserted except for the handful of cars parked in isolated spots under the trees. The freeway was on the far side of the creek and screened out by the thick stand of oaks there, and downtown was just over the hill to the south. Still, if you hadn't known better, you could have easily sworn you were miles from the hustle and bustle of the state's third largest city.

The quiet grating on his nerves and setting his heart thumping in his chest, Blake tightened his grip on the tire iron and jogged across the street and down into the creek bed that meandered all the way to the spot where Vanderbilt had Sabrina hidden among the trees. There, out of sight of the park's occupants and anyone else who might be watching, he began to run.

Chapter 12

"This is all your fault," Louis lashed out as he forced Sabrina out of the car and dragged her through the bushes to a small clearing that was totally cut off from the rest of the park. "*I loved you!* Do you know how many women I've said that to in my lifetime? Just you." His eyes tortured behind the lenses of his glasses, he glared at her accusingly. "You're the only one. The only one I ever wanted, the only one I ever dreamed about, the only one I wanted to share my life with. But you didn't even know I was alive."

Her gaze locked on the gun he was waving wildly about, fear churning like a storm in her stomach, Sabrina struggled not to panic. If she could just get him to drop his guard—and the gun—for a second, she might be able to escape into the bushes and lose him. It was a long shot, but the only one she had. No one knew she was here or in danger. If she was going to get out of this alive, she had to do it all by herself.

Facing him in the middle of the clearing, she fought to remain calm, but it wasn't easy, not when she could see the madness in his eyes. "That's not true," she said quietly. "I always knew you were just next door if I needed you—"

"But you never did," he cut in harshly. "The only thing you ever needed me for was to fix a leaky faucet or give your car a jump when your battery was low. You didn't need my arms about you or the security of knowing I was there beside you in the middle of the night. You didn't need anything but your job."

"I had to work, Louis. I have bills to pay just like everybody else."

"But you didn't have to love it!" Anger tightening every line of his body, he said bitterly, "You didn't have to drop everything and go running to it in the middle of the night just because some idiot beat up his girlfriend or a convenience store was held up. You shouldn't have been darting around town chasing stories at all hours of the day and night, putting yourself in danger and worrying me to death. You should have been home, with me, where you belong, talking about our future, planning children. I'm not too old to have children, you know. I used to dream about the babies I would give you...."

A loving smile playing about his thin mouth, he described the children he'd planned to have with her, the two boys and a girl that she would stay home with and take care of like a good, dutiful wife and mother, and Sabrina could do nothing but stare at him. How could she have lived next door to this man for years and not realized that he was totally and completely out of his mind? How could she have been so blind?

"Louis..."

He blinked, his expression changing from dreamy to angry resentment in a split second. "But we're never going to have those babies, are we? We're never going to have anything. Not children. Not a home together. Not a future. Because of you."

Bitterness twisted his mouth. "God, what a fool I've been. You don't want me. You never did. You never will. All you want is Nickels."

She didn't have to justify herself to him, didn't owe him any explanation about her private life. But he was so close to snapping, she had to do something before he went completely ballistic. "Blake and I are friends—"

He snorted. "Is that why your face lights up like a Christmas tree every time he comes anywhere near you? Damn you, I'm not blind!" His thin face flushed with fury, he turned on her, brandishing the gun in her face, the haunted look in his eyes wilder than ever. "You love him," he snarled. "Oh, you might not think you do, but I know you. You don't give your heart lightly, and you've given it to Nickels. And that can't be tolerated. Not after all that I've done for you."

What had he done for her except kill four innocent women? she wondered in confusion. The coppery taste of fear thick in her throat, she said, "Please, Louis, you're twisting this all out of proportion—"

"So this is all my fault? Is that what you're saying?"

"No!" she said hastily as his silky tone slid over her, making her skin crawl. "I'm not saying anything of the kind. We're just both upset. Why don't we go somewhere and get a cup of coffee and discuss this rationally? I'm sure we could work it out if we could just—"

The sudden snapping of a branch in the bushes was as loud as a gunshot. For a second, neither of them moved, then quick as a striking snake, Louis whirled, his eyes crazed as he searched the surrounding brush for an intruder. "He's out there," he said, half to himself. "I can feel him. Go away, Nickels! Leave us alone!" And with no more warning than that, he fired into the bushes.

Sabrina screamed. "Louis, no!"

Hidden in the thick undergrowth, Blake threw himself behind a tree just as the bullet whizzed past his shoulder. Cursing himself for not watching where he was putting his feet, he leaned against the tree, waiting for his heart rate to slow. He didn't think for a second that Louis had seen him—the surrounding brush was too dense and he'd been careful to keep out of sight as he'd worked his way toward where he could hear them talking—but the old man was obviously paranoid where he was concerned. And not so crazy after all if he knew that he would eventually come after him for Sabrina.

Chancing a quick look around the oak, he spied Louis standing with his back to Sabrina, his face twisted with fury and madness as he studied the surrounding brush off to Blake's right. For the moment, at least, he was distracted and didn't even realize that Sabrina was slowly backing away from him. If Blake could keep the old man's attention away from her long enough, she just might have a chance to slip into the trees and hide.

Glancing around, he found the fallen branch he'd stepped on and picked it up. Barely two feet long and not quite as thick as his wrist, it was half-rotten but would still make a nice loud crash when it hit the ground. Silently praying that Sabrina was on her toes and ready for anything, he hefted it by one end and tossed it far to the right of him. As it came down through the trees, it sounded, at least for a few seconds, like the cavalry was breaking through the underbrush.

As jumpy as a first-time bank robber, Louis whirled, his

eyes wild as he scanned the bushes for a threat he couldn't see. "Go away!" he cried, and fired wildly into the trees.

Blake didn't wait to see more. "Run, Sabrina!" he yelled, and dove into the thick stand of oaks off to his left in an effort to draw the old man's anger away from Sabrina to himself.

From the corner of his eye, Blake saw Sabrina take off at a dead run, but she'd barely reached the edge of the clearing when Vanderbilt realized that he was losing her. "No!" His scream echoing eerily through the trees, he spun on his heel to find her racing for the concealment of the bushes. Snarling, he lifted his pistol and fired just as she threw herself into the trees.

"You bastard!" Rage roaring in Blake's ears, fury blinding him to everything but the need to kill the old man with his own hands, he threw the tire iron and hit him right on his wrist. The gun went flying, and before he could do anything but cry out in pain, Blake was on him.

"You miserable piece of trash! If you hurt her, I'll make you wish you'd never been born."

Out of his head, his only thought to get the gun, Louis was stronger—and wilier—than he looked. Kicking and scratching and ranting like a wild man, he slipped out of Blake's hold and scrambled for the pistol, which had fallen under a bush at the edge of the clearing. His breathing ragged, sweat dripping down into his eyes, Blake launched himself at him, grabbing him just as the old man's hand closed around the barrel of the gun.

"Drop it!" he growled, jamming one hand under Louis's chin while the other locked around his wrist. "Drop it or I swear I'll put my fist through your face."

Past reason, Louis only grunted, his lips drawn back in a snarl as he fought to hang on to the gun. Swearing, Blake rolled over the ground with him and finally came up on top as sirens wailed in the distance. With a vicious oath, he slammed the old man's hand down on a rock. Just that quickly, the fight was over. The pistol fell from his grasp, and in the next instant, Blake had it and was towering over him.

"Just give me an excuse to pull the trigger," he said coldly, pointing the gun right at his head. "Please…just one. That's all I need."

From behind him, there was a crashing through the underbrush, but Blake never took his eyes from Louis, who didn't even try to get up but lay in the dirt like a beaten old man. "Don't do it, Blake," Sam Kelly said as he and four uniformed officers pushed their way into the clearing. "He's not worth it. Let us take over from here."

"Only if you promise to damn well keep him away from Sabrina," he said coldly. "He's scared her for the last time."

"He won't be scaring her or any other woman for the next thirty or forty years by the time we get through with him," Sam assured him confidently as he stepped to his side and took the gun while two of the uniformed officers jerked Vanderbilt to his feet and slapped handcuffs on him. Glancing around while the old man was read his rights, he frowned. "Where's Sabrina?"

Blake started toward the thick stand of mountain laurels where he'd seen Sabrina dive for cover. "Hiding over here in the bushes unless she ran to get help. I distracted Vanderbilt long enough for her to get away, and that's the last I've seen of her."

Half expecting her to come bursting out of the undergrowth and throw herself into his arms any second, he pushed his way through the bushes. "Sabrina? Honey? It's okay, you can come out now," he called, but his only answer was the whisper of the wind through the leaves.

Uneasiness curled into his stomach like a damp fog. "Sabrina?"

He heard it then, a soft moan that could have been his imagination…except that Kelly heard it, too. He saw the other man stiffen, then they were both fighting through the bushes, searching. Ten minutes later, Blake found her. Sitting on the ground, her back propped up against a tree, she was as pale as death and covered in her own blood. She'd been shot.

Later, Blake didn't remember Kelly calling for an ambulance. All he saw was Sabrina's bloodless face, the total lack of color in her cheeks, the pain that darkened her eyes. She stirred at his hoarse cry, a weak smile pushing up one corner of her mouth as he whipped off his shirt and dropped down beside her to press the cloth to the ugly exit wound in her left shoulder. "I-I'm all r-right," she whispered.

"Shut up." Rage tearing at him, his fingers shaking with fear, all he could think of was that the son of a bitch had shot her in the back. In the back, goddammit! And so close to her heart that if he'd hit her two inches lower, he would have killed her instantly. And she hadn't said a word. While he'd been fighting the bastard for the gun, she'd been quietly bleeding to death. Dammit to hell, hadn't anyone thought to call for an ambulance?

"Blake, the ambulance is here," Kelly said grimly, touching him on the shoulder. "You've got to let the paramedics take over from here."

Another voice, a woman's, said firmly, "You've done all you can for her, sir. Let us do our jobs and she's got a good chance of pulling through this."

He didn't want to step back, to trust her care to anyone but himself, but suddenly, there were hands to take over for him and keep pressure on the wound, and he was in the way. He stumbled back, his eyes burning with emotion as he watched the paramedics work over her with sure, skilled hands. He couldn't lose her, he thought fiercely. But God, how could she lose so much blood and still live?

"Come on," Sam told him as Sabrina was loaded onto a stretcher and quickly transported to the waiting ambulance. "I'll give you a ride to the hospital. You're in no shape to drive."

He would have preferred to ride in the ambulance, but there was no room, and time was at a premium. Nodding, he said tersely, "Let's go."

With sirens blaring and lights flashing, they went through every light with the ambulance. His face haggard, his gaze locked on the window in the back door of the ambulance, where he could see the paramedics working fiercely over Sabrina, Blake never heard Sam speak to him or try to assure him that Sabrina was in good hands. Numb, fear gripping his heart and squeezing painfully, he prayed like he had never prayed in his life.

They reached the hospital in record time, but it seemed to take forever. Then Sabrina was whisked away from him, upstairs to surgery, and all he could do was wait. It wasn't something he was particularly good at. Kelly had to leave and get back to the station, but he promised to return when he could. Pacing restlessly, unable even to think about striking up a conversation with the three other occupants of the waiting area, he watched every tick of the clock and never felt so alone in his life. What was taking so long?

"Blake? Are you doing okay, son? I got here as soon as I heard."

Glancing up at the familiar sound of his grandfather's voice, he blinked as if coming out of a daze. "Pop! What are you doing here?"

"Detective Kelly called me," he said gruffly. "I figured you needed me."

He had, and he hadn't even known it. Emotion clogging his throat, he hugged the old man tight. "I can't lose her, Pop. I love her."

"Well, of course you do," his grandfather murmured affectionately, returning his hug. "You just now figuring that out?"

Blake gave a choked chuckle and blinked back the sting of unexpected tears as he drew back. "Yeah, I guess I am. I don't even know how it happened. I certainly wasn't looking to get involved with anyone so soon, especially after Trina."

With a click of his tongue and wave of his bony hand, the old man dismissed his ex-girlfriend as easily as if she'd been nothing more than a piece of fluff. "I never met the woman, but I could have told you she wasn't the gal for you. Not after you went with her for four years without even giving her a ring or anything. A man doesn't need that kind of time to decide if he's found the right woman— not if he really cares about her. Why, with your grand-mother, I knew in the first week. For the next fifty-three years I never looked at another woman."

"Those were different times, Pop."

"Hogwash," he snorted. "Love was love, and it hasn't changed. Your grandmother didn't just fall into my lap, you know. She had plans and was all set to go to some fancy college in New York when we met. And let me tell you, it took some pretty fast talking on my part to convince her that she didn't want to go anywhere without me. But I knew as soon as I saw her that she was what I wanted when I hadn't even known I was looking. Anyone with eyes can see you feel the same way about Sabrina. When it's right, you just know."

Blake couldn't argue with that. He'd come to San Antonio with a bruised heart and ego, determined not to look twice at anything in a skirt. So much for his fine resolve, he thought ruefully. One look at Sabrina, and he'd gone down for the count like a boxer with a glass jaw. No one, not even Trina, had ever dominated his thoughts the way she had, distracting him at the damndest times.

And then when he'd seen her in Louis's clutches and realized that he could lose her before he ever had a chance to tell her what she meant to him, he'd wanted to kill Vanderbilt with his bare hands. The strength of his rage still stunned him. Because of his job, he saw violence and its aftermath every day of the week; he would have sworn he just wasn't capable of that kind of fury. He'd been wrong.

God, he loved her. So much that it scared him. He wanted to spend the rest of his life making her laugh, loving her, going to bed beside her and waking up with her in his arms. But even if she was able to pull through the surgery and make it, he might not get the chance.

Sinking into a nearby chair, he said, "Try telling Sabrina that. Even if I can get her to admit that she loves me, she's got this thing about marriage. Her mother and grandmother have walked down the aisle more times than Elizabeth Taylor, and she's convinced she just doesn't have what it takes to make a marriage work."

"So change her mind," his grandfather said simply. "If she loves you, she trusts you. And that's what marriage is all about, son. Love and trust. Not even the strongest attraction can work without that."

He made it sound so easy. But as an hour passed, then another, and people in the waiting room came and went and he and his grandfather still waited, he couldn't worry about the future when he didn't even know if Sabrina was going to make it through the rest of the day. What was taking so long? Unable to just sit there, he prowled around the Spartan room, watching minutes turn to hours, and had to fight the need to throw something.

Finally, three hours after Sabrina was rushed upstairs to surgery, her doctor, still in his green scrubs, stepped into the doorway of the waiting room. "Mr. Nickels?" he said as Blake turned toward him expectantly. "I'm Dr. Richardson. I understand you're Sabrina Jones's fiancé?"

Blake nodded, promising himself that the small lie would be the truth before too much longer. "How is she? What took so long? Is she conscious? When can I see her?"

He threw questions at the doctor like darts, not giving him time to answer one before he thought of another. Laughing, Richardson held up a hand in protest. "Hold it! Let me tell you what I know, then you can ask any questions you want." His twinkling eyes turning serious, he said, "Sabrina's a lucky young woman, though I doubt she'll feel like one for the next couple of days. That bullet came awfully close to her heart."

Blake paled. "But she's going to make it?"

"Oh, yes. She lost a lot of blood, and she's going to have to take it easy for a while, but she's young and strong. Barring any unexpected complications, I don't see any reason why she shouldn't live to see her great-grand-children."

Deep inside, the knot that had tied itself around his heart loosened. She was going to be okay. He felt his grandfather's hand on his shoulder and laughed shakily. "Did you hear that, Pop? She's going to make it."

"I never doubted it," the old man said, squeezing his shoulder reassuringly. "She may not be big as a minute, but she's tough. I knew it the second I laid eyes on her."

"When can I see her?" Blake asked the doctor. "I won't stay long," he assured him when the other man hesitated. "I just need to see her, touch her. Two minutes, tops. I promise."

"She's still in recovery. She won't even know you're there."

"That's okay. *I* will. C'mon, doctor. If she won't know I'm there, what harm can it do?"

"All right," he said reluctantly. "But only *one* minute, and not a second over. Ms. Jones might be tough, but a gunshot wound isn't something you bounce back from the next day. Once you've seen for yourself that she's really still breathing, I want you out of here for the rest of the day. Got it?"

Blake nodded. "One minute, no longer. Scout's honor."

He would have agreed to just about anything short of murder to get within touching distance of her, but once he was in the recovery room, standing at Sabrina's bedside, he didn't know how he was ever going to leave her. God, she was pale! And so still. The sheet covering her barely moved as she breathed. His throat tight, he reached out and closed his fingers around her limp ones. She never moved.

"Hang in there, sweetheart," he whispered roughly. "You hear me? You're going to be all right."

"You have to leave now, Mr. Nickels," the recovery-room nurse said quietly from behind him. "Dr. Richardson said one minute."

"I know. I know. I'm going."

But he didn't. Not for another thirty seconds. Not until he took one last long look at her, committing every inch of her to memory. It was all he would have of her for the next fifteen or twenty hours. God, how was he going to stand it?

Turning away, he growled, "I'll be back," then walked out the door. It was the hardest thing he'd ever done.

Sabrina shifted slightly in her hospital bed, only to suck in a sharp breath as her shoulder seemed to burn. The doctor had given her something for the pain, but it only made it bearable as long as she was relatively still. Whenever she inadvertently moved the wrong way, she paid for it.

Sweat breaking out on her brow, she squeezed her eyes shut and waited for the throbbing to ease, silently cursing her own weakness. She didn't have time to be laid up, she told herself. Not now. Not when the biggest story of the decade was wrapping up and she had the inside scoop. She had to get out of here and over to the *Daily Record*. Nearly twenty-four hours had already passed since Louis had deliberately shot her in the back, and if she didn't get her version of the story out soon, it was going to be old news and worthless.

Fighting pain and exhaustion, she'd read both papers from front to back page, cursing what she was missing. After Louis's arrest, the police had searched his house, where a diary was found hidden under the mattress of his bed. In it, he'd described how he'd met his victims at the bookstore and grocery store, even the flower shop and a singles' club, then proceeded to make friends with each of them. And when they didn't fall in love with him, he killed them.

With her out of commission, Fitz had assigned someone to follow up the story—a cub who had done a decent enough job and who would, with time, develop his own style and ask all the right questions. But for now, he'd missed more than a few pertinent details, which made Sabrina itch to get out of bed and reclaim her rightful spot in the pecking order. He didn't do the job like she did and wasn't even in the same ballpark, let alone the same league, with Blake.

Her heart constricting just at the thought of him, she felt stupid tears well in her eyes and quickly blinked them away. She would not, she told herself fiercely, cry over the man. Just because he was too busy writing up the rest of the news about Louis to come and see her didn't mean she was going to get all watery-eyed. He'd get around to visiting her eventually. And when he did, she'd tell him what she thought of a man who took advantage of a woman with a bullet in her shoulder just to win a bet.

It wasn't as if she cared about him, she thought as a hurt ten times more powerful than the one in her shoulder lodged in her heart. Okay, so maybe she had let him get to her just a bit. She wasn't made of stone. The man was damn attractive and the kind of lover that most women would sell their soul for. If her heart wanted more from him than a few nights, a few weeks, in his bed, then no one would ever know that but her.

Staring blindly out the window as the day began to fade, she swallowed the lump in her throat. She wanted to go home. She knew it was too soon—she couldn't possibly take care of herself yet—but she needed some time to herself. She had a private room, but people still came and went at their own discretion, often without bothering to knock. If she could get home, at least she could cry in peace without anyone walking in on her.

As if on cue, the door opened behind her, but she didn't spare so much as a glance for her visitor. Meals were delivered like clockwork, and she'd heard the familiar squeaky wheels of the food cart as it was pushed down the hall ten minutes ago.

"You can just put it on the table," she said quietly. "I'm not very hungry. Maybe I'll eat it later."

"You sure?" a teasing male voice asked from the doorway. "I went all the way downtown to get you a George's special, and even had the nurse heat it up in the microwave in the staff break room. It'd be a shame to waste it."

"Blake!" Startled, she turned too quickly, only to groan as her wound clenched like a sprung trap. "Oh, God!"

Cursing himself, Blake swore and hurried to her side. "I'm sorry! Dammit, I should have said something, but I wanted to surprise you. I guess I did." Tossing the foam container of Mexican food on the bedside table, he leaned over her worriedly and gently brushed her hair back from her face. "Are you okay? Damn, you're as white as the sheets. Maybe I should call the nurse."

"No!" She didn't want the nurse. She didn't want anyone but him and it scared her silly. Her shoulder was on fire, the pain raw and biting, but all she could think about was leaning into his strong, sure hand and letting him make everything feel all better. But she couldn't do that. Her emotions were too volatile, her need for him too strong. And there would come a day in the not too distant future when he wouldn't be there for her. As much as she wanted to, she couldn't let herself depend on him.

Blinking back foolish tears, she had to force herself to pull back slightly. "I'm fine," she said thickly. "Really. Just a little sore. The doctor warned me I should move in slow motion for a while. I just forgot."

Not sure he believed her, Blake stared down at her searchingly. The last twenty or so hours had been the longest of his life. He'd lost track of the number of times he'd started for the hospital, his only thought to see her, when he'd suddenly remembered that she needed to rest, to recoup her strength. So he'd stayed away and filled the time haunting the police station and writing stories that only made sense by the grace of God, unable to concentrate on much of anything but Sabrina.

She was okay. He could see that now for himself, but it was going to be months, maybe years, before he'd be able to push the image from his mind of her lying in the bushes, covered in her own blood. Just barely resisting the urge to snatch her close, he had to content himself with taking her hand instead.

"You, slow down?" he teased. "Because of a bullet? I would have sworn that it would take nothing less than getting run over by a freight train to take the starch out of you, Jones. In fact, I expected to come in here and find you pounding out the story on a laptop."

"Don't think I haven't thought about it," she retorted sassily. "I saw your byline—it was good. But my version will be better, so don't go making the mistake of thinking I'm out of the running to win our bet, Nickels. This is just a temporary setback." Glancing down at their joined hands, she frowned in bemusement. "What are you doing?"

He grinned and tightened his fingers around hers. "Holding your hand. You got a problem with that, Jones? Because if you do, you'd better speak up. From now on, I plan to touch you every chance I get."

Her eyes widened at that, but she quickly recovered. "I might have something to say about that, Nickels."

"You're damn right you've got something to say about it. I'm hoping it's 'yes.'" His smile fading, he said gruffly, "I thought I'd lost you, sweetheart. Dr. Richardson assured me after the operation that you were going to be fine, but you'd lost so much blood—"

"You were here?"

"Hell, yes, I was here!" he said, surprised. "Where else

would I have been? Over at the *Times* writing up the story while you were fighting for your life?''

''I don't know. I didn't know—''

''Because you were still out cold when they let me in to see you,'' he said. ''Richardson gave me one minute with you, then threw me out of here. Honey, I've talked to your nurses at least six times today. I couldn't come visit you until Richardson gave me the okay.''

''Oh. I thought…'' She swallowed, shaking her head as foolish tears stung her eyes. Obviously what she'd thought didn't need to be repeated. Of course he would check on her and make sure she was all right. He was a caring man—she'd seen the way he looked out for his grandfather and knew from firsthand experience just how gentle he could be. He wouldn't dump a wounded woman on the hospital steps, then head for work as if nothing had happened. ''Forget I said anything. I guess I was just feeling sorry for myself.''

''Considering what you've been through, I'd say you were entitled,'' he replied. ''I guess you heard Vanderbilt confessed.''

''No! When?''

''After his diary was found. He won't ever hurt you again, honey,'' he assured her quietly. ''In fact, Kelly said the D.A. is going to make sure he spends the rest of his life behind bars.''

Relief coursed through her, but the news brought her little joy. The women Louis killed weren't the only ones who lost their lives—he'd lost his, too, and she couldn't help but feel sorry for him.

''I'm just glad it's over.'' She sighed. ''Maybe now life can get back to normal.''

''Actually, I was thinking you should take a vacation.

when you get out of here and just forget all this for a while. It'll do you good to get away.''

Surprised, she smiled faintly. ''There's the small matter of my job, Nickels. If I left now, you'd steal all my readers while I was gone, then I wouldn't have a job to come back to.''

''Then I guess I'll just have to go with you. Tell me where you want to go and I'll take care of the reservations.''

Stunned, Sabrina just stared at him, sure he was teasing. But his eyes were dark with an emotion that set her heart tripping, and she'd never seen him more serious. Suddenly breathless, she said huskily, ''You want to tell me what's going on here, Blake? I think I missed something.''

For an answer, he drew her hand to his chest and pressed it to his heart. ''You didn't miss anything, sweetheart. I just never asked a woman to marry me before and I'm not doing a very good job of it.''

Sabrina couldn't have been more stunned if he'd asked her to do a striptease in front of the Alamo. He wanted to marry her. Her heart turned over at the thought, joy flooding her. Then she remembered, and the smile blooming on her face vanished.

''Blake, you know how I feel about marriage—''

He cut her off with a kiss, stealing her protests and her thoughts before she had a chance to put up her guard. Softly, sweetly wooing, his mouth played with hers, gentling her, seducing her until her head fell weakly back against her pillow and her blood hummed in her veins. And when he finally let her up for air, it was to discover that he'd stretched out with her on the bed on her good side, uncaring who might walk in.

''Blake, please...''

''Oh, I plan to, Jones,'' he groaned, nuzzling her ear.

"Just as soon as you're strong enough, I plan to please you until neither one of us can move." Lifting his head, he gazed down into her eyes. "I love you, sweetheart. You've got to know that."

She did. Somewhere deep inside, she'd known it the first time they'd made love. She'd felt it in his touch, his kiss, seen it in the heat of his eyes and recognized the same feelings in herself.

The truth hit her from the blind side, shaking her to the core. No, she thought, swallowing a sob. She couldn't love him. She could care for him, want him, need him more than she needed her next breath, but she wouldn't, couldn't let herself love him. Pain squeezing her heart, she pressed trembling fingers to his mouth. "Please, don't say that," she whispered in a voice that had a tendency to crack. "It can't change anything."

"Honey, it changes everything if you love me, too," he argued earnestly. "If you don't, tell me now. I won't bother you anymore."

One word, a simple no, from her and he would walk out, just like that. He wouldn't pressure her, not if she didn't love him. He'd laid his heart on the line, and the next move was hers. If she couldn't return his feelings, he'd wish her a nice life and that would be it. They would be finished.

It would come to that eventually when he found out he couldn't change her mind about marriage, but she wasn't ready to say goodbye to him. Please, dear God, not yet. And what would it hurt to tell him, anyway? she reasoned. It wouldn't change anything, not in the long run.

"It isn't that I don't love you—"

"Then you do?"

"Yes, but—"

"I don't care about the buts," he said quickly, kissing

her fiercely. His grin broad, he cupped her face in his hands and kissed her again. "You're not your mother or your grandmother. Just because they made mistakes doesn't mean you will."

"I already have," she reminded him. "Or have you forgotten Jeff?"

He dismissed that with a flick of his hand. "Harper's not even worth bringing up. You married a man you didn't have a damn thing in common with. The two of you together were doomed from the start, and I certainly don't blame you for having the good sense to quit beating a dead horse. I am not Harper."

She had to laugh at that. "No, you're certainly not." He was as different from Jeff as West Texas was from the Gulf Coast. "But there was a time I thought I loved Jeff, too."

"As much as you love me?"

Caught in the trap of his eyes, she couldn't deny him the truth. "No," she said huskily. "I never loved anyone as much as I love you."

"Then listen to your heart, honey. We were made for each other—you know we were. We think alike, work alike at the same jobs, we even like the same restaurants. We respect each other and love each other. With so much going for us, how can we fail?"

She wanted to believe him, God knew she did. And her heart was on his side—it had been for weeks now. She only had to look into his eyes and feel his hands on her to know that if there was one man on this earth she could spend the rest of her life with, it was Blake Nickels.

Knowing she was going down for the count, she grasped at one last feeble straw. "What about your family? Your parents are expecting you to eventually come to your senses and go into politics, and I just don't think I'm cut out for that kind of life. I would ask too many questions of the wrong people or say the wrong thing and embarrass the country—''

Stunned, he eased her back into his arms, chuckling softly. ''Sweetheart, I've found my niche in life, and it's right here. My parents know and accept that. And my grandfather adores you. If he were twenty years younger and you were thirty years older, I'd have some real competition on my hands.''

He'd shot down her last argument, and they both knew it. Dragging her hand to his heart, he asked solemnly, ''Will you marry me, Sabrina Jones? I'm crazy about you and want to spend the rest of my life with you.''

Tears spilling over her lashes, all her doubts swept away by a tide of love so strong that it seemed to steal her breath along with her heart, she grinned up at him. ''I think I should warn you that I intend to keep working for the *Record*. Do you think you can handle competition from your wife?''

His eyes flaring with heat, he chuckled. ''Jones, haven't you figured it out yet? I can handle anything you can dish out.''

''We'll see about that, Nickels,'' she retorted. Sliding her arm around his neck, she pressed a teasing kiss to his mouth. ''If I remember correctly, we still have a little matter of a bet to settle. Just because we're getting married doesn't mean I'm going to let you off the hook. I plan to beat you soundly.''

He laughed, delighted with her, and pulled her close for a deeper, hotter kiss. He could see already that the next forty or fifty years were going to be very interesting. He could hardly wait.

* * * * *

SILHOUETTE SPOTLIGHT

Two bestselling novels in one volume by favourite authors, back by popular demand!

Bells merrily ringing…kisses under the mistletoe—
that's what Christmas weddings are made from!
Here you go, this is December Spotlight.

Available from 21st November 2003

*Available at most branches of WHSmith,
Tesco, Martins, Borders, Eason, Sainsbury's
and all good paperback bookshops.*

1103/064

▼ SILHOUETTE

*Celebrate the joys of Christmas
with three wonderful romances
from favourite Silhouette authors*

Midnight
Clear

Debbie Macomber

Lindsay McKenna

Stella Bagwell

On sale 21st November 2003

*Available at most branches of WHSmith,
Tesco, Martins, Borders, Eason, Sainsbury's
and all good paperback bookshops.*

1203/55/SH63

He is every inch a Desperado.
But this time the job is personal.

Diana

Palmer

DESPERADO

On sale 21st November 2003

Available at most branches of WHSmith,
Tesco, Martins, Borders, Eason, Sainsbury's
and all good paperback bookshops.

1203/047/SH60

1203/SH/LC76

 **SILHOUETTE**®

is proud to present

a brand-new series

The

Country Club

**Dangerous, intense and seductive.
These stories are ready to introduce the
unsuspecting into a world where wealth
is power and deception is rife.**

December 2003
Once a Father by Marie Ferrarella
Silhouette Sensation

January 2004
In the Line of Fire by Beverly Bird
Silhouette Sensation

February 2004
Moment of Truth by Maggie Price
Silhouette Sensation

March 2004
**The Country Club: The Debutantes
by Ann Major, Christine Rimmer & Beverly Barton**
Silhouette Books

**Now prepare for more action with the twelve-book series...
Coming in March 2004.**

SILHOUETTE®
SPECIAL EDITION™

proudly presents

a brand-new five-book series from
bestselling author

SHERRYL WOODS

The Devaneys

*Five brothers torn apart in childhood,
reunited by love.*

RYAN'S PLACE
December 2003

SEAN'S RECKONING
January 2004

MICHAEL'S DISCOVERY
February 2004

PATRICK'S DESTINY
March 2004

DANIEL'S DESIRE
April 2004

1203/SH/LC75

Maitland Maternity

Where the luckiest babies are born!

Guarding Camille
by Judy Christenberry

A newborn baby… A mother in danger…
Her strong protector.

Jake Maitland has always been a loner. Only Camille and her little boy have ever touched his heart. But he keeps telling himself protecting them is just his job...

Camille Eckart: With a newborn baby to care for she has to rely on somebody. And that somebody is Jake! But is the attraction she feels just a result of their dangerous situation?

Judy Christenberry
Guarding Camille

Hugh Blake: The Maitland family lawyer has had a lot on his plate in recent months. But does he have more than a professional interest in the well-being of the clan?

Maitland Maternity

Where the luckiest babies are born!

The Toddler's Tale
by Rebecca Winters

A toddler in danger… A dramatic rescue!
A hidden desire…

Max Jamison has been so busy trying to get
Chelsea Markum—and her TV camera—out of
his life, he hasn't realised it's the last thing he
really wants!

Chelsea Markum has good reasons why she's
worked so hard on her career. But lately, she's
beginning to wonder if she
hasn't missed out on
something along the way—
like a family...

Lacy Clark: At last the
abandoned baby's real
mother is found. But now
her little boy has been
kidnapped—again!

proudly presents

a brand-new trilogy from

RITA HERRON

NIGHTHAWK ISLAND

*This is one place where you
won't want to fall asleep...*

November 2003
SILENT SURRENDER

December 2003
MEMORIES OF MEGAN

January 2004
THE CRADLE MISSION

1103/SH/LC73

SILHOUETTE®
INTRIGUE™

proudly presents

a brand-new series from

DEBRA WEBB

If you're enjoying her COLBY AGENCY stories, you'll love

THE SPECIALISTS

This elite group of covert agents will take on anything.
Nothing is too dangerous...except falling in love.

UNDERCOVER WIFE
November 2003

HER HIDDEN TRUTH
December 2003

HEIR TO SECRET MEMORIES
January 2004

GUARDIAN OF THE NIGHT
February 2004

Look out for more Colby Agency stories—
coming soon!

1103/SH/LC72

SILHOUETTE®
SUPERROMANCE™

is pleased to present

Girlfriends

by

Judith Bowen

Three women who've been best friends for ten years decide to look up their first loves. Find out what happens in...

Zoey Phillips
September 2003

Charlotte Moore
November 2003

Lydia Lane
January 2004

0903/SH/LC70

0803/SH/LC66

THE COLTONS

ARE BACK!

The Coltons—When this most talked about dynasty is threatened, only family, privilege and the power of love can protect them!

Look out for these wonderful spin-off stories:

WHITE DOVE'S PROMISE by Stella Bagwell
August 2003 - Silhouette Special Edition

THE COYOTE'S CRY by Jackie Merritt
September 2003 - Silhouette Special Edition

WILLOW IN BLOOM by Victoria Pade
October 2003 - Silhouette Special Edition

THE RAVEN'S ASSIGNMENT by Kasey Michaels
October 2003 - Silhouette Desire

**A COLTON FAMILY CHRISTMAS
by Judy Christenberry, Linda Turner
and Carolyn Zane**
November 2003 - Silhouette Books 3-in-1

**SKY FULL OF PROMISE by Teresa Southwick
THE WOLF'S SURRENDER by Sandra Steffen**
December 2003 - Silhouette Desire